Queen of Earth and Stone

Crescent Queens

Book One

Tricia Meyers

ISBN: PB: 979-8-218-22662-6

Cover designed by GetCovers

To everyone who cheered me on along the way and supported this wild dream of mine, and to all the wonderful writers who helped me learn and grow, you all mean more to me than you know. Thank you.

Content Warnings

Please review these content warnings before reading.
- violence
- explicit sex
- blood
- on page death
- the death of a parent
- drowning
- mild torture
- strong language
- sexual threats/threats of SA
- PTSD/panic attacks
- animal death

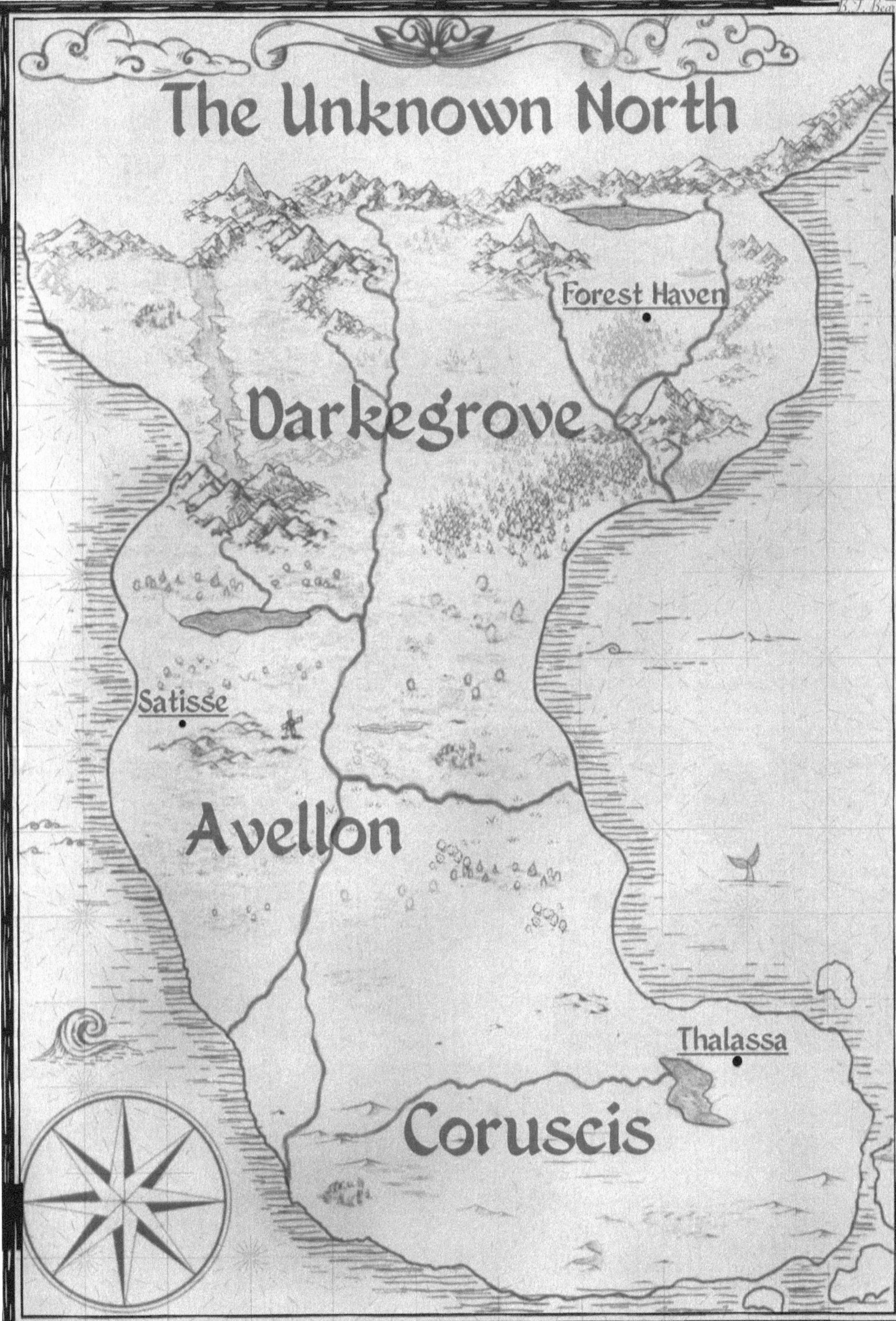

The Unknown North
Darkegrove
Forest Haven
Satisse
Avellon
Thalassa
Coruscis

Pronunciation Guide
Queen of Earth and Stone

Evelyn- eve-lin
Riona- ree-oh-na
Darrow- dare-oh
Callan- cal-in
Aldrich- awl-drich
Sylvie- sil-vee
Leysa- ley-za
Valerian- vuh-lair-ee-in
Cathal Vaderyn- cuh-hall vuh-dare-in
Emilia- em-eel-ee-uh
Dallin- dahl-in

Prologue

The Queen Consort of Darkegrove had no doubt her husband was dead. There could be no other explanation for this clandestine meeting. Only the desire to allow the news to reach her ears in a somewhat private place before it was announced publicly would have them calling her here. Leaves danced across the stone of the courtyard, the strong autumn winds setting them to spin in small cyclones around those gathered in the afternoon sun.

Among them were Queen Consort of Darkegrove Riona Darrow and her husband's most trusted advisors. They gathered in one of the few areas of Castle Stoneweald with an open sky above, a blessing Riona relished as the sunlight warmed her cheeks. She had been born in the forests of Darkegrove but had rarely spent any significant amount of time there. The daughter of an emissary, Riona viewed Darkegrove as home in name only. She was a child of Avellon, the Halcyon Vale, as far as she was concerned, and though she'd spent most of her adult life in the north, she still fiercely missed the bright light and open spaces of the midlands.

"It is as we feared, my lady," Eldred spoke quietly, wary as ever of prying eyes or ears. He was the most senior of King Viktor's advisors, not only in rank but in age, nearing ninety years, if Riona's memory served her well.

"They were overtaken somewhere near the gorge, as far as our scouts can tell, but, well... You know..."

Despite the cool temperatures, the afternoon sun shone brightly above them, setting the Queen's auburn hair ablaze in the light. The slight shake of her head only strengthened the illusion that inspired Viktor to call her a flaming temptress, so many years before during their courtship.

A lift of her hand stopped any further explanation. Of course, she knew, everyone knew, what the cursed creatures that lived in the gorge could do to their victims, and to speak of it now would do nothing more than weaken the steely facade she would now need to wear. Any number of creatures could be responsible, from the giant serpents that stalked the gorge on stormy nights, whose venomous sting could fell a horse in a single strike, or the cusith, wolves that grew to terrifying proportions in the deepest reaches of the northern forests.

Attacks were rare enough in recent years that many supposed the gorge had gone quiet, a complacency that made her husband feel it safe to make the journey; a complacency that had gotten him killed.

She knew what matter they would broach next, the matter of the heir. Certain expectations would be held, and things would need to happen quickly now. It was something she and Viktor had prepared for, had prepared their daughter for.

"My lady," another, only slightly younger man cut in. Though she had thankfully only spoken to him a handful of times, she knew exactly who the narrow face and wispy brown hair that did little to discourage the rude, albeit fitting, nickname that Viktor had once assigned him belonged to. Lord Ward, Reynard the Rat.

His nickname was not only fitting in appearance but demeanor as well, and something about the man had always unnerved her. Despite her husband's assurances that he could be trusted, she didn't, not entirely. It took a mere glance from the lady's ice-blue gaze to silence him. Perhaps the mouse would have been more fitting, she thought.

Eldred merely sighed at his counterpart, forging on with the difficult topic at hand. Reynard pressed on, in a tone that conveyed both his regret at having to broach the subject and his desire to have this quickly done. "My lady, it is the matter of the heir…"

The queen's tone matched the coolness of her gaze when she finally replied, having left the pair in silence for several seconds. "I am well aware of what is required of my daughter, and so is she." A brief glance toward the castle, tucked into the trees just behind them, had her frowning. How small it looked from here, she silently mused.

It was all stone, mined from the Sgiath Mountains not far to the north. Shades of deep browns and grays helped the structure blend into the thick forest that surrounded it. Designed, she supposed, to keep it safer, more difficult to find by those who may wish its inhabitants harm. If it had once been successful, she couldn't say, but now it was essentially a useless notion. Everyone knew where Stoneweald stood. If they wanted to find it, they would.

Now, they needed to depend on much more active manners of protection. Archers and scouts regularly patrolled the forest, acting as the first line of defense, before the more recently added high walls and guard towers even came into view.

"My lady?" Eldred prodded, drawing Riona from her thoughts.

"Evelyn knows what is required of her." Riona sighed, turning her attention to them once more. "She will do what she must."

Without waiting for a reply, she turned and began making her way back to the castle, not once looking back.

Chapter 1

Her world was changing faster and far earlier than expected. Her father was dead, and she was about to be crowned queen. At not even twenty-two years old, Eve Darrow was mourning her father when she should have had many more years with him. Years to learn to become who and what a queen was supposed to be. But fate had other ideas according to the priests, determined that though the gods were gone, some cosmic power still decided things for mere mortals. She didn't much believe in things like fate, since the gods abandoned their children a long time ago. Whatever care they'd had for humans had vanished alongside them.

"How's this, my lady?" Sylvie smoothed the skirts of her mourning gown. The maid beamed at the princess. Sylvie's soft, round face practically glowed with pride, a few tears welling in Sylvie's gray eyes.

Black satin pooled around Eve's feet, spilling from a tight bodice that resembled a corset, though it had puffy, nearly transparent sleeves attached. It held no decoration save for some intricate stitching along the bodice in the design of a vine with small blooms, yet it was still lovely, despite being a color she hardly wore. It made her skin appear at least a shade paler than it really was, making Eve feel as though she were the walking ghost she sometimes felt she was. Going through the motions, doing as expected with little direction of her own.

"It's perfect, thank you." Eve lingered in front of the mirror as Sylvie bowed and stepped away to tell the steward they would soon be leaving. Deep red hair had been swept back in a pretty, but simple braid that wrapped around itself at the nape of her neck. A few loose curls had been left to frame her heart-shaped face.

Pausing a moment to dab her favored perfume, jasmine and lemon, behind her ears, the princess set out to meet with the council. As far as everyone else knew, her life had been a straight and simple path, laid at her feet the day she was born. Not a soul, not even her mother, knew exactly why the princess had decided to change course only a few months ago—as if some small, ancient instinct had known what was about to happen.

The Dowager Queen, of course, knew what she was going to say to the council, and had even helped her prepare. Despite her words of encouragement, reminders that below the soft exterior lay a woman of strength, Eve's heart pounded in her chest as she made her way to the council chambers, down the hall, and then down the grand staircase that would take her to the lower floors, where all the public areas were.

Self-doubt raged so powerfully she hadn't realized she had already come to a stop mere feet from the council chamber doors. A deep steadying breath helped, as Eve reminded herself of who she was, how strong and how sure. No matter how much it frightened her, she had to do this, this was right and would bring change to a kingdom in desperate need of it.

"My lady?" The gentle prompting of a guard posted at the door drew Eve from her thoughts at last, and she turned, offering an appreciative smile. He dipped his head low, his face a picture of confusion. *Great, now they'll think I'm mad,* she thought. Standing silently and staring at closed doors, especially when this was supposed to be nothing more than a formal acknowledgment of long-held traditions, must have looked bizarre. By tradition, the council would present the princess with her choices, and then the planning would begin for the coronation. What little control of her life she had would be gone.

"I'm ready." The simple statement signaled the guard to open the double doors leading into the rather large room that housed Darkegrove's most trusted advisors, the Council of Nine. It had been this way for so many years that none of their scholars could agree on exactly when it had been formed. Another old rule followed simply out of tradition and unwillingness to change. It was nothing compared to the one she now stood to break, of course, but perhaps still a symbol of the stagnation that held Darkegrove in a vice. Nothing ever changed here. Nothing new was ever welcomed, and yet here she stood on the precipice of the most vital and terrifying change her kingdom had ever faced.

Breathe. You can do this. She repeated her mother's encouraging words silently, with each step into the room, growing more assured of her purpose as she approached the council, all seated by the oaken table that had dominated the room for as long as anyone could recall.

Their chatter had been animated, muffled as it was by the doors, as they had awaited her arrival. The moment the doors had been opened, however, they fell silent. Each offered varying degrees of welcome with their gazes. Some appeared open and friendly, mostly the younger of them, she noted, not entirely surprised by that. It seemed the older the men of Darkegrove got, the more surly and silent they became.

Stagnation. The word raced across her mind, unbidden, as she gazed back at the council. Eldred, their elected leader, cleared his throat, and Eve once again donned the mask of quiet passivity she wore as armor.

"Princess Evelyn, welcome, and thank you for coming." Wrinkled features arranged into a friendly smile. *As if I had any choice,* Eve thought, though she didn't let the thought slip past her lips or show on her face as she listened.

"We have chosen two quite appropriate suitors for you to consider." A few of the councilmen sat straighter, offering their neighbors slight smiles, nodding along with Eldred. Self-important, self-congratulatory fools. "One is the son of Lord Clarke, the eldest of his three. He is an accomplished soldier and hero of the last war."

He must be much older than me, she realized, if he were a hero of that skirmish, as most preferred to call it, as it had occurred many years ago. Invaders from the east had come, as they sometimes did, by ship and in large numbers. A test, the elders had said, of Darkegrove's strength. A full-scale invasion may come one day, though nobody knew exactly when. Still, they had lost many, and it had rattled their sense of security. They may not have seen war with their southern neighbors in many years, and the Sgiath Mountains to the north may have protected them from the unknown dangers that lurked there, but there were still others out there who wished to take what Darkegrove had.

"Graham Clarke is fair, just, and well-educated." Eldred leaned forward in his seat and continued, though Eve was far beyond caring at this point. "And handsome, I am told." The slight grin he donned was supposed to draw a smile from her, she assumed, and make her weak woman's heart flutter at the idea of such a handsome and just lord taking her hand in marriage, but if anything it made her want to reach across the table and smack him.

The disdain she felt must have been well hidden, or perhaps they simply didn't care about her opinion, as none of them showed they realized the direction of her thoughts. Pressing on, he glanced toward the councilman to his left, a subtle nod indicating that he was yielding the floor.

Reynard, Lord Ward, had joined the council under Viktor's rule some decades ago and had served him well by all accounts. Her father had trusted his council and had considered him a great asset.

"Princess." Though he lowered it briefly, she felt his gaze more acutely than the others. Deep brown, almost black, and small, his eyes were uncomfortable to look at for more than a moment. It wasn't a question of appearances, but a feeling of being studied like an insect under a magnifying glass. The urge to squirm, to move from his gaze was difficult to ignore. Straightening her spine, Eve settled for gazing at the window behind him instead.

"Lord Adelio Almont comes from an old family from the western isles. He would bring with him a critical alliance, a barrier between our shores and the far eastern nations that still seek a way to conquer our peaceful home."

She let him talk. Going over this Lord Almont's achievements, his strength in battle and education, though she hardly heard a word he said, focusing instead on the rain that fell outside. Eve wished she could be in her garden, to smell the damp earth, to feel the cool rain hitting her skin. Honestly, to be anywhere but here, about to make the most important and life-altering decision of her life. She wanted to run, to flee, even a secret, small part of her coiled like a snake in response to what was about to happen. *Yes,* it seemed to say, *yes, here we are. Finally, here we are.* A tiny voice within, in stark contradiction to the fear she still felt.

"My lady?" Eldred chimed in, taking over from Reynard once more. He gazed at her expectantly. She had been asked a question and had not heard it, so lost in thoughts of rain and freedom. "Do you need time to consider? We have little time but we can allow a day or two to make the choice, of course." Eldred's tone was gentle. He was bestowing kindness, a gift, on her. All nine members smiled now, proud and preening. All benevolence and charity. How generous, how wise, they considered themselves. She hated the lot of them for it, though she knew it was unfair. They simply followed tradition. This was the way things were done.

"I'm ready to make my decision now." The calmness of her own voice surprised Eve. She had expected to sound as nervous and unsure as she felt within, but she sounded strong, assured. "I will not marry."

A chorus of nervous laughter filled the room. Eldred lifted his hand, silencing them. "My lady, if neither suitor is to your liking, I suppose we could find a third, but with such little time I must implore you to reconsider..."

"You misunderstand me, lord councilor. I will not marry at all. I will rule alone." Like a rock dropped into a pond, the impact of her words rippled through them, nearly visible as the attempted smiles all vanished, replaced instead by shock, leaving many of them open-mouthed and gaping.

It was Reynard who broke the silence some seconds later. "A jest, my lady, surely." He glanced to his left and right, nodding as if to reassure his companions of the truth of his words. "You will marry."

As he turned back to the princess, Reynard fixed her with a stare so intense that it made her skin crawl. There was no question. It was a declaration edging toward command. His stare continued, unyielding until she finally broke, returning her attention to the rain outside. "You will marry," he repeated, leaning forward to add emphasis to his statement, his command, as others joined in murmuring their agreement.

"It simply is not done."

"You must, my lady."

"Yes, you must!"

Eve stopped looking at them, stopped hearing them as they all chimed in, pushing for her acknowledgment, her acceptance of this tradition. Of this stagnation.

CHAPTER 2

"No." The simple statement echoed around the council chamber. Though her tone was direct, Eve's gaze remained on the window just past where the council now sat, behind the large oak table. She couldn't face them directly, though it had been what her mother had advised. This decision, though it felt like the right choice, was difficult. The nine men who now stared at the princess in stunned silence sought to dictate not just her future, but that of her kingdom. The council had begun, from the moment she had turned sixteen, looking for the man who would become her husband, and eventual king of Darkegrove.

For several seconds, the only sound was that of the rain falling heavily outside, beating against the glass. A persistent drumming with no end in sight. It had rained for three days straight since the day of the king's funeral. The priests said it was a sign that nature was grieving. It made no sense to Eve, as they also claimed the gods had departed long ago and no longer paid their human children any mind. Not since the fae had vanished from the middle realms.

She was inclined to agree with that at least. The gods were gone. If they were real and they watched, Eve wouldn't be standing here now. They would've put an end to this absurdity long ago. The mistake of one person was hardly reason enough to punish all future generations, and frankly, if they had cared, that mistake would never have been made. If they cared, they would have intervened.

"My lady?" The man who had been brave enough to speak glanced at his peers on the council before turning his confused gaze to her again. "But you must...it's the way things are done." One by one, the other councilors nodded their agreement. All nine of them were men old enough to be her father, some even old enough to be her grandfather, and each of them had served the king, some of them his father before him. This was exactly the reaction she expected. It was the way things had been done for nearly six hundred years.

A queen ruling alone had nearly allowed the kingdom to be destroyed, and they simply could not allow that again. No queen had ruled alone since *she* had.

They taught the children of Darkegrove the story early on and reminded them frequently of the dangers of a woman's heart. Women were far too emotional to lead the kingdom without the guidance of an appropriate husband. A charming man with ill intentions could sway a woman. A queen whose name was never to be spoken, whose name had been struck from most history books soon after her betrayal, only to be referred to as the Queen of Despair for the rest of time, had ruled alone.

For several years, her reign was peaceful and prosperous, and then she had fallen in love with a fae male, from the old fae realm that had once held the westernmost part of what was now her own kingdom. Now, of course, all that remained of their existence were crumbling ruins of a massive palace near the great gorge, and remnants of roads, according to the scouts and hunters that dared venture that far west.

The council and the queen herself had immediately welcomed him with open arms, few within her court doubting his good intentions because the six kingdoms had lived in peace alongside one another for many centuries. Soon, she married the stranger, and prosperity and peace soon turned to war and despair. He sought to conquer our neighbors to the south, something that had not happened in so long that none alive could recall it.

The gods, they said, had blessed the old fae and human leaders with the wisdom to see the benefit in peace, and their descendants had followed suit, as much from tradition as from some bone-deep instinct every one of them felt. The fae prince, whose name had also been struck from history, desired only power and cared little for the tradition of peace between the kingdoms. What had happened to the two of them after the council had seized control was lost to history, or destroyed. For the long centuries that followed, the Council of Nine had been the guiding hand that took over when the kingdom was left without a leader. Only twice had the reigning king been left without an heir, leaving the council to choose a suitable replacement; always a male.

The story made so many afraid of the consequences of a woman's rule that most still opposed a solitary queen.

"I believe 'no' is a complete sentence." No amount of practice had prepared her for just how nervous she would feel at this moment. She had said no to a thousand years of tradition, declared her intent to take the throne and rule alone; and had just placed a huge target on her back. Preparations had begun the moment she'd informed her mother, the day of her father's funeral. Those loyal to Riona had been called upon to support her daughter's cause. Tradition or not, there were plenty in the north who felt the unwritten rule to be archaic and unfair, and they too had been called upon to help support Eve's claim and keep her safe.

Her life would be easier and safer if she had agreed. But to be forced into a marriage she didn't want, to someone she barely knew and didn't choose? Eve couldn't bear the thought. Being queen, responsible for so many lives, terrified her, but it was far less terrifying than the idea of being forced into a cage. Marriage was a prison, one she had no intention of ever being forced into.

Riona had instructed her daughter to hold her chin high. No matter how nervous she might be, she would not let them see her as weak. She was her father's daughter and had every right to speak her mind and make her own choices. Though nearly her mother's twin in appearance, with deep auburn hair and freckles sprinkled over every inch of her, she was his in personality. Eve was willful, they said, stubborn as a mule, and spoke her mind too freely. All of which, the council claimed, made her unsuitable to be queen as if they would allow it anyway. Somehow, none of that had mattered when her father had ascended to the throne.

"It simply isn't done." Reynard's outraged voice rose an octave, drawing her from her thoughts. "My lady, I know you are nervous, as most young ladies are before their marriage, but I assure you the men we have selected are most chivalrous, and either will make an excellent husband and king." The Rat offered a smile that made Eve's stomach churn as he regained his composure. He was loyal, her mother insisted, even if a traditionalist. He would push back, but ultimately he would fall in line.

Fighting the urge to do something that she would regret, she instead settled for a tight smile. "My answer is no. I will not marry them, or anyone. I understand the reason for your fear, and I assure you I will not make the same mistake. I will never marry."

The doors behind her opened suddenly, the click of heels on stone announcing the arrival of the queen. "I believe Princess Evelyn's decision has been made clear." Riona's voice carried a weight of authority, one that immediately drew the attention of all in the room.

This time it was Eldred who spoke up, turning to the queen with a pleading gaze. "My queen, surely you must agree," he implored. "You know well the dangers of–"

"Preparations have already begun, and they will continue as planned. Evelyn will be crowned as soon as possible, and there will be no wedding." Speaking with ice-cold stoniness that Eve could only hope to achieve, her tone left no room for argument.

Eve's heart was pounding in her chest as they left the council in outraged silence, retreating to one of the few places they could be reasonably sure of privacy, Riona's private chambers.

In all their years of marriage, her parents had never truly shared a room. One look at the room made it clear that Viktor's influence had not reached this part of the castle. Every piece of furniture and fabric was lush and lovely, in varying jewel tones. Two oversized emerald green chairs sat near the fireplace carved from a deep gray stone, no doubt mined in the hills just north of Stoneweald itself.

Images of gods and goddesses were on display in tapestries hung about the large room, with their backs turned to the viewer as they were always portrayed. Few of their features were ever visible, as the fae had destroyed nearly all accurate depictions of them when the gods left their children forever, long before Eve had been born.

Taking a seat with a grace the princess envied, Riona gestured for her daughter to join her. "You must stay strong, my love. Do not ever let them see you cry. They will be looking for a way to prove your supposed weakness, and it will only be harder from here."

Ice-blue eyes so very different from the forest green Eve had been blessed with met her own. As much as they resembled one another, that was the one stark difference between them. "You have chosen the most difficult path, and while I cannot express just how proud of you I am, my darling, I am also so terrified for you." The truth of her words was etched on every line of her face. The normally calm and controlled mask she typically wore was slipping, and for the first time in Eve's life, she could see the heavy burdens she carried beginning to weigh her mother down. "Your father is gone. If I am all that is left to stand between you and disaster, then I will do everything in my power to keep you safe, no matter the cost." She paused, giving her daughter a pointed look that told Eve she wouldn't like what she was going to say next. "I've brought in guards specifically for you, ones who can be trusted."

"No!" Eve all but shouted, rising from her chair. There was no way she was going to have what little privacy she had be invaded by people she didn't even know, to be followed around at all times. She had seen enough of this when she traveled with her father to the southern kingdoms. She would certainly not allow it in her own home, safety be damned. "Mother, I cannot-"

"Sit down, Evie. You must, and you will," Riona commanded, silencing Eve with her firm tone. Lowering her voice, she urged her daughter to sit again with a wave of her hand. "You are still so much a child, and I wish I had more time to prepare you, to make you understand just how much danger you are in now. You think you understand, but you do not. They will want you dead for your refusal alone. They will never allow another woman to rule alone. Until you are seated on that throne, with a crown on your head, your rule is not secure. You may never be truly safe again."

The urgency in her mother's tone and the fear in her eyes surprised her. Eve had expected grief for her father, and perhaps some degree of fear for her safety, but not to this degree. Doubt rippled through her briefly. A part of her thought the worst of it was over. Proclaiming her intent had been hard. Ruling alone, and living a solitary life, those would be hard. Somehow she hadn't truly considered what would need to happen to make sure she made it that far. Loosing the breath she'd been holding to steady herself, Eve sat back against the cushions. "Yes, you're right, of course. What must I do?" She was resigned, for the moment, to listening to her mother's wisdom.

"I've asked for help from some of our closest and most trusted friends. Many will simply speak up on our behalf. It is the most they will offer. A few, however, have sent sons and daughters to act as our eyes and ears. I will not tell you who all of them are, but there are some people I want to introduce you to."

Spies? Eve couldn't think of what use this would be when those who opposed her taking the throne did so openly, but now wasn't the time to question, she supposed. Seeing the doubt on her face, Riona shook her head.

"Your enemies will not always make themselves known to you, darling. Remember that." An hour later, her head spinning from all the new information and plans, Eve emerged from her mother's chambers, only to run into, almost literally, a strange man lurking outside the door.

The man, who now stood staring at her with a raised brow, was taller than any she had met before, standing a few inches taller than her. Of just over average height herself, it was rare for Eve to have to look up at someone, but here she was now, gaping at this stranger and feeling utterly foolish. It certainly didn't help matters, she realized with annoyance, that he was attractive, with shoulder-length, inky black hair, warm, golden brown skin, a strong jawline with what she guessed was a least a few days' worth of stubble, and a full mouth, now pressed into an annoyed line.

Deep-set eyes as blue as the stormy seas surrounding their continent stared down at her with more than a little annoyance. "In a hurry?" His tone was cool, aloof, and deep enough that at another time, the princess may have found it intimidating.

"Yes, actually, I am." She hated how flustered she sounded as she retreated a step or two, smoothing the front of her viridian-colored gown. "Are you looking to speak to the queen?" It would be strange for her to accept a visitor, especially an unknown man, in her private chambers, but she supposed today was a day for throwing out tradition.

"No, actually, I've come to introduce myself to you, my lady." He spoke with a lazy drawl that suddenly annoyed her for no reason. "I am to be your new guard, I believe you were to be told...?"

She winced at the word. Guard. More like... well, was there a word for one who invaded privacy professionally?

Regardless, to look at him he certainly did not fit the image one would hold of a guard of any sort. Stoneweald guards all wore uniforms of a deep slate color and were conspicuously armed, whether it be with a sword or with a bow. While she didn't expect him to be uniformed, she certainly didn't expect him to be dressed like a nobleman, in black trousers and a moss green button-up shirt that fit like it had been tailored to him.

At least he was built like a soldier, lean and muscled from what she could tell. No sword rested at his side and no bow at his back, so Eve could hardly tell how he planned to protect her if the need arose, and she wondered if he were here to serve as more of a babysitter than an actual guard.

"Yes, I was. I wasn't expecting you so soon, or to be so..." She waved a hand in his general direction leaving the sentence unfinished.

He chuckled, lips curving at the corner only so slightly. "Apologies, my lady."

"Ah, so I see you've met already," Riona's voice sounded from behind them. "Lord Callan Thorne, my daughter, Lady Evelyn Darrow, Princess of Darkegrove; soon to be Queen Evelyn of Darkegrove."

Callan inclined his head, offering Riona a respectful smile. "Lady Darrow," he said in greeting. "A pleasure to see you again. I apologize for the rather abrupt introduction," he added, turning his attention to Eve. Something similar to amusement briefly passed over his features before settling into a rather stoic countenance. Eve was beginning to suspect the smile he'd offered her mother was far from his normal expression.

"Apologies are unnecessary." An attempt at politeness, even if she was still displeased with the very idea. If he was to be her guardian, being rude would only serve to make it more unpleasant. "And will the others be arriving soon as well?" Eve turned to her mother, assuming she held the answer to that particular question.

"I'm afraid there has been a...difficulty on that front," he interjected.

"What?" Both women blurted simultaneously, earning a raised brow from Callan.

"What difficulty?" Riona pressed. The mask was slipping again, a spark of fear lighting in her eyes once more.

"Nothing too serious, I assure you. A delay is all." Glancing about the long corridor, he shook his head. Though they were alone, with nothing but tapestries and candlesticks along the walls to keep the pair company, he seemed to know the castle walls had ears everywhere. "Perhaps it's better if we do not speak of it just now, as I'm sure my arrival has brought enough scrutiny."

Nodding her agreement, Riona sighed. "Yes, of course. Lord Thorne, would you join us for dinner this evening? It would be better, I believe, for all of our sakes, if you appear to be little more than our guest for the time being, don't you agree?"

"Callan, please. If we are to be friends, then let us make every effort to appear as such," he corrected gently, lips curving into something nearing a smile.

"Callan," she conceded, offering him a warm smile. "We will dine at the sixth evening bell. I'll be certain to alert the staff that we have a guest. I'll assign you to the room directly beside Eve's, which is a bit unconventional, but I doubt anyone will question it."

"Well, if that's settled, then I would like to go and lie down for a while. It's been a very long day." Without waiting for permission, Eve turned on her heel and headed down the hall to her room, at the far end. She had had enough of feeling like a puppet today. She knew her mother held her best interests at heart, and honestly, knew she was right. But in the end, she couldn't help but feel she was trading one cage for another. Certainly being guarded at all times was a far less confining prison, she supposed, but it was still a prison. She had known, had been taught, for all of her life that freedom to do as she pleased when she pleased was not a luxury she would have for long. She was born to this, born to be the heir of the dark forest, and it was her responsibility to behave accordingly.

She had managed, through her own stubbornness and the help of her mother, to push back against the heaviest of the chains, but she was far from free. She was still trapped in a cage, albeit a gilded one, and still had to play by certain rules.

She knew she wanted to do what was right for her people, and her family, but the weight of it all was frightening. What if she failed? With that thought in mind, Eve stalked into her room, careful not to slam the door and draw attention she desperately did not want right now. Once inside, she sank to the floor and let fall the tears she'd been holding back all afternoon.

She was angry. She was frustrated. She was grieving her father. And above all, she was scared.

Chapter 3

Riona

Nothing was going according to plan. She had been promised three seasoned warriors to protect her daughter until she was seated on the throne that was rightfully hers. Riona paced within the sitting room of her private chambers, pine green skirts swishing angrily in time with every step. She had trusted them, trusted *him*, to keep that promise.

"What happened?" She demanded quietly. Eve had retreated to her room so quickly, an attempt, Riona knew, to hide how she felt about her new guardian. Her daughter had every bit of her own fierce independence, she mused with a slight smile. Any bit of humor had disappeared by the time she turned to face the warrior leaning against the arm of her couch.

Callan opened his mouth to reply, but Riona silenced him with a raised hand. "Please, do not tell me there were delays. You know I need more than that." With a sigh, she lowered her hand once more, a signal for him to continue.

He waited a beat, considering his response, before starting again. "I understand. I do. But you know that I can only share so much, even with you." Anger flooded her, but before she could tell him exactly how she felt about that particular part of her agreement, he forged on. "What

I can tell you is they are coming. Leysa will be here within the week, and Valerian will come soon after. They're coming as soon as they can."

Riona snorted. Annoyed and fearful as she was, the knowledge that another of them would be arriving so soon did make her feel a little better. Leysa Ashford's reputation as a warrior was astounding, to those who had knowledge of the trio, anyway. A number that by now was staggeringly small. So few of them remained. The keepers of secrets.

Riona could feel him watching her. She needed a moment to think, to consider her options now that things were changing. Her only child was in danger, and the three of them were the only ones who she could trust to keep her safe.

"How much does she know?" She bristled at the question, the judgment behind it as if he already knew the answer.

"Nothing," she replied, turning to face him. She held her chin high as the word hung between them for a moment.

Callan stared, but Riona showed no shame for the fact of it. She'd left her daughter utterly unprepared, and the knowledge would find its way to her one way or another. She knew that. Knew that it would have been better to be told by someone she loved and trusted than have the knowledge dumped on her in some other way.

But the choices she made were for a reason, even if it was a self-serving one. Admitting the truth to her only child, how much she knew, and how truly difficult things were about to become for Evelyn...the very idea of it terrified her. She wanted time, just a little more time of normalcy before the truth pushed their relationship to the breaking point.

The queen simply stared back. A challenge. Daring him to judge her for her choice. This was not a fight he wanted, not right now, and frankly, it wasn't his decision to make. Her daughter, her choice.

"Well," he sighed. "Not what I would've done but it's your decision, Your Majesty." He wouldn't challenge her, she could see that now, but he didn't back down either, meeting her stony gaze with his own. Two sets of blues eyes locked, one icy and one deepest cobalt. A silent agreement made.

She should've told Eve everything, or at least something, a long, long time ago. But the time for truth had come and gone. Telling her now would only further complicate an already complicated matter. Riona tugged her hair over one shoulder and moved to take a seat on the couch. Why did Viktor have to go and do something as foolish? He should still be here. They should have had more time. Not just more time together, but more time to prepare Eve. To tell her the truth.

"She can't know," the queen said finally, her voice little more than a whisper. "I'll tell her when the time is right, but she can't know, not yet." She was tired, so tired. Tired of the lies, the secrets. A small part of her, one she would never acknowledge, was thankful Viktor had died and set things into motion. She would only have to guard these secrets for a little longer before everything changed and none of it mattered.

"It's your choice," was all he said, before heading for the door. "But some free advice? I wouldn't wait too long. She won't thank you for it."

"I saw the way you looked at her," Riona said, just as Callan reached for the door handle. "Not today, but that first time." He would know the day she meant. A birthday party, not so very long ago, held here in this castle. Callan froze but didn't bother to turn and look back at her. His posture was casual, though his jaw tensed at her words. The queen paid close attention, to every move, every breath. "You know why that can't ever happen."

He nodded once, a brief motion that she might've missed if she hadn't been watching for it. "I know," he said in a low tone as he left.

Chapter 4

Dinner at Stoneweald was nearly always a formal affair. On most evenings, the smaller of the two formal dining rooms would be open to guests, generally a few courtiers or council members and their spouses or guests, and the royal family. The king's untimely death had done little to change that tradition. Some, eager to thrust their eligible sons into the view of the queen and council, had gone to great lengths to secure a seat at an evening meal with the royals. Even more of them, upon hearing of Eve's refusal to marry, had done so in an effort to catch a glimpse of the defiant princess in person. Either to put a face to the rumors or to decide their own feelings on the matter.

Callan's arrival had added fuel to the flames of the latter. Before drinks had even been served, whispers had started, speculating about the nature of his relationship with the royals. Could he be a potential match for the princess? Merely a lover, waiting to see which way the wind would blow? Or perhaps, some wondered, he was not the princess's lover, but the queen's. None could be sure as none of the royals nor their strange guest gave any indication.

Eve had, by a stroke of luck, managed to avoid conversation with any of the courtiers gathered. Drinks had been served on the adjoining terrace, and blessedly her mother had kept her busy in conversation with two of the councilors. They were dreadful bores, prattling on about the weather and whether or not it would turn to winter soon, but at least they weren't gossipy and allowed her to stand in silence. Her mind had drifted elsewhere, of course, but they wouldn't notice. She'd had years of practice offering them bored smiles and appropriately timed sounds of demure agreement. She hardly even needed to think about it anymore.

A cool wind drifted through the gathered crowd, eliciting gasps and some laughter from the ladies. As was expected of them, all were dressed in gowns that offered little protection against the elements, and though the terrace had braziers to keep its occupants warmed against the worst of the chill, they did little against the wind.

Eve's own skin pimpled along her bare arms. Her gown, deep green with a glittering gem overskirt, had only tiny sleeves and a low neckline. She was pretty certain she'd freeze if the servants didn't ring the damned dinner bell soon. Tradition dictated they enjoy the terrace and drinks until then, an old ritual based on the belief that inviting the forest spirits into their meal would bring prosperity. Another tradition she would like to see changed when she took her throne. But for now, she'd let it rest, she supposed. It wouldn't do to rock the boat too much.

"You're going to freeze in that dress." The quiet remark caught her completely off guard, his voice hardly a whisper just behind her. His warm breath kissed her skin where her hair had been swept up leaving the column of her neck bare, and suddenly she was shivering for an entirely different reason.

"Yes, well, we women suffer for fashion, don't we?" She remarked, turning to him with a grin. Something in her chest sighed at the sight of him, a strange sensation she couldn't identify settling over her. He had dressed in black, in fine clothes befitting a man of his supposed station. Had all of his clothes been tailored so perfectly? She wondered, noting he must be a man of some means to afford the finery he possessed. A *Lord*, she reminded herself. Strange for a hired guard.

"Lord Thorne!" Her mother was saying now, a bright smile on her lovely face as she greeted their guest. "I'm so glad you were able to join us. I had worried the journey might've been too tiring."

Callan offered the queen a smile in return, inclining his head deferentially. "Your Majesty, how could I decline the opportunity to dine with such lovely ladies?" His gaze remained solely on the queen, and utterly polite. Eve rolled her eyes at the over-the-top compliment, earning a wink from Callan that surprised her.

"You, my lord, are going to cause all the ladies of Stoneweald quite a lot of trouble," the queen laughed, though her eyes had taken on a slight edge. "If any catch your eye, do let me know, I'll be happy to make introductions."

Before Callan could reply again, the sound of bells from the dining room signaled the beginning of dinner. Eldred stepped forward then, offering his arm to the queen. As the eldest member of the council, he would serve as her escort for the evening. Falling into step just behind them, Callan offered his arm to Eve. For a heartbeat, she simply stood and stared, contemplating, before placing her hand on his arm. "You're a flatterer," she remarked. "My mother will see right through that."

"Oh, I do not doubt that my lady," Callan replied in the same bored tone he'd used earlier. He looked ahead as they walked, not bothering to spare her so much as a glance as they moved into the dining room, not even as he pulled out her chair for her and settled into his own.

The seat at the head of the table had been left empty since her father's death, and her mother had taken the seat she had always used, to the left of the king's, with Eve directly across from her at his right. Callan had been given the place to Eve's right, with Eldred across from him. The rest of their nearly twenty guests were seated by rank, down either side of the table, starting with council members nearest where the queen and princess sat.

Soon after the guests were seated, chatter began, and servants bearing trays laden with food entered the room. The first course, small plates bearing olives from the Strand and varying cheeses from the Vale, along with paper-thin slices of apple. Just a taste for their guests, the real point of the course being conversation and preparation for the more elaborate dishes yet to come.

The queen and those closest to her were the first to be served, of course, and as the servants made their way past him, Lord Eldred Gray leaned forward to speak to Callan. "Lord Thorne," he said, placing his wrinkled hands on either side of his plate for stability. "How do you find the capital? Is it very different from your home?"

A seemingly innocent question, but given the sharpness in the old man's gaze, and the equally sharp wit Eve knew he still possessed, it was far more pointed than it appeared. Eldred offered Callan the same patient smile he had given Eve earlier in the day, playing the part of a polite elderly gentleman well.

If Callan noted the true meaning of the elder lord's words, he gave no indication, simply tilting his head to the side as if considering the answer. "It is not so very different, to tell the truth, my lord councilor. A bit more crowded, perhaps." Still unsmiling, Callan met Eldred's gaze with his own, steady and unreadable. A heartbeat passed in silence before Callan plucked a large olive from his plate and took a bite, as much an ending to the conversation as anything else.

"What's your home like?" Eve asked, raising a brow.

A muscle in Callan's jaw feathered. "Quiet," he replied after a beat. "And as I said, not nearly as crowded as the capital."

Unwilling to let him off that easy, Eve pressed on. "And your family? What are they like?"

A shadow passed over his features briefly. "Complicated." At Eve's weighted stare, he continued. "My parents are gone, they died a long time ago. I have a younger sister back at home who is..." His shuttered features shifted into a small smile. "She's a bit wild, and carefree, but kind."

"Is it just the two of you then?" Eve asked with interest. She wondered for a moment what it would be like to have a sibling, especially one she could think of fondly as Callan obviously did.

Callan's expression darkened again. "No, I–"

"Darling," Riona said, interrupting their refreshingly normal conversation, as she addressed her daughter. "Do you recall Naia Colvari and her sister, Maren? Well, Naia was crowned yesterday, and Maren has been appointed her emissary. We should be seeing more of Maren soon, I expect."

A formidable family, the Colvaris had ruled the thriving port cities and desert settlements of Coruscis for generations, as her family had in

Darkegrove. The news of Naia and Maren's change in rank was not at all surprising.

It had been expected long ago, truthfully, but some trouble amongst them had kept Naia from ascending to her throne when she had been expected to. Nobody knew exactly what sort of trouble, of course. The Colvaris guarded their secrets more fiercely than dragons had guarded their hoards, or so the stories said. But the rumors that had managed to come out of their shining palace by the sea claimed it had to do with a man.

"How lovely," Eve said, only half truthfully. She liked Maren well enough. She was kind, and though she was just as outspoken and brash as the rest of her family, she was also much more level-headed and slower to anger than her sister. Eve couldn't help but wonder if the right sister was sitting on the throne. In any case, they hadn't had to fight to take it. The heir was simply handed the crown when the previous ruler deemed they were worthy, regardless of sex.

The conversation carried on around her, Eldred addressing her mother now, discussing some matter related to the coronation, and the courtiers farther down the table setting to work gossiping about both their neighbors and the royal family. Eve pushed food around on her plate, not particularly interested in the overly ripe-smelling cheese that took center stage in this course.

"Are you not hungry, princess?" Callan asked, leaning closer to her. His gaze was on her now, for the first time since his arrival, appraising her.

"I'm fine," she replied, huffing a breath. "They're all discussing me, you know," she said, gesturing down the long table with her chin. "Some are probably calling me names, saying I'm going to ruin the kingdom. Most are probably calling what I'm doing a child's tantrum and assume I'm going to be pushed into marriage after all. Others are probably wondering if you'll be in my bed tonight." She turned to him, lifting a brow slightly. There was no humor in her tone or features, simply frustration.

Callan opened his mouth to reply, but it was her mother's voice she heard first. "I hardly think that is an appropriate discussion to have right now," the queen said quietly but firmly.

And that was that. She wouldn't argue with her mother, not in public, so she simply shut her mouth. The look Callan gave her suggested he wanted to say something more on the topic, but with a single glance from the queen, he too kept silent.

Soon after Riona's effective shutdown of the conversation, the next course was served, a forest vegetable soup, followed by a salad of fresh greens and more of the same vegetables. The course passed in silence for Callan and Eve, neither willing to risk the queen's wrath and content enough without further small talk.

The chatter around them continued as the next course arrived, braised lamb and more vegetables, accompanied by a deep red wine nearly the same color as Eve's hair. Finally, Callan spoke up, drawing Eve from the place her thoughts had drifted. Thoughts of a gorge and her father.

"How many courses are these meals usually?" He asked, his voice low. His brow was raised as he eyed the long table.

"A few," she replied, knowing there would be at least one more after this one, possibly two. "Is it not to your liking, Lord Thorne?" She asked, eyes narrowing slightly, challenge in her tone. She wasn't offended, not truly, but she certainly didn't like the reproach she'd heard in the question.

"It's just...I haven't experienced a dinner like this for a long time," he replied lightly, turning away as a shadow passed over his features, so briefly she thought she may have imagined it.

What that was supposed to mean, she had no idea, but now didn't seem like the time to push it. Not when she could feel two pairs of eyes on them from across the table. Though they spoke of mundane things, preparations for the coming winter, she knew both her mother and Eldred were closely watching her exchange with Callan. She certainly didn't want to think about that too hard, so she turned her attention to the wine, drinking deeply. Unwilling to poke that particular bear, Eve settled into irritated silence.

Chapter 5

Despite the meager amount of sunlight the gardens at Stoneweald received, plant life flourished. Most everything that was grown in the areas open to visitors was of little use outside of being pleasing to look at, but the smaller, more intimate garden tucked away near the west wing was a different story.

Many of the blooms and foliage there were quite lovely, and some were equally as deadly. For as long as anyone could recall, there had been a private garden here, not only for beauty but also used as either medicine or poison. Her father's ancestors had kept gardens surrounding Stoneweald for as long as anyone could remember, longer than written history recorded and longer than the castle itself had existed.

Darkegrove had remained at peace with her neighbors for centuries, but her proximity to the Sgiath mountains where small warring clans and raiders still existed, did sometimes put her citizens at risk. The occasional need for healing herbs and poisons had driven the castle's occupants to keep the small, yet useful, garden thriving. The scholars believed the gardens had perhaps originally served as some homage to wherever they had hailed from before landing on the continent they now resided.

· · ·

Eve had spent so much time in this garden, cultivating and learning about the many plants it housed from the gardener, that it had become her own private space in a way. She was rarely interrupted during her time here, even by her parents.

A desire to be alone, and outside where she could feel the breeze; away from prying eyes, had drawn her here for some time alone. The rain had finally stopped leaving the stone walkways glistening and slick. She would have to be careful, Eve reminded herself as she stepped outside into the walled garden.

Made from the same stone as the rest of the castle, the garden walls here were tall, designed for privacy for the royal family. Raised beds lined the walls, and in the center, one large circular bed was intended to make working in the garden more comfortable. This time of year, only a few plants offered blooms, but the foliage was still present.

Varying shades of green in all shapes, from long and spindly leaves to full, broad ones nearly the size of her hand, filled each of the beds.

The most numerous of the blooms that remained this late in the year were mostly red, small, and growing in clusters on tall thin stalks. Death's Tears. The blooms were often dried and crushed into a powder useful for treating headaches and sleeplessness, but it could be deadly in high enough doses. They would be glad for the rain, she mused, moving through the winding path, around corner after corner, to her favorite bench, tucked into a niche out of view of the door from which she had entered.

Night was descending, and though it was far from fully dark yet, the autumn sunset had come and gone long enough ago that Eve's sight was somewhat limited despite the last rays of light trickling through the canopy of trees and sparse torchlight offered by the guard towers nearby. She could have had the many lanterns that lined the walk lit before she had arrived, as propriety would insist, but she had chosen to come here for a reason, and bringing attention to herself would defeat the entire purpose.

Seated on the bench with little care given to the effect the wet stone would no doubt have on her gown, Eve tilted her chin skyward, eyes closed, and let the damp air surround her. Here she could pretend to be somewhere, anywhere else. Even if for just a few moments.

A deep breath in and out, and she was soaring skyward. Her body was replaced by a broad trunk, feet shifting into thick roots that plunged into the damp earth, spreading far and deep. Branches splayed wide, deep green leaves springing to life along them.

Higher and higher she grew, taller now than even the oldest trees in Darkegrove. Wider, her roots spread, beneath the loamy earth. The tree she'd become in this waking dream was connected to the very heart of Aestera, every living thing that scurried below, or walked or soared above was hers. She could feel each of them, as keenly as her own fingers.

A raven cried somewhere in the distance, hidden in the forest beneath her canopy. The part of her that remained human in this dream longed to search for it, to call the night-black bird to her, but she was only a tree and–

"Don't worry, it will be handled, one way or another."

A masculine voice she didn't recognize drew her attention. From the direction of the voice, she knew they stood just on the other side of the wall from where she sat. Far enough from the nearest tower that it couldn't be a guard who she now heard speaking. Soon, another voice joined, more familiar but speaking so low she still couldn't quite place it.

"You heard what happened, she said no. If she doesn't–"

"I am aware, but she will change her mind. We will make certain of it."

"And if she doesn't?"

A short bark of a laugh. "Well, then you know what must be done."

A grunt of acknowledgment, then the sound of two sets of footsteps retreating were all that followed. Heart pounding in her chest, Eve exhaled slowly. They were talking about her, they had to be, she realized, folding her arms across her chest to chase away the sudden chill that had settled over her.

You know what to do.

Her mother had warned her of the danger she would now be in and yet here she sat in a dark garden, alone, only feet away from men who wished to harm her if she didn't fall in line. How foolish she had been, in her desperation to escape for a few moments. She had known, of course, that she would be putting herself in danger by choosing this path, but she had not truly known or understood, the seriousness of it.

As if night herself had sensed the shift in mood, the last bit of light left from sunset had vanished, leaving Eve in near-total darkness. The nearest torch seemed much farther away than it had when she had first entered the garden in what she knew could only have been little more than a few minutes prior, but which now seemed like hours.

She had to suppress the urge to jump up and run away. What if those men were still nearby? Was there a door somewhere near where they had been standing that entered the garden? Eve couldn't recall, despite how much time she had spent here. Fear, it seemed, had clouded her memory.

Taking a steadying breath, she gathered her skirts in hand, prepared to move. *I am not a child,* despite what her mother felt. *I am brave, and I am smart.* She could face this, and any threat, standing before her with her head held high just as she had been taught. She could fight a little, her mother had seen to that. When her father was away she had trained as much as was possible without his knowing, thanks to her mother and a few understanding guards; and she was confident that while she may not win a fight, she could at least last long enough for guards to come. *I can do this,* she assured herself, as she rose to her feet and took the first step forward.

"You look as though you've seen a ghost."

Fear was a cold finger down Eve's spine. Her mind raced, running through the steps of self-defense she'd been taught.

A man stepped into view, and relief flooded her as recognition clicked. *Callan.* Somehow he had just appeared in front of her, just a few feet down the path. Where in the hell had he come from?

"Damn it," she breathed, hand on her chest, as he looked her over silently. "Why do you keep appearing out of nowhere like that?"

She hated the slight edge she could still hear in her voice and the way her pulse still raced. She shouldn't be afraid, not like this, and not in what was supposed to be a safe place.

Callan was frowning at her, that damned brow raised again, as he took in what she was sure was her disheveled appearance. She could only imagine what a sight she made with the damp hem of her gown bunched up around her knees, hands grasping the skirt like a lifeline.

"One of the maids saw you come out here alone and was

concerned," he explained in a lazy tone that somehow irritated her. "She was on her way to find a guard, and I told her I'd check in on you."

Right. That would be his job, as a babysitter. Guard. Whatever.

She knew she should be thankful for his presence, and to be honest, a small part of her was, but she was also annoyed. She shouldn't need this. She should be safe in her home and in taking the throne that was her birthright. She wanted to scream. She wanted to curse the Queen of Despair, her hateful lover, and every single man who had decided that one woman's mistake should damn them all. Most of all, she wished she could stand before the fae king who had sent the Queen of Despair's hateful lover and curse him to his treacherous face.

Callan shook his head. "I know you don't like having me here, and I understand that, but it is necessary." The corner of his lips tugged upward gently, the hint of a smile catching her by surprise and distracting her from the anger. "I promise I'll try not to get in your way or invade your privacy," his tone was calm as he scanned the garden.

"But something scared you?" By the time the last couple of words left his mouth, the easy tone had shifted into something else entirely. His jaw was set, as he looked past her into the darkest parts of the garden. For a moment she could've sworn his eyes had taken on almost an amber tone, but surely that was just the dim light playing tricks on her. She dismissed the absurd notion with a shake of her head.

"Yes, actually," she admitted. A part of her wanted to deny it, to maintain the air of bravery and pride she usually did, but there was a line between being proud and being stupid, and she wasn't about to cross it.

"I heard some men speaking on the other side of the wall. It sounded like they were talking about me and...well it doesn't sound like they're throwing me a party." Eve gestured in the direction from which the conversation had come, glad to be looking anywhere but at him for once. Something about his quiet intensity was setting her on edge.

"I'm sure it's nothing," he replied, that lazy drawl returning. She kept her gaze on the wall, replaying the conversation in her mind once more. Maybe he was right, she supposed, but it certainly felt like something. No names were ever mentioned, so it was possible, however unlikely, the men were discussing something else. Whatever the case, there was nothing she could do about it now, especially if her guard was going to be so little help. With a nod, she turned her attention back to him only to find him looking at her curiously.

He offered Eve his arm, and with a sigh she accepted, placing her hand there. Through the thin sleeve of his shirt, she could feel the toned muscles of a warrior. For a brief flicker of a moment, she wondered what it might be like to have those arms around her. She dropped his arm as the image of them tangled in sheets popped into her mind unbidden. She couldn't allow herself to think like that, not now. That simply couldn't happen.

When he raised his brow again, still watching her curiously, she just frowned at him and began walking. He silently fell into step beside her.

It wasn't that she couldn't take a lover, she could. After marriage, it was permissible, even encouraged, for a queen to take a lover. In fact, most had after being forced into an arranged marriage with a virtual stranger.

As the cool autumn breeze kissed her cheeks, warmed by embarrassment, her mind drifted to Brodie, and how fiery and passionate their entanglement had been. It had been love for him, and something just shy of that for Eve. They had both known that no matter their feelings for one another, there lay no true future for them. He would never have been happy with what little she could offer him after the marriage she was destined to have, regardless of how he insisted he would be.

As the son of a merchant, he didn't rank high enough to even be considered a possibility for marriage by the council. He wanted marriage and children together. They'd have to choose between a life together, marriage and children, on the run for the rest of their lives, or with her married to someone else, sharing his bed only after her king got what he wanted from her. She would never ask, never allow, him to settle for so little.

So she had let him go nearly two years ago now. Emilia had told her he had married a lovely girl from Coruscis and lived there with her, safely away from the madness of Darkegrove. Eve couldn't help but wonder if he was happy.

"I met a friend of yours this afternoon. She was quite happy to hear your mother had invited a guest to visit. She believes I am to be your husband." Callan was a step ahead now, slowly moving through the dark garden, a meandering pace that she was grateful for. She needed the time to compose herself before anyone saw how shaken she still was.

"Oh no." Eve could only imagine what had been said if Emilia Danwell had managed to corner him, and considering the way he smirked now, she had little doubt in her mind it was Emilia whom he had encountered. Few others at court would have been brave enough to approach him without introduction. A horde of bored noblewomen with little else to do with their time had made a beeline for the castle as soon as word had begun to spread that Eve had a very handsome guest. This, combined with her refusal to marry, had set many tongues wagging.

"She's very...friendly," he observed, as they walked toward the door that would take them back inside. "I was told all about the castle, and the visiting nobles. She had a little to say about you as well."

"Yes, she is," Eve admitted cautiously. "I'm not surprised to hear she believes that. Most people probably will, outside of the council. They will know the truth, and frankly, you probably make them extremely nervous. They'll worry I'm going to marry you and ruin the world again."

A guard coughed somewhere beyond the wall, and the sound of it surprised her enough for Eve to take her eyes off the slick stone path, causing her to slip. Instinct had her reaching out, only to be caught by her arm in his strong grip.

"Well, let them worry. I'm only here to do a job, Princess, and that is to keep you alive," he replied, giving her a pointed look. "You're as skittish as a little dove."

Damning her clumsiness, the rain, and the guard who'd distracted her, Eve shook her arm free and offered a tight smile in thanks. "Why did you agree to do it? I know you're not the only one. The others are coming, right? Not many agreed to help us." She couldn't blame them, not really. Any who shared her view of things would be sorely outnumbered and treading into dangerous territory here at court, surrounded by those who at best disagreed, and at worst would likely want to see them gone, in one way or another.

Callan lifted a shoulder lightly, turning to glance at her sideways. His gaze was as inscrutable as always, ocean-deep eyes scanning her face as if searching for something a moment before he replied. Every word, it seemed, was carefully weighed and considered before being voiced aloud. She couldn't help but be a little envious of the amount of self-control that must take, a trait she sorely lacked.

"I was asked, so I did."

The statement was simple, yet carried a weight to it she couldn't help but feel responsible for. How many people were going to put themselves in jeopardy because of the stand she had taken? Not many, she guessed, but enough. It wasn't just her life she had put in danger with her refusal, and while she had known this, it was the first time she had to face the idea. It left her with a feeling of guilt that weighed on her like an iron shackle. It *was* the right thing to do, not just for Eve but for every female heir after her. If she took this stand now, no woman after her would have to do it. But it didn't make the potential sacrifice of others an easier burden to bear.

"How old are you?"

She blinked at him. The question caught her off guard and surprised her that he didn't know. "Twenty-one," Eve replied cautiously, unsure where he was going with this. "I thought everyone would know that."

It wasn't vanity that had her assuming so. Her parents had tried for ages to have a child, she had been told, and had decided it would never come to pass when suddenly they were able to conceive. While it wasn't uncommon for humans to struggle to conceive for a time, the king and queen had waited far longer than most.

Because of this, her mother held a grand celebration every year to mark the day of Eve's birth in the forest at the site of Black Pool. It was the last remaining place of worship, used mostly by priests and priestesses, but a few other devout believers remained.

Temples left behind when the fae vanished had been nearly destroyed. All likenesses and recorded names of the gods and goddesses the fae had once devoted their lives to, gone. The jet-black waters of the pool were said to be the tears of ancient gods, mourning their departure from the realm. A few of them were scattered around the continent, but nobody could be certain how many existed; or how deep any of them were as it was strictly forbidden to enter them, not only out of respect but of fear.

All manner of lower faerie creatures stalked the areas around the pools, making them quite dangerous to venture to alone. Legends had told of men and women being lost to them–strong swimmers who simply disappeared beneath the surface of the water never to be seen again.

Eve didn't understand why her mother had chosen such a dangerous place to celebrate the birth of her child, but she always assumed it had been a way of thanking the gods, just in case they were still paying attention.

"You are carrying a great deal of responsibility for someone so young," he remarked, apparently ignoring Eve's confusion. It made little sense, given that he looked not much older than her himself, but she supposed it would be rude to remark on it.

He came to a sudden stop, falling behind, though they were still several feet from the door. She turned to face him, prepared to tease him about slipping himself, but instead found him taking a half step toward her. They were close, almost close enough that their bodies were touching. "Why did you choose to say no, instead of doing what was expected of you?"

For the first time, Eve could see some semblance of readable emotion on his features. There was an intensity to his eyes that made them come alive, and once again, she could almost swear they changed color, appearing, for a split second, to be rimmed in gold.

Callan was looking past her, and a glance over her shoulder told her what he saw. A guard in the nearest tower to them had paused his patrol to watch. Standing so close to Callan, she could only assume what it must look like they had been doing. Instead of retreating, as she expected, Callan remained in place.

"Because it was the right thing to do," she replied, taking a minute step back. It wasn't that she necessarily cared what anyone else thought, but the conversation she had overheard remained a stark reminder of the danger she was in. There was no need to add fuel to that particular fire.

"And," Eve added after a beat. "Because I...because I don't want to continue to live my life in a cage. My parents loved each other dearly, and they had a happy marriage, one they went into because they wanted it. But it was still a cage for my mother. She gave up a lot of freedom for that marriage, even if it was a happy one. For me, it would be all duty, and I would be forced to hand my crown over to someone else to pay penance for a sin that isn't even my own. It's bullshit."

Callan blinked, surprised, she guessed, by her choice of language.

"You are-" He began, presumably to tell her how foolish she was, or brave maybe, she supposed, pushing away at the self-doubt that still clawed at her. Shouts from within interrupted whatever it was he had been about to say.

Curiosity and fear spurred her into action, driving her toward the doors. As she reached the inner hall, a breathless steward appeared. His face was bright red, and his livery wrinkled. He had to have run quite a distance rather quickly to be left in such a state, and the continued shouts and sounds of several guards approaching told her something was deeply wrong.

"What has happened?" the princess demanded as Callan came to stand just behind her.

Before the steward could answer, Reynard appeared from around the corner, stepping between them. In contrast, the councilor seemed entirely composed. Not one hair was out of place, and though his tone was serious, he spoke calmly.

"I am sorry, my lady, but there has been an incident."

CHAPTER 6

The incident, as Reynard had called it, had occurred in Eve's chambers. She was led there by the councilor, solemn-faced and silent, along with four guards. Callan hovered nearby, silent as well, and never more than half a step from her. She couldn't help but be keenly aware of his proximity. Judging from the occasional glances of their current companions, they had noticed as well. After what she had said in the council chambers, the declaration of her freedom, Eve had to let them see her as above reproach as possible. There could simply be no indication she was following in *her* footsteps, so she quickened her pace ever so slightly, putting another half-step between the two of them. Callan allowed the larger gap, slowing his gait slightly. Remaining close, but not too close.

When they arrived at her door, Eve froze. Fear danced along her spine, cold fingers spreading like a spider's web. Blood was pooling on the floor just inside the door, thick and dark. The coppery smell of it hit her nostrils and she was keenly aware of the sound of someone retching nearby. One of the guards uttered a quiet curse, though the rest remained stony-faced and silent.

"Who?" She spoke to no one in particular as she moved through the group, and the guards in front stepped aside to let her pass. Whatever their opinions about it, they wouldn't stop her. "Who has been hurt?"

"No one has been hurt, it's just– my lady, perhaps it is better left to the guards..." Reynard's already pallid complexion had turned a peculiar shade that edged toward green.

"I need to see," she stated, her tone leaving no room for argument. "But remain here if you wish, or go and inform the others," she added more gently.

Nodding his thanks, the councilor scurried away, and unbidden, her father's voice sounded in her mind. *"Reynard the Rat," he was laughing. "Scurrying about, always watching."* She frowned at the memory, shaking her head in an attempt to clear the thought. Eve moved to the doorway, covering her nose and mouth with the back of her hand in an attempt to block out the coppery smell of death.

Blood. There was so much blood. The pool by the door was just the beginning, and as she lifted her gaze, she saw the truth of what had occurred.

It was everywhere, a garish contrast to the tranquility she had felt here up until this moment. Hardly a surface was left untouched. Blood, in spatters, pools, and grotesque smears everywhere she turned. The source, a handful of small game, rabbits, squirrels, and pheasants, had been scattered across her bed, in pieces, from the pillow she had laid her head to rest on for most of her life, all the way to the dressing gown neatly laid out by Sylvie at the foot.

Images of another bloody scene, one she had not personally seen herself, flashed into her mind. Men and horses were shredded, skin and muscle flayed from their bones by the claws of whatever beasts had climbed out of the gorge to hunt them. Is this what had been done to her father? To the men that had gone with him?

She knew little of what had happened, having been shielded from that information by both the council and her mother, but she had learned enough of the gorge and the monsters that called it home for her imagination to run wild, filling in the gaps of her knowledge. She couldn't help but stare, her gaze roaming over the horror of it all, even as her stomach dropped, bile rising high in her throat. *I'm going to be sick.*

And there it was, lying neatly in the center, a single piece of parchment. Callan protested as Eve stepped closer, reaching for the note.

"Evelyn," he warned, moving to stop her. She didn't know if he was afraid of some sort of poison or something more emotionally damaging, but she was beyond caring at that moment. She needed to know, to see what message whoever had done this wanted her to see. Had needed to do all of this to convey.

'This is the first warning. We are watching.'

Bile rose in the back of her throat, sudden and burning. The ground beneath her feet was suddenly uneven, and she began to sway. She was going to vomit, she realized, if she didn't leave this room right now.

Strong hands were suddenly on her, steadying her. One caught her elbow, the other her waist, pulling her closer to him, back onto still unsteady feet.

"I've got you," Callan murmured for her ears only, pulling her so close that she could feel the warmth of his breath against her bare neck, his steady heartbeat against her back. The scent of the forest, cedar, and sage surrounded her. His scent. The realization had her pulling away, forcing herself to regain composure.

"Where can I take you?" he asked, pulling away as she steadied. "Where do you want to go?"

"Still think it's nothing? I need to see my mother." Eve didn't care if it made her sound like a child as she handed the note to the nearest guard. She had no idea which of them it was. Didn't see. Didn't want to see, or think about what had happened any longer.

Callan led her down the hallway in silence. She had never been more grateful for the closeness of her mother's chambers to her own. Her knees threatened to buckle again with each step, but Callan's gentle yet firm grip on her elbow assured her that even if they did, she'd never hit the ground. Despite it all, because of it all, she realized, she was grateful for him. Babysitter or not.

Maids and other servants had already begun to arrive from other areas of the castle, no doubt tasked with cleaning the horror and gore from the princess's bedchamber. Not that she was likely to ever step foot inside that room again. Eve couldn't help but shudder at the thought of it.

As expected, extra guards had been posted outside the queen's chambers. Two that she saw, though she wouldn't have been surprised to see more lurking somewhere nearby as well. Their approach was met with bows and murmured sympathy, as well as speculating glances at Callan's hand, still holding her arm, offering her his strength should she need it. Less than an hour ago, she would have cared, would have shied away from his touch, at their gaze. But for now, at least, she no longer had it in her to care what they thought, what conclusions they may incorrectly draw from the gesture.

"I need to see her." It was command enough to have the guards stepping to the side, one of them opening the door wide for them to pass. The moment Riona spotted her daughter she flew from her chair in the receiving room and raced to greet them. Gentle hands suddenly cradled Eve's cheeks, and she felt Callan's hand fall away as he took a respectful step back. Still close, but allowing mother and daughter the space they needed.

"Are you hurt? They told me what happened. They said animals were butchered in your room. I was assured you were okay but, are you?" Her face was a picture of concern as she stepped back slightly, moving her hands from Eve's face to her shoulders as Riona looked her over; apparently needing to see for herself that she remained unharmed. Frosty blue eyes scanned her face next, searching for a sign of what she was feeling, what she wasn't saying, Eve knew.

"I'm okay, I'm okay," Eve assured her, as she stepped into her mother's outstretched arms. "I'm okay."

Riona held Eve close, rubbing her back in gentle circles, just as she had when she had nightmares as a girl, frightened and alone in the dark.

"They left a note," Eve said quietly. It wasn't a secret, and she was sure that Callan could hear, though he had moved slightly closer to the door in an attempt to give them some degree of privacy. She suspected he would remain close by for quite a while.

"What?" Riona demanded, pulling back, grasping her shoulders once more as she stared intently. "Tell me exactly what it said."

So she did. The threat was simple and clear enough that Eve knew precisely what was being warned against. Fall in line, or pay the price.

The shift in the air had been felt by all three of them, and they moved simultaneously to chairs near the fire, each taking a seat without a word. For several moments they simply sat, Eve's gaze on the fire, ignoring the two sets of eyes she could feel watching her. The fact that threats were coming so quickly was a shock. *I have been so naive.* "Who would do this?"

"The council comes to mind," Callan began, glancing between the two women. Eve could feel the intensity of his gaze, watching for any sign of how she felt about the accusation, even if his features remained stoic as usual.

"Yes," the queen conceded. "Of course. But I don't know who, or how many of them. There are those I believe are sympathetic and loyal enough to our family to not be a real threat. Eldred Gray, Alder Clarke, and Reynard Ward, specifically, have served us for decades. They are traditionalists but I cannot imagine they would resort to this."

Callan grunted, rising from his chair and facing the fire.

Falling back in her chair, Eve sighed. To hell with sitting like a lady and to hell with this entire day. She couldn't fathom how her mother remained so poised, so calm. "It could be anyone. Anyone inside this castle."

Two pairs of blue eyes turned to her at once.

Riona sighed, resigned and sad. A shadow clouded Callan's features. Perhaps he was reconsidering the job he had taken on now that the real risks were being laid at their feet. Eve watched the two of them closely, the only two people in the kingdom who she currently trusted.

"Most of this kingdom remains traditionalist. Many agree with what I am doing, and many more, I believe, will change their minds when they see it can be done, that no disaster will befall us for simply having a woman on the throne alone." She was right, she knew it, in that deep instinctual part of her soul. She could prove it to them all. She could prove that she was capable. That women were capable. One woman's mistake did not need to damn them all.

"Then there's no way to be sure." Her mother's voice was tired, much smaller than she'd ever heard it. As if the weight of Eve's decision was beginning to take a toll.

"Not yet," Callan added. His voice was even, deadly calm, his expression as unreadable as ever. What would he do, she wondered. Would he leave? If things got worse if more *warnings* were issued in the days leading up to her coronation, would he leave?

She had no idea what her mother had promised him in return for his help, gold she assumed, perhaps some territory that he would receive as soon as Eve was crowned, but she wondered if it would be enough to repay him for the danger he now took on.

She was staring, she realized, and averted her gaze. For a long moment, she stared at the fire. Is this what my life is to become? Constant threats and an ever-hovering bodyguard.

Turning her attention to him once more, she frowned. As if in answer to her unspoken thoughts he shook his head, and the deepest blue eyes she'd ever seen watched her intently, as if she were a puzzle he needed to solve.

"I'll understand if you no longer want any part in this. If you want to return to your home."

The words had no sooner left her mouth and he was answering, in that quiet, intense way of his. "I'm not going anywhere. I made a promise, and I'm staying here. Until you are safe." There was no more room for argument, for questioning. "Though I believe the time for the pretense of simply being a guest has now passed."

Eve simply nodded and turned to her mother, who had been regarding them intently, in silence. "What do we do now?"

CHAPTER 7

CALLAN

They had talked for hours. He and these two royal women he was now tied to. The Queen had enough of an idea of who could be trusted, and who she didn't believe could be trusted to give them a place to start. Without solid leads though, there was little he could do but continue watching over Eve. When Leysa arrived, which he hoped would be sooner than she'd anticipated, he could get to work on actually investigating. He could leave Eve's side long enough to do that once she was here.

He found himself prowling in the hall outside the queen's chambers, having stepped out to give mother and daughter a moment of privacy. After checking the room for other entry points, of course. Her room was high enough off the ground, with no balcony and no other entrances, to make him feel safe enough to leave them for a few moments anyway. Besides, if he didn't take a moment away from those piercing green eyes of hers, he'd never make it through the night, much less the next several days.

He dragged a hand through his hair and sighed, drawing a curious look from one of the guards stationed by the queen's door. Resisting the urge to bare his teeth at the slender young man, he instead stared back until the guard cleared his throat and looked away.

He'd used his gifts tonight, twice. He had known not to use them unless necessary, and here he had done so twice in one night, all because of her. He had needed to check for danger in the garden, he told himself, needed to make sure it was safe. It had been, thankfully, no sign had remained of the men she'd heard. He had only been able to sense something small, likely a lower fairy, tending to one of the flower beds.

The second time. Well, that one, Callan had to admit, was a mistake. He could practically see the sneer from the guard who had watched them in the garden. What right did anyone have to judge her for anything she did? From what he'd seen of this backward kingdom, a farmer's daughter had more rights and freedoms than they'd offered their princesses. It was ridiculous. He was still fighting the part of himself that wanted to find that damned guard and kick his ass for looking at her the way he had.

He couldn't explain why he felt such a strong need to protect her not just from physical harm, as he'd promised to, but also from the judgments and criticisms of the small-minded. *It's just part of the bargain.* Part of the promise he'd made to an old, old, friend. A part of him still questioned why he'd agreed. He owed nothing and had no real reason beyond honoring a friendship from a long time ago, but he felt drawn to this place, like an invisible thread had been pulling him closer, urging him to agree so that he could find himself here. A strange and unexpected feeling.

He glanced toward the closed doors of Riona's chambers. The strange tug had disappeared that morning when he'd arrived at the gates of Stoneweald. As if he'd reached the end of the tether. He hadn't brought it up to the queen, not yet. There hadn't really been time, and with all the events of today, it hadn't seemed important. They hadn't even made it to their dinner, and the planned conversation between himself and the queen, before shit had gotten interesting. Things could, and likely would, get worse, he knew, making a mental note to find the time to speak to her about not only that but the reminder she'd issued earlier.

He hadn't forgotten that night, the first time he'd laid eyes on the princess, and it wasn't likely he would. How strange, he mused silently, that the pull to this place hadn't started then nor the many times over the years he'd been either in or near Stoneweald. Maybe he'd speak to Leysa about it, or Valerian, if he arrived in time. They might have some thoughts on the matter.

He had noticed her expression, seen her looking a little harder at his eyes in the garden as if she'd noticed something strange about them. He had to be much more careful. Everything would fall apart if she found out.

The sound of footsteps approaching drew his attention. A maid, Sylvie, he thought her name was, had arrived, and now spoke in whispers to the young guard at the queen's door. Callan took a position by the window, leaning idly against the frame. He could hear every word, of course, but kept his attention on the rain beating on the nearby window. They didn't need to know that he could hear what they were saying.

"Her room is...it's a disaster, Dallin. It's awful. She must be so frightened. Who would do this?" He hazarded a brief glance at the maid, curiosity getting the best of him. Her face had lost all color. He'd only seen her twice during his brief time here, but she had been cheerful and smiling both times. All of that innate happiness she seemed to have had disappeared. Understandable given the night's events.

Dallin frowned, shaking his head and casting a glance toward Callan, who didn't immediately look away, offering instead a polite nod before slowly turning back to the window. He may be young, he noted, but the guard was observant. Good.

"We'll talk later, love," Dallin said to Sylvie. "At home?" The guard and the maid, Callan mused with a little humor. Interesting. He'd made it a point to learn all of the ins and outs of Stoneweald's court, and knowing the relationships between its inhabitants could be useful.

Sylvie murmured her agreement and headed back down the corridor. If she had looked his way, he didn't know, didn't particularly care. He'd have to watch her closely, of course, given her proximity to Eve, though both the queen and the princess had assured him that the maid could be trusted with absolute certainty. Their opinions held weight of course, but ultimately it was up to him to decide.

Left in relative silence again, he allowed his thoughts to drift once more as he stared out at the rain-drenched forests that surrounded the castle. Riona's warning earlier had gotten to him, more than he'd let on. More than he liked.

It had happened a few years ago, during his last visit to Stoneweald. He hadn't stepped foot in the kingdom of Darkegrove for years, nearing decades, before that. Callan had been asked to deliver a message to Riona, one only he could be trusted with, and it had just so happened the princess was celebrating her birthday that evening. He didn't know which one and hadn't bothered to ask. It wasn't relevant to the reason he'd come.

The family and a few guests had already partaken in the ritual celebration by the Black Pool and had moved on to the ball that followed. He had managed to find some time to speak alone with the queen, away from the attention of her husband and other prying eyes and ears, and relayed the message. Riona had graciously offered to let him stay the evening and enjoy the festivities before he returned home the next morning.

Parties had never held much interest for him, but he had agreed anyway. It was a long ride back to Valengard. Good food and drink, as well as rest, would be welcome.

A string quartet played lively music and the younger members of the court had mostly taken to the dance floor. The sun had set hours before, and the cool spring breeze drifted in through the open archways that led to the terrace and gardens outside. Every window had been left open, both to keep their guests cool as they danced and to invite nature into the celebration, he had been told by Riona when he arrived that night. The citizens of Darkegrove had always held a close relationship with the forests and mountains they called home, and he was pleased to see some of this particular piece of tradition remained.

"A dance my lord?" A courtier had been asking, desire and mischief twinkling in her hazel eyes. He had been about to agree when a flash of silver caught his eye. She had entered the room finally, the princess they were all there to celebrate, and the lovely girl standing in front of him had been all but forgotten. He hadn't even noticed her walking away, irritation lining her expression.

His gaze roamed over the princess; deep auburn hair, swept up, leaving the column of her neck bare, a slash of kohl across her lids, and red lipstick. Her gown was pure starlight, impossibly silver, and moving like liquid around her body, fitted to every ample curve. A sudden, sharp, intense pull in the center of his chest urged him toward her. He managed all of one step before the queen was suddenly in front of him, bearing a forced smile on her face that was so like Eve's, but more polished and calculating.

"You must be quite tired, Lord Thorne," she had said, offering him a pointed stare that left no doubt of the true meaning of her words. *Off-limits*, her cold gaze said. So he had listened, leaving quietly through the door at the back of the ballroom. She'd never noticed him and had not laid eyes on him until he'd arrived to protect her, at the request of her mother.

Playing the stranger, hiding his thoughts from her had been easy enough so far, but with every minute in her presence, with every questioning gaze, it got more difficult. He needed to know why he'd been so drawn to her, why he'd felt pulled to this place, and why, when he thought about leaving when all of this was done, an ache settled deep in the center of his chest.

Leysa and Valerian need to hurry their asses up.

The door opened finally, and he turned away from the window. That thing in his chest lurched as she stepped into the hallway. She looked exhausted, poised as she always was somehow, but exhausted. "Are you ready?" Eve asked, voice quiet. "They should have our room ready now."

Why had he insisted on sleeping near her? To keep her safe, of course, but gods, that was going to be torture. There'd be a door separating them, but knowing she was so close. It was going to be hell.

"I'm ready," he said, forcing the flat, disinterested tone he used as a mask.

CHAPTER 8

It had been a long day. Eve needed a bath, and then as much sleep as she could get. Though none had touched her, she felt as though her hands were coated in the blood of the creatures that had been slaughtered to frighten her into submission. She felt dirty and responsible. No matter how sure she was of her choice, or how right it felt when she'd declared her intent to the council, she couldn't discount the danger. People were willing to spill blood, to terrorize not just Eve, but also Sylvie who, she'd been told later, had been the one to find the mess.

The conversation in her mother's rooms had dragged on for hours. Every possibility and course of action had been weighed and carefully considered. Through most of it, Callan and her mother had done the talking, leaving Eve to listen, to absorb the knowledge they shared. Once again, she felt naive, unprepared for the hornet's nest she'd kicked.

The first order of business had been to have new rooms prepared for her. A suite this time, as Callan flat out refused to be housed even as far as next door. He'd said, *I have a job to do, and I am damn well going to do it the way I see fit*. There had been no arguing with that, especially when her mother had voiced her agreement, however reluctant. So a suite on the floor above had been chosen, one with a large and comfortable sofa in the sitting room had been prepared. Their discussion left her with little care for what others may think of the arrangement, and to at least put some of the rumors to rest, her mother spread the word to the court that Callan was, in truth, there to protect Eve. Few could argue with the practicality of the choice, though the council would likely be watching especially closely from now on, fearful as they were of a weak, feminine heart.

Callan and Eve were making their way to those very chambers, in silence. She had never been one who needed constant conversation to feel comfortable. In fact, she often sought out the peace that being alone offered her. Her garden had been her haven largely for that reason, when Emilia had been a little more than she could handle, gossiping about some nobleman or another or lamenting over a dress the seamstress hadn't made to her exact specifications. She didn't feel that her friend was entirely a shallow person, but sometimes Eve needed a break from the world itself and all of the shallow trappings of her gilded cage.

Thankfully Callan seemed content with the silence. He was walking close to her again, now that the ruse of him simply being a guest was dropped, and watched any who approached them carefully, from servant to courtier. Any one of them could have been behind the threat.

They were nearly there, rounding a corner when a familiar feminine voice called out. "Evie! Evie!"

Emilia. Eve barely suppressed a sigh. She hadn't seen her friend since before she had met with the council, and she couldn't deny it was at least partially by design. As much as she liked Emilia, her unending cheerfulness and love of gossip wore on Eve at times. Callan, again seeming to sense the direction of her thoughts, tilted his head in silent question. Did she want him to intercept?

Eve shook her head. She knew she would have to speak to Emilia eventually, and it may as well be now. As Emilia approached, Eve offered a strained smile. "Hi, Em."

"'Hi Em?!' Hi Em?!'" Shaking her head in disbelief, russet brown curls bounced merrily.

With a flawless heart-shaped face and a slender figure that many women at court envied, she was lovely, the picture of what a woman of Darkegrove was expected to be. Certainly not the soft, curvy shape of Eve's own body. Another way she upset the norm, though she was hardly alone. She simply didn't fit the standard of beauty held by the same people who thought it ridiculous that a woman could be strong enough to rule a kingdom. Small-minded idiots.

"That's all I get?" Emilia demanded in mock outrage. "After all that has happened, that's all I get?"

She stared Eve down a moment, waiting for a reply. Eve opened her mouth, ready to offer a vague apology, but Emilia was already turning her gaze to Callan, openly appraising him.

"Hello again." Emilia was a cat and Callan a mouse. Eyes the color of warm chocolate narrowed suspiciously. Whatever she thought was going on between the two of them, Emilia had decided to make it her mission to get to the bottom of it. The slow sweep of her gaze told Eve that Emilia would pounce if she determined he was fair game. She hated the way her fist curled in response and chose to ignore it, along with the pounding of her heart.

"Hello." Callan's reply was flat, offering not one ounce of friendliness in her direction.

"I'm sorry, truly. Just...so much has happened, and I couldn't tell anyone what I was going to do. To keep you out of it," Eve explained, weariness creeping into her voice. "Can we talk tomorrow? It's getting late, and I desperately need to sleep." Her gaze shifted between Emilia's sharp stare and Callan pointedly looking elsewhere.

Emilia ever so slowly dragged her attention back to Eve, her predatory smile shifting to a frown. "Of course, I understand. Find me tomorrow and we can talk then. Maybe I'll see you in Forest Haven?"

Nodding her agreement, Eve reached for Emilia's hand, giving a gentle squeeze, one that was returned instantly. As she turned, Callan following just behind, Emilia snickered, so quietly Eve couldn't be certain it was her. She glanced back, to where Emilia had been, but she had already gone. "Oh, everyone is going to hear all about you," Eve sighed.

"Let them talk." He shrugged, the picture of nonchalance. "Your mother will ensure that the truth is spread, and frankly, I don't care what they think."

"I wish I could say the same." It was the truth. For as long as she could remember, everything she did was under scrutiny. Any misstep could be fodder for gossip, something used to embarrass either Eve herself, or more importantly to some, her father.

She had been allowed some freedom, to a point, but while certain things, like dalliances with merchants' sons, were acceptable as long as they were kept quiet, others were not. Like speaking openly on political matters or challenging tradition. Callan, with his standing as a lord, would be seen as much more of a threat to the tradition the council was so intent on holding to than Brodie ever had.

"You get used to it, after a while," he remarked to her surprise.

"You've been the center of such gossip before?" she asked doubtfully.

The corner of his lips twitched upward slightly. "Well, not exactly the same, but yes." He paused a beat, as if deciding whether or not to continue. "As the son of a very important man, I was under a lot of pressure to be certain...example to others." At her raised brow, he added, "Nothing like what you're facing obviously. But there were certain... unattainable standards held by both my father and others."

"I imagine you do understand a little, I suppose, as the son of a Lord," she admitted. "Though I'm sure you wouldn't have had to fight for the right to choose who, and if, to marry."

"No, princess, I would not. On that matter, my parents would have no say."

His shuttered expression was at odds with his light words, but before she could remark further, they had reached her door now. Suddenly she felt awkward in a way she hadn't since those first days with Brodie. Standing at the threshold of her private room, with a man she had only just met, her nerves were a mess. As much as he had helped her, he was still a stranger.

"I should check first, just to be sure." Without waiting for a reply, he pushed the heavy oak door open and stepped inside.

He still bore no weapon that Eve could see, and she couldn't help but wonder what exactly he would be able to do if someone lay in wait. Edging closer, she peered inside, watching as he moved about the sitting area with surprising grace. A wolf stalking prey. The only light source in the dark room came from the low burning fire in the hearth, and bright moonlight leaked in through the closed drapes.

With a wave of his hand, Callan beckoned Eve into the sitting room. Disappearing into the shadows beyond the bedroom door, Callan left her alone, standing by the fire. Heat warmed her skin, chasing away the worst of the chill that still haunted her after what had happened downstairs. She was certain it would take a long time to fully rid herself of it.

A log snapped in the fireplace, and she jumped, letting loose a quiet curse.

"That's not very ladylike." Callan teased, surprising her with more humor than she'd heard so far, which wasn't saying much, truth be told.

"Did I ask?" Eve spun to look at him leaning against the doorframe, hands in his pockets. How did he always manage to look so casual with everything that was going on?

"Why don't you carry a weapon?" It wasn't the question she really wanted to ask, the one that had been on her mind since the garden. *What was he promised in payment for protecting me?* She had a suspicion whatever reply she got would be vague, a nonanswer designed to deflect. Maybe she would ask her mother instead; she would either answer truthfully or simply tell Eve to leave it alone.

"Who says I don't?" His gaze drifted from her face downward slowly, not a lustful gaze but a curious one leaving her feeling suddenly chilled for an entirely different reason.

"I need a bath. I assume no armed assassins are lying in wait in my bathtub?" She lifted a brow, waiting only a moment before heading toward the bedroom. Toward him. She couldn't say for certain why, but annoyance at his presence flared brightly once more. He hadn't actually done anything to deserve her ire, the opposite in fact. He had been there to support her when she needed it, and she had shown little gratitude for the fact.

"Enjoy your bath, I'll be out here." It was dismissal enough for Eve, and as she neared the doorframe, he moved, passing her just before she crossed the threshold. Cedar and sage trailed in his wake, faint, almost imperceptible, and for the second time, she ignored the racing of her heart.

Callan was seated on the sofa facing the fireplace when she returned, relaxed with one arm draped over the back. As nonchalant and calm as he'd been most of the day. For a moment Eve simply stood in the doorway, looking him over. She had been in the bath so long she half expected him to come and check that she was alive. Every inch of her skin had been scrubbed nearly raw, trying to rid herself of the events of this evening.

Too much had happened. Too much awfulness. She didn't know if she would ever truly feel the same again, but she had at least managed to feel somewhat more normal, despite the weight that had settled itself on her shoulders.

"I was beginning to think I may have missed an assassin after all." He didn't bother to look at her, but she could hear the smirk in his tone.

Eve snorted. "No, it seems you are sufficient at your job." More than sufficient, obviously, if he had heard her quiet approach so easily. Though she hated to admit she was grateful for his protection, she could at least admit it seemed as though he knew what he was doing.

"I appreciate the glowing praise." Callan offered a dismissive wave of his hand, not bothering to turn around. "You didn't tell your mother about the garden."

"No, I didn't." Eve tightened the robe around her waist just a little. She had considered dressing, but it was late, well past midnight if she had to guess, and the plush blue robe was too comfortable to pass up, especially when she intended to be sleeping in just a few short minutes.

"Are you going to ask me why?" She took a seat in the chair closest to the fire. So she could dry her still wet hair a little, she told herself, not to be near to him. She was less annoyed by his presence than she had been earlier, thanks to a hot soak and time, she supposed, but the irrational feeling was still there.

"No, I don't think I will." Turning toward her finally, he offered a slight smirk. "I can guess your reasons, and I don't blame you." Tilting his head to the side he paused a moment to examine her face.

Irritating man. She resisted the urge to turn away, to break the eye contact he now made. Instead, she lifted her chin a bit higher.

"I'm glad you approve," Eve replied, lifting a brow. "If I ask you something, will you tell me the truth?" A pointless question, but she had to ask.

"How do you know I won't just say yes and then simply lie anyway?" he countered, head tilting. "Go ahead and ask your question. I'll tell you the truth, if I can." His tone was as dispassionate as it always was, but his eyes had taken on an intensity she had not seen before. Somehow so dark blue now they neared black. *Just a trick of the light*, she supposed, but it was strange.

"Why are you here? Protecting me. You said you came because you were asked to, but everyone has a price. I imagine yours must have been high, to come into the middle of this conflict, and for someone of your standing..." Eve trailed off, letting the rest of the sentence hang between them unspoken.

"Are you asking how much I'm being paid?" Intensity gave way to amusement, and now those blue depths lightened, nearly sparkling. Eve thought she might fall out of her chair from shock.

"No. Well, yes. I suppose I am." Embarrassment flooded her cheeks, and she finally broke away, looking instead to the fire.

With a sigh, he sat up, forearms leaning against his thighs. "I'm not. Being paid, I mean. I think you're doing the right thing. More to the point, I made a promise to protect you, and I keep my promises, Eve."

It was the first time he'd called her that. *Eve.* Formally, she was always Evelyn, and even amongst family and friends, Evie was usually the preferred nickname. Something about it, about the way he said it had goosebumps dancing over her skin. She waited for an explanation, for him to expand on the statement, but he remained silent for so long that she finally looked at him again.

He was gazing into the fireplace, expression shuttered. Any amusement that had been in his eyes before had vanished once more, and she couldn't help but feel disappointed in its absence.

Whatever he was thinking, she doubted it was likely he would share, and she suspected she was pushing him enough as it was. *We are strangers*, she reminded herself again, thoughts drifting back to the sleeping arrangement he had insisted on.

Weighing the importance of this answer against possibly annoying the man who would literally stand between herself and danger, Eve pressed on. She needed to know. Whatever the price he paid, the promise made, it had to be huge.

Even if she had been too naive to expect real danger, her mother and Callan had not. In fact, neither had seemed surprised at what had happened. Upset, afraid, yes, but not surprised.

"To whom? Why?" She watched closely, as if she could glean anything from his demeanor that would help her decide the truthfulness of his response. Despite his declaration, Eve had no way of knowing for certain she could trust him, though a small part of her already did.

"I can't tell you everything, and I told you I wouldn't lie," he replied quietly, rising from his seat. Before she realized what he was doing, before she could protest, he was standing directly in front of her, hands on the armrests on either side of the chair. He was so close, leaning down so they were face to face, that she couldn't help but meet his gaze again. When he spoke, his voice was little more than a whisper. "I may not be able to tell you everything, not yet, but I will keep you safe. Always."

Always. That single word was a promise in and of itself. One that both thrilled and terrified her. They were so close now that if she had wanted to touch him, to press her lips to his, she would need only move ever so slightly. The image of the two of them tangled in sheets flashed into her mind once more as cedar and sage filled her nose, setting her pulse at a gallop.

Damn it.

Eve didn't trust herself to speak, so she settled for a nod. After a beat, he pulled away, still standing in front of her but leaving plenty of room for her to move if she wanted.

"We should sleep," she muttered, rising to her feet. "I'm expected in the city tomorrow for an appearance. It may be a long day." She didn't dare look at him again, too afraid of what she might do if she found those blue eyes looking at her as intensely as they just had been, so she made her way directly to her room.

"Sleep well, dove," he called quietly, as she shut the door.

CHAPTER 9

Coronations were rare enough events in that when they did occur, they were momentous events. Receptions, dinners, parties, and public appearances, all had to be packed into a short window before the new monarch could take the throne. The first of these, an appearance in Darkegrove's largest city, Forest Haven, was due to happen this afternoon.

She would be expected to give a brief greeting to the citizens, who would then offer words of blessing and gifts, which would then be passed on to a charity of her choice. It was tedious and sometimes took the entire day, but it was necessary to allow the people of Darkegrove to feel at least somewhat connected to the person who would be leading them.

Sylvie arrived shortly after dawn. The maid moved about the room humming quietly to herself as she laid out the gown that had been chosen for the occasion.

Eve peeked from beneath the blankets that remained pulled over her head. For a moment she considered simply staying in bed for the rest of the day. Responsibility be damned.

"It's time, my lady," Sylvie prompted gently.

Heaving a breath, Eve rolled over, tossing the blankets away dramatically. "Has Lord Thorne…Is he out there?" Eve glanced toward the closed door of her bedroom. Heat flooded her cheeks at the thought of their rather intense, albeit brief, exchange the night before.

"Lord Thorne stepped out a few minutes ago, my lady," Sylvie replied. Eve could feel the maid watching her curiously and despite her decision last night to adopt his carefree attitude regarding the opinions of others, she still felt a bit self-conscious. She dreaded the idea that even Sylvie, who knew her better than most, would make the same assumption so many others would regarding their non-existent relationship. Eve scrambled to find a way to show Sylvie just how wrong the idea was.

"Well, I hope he'll return to his post by the time we need to go." It was a lame attempt, she knew, but it was the best she could think of at the moment.

"I'm sure he will, my lady." Offering a grin that told Eve her attempt had been an utter failure, Sylvie returned to her task selecting matching shoes to go with the gown.

Later, after she'd bathed and dressed in that soft blue robe again, Eve took a seat at the vanity. Sylvie set to work on her hair, braiding it slowly as Eve watched in the mirror.

The faintest hint of dark circles had appeared beneath her eyes. That would have to be hidden with makeup. Regardless of what she felt, the fear and exhaustion, it was her duty to appear strong, without doubt. Any sign of weakness would be seen as a reason to stand against what she was trying to do and would give support to the claim that women were far too fragile to bear the burden of the crown alone.

It didn't take Sylvie long to style Eve's hair, braided and then wrapped like a crown around the top of her head. Strategically placed flowers hid the pins that held it up, and a few loose ringlets softened the look.

"Can I ask a question, my lady?" Sylvie's typically self-assured tone was quiet and nervous. Setting the brush she'd been using on Eve's cheeks gently on the vanity, Sylvie wrung her hands.

Eve had never enforced strict social protocols with Sylvie, or any of the staff, so there was no reason she could think of for Sylvie to be afraid to speak freely. "Of course, anything." Two sets of eyes met in the mirror, one confused, one anxious.

"You're being careful, my lady? I think what you're doin' is great, but with what happened in your room. Well, I know a lot of people around here are so angry with the choice you made. I think you're very brave, and what you're doing is right, but–" Sylvie bit down on her lower lip, hands still wringing in front of her. "I worry, my lady."

A weight lifted from her shoulders immediately. Sylvie hadn't asked about Callan, about any supposed entanglement between them as she had expected. More importantly, she hadn't tried to talk her out of her decision to refuse marriage. "I am, and I will continue to be, I promise." Nodding, Sylvie offered a smile that still did not quite reach her eyes.

Eve was stepping into her gown when she heard the outer doors of the suite open, followed by Callan's low voice, presumably speaking to the guards stationed outside. "...and three following behind. I want her kept safe today."

She finished dressing quickly, tugging the dress up and sliding her feet into her heels as Sylvie fastened the buttons that trailed along her spine. The fabric was lovely, a shade of green so dark it neared black. The bodice was fitted, with a heart-shaped top and a flared skirt. Around her waist, a jeweled belt of silver, with tiny, crystal clear gems attached. The effect was stunning. Eve had opted for simple emerald earrings for jewelry, a complement to the gown and belt.

"Ready my lady?" Sylvie asked, taking a step back. Folding her arms in front of her skirts, she smiled, pride etched in her features. They glanced toward the door to the sitting room at the same time. "Please, be careful today. My prayers are with you."

Appreciation had Eve smiling warmly. "That means more to me than you know," Eve said, inclining her head briefly before moving to the door. "Here we go."

Whomever Callan had been speaking to was gone by the time she had finished getting ready. He was alone, staring out the terrace doors when she emerged. He didn't bother to turn at first, which gave Eve a moment to look him over.

For the first time, he had not dressed the part of the nobleman, but of the guardian. Sleek, black-scaled armor that must have been tailored specifically for him. Well fitted so that it hugged his muscled form perfectly, and well made enough to leave little doubt that the armor was not simply for show. Twin blades, their ornate black handles adorned with rubies, had been sheathed at his back in the shape of a pair of wings.

"Are you ready to go, Princess?" he asked, in the same lazy drawl he always used. So out of place with the picture of a deadly warrior. Turning slowly, he finally looked at her, and Eve could have sworn something like surprise danced across his features before disappearing so quickly.

A witty reply died on her tongue as he looked her over. The tingle along her spine at the intense gaze he fixed on her was beginning to feel familiar, and not altogether unpleasant. Slowly, so slowly, his gaze slid over her from head to toe and back again. She was once again a puzzle he wanted to solve. When their eyes finally met, they simply stood in silence appraising one another for a heartbeat.

"We should discuss safety before we leave," he said suddenly, dragging a hand through his dark hair, and tearing his eyes away from her to look at the door. "I will stay by your side, and there will be several guards surrounding the carriage, and you, at all times. The city guard has already been doubled up for today, and the streets we'll be taking are cleared of foot traffic." He turned his attention to the ornate clock above the mantel, frowning at the time. "They know a threat has been made, and while most of them were pissy about it, they'll do what they're told."

Turning his attention back to her once more, he added, "They aren't happy with your choice, but I don't think it will be a serious problem today."

"Thank you. For all of it, I mean. Not just for today." Eve smiled, hoping to appear calm and collected. Not at all like the nervous mess she suddenly felt. Her stomach was doing flips, and her hands were trembling. Thanking the stars for Sylvie, she hid them within the hidden pockets of her skirt and fiddled with the little surprise the maid had tucked inside.

"I made a promise," he said simply. Repeating the phrase she'd heard several times now. Eve still didn't understand, and it drove her mad. *A promise to whom? Mother? Why?* Not knowing was going to drive her mad.

"To whom?" Eve pressed, though she knew he wouldn't answer, not after last night.

"Don't." Almost as much a plea as a command. Callan's eyes had taken on an intensity Eve didn't think she would ever get used to. They were a depthless sea she could drown in. His gaze was unwavering as he silently awaited her acknowledgment.

"I know, you can't tell me everything right now," She sighed, echoing his words from last night. "But you will?"

For a moment he didn't respond, didn't look away as his gaze roamed over her face, searching for something. She had no idea what he sought or if he found it when he finally said, "Trust me."

How? They were strangers thrown into a situation that, despite being of her own making, she had little control over. Yes, she had trusted him with her life. She supposed she had made that decision the moment she met him and accepted he would be her guard. But deciding to trust him when he said he would never lie to her was an entirely different sort of trust, one that left her feeling both weightless and chained down at the same time. It was terrifying, more so than the threat left in her room just yesterday. She wouldn't allow herself to think too hard about why that was or why a very small, but ever-growing, part of her said, *Yes, I trust you.*

She realized he was still waiting for an answer, for some signal that she understood, so she nodded, and turned for the door. "I'm ready," Eve said finally, quietly, not entirely certain she meant ready to leave.

Unlike before, the silence they walked in as they made their way to the waiting carriage was stifling. She'd agreed to be patient, to wait until he could provide her with the answers she desperately wanted. Partially out of desire to avoid annoying the man tasked with keeping her alive, but mostly because a small voice told her she didn't want to know, not just yet. Despite that, curiosity was still a burning ember within her. The few glances she had hazarded his direction told Eve nothing about what he was thinking, not that she had expected to be able to glean much from his stony features.

The courtyard and surrounding gardens were drenched from the rainfall that had finally abated the night before, and the smell of sodden earth flooded her senses. The sky above remained cloudy, devoid of any real sunlight. Darkegrove was certainly earning her name.

As Callan had ordered, three of the household guards waited behind the carriage, already astride their horses. Two others waited ahead of the carriage, and a large chestnut stallion she assumed to be Callan's stood at the bottom of the steps, a rather spindly-looking stable boy holding his reins.

As they reached the bottom of the stone stairs, Callan stopped short. "I'll be riding alongside the carriage. I want to be able to keep an eye on things, and I can't do that from inside." His gaze roamed over the gathered party, inspecting them before deeming them satisfactory with a curt nod.

"It's time to go." At Callan's command, a pair of footmen Eve hadn't noticed before immediately complied, opening the door to the carriage. Eve had no idea when he'd taken command of her men, but judging by how quickly they obeyed, and the fact that none of the more senior guardsmen seemed to argue, he had to have done something to earn their respect. Yet another question she would want an answer to.

Callan held a hand out for her, silently raising a brow, impatience written all over his face as he said, "Get in, dove."

Irritation with his presumptuousness flared. "So demanding," Eve remarked, placing her hand in his. He brushed his thumb over the back of her hand, sending a jolt of electricity racing through her very core at the contact. The gesture was so gentle in such stark contradiction to the roughness of his hand, and to the intense apathy he displayed. She couldn't stop her sharp intake of breath.

"You have no idea," he replied, lips curving into a sly smirk. It was all she could do to climb into the carriage, jerking her hand from his as if he were on fire.

"Enjoy the ride, Princess," he said over his shoulder, as he stepped away.

Ass.

CHAPTER 10

The short ride to Forest Haven was relatively pleasant if for no other reason than it was quiet, and Eve was alone. Sort of. She could at least pretend the guards and footmen outside the carriage weren't there, that Callan wasn't just outside. They hadn't spoken since they left, and the only sounds that accompanied them were the rhythmic clopping of horse's hooves and the quiet rumble and creaks of the carriage rolling down the cobbled road.

Sylvie had made sure a cloak was waiting for her in the carriage. Black fur, lined with silk on the inside, with a silver clasp at the throat. She would have to remember to thank Sylvie for her thoughtfulness later. The long sleeves of her gown had kept her warm enough, at least to walk to the carriage, but by the time they arrived in the center of the city, only a short ride from Stoneweald, the cool air was beginning to get to her.

Unlike before, Callan was nowhere to be seen when Eve stepped out of the carriage with the help of one of the younger footmen, Ferris she thought his name was. She thanked the boy, who couldn't have been more than fifteen, with a smile. His mouse brown eyes widened and color crept up his neck and cheeks, but he managed to stammer a shaky, "Y'er welcome, My Lady," before all but tripping over his own feet to move away. The poor boy was going to have a rough go of it with the girls in Forest Haven if he was that shy just speaking a few words to her, Eve mused.

She had fastened the cloak around her shoulders just before arriving, tugging it close around her as a cool wind swept through the street. Though Callan had been true to his word and had seen the street they'd stopped on cleared, the crowds were still present, kept away by temporary barricades set up by the city guard. Well within sight, but not so close that she would have to interact with them yet.

Eve kept her expression calm, schooling her features into the cool neutrality she'd seen her mother wear so often as she perused the crowd. Her heart gave a silly thump as her gaze landed on Callan, standing a few feet away. Where he had come from so suddenly, she didn't know.

He was looking her over, in that slow, methodical way of his. Eve shuddered and gripped the edge of the cloak like a lifeline. It had nothing to do with the cold, she knew, but instead with the intense deep blue eyes now locked with her own.

"Ready, Princess?" The corner of his lips twitched upward slightly and for a moment she had the distinct feeling that he knew exactly what his appraisal did to her. *Ass.*

"Lead the way," she replied, loosening her grip on the cloak. Eve straightened, lifting her chin slightly. If he knew she was lying, he didn't let on. She wasn't ready, not really. She knew what needed to be done and had practiced what she wanted to say, but all the preparation in the world wouldn't calm her nerves.

She had never spoken in front of a crowd before. The fact that for her first time, the crowd comprised of people who may hate her for what she was trying to do only made matters worse. There would be pushback, likely a lot of it. The best she could hope for was some small degree of patience, of understanding, from the people she would lead.

The group made its way down the street, moving toward the main city square where a platform had been built for the occasion. Ahead, throngs of people had been allowed to gather, facing the stage from where the princess would soon be greeting them. The din of the crowd rose higher as it approached. Pounding, thunderous waves crashing on a stony shore filled her ears, all but drowning out the many voices that surrounded her. Darkness flooded the edges of her vision, and her breath came quickly and her pulse raced. She couldn't get air fast enough, her breath heaving hard and fast. *I can't do this.*

"Eve." His voice was little more than a whisper in a storm, heard but not acknowledged. "Eve." More insistent this time, louder. A lifeline in the tempest. She turned to look at Callan finally. The darkness that threatened to swallow her whole began to abate, shadows sent scurrying at his voice as she clung to the lifeline he offered.

When did we reach the stage? How have we been standing at the foot of the wooden steps?

"Eve, look at me." A quiet, but firm, command. She'd been gripping his arm, she realized then, as her breathing slowed.

"Don't be so damn bossy," She retorted, yanking her hand from his arm, though there was no real fire behind it.

A quiet chuckle was her reward. "There she is. You ready to do this?"

Eve met his gaze, inhaling slowly to calm her frayed nerves. The roaring in her ears was beginning to quiet, and her heartbeat slowed to a normal pace.

"I can do this," she said, as much for her own benefit as his. Without another word, he turned, gesturing to the captain of the city guard standing at the top of the platform. The captain silenced the crowd with a wave of his hand. Sunlight glinted off polished black armor.

"My lady," he called, no hint of emotion in his rough voice. "We are ready for you."

There was no room for fear, for doubt. The people of Darkegrove needed a leader who was sure and brave; now more than ever. Summoning every ounce of courage she had, Eve stepped forward. She wondered if her father would be proud, or horrified. He had never wanted her to walk this path, to take the throne alone, but she couldn't help but hope he would be proud of his daughter anyway. Would he see that she was trying to do what she thought was best for his people, her people? Or would he condemn her choice and, like the council, try to force her into a marriage she didn't want or need?

I have a duty, she reminded herself, *to see it through*. Whatever her father would have thought, she had made her choice and now needed to stand by it. She wished her mother could have been here, at least, but the council had requested she stay behind, for security they had said. The threat left in Eve's room had been enough to scare them into taking extra precautions for both their safety. She was on her own, and that was okay.

A deep inhale and she was stepping forward, ready to speak, to offer whatever sense of security and right that she could. The autumn wind swept up dramatically, sending her cloak to fly behind her like dark wings. The cool wind bolstered her determination. *I can do this.*

One step. That was all it took for all hell to break loose.

"People of–"

A woman screamed somewhere in the crowd, then another. A man shouted somewhere to the left. Some of the guards scrambled onto the stage and surrounded the princess, while others rushed into the crowd.

"What is it? What's happening?" Eve demanded of no one in particular, rising on tiptoes to see around the guards.

Smoke, thick and white, was rising from down one of the streets. Far enough away that she couldn't see the source. People were beginning to run, to flee whatever was happening. To the left, down another street, a series of loud pops, followed by more white smoke.

"We aren't sure yet, my lady," a guard was saying, as he gripped her arm firmly. Not enough to hurt, but certainly enough to draw her attention. "We're moving you to safety while we figure it out."

"No, wait," she tried to stop, to turn and see what was happening. People were screaming, running in all directions to escape the fire, or whatever it was. Orders were being shouted above the noise, but she couldn't quite make out what was being said. Fear coursed through her veins, real and deep. He said he would be close by, so where was he? He should be the one leading her away.

"Where is Lord Thorne? Where are you taking me?" This time her questions were left unanswered as she was led through the streets by three of the city guards who had been on the stage with her. The tallest of the three, thin, with muddy brown hair and a thick beard, led the way, still holding her arm in his tight grasp. The other two, a short blond man and a mountain of a man with red-brown hair followed.

The captain, it seemed, had disappeared into the clamor, and Callan was nowhere to be seen. They continued leading her through one alley after another, in an attempt to avoid the larger groups of people still fleeing whatever had just happened, she thought. But why not go to the carriage a small part of her asked, and a new sort of fear blossomed.

"Stop," Eve demanded, and was ignored again. The guard gripping her arm still hadn't released it and she tugged, attempting to pull her arm free. His grip was firm, unyielding, and tight enough now that she knew it would leave a bruise. He didn't so much as look at her as they kept walking. "Let me go." she ordered again, hating the panic that had crept into her voice. "Now."

A snort was his only reply. The blond guard spoke up only when they reached what appeared to be a dead end.

"Here?" he asked the leader, the man with the vice grip.

"Yeah, here. We'll wait here," the leader replied.

Eve jerked her arm once again, and this time he released it. The reality of her situation was beginning to set in, but it still made no sense. What was their plan? To drag her to this alley and murder her? How many people had seen them escort her away? There had to be more to this, but she wasn't all that interested in waiting around to find out.

She couldn't fight them. That would be pointless, not with three of them and one of her. She had been trained to defend herself, and if there had been one of them she might've been able to hold her own long enough for someone to help, or to escape. Against three though?

Regardless of the odds, she had to try. She had to do something. There was no way she was simply going to accept whatever they had planned for her. She was not going to lie down and die or cower in the corner like some simpering coward. She was going to fight back, even if she died in the process. Better to go down fighting than crying and begging for her life.

As they shuffled around, waiting for what she didn't know, she began to formulate a plan. The thing she had loved most about her dress, one of the reasons she had chosen it, was that it had pockets. Finally free of the kidnapper's grip, she dipped a hand into the folds of her gown, into the pocket where Sylvie had hidden a dagger, just in case.

A week ago, she would've been scandalized by it and would have asked Sylvie what in the world she was thinking. Not now. She may have been naive when she took her first step down this path, but she had learned the truth of how much danger she had been in over these last couple of days and was smart enough to be grateful for Sylvie's assistance.

"I don't know guys, it's taking too long…" The blond one was getting nervous.

Eve didn't know what he was waiting for, but instinct and common sense told her she was running out of time. Whatever, or whomever, they were waiting for was not something she wanted to be around for. Blessedly, they hadn't noticed her hand slide free of the pocket, or the dagger she'd produced. It was small but deadly sharp, and she knew how to use it, thanks to her mother and the training she'd arranged for Eve years ago.

The skinny blond one had his back to her now, facing the leader who had moved farther into the alley, leaning against the grimy wall. The one with red hair was facing out, looking in the direction of the street they'd come from. None of them were so much as looking at the princess, having deemed her completely helpless. After all, she was seemingly unarmed, alone, and in a gown and heels. Hardly a threat.

She would have to be fast and damn lucky, but maybe, just maybe, she could get away, and find safety amongst the crowds she could still hear, somewhere out of sight but nearby. Eve eased closer to the redhead who kept watch, stepping out of her shoes as she moved.

"We will wait as long as it takes, damn it," the ringleader snapped irritably, sweat beginning to bead at his brow despite the cool temperature.

"It's too much of a risk. If he doesn't get here soon…what if someone sees?" The blond man paced in front of his companion, shaking his head from side to side.

The two behind her had fallen into an argument, voices low but intense, and were focused solely on each other. Now was her best chance.

Lunging forward, she launched herself at the redheaded guard, stabbing at the side of his thick neck with the dagger as soon as her body hit the brick wall that was his back. Willing herself to ignore the spray of warm liquid over her face, arms, and chest, she shoved away from him, taking off at a dead sprint down the alley, toward freedom, before the other two had a chance to process what had just happened. His gurgled cry of pain haunted every step as she ran.

Forest Haven was large enough to have a rather confusing warren of streets and alleys, but blessedly small enough that she could guess which direction to run with some degree of certainty. Barefoot, she stumbled over loose stones and gods only knew what else as she ran. She didn't give herself even a moment to consider what she was stepping on, what was cutting into her feet as she fled; her only thought was escape.

CHAPTER 11

CALLAN

She was gone. Someone had taken her while he stood not ten feet away. At the first sign of fire, when everyone had started screaming, he'd been distracted, only for a moment but it was long enough. The city guard had taken charge of the scene, clearing the square as best they could of panicked citizens. A few had taken off in the direction of the fires, only to report back within minutes. Just some burning garbage and a few noisemakers, small bombs that were mostly harmless, generally used to play pranks. Nothing that would cause any real damage. It was an amateur, but effective, distraction.

When had she been taken? Dragging a hand through his hair, he recounted the last time he'd had his eyes on her. The smoke had come first, then the screaming, followed by the noisemakers.

He'd turned his back for a mere moment when the screaming started, had started toward the fire to help, a stupid mistake. She'd been on the stage surrounded by guards, about to speak to the crowd. He'd turned around and– realization dawned.

Callan pushed his way through the guards gathered near the podium, awaiting orders from the city captain who had just returned to his post by the platform. "How many men did you have on the stage with her?" Callan demanded. The captain frowned, the expression deepening the lines of his aging face.

"Eight, in total. Four on each side. Tried to keep 'em to the sides to not obstruct the view. Why?" He eyed Callan suspiciously. Clearly, he didn't like where Callan was going with this. To hell with him.

"How many of them are here now?" Callan stepped closer to the captain, gesturing to the gathered guards. "Are they all accounted for? Or are some of them missing?"

Realization bloomed in the captain's eyes, and he scanned the gathered guards. "Shit," he murmured. "I know all of my men, every one of them by name. Three...three of the men I had on the stage are gone."

Callan knew the moment his eyes had shifted. The captain's grey eyes widened with fear, and he took an instinctive step back.

"Find her," Callan commanded, loud enough for all the men gathered here. "If there is a single mark on her, you will beg for the sweet release of death before I end you," he growled, lowering his tone for the captain's ears only. His expression and the unbridled rage radiating from him left little room for doubt about the truthfulness of the threat.

The captain took a breath, steeling himself. "Do it!" he shouted to his men. "Your princess is in danger. Find her."

Callan didn't wait to see if they followed orders or if they protested. He'd look for her himself. He could only pray to the long-forgotten gods that he'd be in time.

CHAPTER 12

Fear had frozen her in place earlier when the worst thing she faced today was speaking to a crowd and convincing them of her worthiness to rule. Now, fear drove her, pushing Eve harder and faster than she had ever run.

She could hear shouting behind her, the sounds of boots growing closer and closer. Gathering her skirts as high as she could, Eve made a sharp right and pushed herself harder. She was getting winded, her lungs burning with every inhaled breath. The main street was so close that she could see it now.

People were still flooding the streets, fleeing the main square she had been taken from. She could only hope they would be salvation and not damnation as she called out for help.

Strong, broad hands gripped her waist from behind and yanked her backward. A wordless scream escaped her lips, and she began kicking blindly, fighting for her life. For a moment she couldn't think, couldn't breathe. The dagger whistled through the air as she swung blindly.

No, please, not like this. She didn't know if she'd screamed the words aloud or if they'd only been panicked thoughts as she fought as hard as she could, kicking backward and aiming for the one part that might down a man long enough for her to run again.

The world spun as her attacker's grip changed, moving from her waist to her shoulders, twisting her to face him. This was her only shot at escape. So close, she had been so close to safety. Another scream erupted from her as she was shoved against the brick wall behind her, and her attacker grabbed her wrist with one hand, leaving her unable to swing the dagger anymore. The other hand held her shoulder, pinning it against the rough brick wall behind her. The wall was cold and scraped against the back of her head, despite the care her attacker was taking not to hold her too tightly.

"Eve! I've got you, dove, you're okay." Callan's panic-edged voice stopped her dead and she opened her eyes, unsure when she'd even closed them. Eve dropped the dagger to the ground and slumped back against the wall. Relief washed over her like a winter breeze.

"Who did this to you? Where are they?" Callan's voice was low and filled with barely contained fury. His eyes had taken on the color of midnight, so blue they neared black, promising a slow and painful death to whomever was responsible.

Tears fell freely now, exhaustion flooding her. "I don't know. I think I killed one, but there were two more." She heaved a shaky breath and looked down at herself. Blood soaked her neck and chest, and judging from the stickiness she could feel on her cheeks, splattered across her face.

"Where are you hurt?" His murderous gaze dropped from her face, and he released his hold on her wrist, instead sliding both hands over her shoulders and arms, searching for the source of the blood.

"It's not mine...none of it... I'm okay but–" She lifted a shaking hand to her temple, closing her eyes and taking a deep breath. She'd never get through all of this if she couldn't get her breathing under control.

"They were guards, or dressed like them at least. They were behind me...there were three of them. I think I killed one. Callan...I've never killed anyone. I think I killed him. They took me away from the crowd, to safety they said, and.... What happened anyway? Why was everyone screaming?" She was rambling, the full weight of her ordeal catching up with her now. Her voice was shaking, and words were tumbling free without thought. "Where were you? I asked them, but they said...And then they took me…What happened?" She was beginning to tremble now. Shivering despite not feeling the cold.

Callan stopped his search for wounds that weren't there, instead laying a palm against her cheek gently. "You're okay, you're safe."

It was a short-lived gesture of comfort as he quickly stepped back, crossing his arms across his chest. Shaking his head he glanced toward the street where the flood of people had slowed to a trickle. Somehow, nobody had bothered to look toward them, or if they had they hadn't noticed the blood that was quickly drying on her skin, or who she was. The alley was dark, darker than she thought it had been before, but it was likely she simply didn't remember correctly, considering she had been running for her life.

There's blood all over me. Panic rose like bile in the back of her throat. She swiped and scrubbed desperately at her chest and neck, sobbing. She'd killed someone. It had been a matter of survival, yes, but he was still a person, and she'd stabbed him. She'd ended his life.

"Get it off," she pleaded. To herself, to Callan, to the nameless, faceless gods.

Without a word, Callan tugged a water skin attached to his belt free and set to work, pouring water on her chest and wiping gently with his sleeve. Not one ounce of judgment or pity shone in his blue eyes. Within a few moments, the worst of it was gone, or at least hidden so enough that she couldn't readily see it. There was little to be done about the dress, but she tugged the cloak tighter, hoping to hide it from view.

"It was a distraction. Someone started fires to create a panic so that they could take you away." His gaze roamed over her face, deep blue still simmering with rage and a shadow of something else Eve couldn't identify. "I assumed you were safe, and I shouldn't have. I should have stayed at your side. It's a mistake I won't make again."

She nodded, too exhausted to analyze that too deeply. "Can you take me home? Is the carriage nearby?"

"Fuck the carriage," he growled. "You're riding with me."

"YOU MUST BE JOKING." CALLAN SAT ATOP HIS HORSE, HAND extended toward Eve expectantly. "I'm not getting on that horse with you, Callan." She stared at him incredulously. She was still wearing a gown, and her shoes had been long forgotten. "Everyone will-"

An irritated snort cut her off and he sighed, dropping his hand to rest on his thigh. "Gods be damned, Eve. Why do you care?" He had a point, but she still hesitated.

They had managed to get out of the city without incident, thanks to the deep hood of her cloak hiding her face and the now-dried blood from view. Callan had hurried her out, not bothering to seek out any of the city guards. He didn't trust them now, and frankly neither did she. The few personal guards they had brought with them would be waiting near the carriage, he'd told her. When the chaos had erupted, they'd gone to prepare the carriage to take her home, assuming as he had that the city guard would escort her to safety, as they had been ordered to in the event something happened.

The clouds above now threatened rain, and the sun would soon be setting. They needed to move quickly, get away from the city and back to the relative safety of the castle before dark fell.

"My lady," Edvard, the most senior of her guards cut in, stepping closer to where Eve stood. Guilt was etched in his weathered features, grey eyes that reminded her so much of her father's clouded with concern. "Lord Thorne and I are in agreement, on this at least. We must get you back home, and quickly. Whoever those men were working with is still out there, and we don't have the numbers to put up much of a fight if they try again."

Eve opened her mouth to protest, to suggest the carriage again as she had a few times before already. "The carriage is gone," Callan interjected before she could start down that fruitless path. "We have no time to retrieve a new one."

"Gone? What do you mean gone?"

Callan sighed. She couldn't tell if his frustration was with her or with the situation they were in. Both seemed likely. "They torched it. Killed the men I'd left with it."

Something in Eve's chest ached. They'd died because of her. The face of the footman, Ferris, flashed in her mind. He had been kind, and so young. Who would tell his mother?

Callan cleared his throat pointedly. They needed to go. Stubborn as she may be, Eve was certainly not stupid. If this was the best way, then so be it. But that didn't mean she had to be happy about it.

Muttering a particularly dirty curse under her breath, she hoisted herself onto the horse, ignoring Callan's once again outstretched hand. She had no choice but to hike the full skirt up high, leaving her legs bare clear to her thighs. She felt ridiculous. Bare legs and feet hanging freely on either side of the poor beast now tasked with carrying both of them to safety.

Settling into her seat, so close to him, was far from comfortable. She wiggled a little, trying and failing to find a more comfortable position in the hard leather of the saddle. Callan was close behind, the firm planes of his chest pressed against her shoulder blades.

"Careful, dove." His voice was a low whisper, his breath hot against her neck.

Confusion had her turning to glance at him over her shoulder. "Am I hurting you?"

Callan simply stared back, brow raised. Realization struck, and embarrassment flooded her cheeks.

"Ass," she muttered in reply, earning a low chuckle from him. Straightening, Callan took the reins in one hand, and they were off; heading home down the same road they had taken earlier in the afternoon before everything had fallen apart.

His other hand came to rest at her hip, fingers splayed against her abdomen. A gentle, yet firm grip. Despite her best efforts at ignoring it, she couldn't help but be keenly aware of the way his fingers flexed, tips pressing against her skin as his thumb made slow, small circles. Her pulse galloped, muscles low in her belly coiling. Just nerves, a side effect of the ordeal, she told herself.

Eve could admit, to herself at least, she was attracted to him, had been since she'd first seen him. It was a physical thing, this attraction, and nothing more.

His hand shifted slightly, adjusting his grip on her waist, drifting slightly lower. The idea of acting on that desire was out of the question, no matter how much she might want to. It would be nice, so nice, to have that release, that distraction from everything, but having to face him every day afterward would be too much. It simply was not worth it.

The part that confused her, that scared her, was how safe she felt with him. She hardly knew him, but a small voice within told her she could trust him. Told her she was safe as long as he was near. It was beyond what she felt with any of her trusted guards, even Edvard, who had been charged with protecting her for much of her life.

She hadn't realized she had relaxed as much as she had. Hadn't realized she was leaning against him until he spoke again, several minutes into the ride. "You can sleep if you need to," he said quietly, for her ears only.

Despite the slow pace they took, for her sake, the ride would be short, too short, to make it worth sleeping. Eve shook her head, starting to sit up again, but his hand on her waist pressed harder.

"Just relax, you need it." It was a command, albeit a gentle one. She was too tired to argue, and honestly, she knew he was right. So she simply stayed where she was, leaning back against him, safe and comfortable with the sound of the horses' hooves against the packed earth of the road a lullaby, urging her to rest.

It was well into the afternoon hours by the time they finally arrived back at Stoneweald. One of the guards had broken away, riding ahead to alert the guards at home to their early return, and the reason why. It was no surprise, then, when they arrived to find guards waiting outside the gates. What was surprising, however, was the crest that some of them bore. Soldiers of Avellon were in Darkegrove.

"Shit." She sat up straight, lifting a hand to her throat. There could only be one reason for their arrival. Only one person they could be here to protect. Lia Vallyse was here.

As the eldest daughter of the king and queen of the Vale, Lia was set to inherit the throne in a few months. Unlike Eve's rise, hers was welcomed and celebrated. In the Vale, the eldest child of the monarchs always ascended to the throne on their twenty-third birthday, or upon the death of their parents, regardless of gender. She had always envied that.

Genuinely kind, with warmth to both her spirit and smile that could rival the very sun, Lia was nearly impossible to dislike. She had a gentle soul but a fighter's strength, and for a moment Eve was nearly paralyzed by the idea of her knowing what she had done in the name of survival. Lia would never judge her for doing what needed to be done to save her own life. It would be worse than that, she would pity Eve and offer words of comfort when she didn't deserve them. She had taken a life and despite the reason she had done so, did not deserve comfort.

"She can't see me like this, she can't," Eve whispered desperately. Callan had helped to get most of the blood off her skin, but her dress was ruined. There was no way of hiding it now.

"Be brave, Eve. Remember who you are, and that what you did saved your life." Callan's voice was low, little more than his breath in her ear. Her heart raced. Not only from fear but also some other emotion she couldn't identify.

They were in the courtyard before she could examine that too closely, and Lia was bounding down the stairs to meet them, as radiant and lovely as ever. The exuberant smile she greeted Eve with was so bright that she couldn't help but smile in return, despite the pang of guilt and worry she felt.

Lia had dressed for a formal visit, Eve noted, taking in her appearance fully. Her light golden gown moved around like liquid sunlight spun into fabric. It draped low in the front and fell loose around her form. A sun goddess draped in molten gold. She wore only a simple pair of gold earrings, twin suns falling from gold chains on either of her ears, and a single sunburst ring on her left middle finger, the symbol of her house.

Lia opened her mouth to call out in greeting, only to stop short as Eve slid from her horse and the ruined dress came into view. Her eyes widened and she rushed toward Eve, her expression a picture of concern.

"What happened? Are you hurt?" Before Eve could respond, Lia wrapped her in an embrace, squeezing tightly.

Eve had forgotten how much she had missed her friend. The familiar scent of apple blossoms tickled her nose, reminding Eve of the sunswept plains of Avellon, the kingdom that Lia called home. "I'm okay, I'm okay," Eve breathed, returning the hug just as intently.

"They said there had been an incident, but that was all they would tell me. Are you sure you're not hurt?" Concern clouded her eyes, the color of the summer sky, and she stepped back to examine Eve. "There's blood all over you!"

Shame colored Eve's cheeks. "It's not mine," she said quietly, frowning at Lia's dress. "I've ruined your gown." A fresh wave of embarrassment flooded her. *Queens don't go around ruining the gowns of visiting monarchs*, she mused to herself humorlessly.

"It's fine," Lia's tone was matter-of-fact, utterly unconcerned by the destruction of her dress. "What matters is that you're okay, no matter what." Her gaze slid to Callan finally, taking in the sight of the armor-clad warrior behind Eve. The man was most certainly not one of the household guards. "It seems like there is quite a lot we need to catch up on." After a moment's appraisal, she offered him a smile and linked her arm with Eve's. "You need a bath and something to eat."

Eve barely resisted sagging with relief as Lia began to lead her inside. Her legs ached from the run and the ride back. Each step sent a fresh wave of pain through her feet, and she desperately did not want to think about the reason behind that. The gods only knew what had been in that alley, what had possibly cut open the soles of her bare feet.

A bath sounded like exactly what she needed right now, but she wasn't going anywhere without Callan. As irritating as he was, he made her feel safe, and after what had happened in the city she didn't trust anyone else to do that.

"He's coming with us," she said to Lia, her gaze on Callan who already trailed silently behind them. His expression was as unreadable as always, though some emotion she couldn't identify darkened his features for a brief moment.

Lia nodded, brow raised as she glanced between them. "Well, this is shaping up to be a very interesting visit."

CHAPTER 13

"I thought I was going to die." Eve swatted at a floating bubble, hovering just above the steaming bath. Maids had come and carried away the dirty water, replacing it with fresh, steaming water, fresh oils, and bubble bath twice already.

She'd been escorted straight to her chambers by Lia, followed by Callan of course, and instructed to get straight into a hot bath that Sylvie had already prepared. Eve made a mental note to thank Sylvie for that later as well.

Her mother was wearing a path in the carpet of the sitting room, hot chocolate on its way up from the kitchens. After tearful hugs and assurances of her health, Eve headed into the bathing chamber and got straight into the large porcelain tub.

Every muscle in her body had been aching, and she'd refused to look at the water as they'd had her step out each time so that the tub could be drained and refilled with clean, hot water. She already knew without looking that it would be red, carrying the taint of what she'd done with it.

"But you didn't, and that's what matters right now," Lia said in that gentle way of hers. Her voice had always made Eve think of early summer afternoons. Warm, inviting, and calm. Something without flaw, impossible to dislike. At some point, she'd dragged an ottoman from the living area and sat herself beside the tub to keep Eve company.

Eve could hear Callan and her mother speaking in the other room, though she couldn't make out what was being said. Probably making plans for adding security, or for finding the men responsible for what had happened in Forest Haven. They'd have to find out who had been behind it all, who her captors had been waiting for. Someone would have to collect his body.

The quiet squeak of her back against the porcelain as she slid downward was the only sound for a moment as Eve's thoughts returned to the alley. She couldn't allow herself to think about that, not right now. "I knew I had to do it, it was my only chance at escaping, but...Lia, it was awful." She shuddered at the thought, the memory of the man's blood hitting her skin, hot and wet. The gurgling sounds he'd made, the shouts of his friends when they realized what she'd done.

"Stop," Lia ordered gently. "Don't do that to yourself, Evie." Her golden-brown eyes were full of concern, of pity. Exactly what Eve did not want at that moment.

Her reaction to that pity must have been clear in her expression because the next thing Lia did was wholly unexpected. Dropping her hand into the tub, Lia narrowed her eyes. Pity was quickly replaced by glittering amusement as she lifted her hand again, now covered in a cloud of fragrant bubbles from the bath.

"What are you–" Eve's question was interrupted by a most unladylike squeal erupting from her throat as Lia blew the bubbles directly into her face. A splash from Eve had both women laughing as the playful gesture turned into a full-on bubble fight between the two.

For a few moments, it was as if nothing bad had happened. As if the blood of slaughtered animals hadn't stained her bed. As if she hadn't murdered someone. As if they hadn't attempted to kidnap her and do gods only knew what with her. For a few moments, she was free of the guilt and the weight of responsibility and fear that seemed her constant companions lately.

The heavy shroud of fear and guilt lightened with every moment as peals of laughter bounced off the walls. Sunlight chasing away the shadows.

A sound at the door halted both Eve and Lia, the latter now nearly as drenched as the former, water and bubbles from the bath soaking her thoroughly.

The queen stood in the doorway, shaking her head slowly, but not with judgment. Amusement and relief were clear in her ice-blue gaze. Standing at her side, Callan watched with a raised brow, expression as unreadable as ever.

Suddenly aware of her own nakedness, Eve gathered the remaining bubbles, pulling them closer as she sank deeper into the water, shielding herself from view as much as possible.

Realization dawned on Riona at nearly the same moment, and she cleared her throat. "Lord Thorne, if you would be so kind as to wait in the other room..."

He simply inclined his head and turned away, but not before Eve caught the faintest hint of a grin lighting his normally stoic features. The sight was enough to set her heart skidding and thoughts of him racing to the forefront of her mind. The feeling of his body against her back as they rode back to Stoneweald. The way he had gently helped wash away the blood after finding her in the alley. The way he'd cupped her cheek. The way his voice had sounded when he'd assured her she was safe; low and smoky, gentle and strong all at once.

"I think you'd better get dressed." It was Lia's voice that drew her back to reality. "It seems a conversation needs to be had." Eve followed Lia's gaze to her mother, still hovering in the doorway, waiting. A nod from her mother told Eve that Lia's guess was correct.

She'd wrapped herself in another plush robe, deep emerald this time, her towel-dried hair twisted quickly into a braid that now hung over one shoulder.

Lia, who had stepped out to give her privacy to dress and change out of her own bloodstained gown, was now seated next to the queen on the sofa near the fireplace.

Callan took a chair across from them, Eve the twin to his, on his left. Her gaze flitted between the three of them.

The fireplace was lit, warming the room against the chill of autumn as well as providing most of the current light. Only a few candles had been lit, and the low light gave the little meeting they were currently having an even more mysterious, and serious, feeling. Riona sat as straight as always, but the tension around her face was more pronounced than usual. Whatever she had to say was going to be bad.

"They can't find them," the queen said finally, earning a puzzled frown from her daughter. "The men that took you. None of them. Not even the one you..." She trailed off, leaving the rest of it unsaid.

A fresh wave of guilt washed over Eve, followed quickly by fear. She couldn't explain why she felt it. Not the guilt at least. It was self-defense, she knew that. She did what she had to do to escape, as Callan had said, as everyone had. But a life was a life, and she had *taken* his. This man whose name she didn't even know. *How can anyone forget that, and forgive themselves?*

"I'll find them." His voice was so low, so full of ice-cold fury that Eve's attention snapped to him immediately, as had her mother's and Lia's. Silence raged for a moment, his fury nearly palpable.

It was Eve who broke the silence. "No." Her voice was calm, and steady, with no sign of the building worry she felt rising to the surface. "I want you to stay here with me." A flush of heat crept up her neck, rising towards her cheeks. Whether it was from embarrassment or the other thing she felt building within her, the thing she didn't dare acknowledge, she wasn't sure. She didn't want to think about that right now.

Riona pressed her lips together tightly but nodded her agreement. "Though I do believe you'd find them, certainly faster than the city guards, you need to stay close to her." The queen looked between them watching, for what Eve didn't know, and supposed she likely would never know. Whatever Riona's thoughts were, she doubted her mother would share them.

"Well, if uh, that's all you need to say about that," Lia broke in, interrupting the heavy silence that had settled over them. "I did have something I needed to share with you both." She cast a nervous glance toward Callan.

Riona shook her head lightly. "He can stay, Aurelia darling. There are few secrets our Lord Thorne isn't privy to."

Eve frowned but didn't question it. There was enough going on now, enough confusion and chaos. She didn't want to add to the things she needed to worry about. She'd worry about her mother's weird relationship with Callan later.

"Alright," Lia said, sitting up a little straighter. She'd changed before Eve had finished her bath. Her own handmaid had brought her a gown from the guest room she'd taken a floor below. Smoothing the pale pink gown, she patted her leg nervously before she began speaking. "So, you know my father and his love for ancient knowledge, right?"

Riona and Eve nodded. The king of Avellon was well known for his extensive library, and his seemingly neverending search for relics of the past, ranging from rare books and manuscripts to more mundane things like pieces of pottery and sculptures. Anything, it seemed, that connected humans to their fae friends and neighbors, lost to them so very long ago. Callan simply sat back and listened. If he'd heard of the king and his interests, he gave no indication.

"So yeah, he found something new. Some*one* new."

Confusion swept Eve as she glanced at her mother. A person? He'd found a person? Both Riona and Callan had gone very, very still. Eve turned back to Lia, waiting for her to continue.

If Lia had noticed their reactions, she didn't pay them any mind as she continued. "He says she's a seer."

"That's a thing?" Eve asked incredulously.

"I didn't think so at first," Lia snorted. "I thought he'd been taken in by a con artist. But then she gave him a prophecy." That wouldn't have been shocking, not the part about the 'seer' being a con artist anyway. There certainly were plenty of those around. It would've been shocking though, for a man as smart and perceptive as Aldrich Vallyse to be tricked by one.

Lia sighed then, sitting back against the couch. Riona and Callan had remained so still and quiet that for a moment Eve wondered if they were breathing. But as she watched her mother, who sat staring into the fireplace, a sort of awareness pricked over her skin. Turning, she found exactly what she'd expected. Callan was watching her, intently. A puzzle to be solved again.

"A prophecy?" She prodded Lia, tearing her gaze from Callan as she did. "What kind of prophecy?"

Lia laughed lightly. "A weird one. Let me see if I can remember it, *'When the gods touch the crescent once more, the lost children will return and herald a new age.'*" She shook her head briefly, then rested her elbow on the arm of the couch and propped her chin on her hand. "Told you it was weird, right? Makes no sense. The only reason I believe she *might* be for real is that he found a book in his library that makes mention of the same prophecy. He insisted I come at once and share this with you. He sent Aelius to Coruscis to tell the Colvaris."

"A new age," Riona murmured. Eve's attention shifted to her mother then, as did Lia's. As if something had snapped, Riona changed. The quiet stare was gone, and her expression turned immediately to a smile. "Well, how interesting. I hope he enjoys the new puzzle he's found, though I can't imagine why he thinks I would be able to decipher it." Her light laugh was brittle at the edges, as was her smile. "Shall we retire for the evening? Aurelia darling, I know you must be exhausted from your trip, and you two," she said sliding her gaze from Lia to Callan, and then to Eve, "are in desperate need of rest, I am sure."

There was no argument there. They all wore the signs of exhaustion, plain as day, and it was already getting late, as evidenced by the growing shadows of the room.

It was Lia who agreed aloud. "Sleep would be good," she said, hiding a yawn behind the back of her hand. "I so look forward to dreaming about weird prophecies and creepy seers," she laughed.

Riona stood, followed by the others as she did. "Well, then I will say goodnight, my darling." She embraced Eve in a tight squeeze before lifting her palms to cup her daughter's cheeks and pressing a kiss to her forehead, just as she had done so often when Eve was a girl. "I am so relieved you are safe, my love. I will see you in the morning." She stepped back, offering Callan a brief nod.

Lia offered Eve a quick hug and Callan a bright smile. "See you tomorrow," she said as they both headed for the doors, leaving Eve and Callan alone in the dim sitting room.

After a few heartbeats, she turned to Callan. "I'm going to bed."

Her mother's abrupt departure had been strange, and she'd certainly filed that away along with all the other things she'd think about later, but for now, she was exhausted. Physically and emotionally. The last days had taken a toll, and now sleep beckoned like a lover.

Callan nodded once and turned toward the sofa. "I'll be here if you need anything," he said, his watchful gaze sweeping her face as he took a seat. He'd donned the facade of apathy he so often seemed to wear, but the fire behind his cerulean eyes told her whatever he was thinking was far from unfeeling.

Yet another thing to file away for later.

"Goodnight," she said, instead of the other thing that had nearly bubbled up, passing her lips. The request she knew she couldn't make. He didn't reply as she moved through the door to her bedroom, closing it behind her.

By the time she settled into bed and found herself lying on her back, staring up at the ceiling, the little bit of activity she heard on the other side of the door, the sounds of Callan presumably getting comfortable, stopped.

All of the candles in her bedchamber had been extinguished, and only the most meager amount of moonlight trickled in through the windows. The gauzy white curtains had been pulled back, and if she turned her head just a little, the forest would be in full view. As tall as the castle stood, even the second floor didn't break the canopy of trees.

As beautiful as it was, and it was beautiful, the dense forest that she called home, a part of her had always longed for the open sky, the sea, literally anything open and bright. She supposed that part came from her mother. Some primal longing for another land. But it was unlikely to happen anytime soon, given the impending coronation. *Maybe after, a few years from now, when things are stable.* She sighed. Who knew how long stability would take? She would be lucky to see true acceptance of her rule in her lifetime.

Thoughts of one unlikely, yet desired thing led to another, and suddenly she found herself picturing the man just on the other side of the doors. Was he sleeping? Lying awake like she was? Or maybe reading the book she'd spotted on the low table by the couch? Mundane curiosity led to memories of that afternoon, and the way he'd held her. The way he'd calmed and protected her. Heat flooded her cheeks as she recalled the ride back to Stoneweald, his body had felt so right against hers...and that devilish remark he'd made...

Eve shook her head, stopping the thought before it went any further. That couldn't happen, not right now at least, not when they needed to work together. Maybe when it was all over, she could see. But for now? Bad idea. Rolling to her side, she pushed thoughts of Callan aside. As she waited for sleep to overtake her, she could've sworn the shadows in the corner grew darker.

Chapter 14

It was dark, and someone was chasing her. The winding corridors of her home were unfamiliar to her. Darker than they'd ever been before, choked with vines covered in impossibly long thorns. She was screaming, pleading for help from someone, anyone. A man's laughter was the only reply. He was coming closer and he was going to–

The doors to the room burst open before she could recall anymore. Callan stood in the doorway, wearing nothing more than linen pants. "Was someone here?" He demanded, scanning the room for any threat.

Eve shook her head a bit, before realizing he might not be able to see the gesture. "No," she said hoarsely. Maybe she had been screaming. The faint firelight from the sitting room left him in silhouette, and though she could barely make out his face, what she could see looked downright murderous. Pushing herself to her elbows, she blinked. Shadows danced and pulsed around him, some trick of the waning moonlight blending with the light from the fire behind him. "I was having a nightmare."

He didn't respond, though the rage in his gaze dissipated, shifting into something else she couldn't identify. Her attention drifted from his face, lowering to his chest, rising and falling rapidly. The surprise maybe, or the concern for her safety?

Lower, her gaze roamed over the muscles of his abdomen, to the well-toned vee of his hips, to the band of his pants, hanging indecently low, just above his—

"Eve," he said then. His tone was low, smoky. A warning, or maybe that other thing she'd been ignoring in herself.

Her gaze snapped back up to his, and the intensity of his stare had her breath hitching. Her heart galloped, from the fear of the nightmare, yes, but also that other *thing* building between them. The words that spilled from her next seemed to come without thought, without her meaning to, but taking them back didn't even cross her mind. "Will you stay with me? In here?"

For what felt like an eternity, but was likely no more than a few moments, silence hung between them. Callan cleared his throat finally, nodding once. "If that's what you want," he replied, the smokiness in his tone now giving way to something akin to wariness.

"I do," she replied, scooting over to make room for them both. She wanted him close, needing the sense of security and comfort he brought. People would talk if they knew, the council would have a fit, and her mother, well who knew what she would do. Right now though, she didn't care. She needed sleep, and she needed to feel safe to sleep. Callan could provide that for her.

He settled himself into the bed beside her, lying on top of the blanket rather than under, keeping it as a barrier between them. They lay there, side by side, not moving or speaking, for a small eternity. The only sounds were that of the fire crackling in the other room, the sound drifting in through the now open doors of the sitting room, and the occasional night bird from beyond the balcony, deep within the forest.

"Your mother will disapprove." His tone had returned to normal though his body was tense behind her. He was far from relaxed, even though he had agreed to it.

"I know. I don't care," she whispered. "I need...You make me feel safer." It was difficult to explain without sounding childish, and she struggled to find the words. "The nightmare, I think it was because of what happened today, which I guess makes sense, but, I can't...I don't want to be alone. I'll understand if you're more comfortable out there, though."

Rolling to her side so that she was facing him, Eve studied the lines of his face. She'd found him attractive the first time she'd laid eyes on him, but looking at him now, in the near-total darkness of her room, she realized he was more than that. His nose was proud and straight, his jaw strong, and his mouth, gods his mouth was full and promised decadent, sinful kisses. He still stared at the ceiling above the bed, but she knew if he'd turned to look at her she'd meet those deepest blue eyes, the ones that made her feel like she could drown in them.

"You're staring at me," he murmured, lips twitching into a smirk. The amusement in his tone surprised her. "Most people would find that rude, you know."

"You don't?" she shot back, eyeing his still unmoving form. He hadn't moved, hadn't so much as shifted, but the tension she'd felt from him had somehow lessened.

He laughed, actually laughed, at that. The sound had an altogether unexpected effect on her, sending a sharp tingle down her spine. "No, I don't. I don't find it rude at all." The way he spoke the seemingly innocent words, felt decidedly *not* innocent. That smokiness had returned to his voice, and, she realized as he turned to face her, to his eyes.

"Is it because you like to stare at me too?" She asked, brow lifting. "I catch you staring at me sometimes like you're trying to figure me out."

"Well," he replied with a light laugh. "You're confusing. Sometimes you seem...so naive. But I've also seen you handle shit that would have people much older than you crumbling. You're kind, even to those that many of your station consider beneath them. Other times you're a total smartass. And," he pressed on as she started to object, "you're doing this really incredible thing. This world-changing thing. I can't figure out how to make all of that fit together into the person I see. Frankly, I think that while you're wholly unprepared for what you've done, you're incredibly brave for doing what you think is right."

Well, that was...unexpected. It was also the most she'd heard him say so far.

"I don't know what to say to that," she murmured finally. "But thank you."

"You're welcome. Just don't get used to me throwing compliments at you a lot," he replied with a grin.

"We should go to sleep," she said, barely recognizing her own voice.

It was almost sultry, the way she had said it, without even intending it to be.

"Yeah," he replied, voice rough.

Eve turned away then, putting her back to him. She felt him roll onto his side, facing her back as he did. They were close enough that she could feel his warm breath against the back of her neck, left bare to him thanks to the braid that had fallen forward when she moved. Her heart skittered at the closeness of him, of the heat from his breath on her skin.

He didn't reach out to touch her, didn't so much as move, but something within her felt his closeness and needed to be closer to him. Loneliness, or just a need for comfort after the day she'd had perhaps. She hadn't been doing much thinking in the last few minutes, hadn't considered her actions, and she supposed there was no point in starting now, so she scooted back, edging herself closer to him slightly.

His sharp intake of breath as their bodies touched was his only reply before he shifted, moving his arm so that it was around her head. His other arm slowly came to rest over her waist, just above her hip. Tentatively, allowing her time to object if she wanted. She didn't. They lay like that, cuddled close with no space between their bodies, in silence until both of them fell asleep.

She'd been running again, in the dark, and alone. But this time, she was running toward something. A familiar feminine voice that she couldn't quite place was calling for her, beckoning her farther into the darkness that lay ahead. Eve had almost reached her, the mysterious woman calling out for her, but a strong hand on her shoulder stopped her dead in her tracks. That hand had pulled hard, turning her around–

She woke before seeing their face, with the knowledge that this hadn't been just another dream. It mattered, all of it, but she couldn't make sense of it.

She stretched, raising her arms and arching her back slightly as she tried to reorient herself. Only to suddenly collide with Callan behind her, specifically the hardened, thick, length pressed against the curve of her ass. She gasped, straightening herself and shoving her back against his chest instead as she scooted her hips forward, away from him. From his steady breathing, she guessed he was still asleep; his arm was still slung across her waist, effectively pinning her to the bed, unless she wanted to risk waking him.

She moved again, heat flooding her cheeks, as a different kind of heat began pooling low in her center. He shifted, pulling her closer. That proud length pressed against her rear again, and he stilled.

"Eve," he whispered, lips brushing against the nape of her neck gently. Her name sounded like a plea on his lips or a prayer, for what she didn't know.

"Callan," she returned, her voice little more than a breath as it passed her lips. Slowly, she turned her head to look at him. The bed shifted under her as he sat up leaning over her shoulder, his arm still keeping her mostly in place. They were so close now that their lips nearly touched. He hissed in a breath and tensed but didn't move away.

"We can't do this."

It didn't sound like he meant it. Or at least he didn't want to mean it. She'd been telling herself the same thing, that any kind of entanglement between them would be a bad idea. They had to work together for a while longer, and she'd been trying to avoid rumors and speculation about them because she didn't need to give those who opposed her any more reason to doubt her intention to rule alone, and yet....

"Why not?" People were already going to talk, whether she acted on this attraction or not, and it didn't need to be anything more than a release.

Liar. The word rang through her, with an ache in her chest, a tugging, that echoed the sentiment.

She closed her eyes, willing the annoying voice inside herself to silence. A new sort of fear crept inside her, keeping her eyes closed to the man in her bed, the one she'd just propositioned...more or less. The bed shifted with his movement again, and the weight of his arm at her hip vanished.

Disappointment stung. Rejection wasn't something she'd experienced often, if only because she so rarely put herself in a position to be rejected. Brodie had pursued her, at first, and even the decision to end their entanglement had been hers. Heat flooded her cheeks. *I'm an idiot.*

"Forget I asked–" she began to say, only to be interrupted by more sudden movement behind her.

Not away as she'd expected, but closer. His lips danced across hers briefly, feather-light. The hand that had rested at her waist returned, fingertips tracing a line along the hem of the silk nightgown she wore. At some point it had ridden up, stopping mid-thigh.

She arched her back toward him, needing to feel his warmth, to just feel him against her body. Her reward was another flutter of kisses, this time along her jaw. A light gasp escaped her lips, earning an approving growl from him as he nipped her earlobe gently.

"Gods," she whispered, rolling onto her side so that she was facing him fully. She lifted a hand to the nape of his neck, plunging her hand into his dark hair, urging him closer.

Callan stopped then, resting his forehead against hers gently. For a beat, they lay there like that, not moving, just holding one another.

"We can't...," he repeated, a tinge of regret in his whispered tone as he rolled away from her, tugging his other arm free. He rolled to his side, back facing her now. "I'll stay if it makes you feel better, but this can't happen."

Eve didn't reply as the warmth and comfort of his body moved away from her. She simply rolled onto her side, hiding her face away from him. The sting of rejection was real, and so much worse than she'd anticipated. That place in her chest that made being near him feel so right suddenly ached. Burying her face against her pillow, she shoved it down and willed herself back to sleep.

CHAPTER 15

She couldn't be sure if it was because he'd remained close, as he'd promised, or just luck, but either way, the nightmares hadn't returned. His steady breathing and the lack of movement behind her told Eve that Callan was likely still sleeping. Holding true to what he'd said about the brief moment they'd shared the night before going no further, he hadn't moved closer nor said another word to her for the rest of the night.

The sun had begun to rise, and the first rays of light were starting to stream through the windows. It was as good a time as any, she supposed, to get up. She could rise and quietly dress in the bathing chamber, then sneak out to the sitting area before he woke up, buying herself a little time before they had to face the awkwardness that was sure to follow what had occurred the night before.

With that in mind, Eve slowly began to slip out of bed, moving carefully to avoid disturbing Callan. A chill snaked over her as her bare feet hit the cold stone of her bedroom floor, and she whispered a low curse before standing and turning toward the foot of the bed.

She couldn't help but glance to where Callan still lay. He lay on his stomach, one arm stretched out toward where she'd been sleeping. That strange feeling in her chest surged briefly. She ignored it and headed for the bathing chamber to see to her needs and dress for the day. While lacing the front of the soft lilac gown she'd chosen, she made plans for the day, most of which involved ignoring Callan and altogether avoiding him when possible.

He was still sleeping soundly when she made her way out of the bedroom. She once again shoved down the sting of rejection. With one last glance at his still form in her bed, she moved into the adjoining sitting room.

It wasn't that she was hurt, not really. Mostly, she was embarrassed. He'd been kind to her, he'd done what he had promised to do, and she had taken that kindness and her own need for comfort and tried to turn it into something it wasn't, something more than duty and maybe a little flirtation. She had no idea how she was going to look at him again.

Without putting much thought into where she was heading, Eve stepped out into the long corridor outside her room. She moved down the hall, and then to the back stairs that would take her to the servants' areas and the kitchens.

Maybe she'd steal a scone or one of those amazing gooseberry muffins that Mrs. Elliott made sometimes. The garden would be chilly now, and she hadn't brought a cloak, so the solarium would have to do. Nobody should be there this early anyway, she reasoned.

Eve couldn't recall how many times she'd found herself wandering to the kitchens in the early hours of the morning, or occasionally late in the evening.

She'd grab a snack and sneak off to some corner of the castle where she was unlikely to be found, and then spend her time either reading or simply staring out the windows. Letting her mind wander, a sort of escape from whatever troubled her at the time.

The last time had been her last night with Brodie. He'd wanted to stay, insistent that he could be happy with what little she could give him, but it would never be enough for him, for either of them. The night he'd left for Coruscis, she'd hidden in the library for most of the evening. A plate of mini cakes and a mystery novel were her only companions. It had been two years since he left, but she could still recall the sting of the relationship ending.

Today's hideout was at least a little brighter. The solarium was just a short walk from the kitchens, and far from any of the bedrooms, which meant there were few prying eyes as she made her way there, aside from the guards that haunted her steps like shadows.

This would be different than last time. Last time, she'd allowed herself to dwell on the hurt, on the sadness. Not today. Today she would shove all of that far, far down and think only of the steamy romance novel she'd snagged from the sitting room on the way out. She would focus on her problems later.

The first light of dawn had just begun to break through the trees when she reached her destination, having escaped the kitchens after brief hellos with the cook. The solarium was little more than a small porch covered with domed glass from ceiling to floor. A pair of double glass doors led to a small garden with a path that led into the still-dark forest beyond.

At this hour, the candelabras surrounding the room hadn't yet been lit, and the only light in the room was the rosy-hued sunlight wafting in from the sunrise. She cast a wary glance toward the guards who had taken up a spot by the doorway before plopping into one of the chairs, she set her plate on a table nearby and looked beyond the potted plants lining the glass walls, out to the darkened tree line. Only the outermost trees were visible now, the rest still hidden in inky darkness.

A small, familiar part of her longed to run into the forest, to flee the burden of rule, of the fight that lay ahead, but especially thoughts of what had happened; of the man who she'd killed. Thoughts of Callan and the discomfort of the situation she had put herself in with him were there as well, despite her best attempts at forgetting.

She was curled up in the chair, legs folded under her, when Lia found her. Eve had been nibbling on the raspberry scone she'd managed to snag from the kitchen maids, her second favorite after the gooseberry muffins, which were missing this morning, much to her dismay.

"I see your hiding spots haven't changed," Lia remarked. Eve didn't look up, but the smile on her friend's face was clear enough in her tone that she could picture it. "Nor has your taste in comfort foods."

"Mmf," was the only response given, partially due to the mouthful of that comfort food she had, and partially due to the dread she felt at the idea of telling Lia about what had happened.

Never one to be deterred, Lia took a seat in the nearest chair to Eve's. Unlike her friend, she sat gracefully, straight-backed with the ample length of her pale blue gown pooling around her feet. Lia had an innate sense of grace that Eve couldn't quite match. Not that she was a clumsy lout by any means, but Lia Vallyse was something special, the epitome of what a queen should be, not just in the way she carried herself, but also because of her kind and generous heart, and tack-sharp mind. She would be an incredible ruler for her people.

"I'm not in the mood to talk, Lia," Eve muttered finally, brushing the crumbs from her chest. She felt guilty for pushing her friend away. Especially when their visits with one another were so rare. They had a rare connection, one that Eve hoped wouldn't be damaged by her rudeness.

A few heartbeats passed in silence before Lia spoke up again, her tone gentle and patient. "Is it the coronation, what happened in the city, or something else?" As usual, Lia struck the heart of the matter with unerring accuracy. She had always had a knack for reading a person or a situation.

Eve sighed, leaning back against the chair as she tossed the unfinished scone onto the plate. Turning her attention to the guards, she said firmly, "Leave us." With shared glance, they did as they were told, no doubt simply moving a little farther away to give her privacy while remaining close enough should she need help.

She had meant it when she said she didn't want to talk about it, but Lia's presence had always served to comfort her when she needed someone to talk to. She'd traveled to Avellon on more than one occasion for just that reason. While she'd been afraid yesterday, so certain she didn't deserve her friend's comfort and kind words of reassurance, today she was tired, and despite her desire to hide she simply didn't have it in her to run from this anymore.

"A little of it all, I guess," Eve admitted. "I'm tired, Lia." Her gaze remained on the forest, watching the still lightening treeline. So much as a glance at Lia's expression would shatter what little bit of steel she still had to hold herself together. "I knew it would be hard, but it's a lot harder than I thought it would be. Naive of me, I know."

"You couldn't have known exactly what to expect," Lia said, now following Eve's gaze to the line of trees beyond the windows. "Do you still want it? The crown I mean."

Eve tensed, frowning at the question she hadn't even let herself consider. *Do I still want it?* "I think so," she replied quietly.

"Okay," Lia began, rising from her chair and striding to the double doors. A gust of cool air had Eve jerking her head in Lia's direction finally. Lia had thrown the doors open, leaving the path from Eve's chair to the forest path wide open. "If you could have an easier life, freedom to do whatever you wanted and freedom from the danger you're now in, would you run?"

She knew the answer without even thinking about it. *Of course not.* She'd thought about it once before her father had died and everything had gone to hell. But now, despite all of the chaos and danger, she knew what she was doing was the right thing.

There were moments, of course, where she doubted it, but with the chance to run laid bare in front of her, she knew without question that she wasn't going anywhere.

"No," she said finally. She moved to stand beside Lia at the door. The lingering thought that she hadn't been able to completely bury flowed freely before she could stop it. "I killed a person, Lia. I know it was self-defense. I know I didn't have a choice." She held a hand up before Lia could respond. Eve didn't need to hear the reassurances again. She'd had enough of that the night before, and she'd certainly get more of it from her mother later, maybe even from Callan too. "But it's still....I still did it."

Lia nodded and pulled the doors closed, shutting out the cool breeze that whispered promises of freedom. "Yeah, you did. I can't pretend to know what that feels like, but I do know you. I know you're strong and if anyone can get through this, you can." She leaned against the frame and turned to face Eve. "You're doing the right thing."

Eve trailed her finger along a pane of glass. The coolness of it sent a chill down her spine and had her dropping her hand away. Winter would be here in no time if the cold morning was any indication.

Her thoughts turned to Brodie again, and for the first time in two years, she didn't feel a single pang of longing or regret for sending him away. She wondered if it was warm in Coruscis, or if autumn's touch had chilled the air there as well. She had done the right thing. He was safer, and happy she hoped.

"Callan slept in my bed last night," Eve blurted out before she could stop herself.

"He did what?" Both women spun toward the opposite doorway at once. The demanding, bordering angry, tone had not come from Lia, but from Riona.

Eve had no idea when her mother had arrived, or how they hadn't noticed her. The queen's eyes were narrowed at Eve, her lips pressed together in a thin line. Her normally regal features had taken on an undeniable aura of barely contained fury.

"Mother, it's not what it sounds like," Eve began lamely, feeling very much like a child caught with her hand in a cookie jar. "Nothing happened. I was frightened, and he stayed so that I would feel safe...." Saying it aloud, it felt like a lie. That had been a reason, sure, but certainly not the whole reason; and her mother's expression told her clearly that Riona didn't believe her.

Lia had been watching silently, an unintended witness to a family disagreement. "I think that perhaps I should go write to my father..." she said quietly, moving to make her escape while mother and daughter continued to glare at one another.

"I apologize, Aurelia, for the intrusion," Riona said gently, tearing her gaze away from her daughter to offer Lia a smile.

Eve followed suit, eyes widening in silent appeal to her friend.

Lia inclined her head, silently mouthing "Sorry," before heading out of the room.

The moment they were alone again, Riona took Lia's place by the back door. For several seconds, she simply stared out into the forest. A pair of bluebirds flitted and hopped around the path leading into the treeline, chirping happily. "You cannot be with him, Evelyn."

Riona's use of her formal name startled Eve. Even when angry, her mother generally preferred to call her Evie, like everyone else. She also had been the only person to not make demands of her personal life. When her father had all but demanded she stop seeing Brodie, her mother had never really objected, only worrying for Eve's long-term happiness. She had advised her daughter to consider her decision carefully but had ultimately left the choice to Eve.

"You can't tell me what to do with my love life, Mother." Eve retorted, folding her arms across her chest. "Besides, it's pointless. He turned me down."

Riona sighed heavily, lifting a hand to her brow. "I know I have no right, but please listen to me this one time. Don't pursue this. You don't know him, and you are doing nothing but giving the council more ridiculous accusations to fling at you." Riona placed her hands on Eve's shoulders, squeezing gently. "Please. Now, I must go and see to preparations for the coronation. The dressmaker is coming this morning to help with your gowns for the ceremony and the ball, so head upstairs and prepare yourself soon." She didn't wait for a response from Eve before dropping her hands and leaving the room, leaving her daughter in stunned silence.

Chapter 16

Callan

"You slept in her bed." Callan was dressing for the day when Riona barged into the suite. Standing by the sofa in the sitting area, he had just begun buttoning his shirt when she'd arrived, all but yelling the statement at him. He could sense the fear emanating from her, even without using his gift.

"Only slept," he replied gently. "Nothing more. I intend to keep my promise."

It was the truth, of course. He had every intention of keeping Eve at arm's length. How he felt about her didn't matter, and neither did what she felt. He had to keep her away; there was simply no choice in the matter.

Riona's expression shifted from one of frightened anger to doubt, her hands clenched at her sides. She didn't believe him, not totally, and he couldn't blame her for it. Despite the trust she had placed in him, his actions were reason enough for anyone to doubt his sincerity.

Riona shook her head once. "That's not good enough, Callan, and you know it. Everybody can see how you look at her."

Callan finished with his shirt, tugged on his long black coat, and checked the sword at his hip. He didn't bother to tell her that short of plucking his very eyes from his head, he couldn't stop looking at Eve. No matter how much he wished he could.

"Are you going somewhere?" Her question wasn't a total surprise. He hadn't bothered arming himself while in the castle up to this point, but his plan for today required it.

"To the city," he replied, avoiding her gaze by busying himself with his belt. "I need to find the men responsible for yesterday."

"Revenge, while certainly warranted, is hardly the priority right now, Lord Thorne," Riona replied evenly. "You should be focused on my daughter's safety. We can send men to the city. We can deal with them when they're found."

He wished it had been anger that had carried her to his room, and not fear for her child. Anger was so much easier to deal with than fear and worry. Callan sighed, glancing toward the door once. "I should go, your majesty."

Riona opened her mouth to reply, to say something to stop him again. "I'm not leaving her alone or unprotected. Leysa has just arrived, and Valerian is just behind her. Princess Aurelia's presence alone should be enough to deter any further attacks. She'll be here another week, I'm told, and she has plenty of guards with her. Guards who, unlike your own, have no stake in her rise to the throne and pose no threat."

By the time he'd finished speaking, he found himself standing by the door. He was ready to go, he *needed* to go. They needed to pay for what they'd done to her, but as importantly, he needed to find out who was behind this and prevent it from happening again.

"And no offense," he added, as he opened the chamber doors. "But your guards are useless." Before she could protest, or admonish him for his rude remark, he left.

No more than an hour later, he found himself back in the city. He'd retraced the steps Eve had taken that day, repeating the details she'd given him in his mind.

From the stage, they'd taken her through the winding alleys and back streets, presumably to hide their actions from view of the guards, and any other bystanders who may have intervened. It didn't take long to find the dead end she'd described, where she'd made her stand and managed to get away.

Greyish brown stains on the ground and stone walls surrounding the alley still marked the spot. Her panic-stricken face, covered in blood and terror flashed in his mind briefly. Rage and something akin to fear bubbled up from somewhere deep within him. She had been so gods damned brave, so undeserving of the nickname he'd taken to calling her.

They'd nearly taken her, and he'd failed to be there to protect her when she needed him most. He couldn't understand why she didn't blame him, didn't hate him for failing her. He knew Riona did, could sense it from her. He didn't know why she hadn't spoken up about it just yet, but he suspected it was coming. *That's going to be fun*, he thought with a humorless laugh.

A faint sound, likely undetectable by anyone else, drew his attention to the end of the alley. Someone was coming, several someones in fact, from different angles. He should've seen it coming, the ambush that was about to happen.

If he'd bothered to reach out with his gift, he likely would've sensed animosity and deceit. Hell, if he'd bothered using his damned eyes he probably would've noticed them watching him, following his every step. He'd been distracted, his thoughts on her, on revenge.

His feelings for her had clouded his focus and had led him straight into this situation, and he was going to have to fight his way out of this, against an unknown number of enemies, with no clear means of escape should he need it. *Fucking great.* He pulled his sword free from its scabbard just as the first two rounded the corner at the end of the alley. He could handle two of them, no problem.

A low whistle from somewhere up and to the right of him, atop one of the buildings surrounding the alley, drew his attention. *Oh, great, so not just two, at least eight more of them.*

In the time it took him to realize the seriousness of the situation, three more had joined the original two, and all five were smiling.

This is bad, he thought, adjusting the grip on his sword. He'd hoped to avoid having to unleash the particular gift he was about to have to, but they were backing him into a corner here, literally and figuratively.

He could only hope nobody else noticed. Nobody could be aware of who, and what, he really was.

Decision made, he closed his eyes and began. Despite the fact the sun shone brightly above them, the alley began to darken. The shadows cast by the buildings began to deepen and gather around him, closing in as if night herself had arrived early. He would unleash himself, his true self, on them and they would regret this day.

"I wouldn't bother." The lazy drawl came from the end of the alley. A sixth man had arrived and now stood behind his compatriots. "He told us all about you, what you can do, and how to stop it."

Is he bluffing? "Well, that's a damned shame," Callan laughed arrogantly, cocking his head to the side. "Because if that's true, you know just how stupid it would be to attack me, and yet...here we are." He lifted his free hand lightly, gesturing toward them. "Your mothers must be so proud to have raised such smart little boys."

"My mother was a drunk whore," the fool shrugged, scratching at his greying beard. "Don't particularly care what that cunt would think. But we'll be making our coin, abyss-spawn, and drinking to your death later." The other members of his gang laughed nervously.

Callan's other, less deadly, gift told him that the leader was confident and carried not a trace of deceitfulness or fear. So he was telling the truth, or at the least believed in whatever he was told.

Which led to the next problem. Who had told this man about Callan, and what he could do? He could probably count the number of people in this realm who knew the truth, and none of them would betray that trust.

The ones who knew and would want to do him harm should have been long gone. He dismissed the thought before it could distract him further. If what the man said was true, then this fight would be much more difficult than he originally thought, and he would need a way out just in case.

"Then at least she won't have to mourn you," Callan replied flatly. Shadows continued to swirl and gather around him, even as the men at the end of the alley began to step closer, nothing but resolve and hatred emanating from them. No doubt about their purpose or the fact that they could take him down.

Most troubling of all was the lack of fear at the sight of the shadows that now surrounded him, a shroud of night nearly encapsulating him. Most mortals would be terrified, cowering at the sight of magic thought to be long lost from this realm. Magic had vanished alongside the fae when they had left the humans they'd called neighbors, friends, and even lovers, behind.

They should have been fleeing, crying out to the lost gods for mercy. Instead, they grinned and raised the bows they'd been carrying, the ones he'd all but ignored in his own hubris. The bows, he realized, were nocked with the one thing they shouldn't have known to use, the one thing that could temporarily nullify his powers; white ash arrows. If they were using white ash, then they had to have been telling the truth. Realization set in, sending a chill to his very core.

They knew, they knew everything. And if that was the case, then this *he* that they had mentioned must have been.... Callan's eyes widened and his heart pounded. This was so much worse than he could've imagined.

CHAPTER 17

The dressmaker had stayed nearly the entire morning, and her mother had flitted in and out of the room, fussing over fabrics and gown designs. Though Eve had a suspicion that her real aim was to watch for Callan and to make sure nothing was happening that she believed shouldn't be. When that was finished, Lia begged her for lunch on the terrace, which she'd happily obliged of course. An afternoon without fear, without the stress of having to face the council was welcome. As was the chance to avoid Callan.

He had to be hovering nearby somewhere, she knew, but she hadn't seen him since she'd snuck out like a child to steal a treat from the kitchen. The utter lack of his presence was beginning to make her suspect he was avoiding her as well, or at the very least allowing her to avoid him. It didn't help her feel less awkward, but it was nice to at least pretend she didn't care about what had almost happened between them the night before.

Around the time she was dragged to tour the new gallery with the pair of them, she realized she was being distracted. A week ago, the frivolous things they'd spent the afternoon wouldn't have bothered her or felt out of the ordinary in any way. But now it felt like everything that happened had some meaning. Her choice to say no had been the stone dropped in the still pond, every moment afterward changed by the ripples that spread outward. At least this particular stone had the advantage of being her choice and hopefully setting right a centuries-old wrong. The other stone would've been heavier, tied to a man she didn't know and would drag her under the water, drowning her spirit.

"Where is he?" Eve halted suddenly, spinning on her heel to face her mother. Lia had retired to her chambers four tapestries ago, though Riona showed no signs of stopping. She clearly planned to keep Eve busy with mindless chatter and walking through the seemingly endless galleries and greenhouses for as long as she could.

"I told you, Evie." Exasperation was beginning to creep into Riona's tone, as she answered Eve for the third time. "He's seeing to something, but he will be back soon."

"Well, since you're so determined to keep me busy, and not at all inclined to answer me truthfully, I'll take my leave," Eve replied, crossing her arms across her chest. *Might as well stomp my foot too.* "I'll see you at dinner." Turning on her heel, she strode for her room, wincing at her own childish display.

Night had begun to fall by the time dinner was announced. Eve was making her way to the smaller more intimate dining room she'd be sharing with her mother and Lia, prepared to interrogate the queen until she got the answers she wanted. Callan still hadn't returned from wherever he was, and Eve wouldn't allow another hour to go by without an answer.

She heard the woman's voice before she saw her. "No really! He was covered in it. It was *disgusting*."

Rounding the corner, the woman finally came into view. Just a bit taller than her, with rich brown skin that reminded Eve of the topaz mined from the nearby mountains, she was, in a word, stunning– and also armed.

The daggers strapped to each of her leather-clad thighs drew Eve's attention almost immediately. Though she knew female fighters existed in the southern kingdoms, in high numbers in some places, female warriors were unheard of in the north, and Eve had never personally seen one. It was intriguing and frankly more than a little intimidating.

"Who are you?" Eve demanded, more sharply than she'd intended. She should probably apologize for being rude, and her mother would certainly have expected it of her, but her head was still reeling from Callan's sudden disappearance, which nobody but her seemed to be concerned with. What patience she'd had this morning had been quickly used up.

The stranger, whoever she was, took Eve's rudeness in stride. "Leysa Ashford, my lady. I'm a friend of Callan Thorne's."

A friend of Callan's. Eve hesitated a moment and let the words settle. She couldn't ignore the petty pang of jealousy that flared up at the ridiculously pretty woman's words. As much as she hated herself for feeling it, and as much as she wished she could pretend it wasn't, it was there.

They weren't together and Callan had made his feelings perfectly clear. She had no right to be jealous and no claim to him. Perhaps this woman was why, or perhaps not, but whatever the case it wasn't her business.

Regardless, she was dying to know.

"A friend?" She asked, forcing a smile. "Well, it's a pleasure to meet you." Eve paused a moment, pointedly examining Leysa's weapons before glancing at the guard, who cleared his throat and straightened. While they'd spoken he'd been staring intently at Leysa, obviously enraptured.

"She's been cleared, my lady, by the Queen herself," the guard offered.

"Alright then," Eve replied, irritation with her mother rising once more. " You may go. I believe a room has been prepared already, as we were expecting Lord Thorne's companions soon. I will show her the way."

With what she hoped would pass as a friendly smile, Eve turned back toward the hall she'd come from to lead the warrior to her chambers. "I'll make sure your things are brought to the correct room," she began tentatively. "I was expecting a man, so the room may be a bit... masculine for your tastes. I'm sorry."

Leysa responded with a light laugh and a wave of her hand. Humor lit her amber-brown eyes. "Please, don't trouble yourself. I'm sure my husband will enjoy it enough for the both of us, and frankly, anything that isn't a tent in the middle of some forest is good enough for me."

Husband? A wave of relief washed over Eve, and she turned a curious gaze to Leysa. "Will he be joining you soon?"

Leysa narrowed her eyes slightly, taking a moment to read the expression on Eve's face before responding. Whatever she saw there had the corner of her mouth twitching upwards ever so slightly. "Yes, Valerian should be no more than a day behind me. When Callan called on us, we were together but he had to go and check on something before he could join me here."

"You're all friends then, the three of you?" Eve asked. She couldn't help but wonder what that dynamic must be like. What it would be like for her in the future.

She would remain unmarried while her friends moved on and began families. None of her friends had married yet, not that she had many of them to boast of. Emilia was deadset on a good match, but so far none had risen to the level she deigned to be worthy. Lia was a romantic at heart and longed to find the right person for her, but so far none of her relationships had worked out. And....well that was the very short list of the people she could call friends.

She wondered if she could've once called Brodie a friend, but that title didn't really seem to fit them, at any point in their relationship. They had barely known each other when they'd fallen into one another and then nearly the moment it ended he was gone. There was no time for them to find a way to continue any sort of relationship, much less friendship. Jealousy of an entirely different sort struck her then, and she turned her gaze away to avoid Leysa's stare.

"Yes," she replied, either unaware of the direction of Eve's thoughts or too polite to remark on the shift in her expression. "We've known each other since we were children, all three of us. Our parents were all friends."

"So you must know one another quite well," Eve remarked. "May I ask about the story you were telling the guard? Was that about Callan?"

Leysa's answering laugh was warm and lush, reminding Eve of something wild and wonderful. "Oh, no that was about my husband, Valerian. We were once camped near the great gorge, and this huge thing, I don't even know how to describe it, it was like...a giant slug or something, I don't know. Anyway, it was drawn to our campfire I guess, and Callan went to chase it away. While he was doing that, Valerian snuck up behind the thing, just in case. Well, it didn't want to go, and was trying to take a bite out of Callan."

Leysa paused then, placing a hand gently on Eve's arm, eyes wide. "Oh did I mention it had huge teeth? Like, honestly huge teeth. Crazy huge. Anyway, Valerian just stabbed it...and it exploded. *Boom.* Somehow, I still don't know how, Callan jumped out of the way in time, and the next thing I know, Val is covered in goo. Nasty, nasty, goo. It was gross and hilarious."

Mention of the gorge and its awful creatures brought her father to the forefront of Eve's mind. Unbidden images of him and his men being eaten by a giant slug sent a shiver down her spine. Was that what had killed him? Or was it some other awful thing?

She'd avoided thinking of her father recently, and the guilt over that fact hit her hard. She had told herself that it was so she could focus on the coronation, on keeping the council in check and their insistence on her taking a suitor at bay, but the truth was far more simple.

Grief was too hard, too raw, too real. She was afraid if she allowed herself to feel it, she'd sink into its depths and never surface again. They'd had their differences, but at the end of the day, he'd loved her and had wanted the best for her, even if what he considered to be best was completely absurd in her mind.

As most parents in the North, Viktor had taught his daughter that marrying was the best course of action and the safest, citing the few women before her who had spoken up and tried to take the course she'd chosen. Each of them had changed their minds soon after, likely talked out of the decision by parents or the council, she guessed.

They'd nearly made it to Leysa's appointed room by the time Eve realized she hadn't spoken a word for a few minutes. Like Callan, Leysa seemed to be comfortable with the silence.

Leysa's gaze roamed over the tapestries and various artwork that lined the hall leading to her temporary quarters. Whatever she was thinking, it wasn't clearly written on her face, and Eve was a little afraid to ask, so instead, she chose what she thought would have to be a safe topic. Safe enough anyway. "So, do you have any other stories like that? About Callan maybe? I'd love to have something to tease him with." She could only hope her tone was as light and casual as she'd intended.

Amber eyes turned to Eve once more, and for a moment something like mischief shone in them. "I have lots, but I think this one might interest you the most." They'd reached her chambers now, and the pair of them stepped inside while Leysa spoke. "A few years ago, he was called to visit with some fancy ruler or another. They had some concerns about, well, it doesn't matter. Security of some sort, I guess. Only, the day he arrived, they were having a party." Leysa paused them, lifting her chin slightly and looking Eve over. Some unreadable expression danced across her features briefly before she turned away and wandered towards the window on the opposite side of the room.

"A party?" Eve asked, confused and more than a little irritated by the strange expression. She wanted to do something, needed to do something other than standing around and waiting for Leysa to finish her story. The story which she was now regretting asking for, as it seemed to be going nowhere interesting. At least this was better than trying on a million dresses and being ignored when she asked questions about Callan, she supposed.

There was no sofa in this room, only a single chair by a small writing desk, and the bed. It was a nice room if a little small. Eve wondered how comfortable it would be for a married couple to share. Better than a tent surely, but she would have to ask the steward to find something more spacious for them. Giving up on the idea of sitting, Eve moved to the wardrobe and idly toyed with the brass drawer pulls, shaped like a lion with a ring through his mouth.

Leysa didn't turn to face her, instead settling on staring out at the forest canopy beyond, now nearly invisible in the inky darkness. "A birthday party, I think. It doesn't matter. What matters is the girl." She finally turned then, offering Eve a grin. "There's always a girl, in these kinds of stories, right?"

Leysa didn't wait for Eve to respond before continuing, lifting a shoulder in a light shrug. "Anyway, the way he tells it, he's just making small talk with someone and she walks in. The most beautiful woman he'd ever seen, and the world stopped." Rolling her eyes dramatically, Leysa sighed. "He's hopeless, honestly. So he sees this girl, the world stops turning, blah blah–"

She froze then, mid-sentence, and stared at the door, nostrils flaring slightly as her eyes narrowed. "Move away from the door." Her light, lovely tone had shifted immediately. There was no humor left, and her face was devoid of every ounce of levity.

Eve could hear nothing at all, but Leysa's tone alone was enough to brook no argument, and she moved immediately to Leysa's side. She couldn't help the quickening of her pulse as fear crawled up her spine.

"Someone is coming, in a hurry," she said, sparing Eve only the briefest of glances. "Stay beside me."

"How do you–" She began to ask, to demand how Leysa could know that, only to be interrupted as a guard she didn't recognize burst through the doors.

"My lady, you must come at once. Lord Thorne has returned, and he's injured, he..."

Whatever else he said was ignored as Eve ran from the room, pushing past the stunned guard.

Don't run, it isn't ladylike, her mother's voice chided in her head. *Propriety be damned,* was her silent response, as she ran down the hall.

It wasn't until she'd reached the entrance hall that she realized she had no idea where he actually was. She stood there, surrounded by stunned staff, gaping at their princess for several seconds. Eve could only imagine what she'd looked like, tearing through the castle as fast as she could in heels, dark red curls flying wildly behind her, and her face panic-stricken. He was hurt, who knew how badly, and they had lied to her all day about where he was. Where had he been? How badly was he injured and who had done it?

Questions raged through her mind, not the least of which being where was he now? She spun in a slow circle in the center of the room, fists balled at her sides. She hadn't started crying just yet, but she could feel the tears beginning to well.

There was something there, within her, causing this reaction that she would need to examine eventually. *Later,* she thought, later she would think about that. Not now, not when he was hurt, and she couldn't find him, didn't know where he was. She should ask someone, she realized, surely one of the guards would know. Why hadn't she thought to stop and ask?

"Why so upset, dove?" Callan's voice hit her like a weight.

She spun, turning towards the direction of his voice. He was bruised, his mouth and nose bloodied. Blood soaked his shirt, and his left arm hung limp at his side. Without thought, her feet were moving, carrying her straight into him. She didn't pause to take in his appearance or assess his injuries before crashing against his chest, throwing her arms around his neck.

"Where have you been? What happened? Why are you hurt?" Her words were all but running together, each question coming out right on the heels of the last, not even pausing to breathe.

A pained grunt from Callan stopped her and she stepped back, emerald eyes widened. "What is it? Should I call someone?"

"A healer would be good, but right now I need you to stop squeezing. I've got a little bit of a puncture wound there and I'm pretty sure you're squashing a broken rib or two." His tone was rough. Eve released him immediately, scanning his features. His brows were drawn together as he took a ragged breath. "Ouch."

"Oh, gods. Oh, gods, I'm so sorry." Turning towards the nearest guard, Eve shouted, "Call a healer! Immediately!"

"They've already been called, my love." As composed as ever, the Queen entered the antechamber, Lia alongside her, and Leysa just behind.

In stark opposition to Riona's calm features, Lia's countenance was the very picture of worry. As she spoke, a pair of healers bustled in and began to lead Callan to the healing room. The elder of the two, Mauren, silently took charge, waving a hand for the assembled royalty to follow them as they led Callan into the dimly lit chamber. Nobody spoke as they walked.

Questions burned within Eve's mind, the most pressing being about his health. Was he going to be okay? How was he hurt? She barely managed to keep her mouth closed, biting the inside of her cheek to keep quiet.

Callan took a seat on the raised table in the center of the room with a pained grunt. Celestia, the younger of the two healers, gathered herbs from around the room, while Mauren gestured for Callan to take off his ripped and stained shirt.

"Now, my lord," the elderly woman said gently, her voice low and gravelly. "I'll need to inspect your wounds. It may be painful, and men such as yourself often prefer to have some privacy." She passed a pointed glance in the direction of the assembled ladies.

Eve opened her mouth to protest, to say that she'd be damned if she was kicked out, at least not before she got answers.

It was Callan's voice that stopped her. "It's fine, she can stay," he said gruffly, staring straight at Eve.

It was cue enough for the others to go. Riona cast a wary glance before going, with Lia offering Eve a supportive smile. Only Leysa hesitated, waiting for Callan to speak up again, leaving a few moments later when he remained silent.

The healers worked quickly and efficiently, only murmuring quiet instructions or comments to one another as they set to work bandaging Callan's wounds or applying herbs and salves to the wounds that covered his body. He'd been beaten, badly. It was a wonder to Eve, that he was still upright.

"Are you going to tell me what happened?" Eve demanded. She was anxious, and it showed. Her lips were pressed together firmly as she awaited his response, hands clenched at her sides.

"I got mugged," he replied in a half-assed attempt at a joke. One of the healers, Eve couldn't be sure which, snorted in response as they worked. Did he actually expect her to believe that? She didn't know and didn't care either but it was clear he was full of shit.

"Funny, I would've expected you to be able to handle some muggers. Some bodyguard you are." It was an attempt at humor, to calm her own nerves and bring some kind of levity to a situation that terrified her. She hadn't meant to cause the hurt that so clearly flashed through his eyes. *Stupid*, she thought, realizing the direction his thoughts had taken. "Callan, I didn't mean..."

He interrupted her apology with a light wave of his uninjured hand. "I know," he said gruffly, wincing at whatever salve the young healer was currently applying to one of the many wounds on his back. "You want the truth then? I went to look for the men who tried to take you. Or at the least some information about them. Somehow, someone anticipated my arrival and arranged an ambush. I managed to escape and took a few of them out before I did, but there's something that really concerns me."

Eve's heart skipped a beat. "Who knew you were going to the city?" She bit her lower lip gently casting a slight glance at the healers. *Should we be speaking about this now? If someone had informed the attackers of his trip to the city, it would have to be someone inside the castle. But who?*

"We can discuss that later. I need to think, and frankly you standing there, biting your lip like that, and worrying about me is distracting as fuck." His eyes darkened as he watched her puzzle out what had happened to him.

Her heart raced in her chest, and she immediately released her lip from between her teeth. Along with the desire and confusion sparked by his words, another emotion rose. Anger. How could he say that now, after what he'd said just the night before?

"What is wrong with you?" she demanded angrily. Only the scraping of a mortar and pestle, a reminder that the healers were present stopped her from shouting any further, from slinging every one of the many insults poised on the tip of her tongue.

Celestia and Mauren exchanged a glance, the elder of the two gesturing toward the door with a jerk of her chin. The younger healer quietly exited, casting a sparing glance over her shoulder at the soon-to-be queen. Gentle brown eyes were filled with something akin to pity as she stepped out.

Irritation flared inside Eve, but she forced a slight smile. No reason to be rude to the girl, no matter how much she hated Celestia feeling sorry for her.

Callan remained silent, leaving the question unanswered as Mauren gently applied a grey paste to the most serious of his wounds along his ribs. With deft hands, she wrapped a clean bolt of linen around his torso, binding the wounds and covering the healing paste.

When she finished, the healer grabbed a clean cloth from her work area, and followed her apprentice out the door. The door closed behind her with a gentle click, leaving the pair of them alone finally.

"I do not understand you," Eve began, voice low and calm, despite the fire burning within her.

"No, you don't," he countered. "You have no idea what I want, who I really am, or what I've been through. You know nothing about me."

Eve opened her mouth to reply, but Callan raised a hand and continued. "I'm not saying that to be an ass, Eve, it just is what it is. You don't know me, not really. Do you want to know something? Ask. If I can tell you, I will. As I said before, I can't tell you everything, but I will never lie to you."

Confusion blended with anger, only slightly dulling the raging fire within her. Questions rose within her mind. But which one would he actually answer? A new question, one she hadn't asked before flew from her mouth before she could stop it. "Why did you stop me last night?"

Callan sighed, dragging a hand through his dark hair. "We've been walking on a razor's edge, you and I. If I hadn't stopped, hadn't pulled myself away from you, nothing would've stopped me from tumbling right over the edge of that precipice with you Eve, and that cannot happen."

Eve snorted. "You said it can't happen, and...and that's fine, of course. But if you were spoken for then you should've told me." *Before I made a fool of myself*, she thought. "Before I asked you to sleep in my bed. You could've saved both of us the embarrassment of your lover, whoever she is, finding out like that."

"You have no idea what you're talking about." He replied darkly. His voice was quiet with a deadly sort of intensity she'd only heard him use once before. When she'd been covered in someone else's blood and he had been her salvation.

"What the fuck is that supposed to mean Callan?" She demanded, arms folded across her chest. "I think it's pretty clear that you're involved with someone. Leysa told me, or started to anyway."

Resolve hardened her features and she tilted her chin upwards. She was hurt, more than she cared to admit even to herself, but she'd be damned if she'd let him see that; let him see just how much he made her feel.

Callan laughed then, bitter and humorless. "You think that's why I pushed you away? As if something as small as that could keep me from you?" He moved towards her then, faster than he should've been able to with his injuries.

Before she could question it, he was there, fingertips gently resting against her cheek. "Nothing less than the promise of utter disaster would keep me from you."

The burning in her veins shifted to something else entirely. Anger was quickly replaced with desire, setting her very core aflame.

Callan's touch trailed slowly from her cheek to the column of her neck, before he dropped his hand to his side. "As I said, this can't happen; no matter how much I want it to."

CHAPTER 18

The next morning Eve was still reeling from all that was said, and what he'd done. What disaster could possibly come from the two of them sleeping together? She'd asked him that exact question and received only a shake of his head in response. Apparently, that fell under the 'things I can't tell you' category. Being pulled in and pushed away all at once was maddening and more than a little distracting from the one thing she should be focusing on entirely.

The coronation was only days away, and though her planned public appearances had been canceled after her near kidnapping, she was still expected to attend the grand dinner being held that evening. The captain of the guard would personally ensure that only invited guests were allowed in, and they had doubled the number of guards in attendance.

Though he remained close, still sleeping in her sitting room, Callan hadn't returned to her bed. She'd woken the next morning to find him gone. It seemed the discussion in the healer's room had left both of them resolved to avoid the other.

"What's on the schedule for this morning?" Eve turned toward the sound of the cheerful voice drifting in from the sitting room. Leysa had taken up Callan's post, presumably called upon before he'd even left.

"I'm meeting Princess Aurelia in the gardens this morning. She wanted to see the Black Pool near the castle. Apparently, her father asked her to take some notes regarding its size or something." Finally ready for the day, Eve drifted into the sitting room and gave a little spin to show off her emerald day gown. Leysa rewarded her with quiet applause and a warm smile. "King Aldrich is always conducting research on that sort of thing," Eve explained.

Leysa's raven curls bobbed slightly as she tilted her head. "They are all exactly the same, aren't they?"

She was right, as far as Eve could recall. The pools that had supposedly been formed by the tears of the gods as they departed the known realms were said to be identical to one another. Nobody knew exactly why, or even where the legend regarding their origin had come from when little else about the gods had remained intact with the departure of the fae. A knock at the door interrupted her reply. Leysa stepped closer to Eve as she called out, "Come in!"

Eve had been expecting Lia, or perhaps her mother. The last person she expected was Emilia Danwell, dressed in a sky blue day gown and straw basket on her arm. "Are you ready to go?" She chirped happily, before glancing at Leysa with confusion etched on her features. "Oh, I'm sorry I appear to be interrupting something."

"I didn't realize you haven't met my newest guardian, Leysa Ashford," Eve replied, hiding her surprise at Emilia's arrival with a smile. "Leysa is a friend of Lord Thorne's, here to help when he is unavailable."

Leysa offered Emilia a smile but remained silent.

"It's a pleasure to meet you, Leysa." Emilia eyed Leysa with no less curiosity than she had when meeting Callan for the first time, but with considerably less interest. "I ran into Princess Aurelia on my way here. She's leaving now. King Aldrich sent word that he needs her home immediately. She asked me to pass along her apologies, and sent a message for you." Emilia paused, brow furrowing slightly as she recalled the conversation. "She said for you to speak to your mother, and tell her that her father says 'the crescent is more important than he thought'."

Lia had left without even taking the time to say goodbye. Eve could only guess that something was deeply wrong at home if she had been recalled so suddenly without even completing the task her father had assigned her. It was unlike Aldrich Vallyse to leave something undone, especially when it came to his academic interests.

Concern for her friend washed over her, and for a moment, she considered going after Lia. As if sensing the direction of her thoughts, Leysa quietly cleared her throat, drawing Eve's attention back to the situation at hand.

"I'll go and speak to my mother when she returns from her visit to Forest Haven. Thank you, Em. Where were we going?" Eve hadn't remembered making plans with Emilia today, certainly not when she'd expected to go out with Lia to the Black Pool, but with everything going on she supposed she might have simply forgotten.

"I thought maybe the two of us could go to the greenhouses and choose some blooms for this evening. I know the florists have already made some lovely arrangements, of course, but I thought it might be fun to make one or two ourselves and sneak them in among the others."

Eve couldn't see the fun in that herself, but with her plans for the day already ruined, it would be more fun than anything else that came to mind. "That sounds nice," she replied, glancing at Leysa awkwardly. Emilia's invitation had clearly not been intended to include Eve's new guardian, but she could hardly leave her behind. Not only would it be horribly rude, but also reckless, and she had no doubt the suggestion would be met with a firm refusal.

Emilia's gaze darted between them, warm brown eyes narrowing slightly. She was obviously disinclined to extend the invitation to Leysa, no doubt planning to use the privacy of the greenhouse to gossip with Eve.

It was Leysa who finally broke the awkward silence. "I have some things to do anyway. I can walk you as far as the gardens if that's okay."

"Perfect!" Emilia declared as she set off, not bothering to check if they followed.

Leysa's brow shot up, and she tossed Eve a glance. Eve could only shrug in reply. There was no deterring Emilia when she set her mind to something, and she had long since learned to choose her battles with her friend.

It was only a short walk to the gardens, made in silence by the three of them. The only sounds were the murmured greetings of household staff they passed in the corridors. Once outside, Leysa muttered a quiet goodbye and then headed away, in the opposite direction of the greenhouse.

"Isn't it weird?" Emilia asked suddenly, breaking the silence as they entered the first greenhouse. Stoneweald's hothouses had been built many generations before, and though they remained in good shape, they certainly bore the signs of their age. Rust now blemished her iron bones, and some of the many panes of glass had cracked.

"Is what weird?" Eve asked. Unlike the exterior gardens, the plants here bore heavy blooms and bright green foliage. Gardeners worked tirelessly to maintain a steady source of flowers, fruits, and vegetables for the residents and guests of Stoneweald. Each building had its purpose, dedicated to either food or pleasure, and this particular house was used for flowers alone. A rosebush, heavy with deep red blooms caught Eve's eye and she moved to inspect the flowers more closely.

"Being followed all of the time. I mean, it's not so bad I suppose, when it's a handsome man that looks at you like you are the most important person in the world, but a woman? A woman who carries *weapons*?" Emilia wrinkled her nose, emphasizing the word as if it were dirty. " She's just very...strange. I don't understand it."

Her opinion was hardly shocking, as distasteful as Eve found it. It was the old way of thinking, the same way of thinking that would see Eve handing over her throne to a man, simply for the fact she lacked a cock. For a moment, Eve found herself questioning the long-time friendship they'd had. How would it be impacted by her refusal to marry? Would Emilia stand by her or despise her the way she knew some others would?

A small part of her found it strange that Emilia hadn't spoken against her decision. She hadn't supported it necessarily, but she hadn't been as vocal about her opinion as Eve had expected. Eve turned to face Emilia, who had begun to meander down the aisle of the greenhouse, eyeing the varying roses that this section of the greenhouse had been dedicated to.

"I'm not sure what you expect me to say, Em. Leysa is kind of amazing. She is funny and brave, and frankly, I think it's ridiculous that the women of Darkegrove don't have the opportunity to learn to do the things that she can do. Though you might have to start keeping some of your opinions to yourself if they do," she replied, her tone light and teasing. Somewhere outside a hawk cried, drawing both of their gazes upward. "I hope it doesn't bother the little folk in my garden," Eve muttered, frowning.

Emilia huffed, the basket on her arm bobbing as she crossed her slender arms in front of her body. "That was a little uncalled for, don't you think?" Pink lips pursed together in displeasure. "Sure, that stuff sounds...exciting I guess. I just think it should be left to the men. We have important roles to fill too..." She drifted off, dropping her arms again and floating down the aisle as if she had not a care in the world.

There it is. The real reason for this little outing. Whatever opinion Emilia had been keeping to herself was about to be dropped on Eve's lap like a bundle of stone. Unwanted, heavy, and uncomfortable.

Eve's shoulders tensed, and she gripped the soft fabric of her skirt tightly. It seemed their friendship would be put to the test sooner rather than later. "Just say it, Em."

Emilia continued her stroll, pausing only to examine blooms that caught her eye as she did. *She didn't even bring shears*, Eve realized. It had been a ploy all along to corner her into this conversation. *Great. Just great.*

Finally, Emilia lifted her gaze to Eve. Her typically cheerful face was drawn, apprehensive. "Well, I know that you think you're doing the right thing, of course. I just think that maybe it's not. Look at the danger you're in. Your poor mother had to call in special guards for you because she's so afraid for your safety." Emilia lifted a hand to her heart. "And so soon after our beloved King..." She sighed then, shaking her head gently in admonishment.

Temper flared, hot and bright, within Eve. But alongside it, guilt. She had known how hard all of this was on her mother, had known that her mother was still grieving her father's death. She certainly did not need Emilia using that pain as a weapon to make a point. "You are exceptionally out of line, Emilia."

Emilia froze mid-stride, fingertips resting on a bright yellow rose. "I'm just saying I'm worried about you." Her shoulders were squared, and the fingers that had gently rested on a rose moments before now gripped the fragile bloom tightly. "I'm trying to look out for you, as your friend, and you won't even hear me!" Indignation rolled off her in waves, and before Eve could reply, she started for the door, all but stomping her feet like a child. The basket she'd brought with her banged against her leg in emphasis. "But you clearly don't want my opinion. Just remember, Eve, whatever happens because of the choice you've made is on your head, and yours alone."

"I am well aware of that," Eve murmured in response as Emilia yanked the door open and stepped outside. She'd learned the hard way about the personal consequences recently. Lying in bed at night questioning the path she'd chosen, and her own resolve, Eve had come to realize that she had more strength than she'd known. If she had to be hated, or even harmed while trying to do the right thing then that was fine, she could take it. As long as her efforts helped ignite change in their kingdom, she would take whatever was thrown at her and push through.

Screams from just outside the greenhouse drew Eve from her thoughts. Emilia was screaming and flapping her arms, dancing around like she was on fire and frantically trying to fend off the bird that was dive-bombing her head. Not just a bird, a hawk.

The golden brown bird flew up, then turned, flying directly for Emilia's head. The hawk easily avoided Emilia's flailing limbs, coming dangerously close to the panicked courtier's head before heading toward a nearby tree. From one of the lower limbs, the hawk cried, and a hysterical Emilia scrambled for the safety of the castle.

Eve remained on the threshold of the greenhouse, wary of the bird that now watched her from the branch. *Where are Leysa and Callan?* The screaming should've drawn their attention by now. She would've expected Callan to arrive by now, and wouldn't Leysa still be close by?

"You're not scared of that little bird, are you, dove?" As if on cue, Callan's voice announced his arrival. The hawk cried out again as if offended perched just above where he leaned against a tree, offering Eve an indolent grin. Where had he come from? She could've sworn she looked there just a moment before.

"That is not a little bird," Eve retorted. "And I don't think it likes people very much."

Callan watched the bird as he approached, humor dancing in his cobalt gaze. "She's not so bad," he remarked. Before Eve could ask him how he could possibly know that, the hawk in question took off, calling out once as she did. "I heard screaming so I thought I should come and see."

Eve narrowed her eyes at him slightly. "You took your time. Did the screaming interrupt the leisurely stroll? Or are you so injured that walking is all you can manage?"

A light laugh was his answer to her snark, and he shook his head. "Leysa was close, and I knew you were safe with her nearby."

"She's close by? Why didn't she help Emilia?" Eve demanded, not that she felt any real ire. Emilia frankly deserved it, after how she'd spoken about Leysa. She could handle the judgment thrown her way and had expected it, but to disparage Leysa was unacceptable.

Callan lifted his uninjured shoulder lightly. "You'd have to ask her that when she returns. Valerian sent word. He's in Forest Haven, and she's gone to meet him. They've been apart for a few weeks now, so they wanted some time together." He cracked a smile, then added. "I think she also wanted to go and buy a new dress for tonight. She loves parties."

The idea of Leysa and Valerian being reunited again made Eve smile. She couldn't imagine being separated from the person you loved for as long as they had been. "It's kind of them, to come and help. Of all of you, really. I hope you know that I appreciate it."

Her gaze drifted to the place on his ribs where she knew bandages were now hidden beneath his black shirt. She'd teased him about moving slowly because of his injuries before but now wondered if they were in fact the cause. "How are you feeling?"

"Better I think–" He began to reply, only to be interrupted by a pair of guards bursting through the castle doors.

"My lady!" The first of them shouted, scanning the area. "Lady Danwell said there was a vicious animal in the area. We must ask you to come inside immediately while we ensure that it is gone."

"Princess Evelyn is perfectly safe now, gentlemen," Callan stated calmly. He held his hand out for her, palm skyward. Amusement danced in his blue eyes.

So we're back to this. The flirting, the friendship. Even as she placed her hand in his, Eve couldn't help but wonder how long it would be before he was pushing her away again, telling her how disastrous it would be if they were together. Looking less than convinced, the guard huffed but said nothing further as they walked through the doors together.

The question currently burning at the forefront of her mind would have to wait. There were too many guards close by, warily watching her as Callan escorted her within. How many of these men hated her for what she was doing, she wondered. Her mother had been sure that most of the household guards held strong enough ties to the family to ensure their continued loyalty, but then she had also expected Eve's trip to Forest Haven to be safe enough. Not that it was her fault. None of them could have anticipated what had occurred.

"I need to go and change," she said to Callan, slipping her hand free from his light grasp.

"Of course."

She pretended not to see the way he flexed his fingers afterward, completely unwilling to think about what that meant. "I hope Emilia is recovered by dinner."

Callan only smirked, falling into step alongside her. The walk to her chambers was like so many others they'd taken, silent and all too brief. He was a distraction, one she thought she needed when it seemed to be simple. Now it was complicated, and not just because of her own feelings. He'd said only the promise of disaster could stop him from being with her. That kind of intensity...she had no room in her life for that, not now. What she thought she was beginning to feel for him...she couldn't have that. Not when she was destined to spend her life alone.

And there she was, thinking about the very thing she'd be determined to ignore.

Frustrated with herself, Eve sighed and plopped down onto her bed. She'd left him in the sitting room when they arrived, heading straight into her private room without a word. The crinkling of paper beneath her caught her by surprise. Rolling to her side, she tugged it free and examined the seal along the fold. Deep green wax with ivy relief, her mother's signet. Emilia had mentioned that Riona had wanted to speak to her earlier, likely to explain Lia's sudden departure, or perhaps to give some sort of instruction regarding the dinner this evening.

Eve could only hope it was the former and not the latter. She scanned the letter, frowning at its contents. Riona's flowing script was immediately familiar, strange as the message was.

Darling daughter,

There are things we need to discuss when I return from Forest Haven. Princess Aurelia is departing this morning to return to her father. He requested her return because he believes he has deciphered the prophecy regarding the crescent, and I fear he is correct. There are things I must explain to you as soon as possible, it is vital–

Whatever her mother had begun to write about the prophecy that Eve had nearly forgotten about trailed off there, a smudge of ink trailing across the page. Dark red splatter marred the parchment. Below, in the same bold lettering as the note left in her previous chambers,

'You will not be warned again.'

Dread, cold and heavy, settled in her gut like a weight. *No. No. No.*

The word repeated in her mind, fear leaving no room for any thought beyond that. The paper shook violently in her tightened grasp.

"What's wrong?" She hadn't heard the door open or heard the usual creak of the floorboards, but somehow he was there, standing just beside the bed.

Wordlessly, she thrust the paper at him as she scrambled from the bed. She had to go to her mother.

It must be fake. Except she'd recognized the handwriting as Riona's.

Okay, she thought, running for the hallway now, *maybe they took an unfinished note from her wastebasket.* Her mother was in Forest Haven, safe. Not here. *My mother is not here, she is safe.*

She didn't know if Callan was following, and didn't care. After the threat left in her room, guards had been posted outside of both of their chambers for added security. Something they'd never thought of before she'd made her declaration before the council. The luxury of living in long-lasting peace.

Relief flooded her at the sight of the guard still posted at her mother's door. If he was there, then there was no way anyone had gotten in to harm her.

"Has the queen returned from Forest Haven?" She didn't immediately recognize the man but so many new guards had been called from other posts to serve in the castle, that it wasn't altogether alarming.

"Oh, she never left her chambers," he replied with a slight smirk. "She got what she deserved."

Eve froze, the dread in her gut doubling in size. "What did you say?"

The man turned to face her fully, a malicious grin dominating his rugged features. Recognition tugged at the back of her mind. She *did* know him from somewhere, but she couldn't quite recall where. "I said, the bitch queen got what she deserved and so will you." Looking over her shoulder, fear blossomed in his deep brown eyes, even as he said, "I ain't afraid to die. I did my part."

She could sense Callan behind her now, so close that their bodies were nearly touching. His voice was low and deadly calm when he spoke. "If you even think about laying one finger on her, I will make sure that you live a very long life, and wish for death every moment of it."

Pressure began to build in her head, loud humming drowning out most of Callan's words. "No, she's fine–" He was lying, he had to be. She'd just go in and see for herself...

The guard merely snorted, reaching for Eve as she pushed past him. There was only the faint sensation of rough fingers gripping her arm before darkness exploded in the corridor.

The guard's hand flew from her arm as if he'd been yanked away. Turning back to Callan, she realized she could no longer see him, or anything else for that matter. Night herself had descended on Stoneweald. Darkness like she had never seen engulfed the hallway. The guard, wherever he was, had started screaming in pain or fear, or some combination of the two.

Reaching outward, she felt for the wall. Terror blossomed in her chest, sending her heart skittering and her breath coming in swift, panicked gasps. *What is happening?* The man was still screaming. She had never heard terror like that, had never even known humans were capable of the sounds he made... Had some unknown fae monster made its way into the castle? Were the gods coming to punish Darkegrove for her sins, as some of the more zealous priests sometimes predicted?

Callan was somewhere, in the darkness. Though she couldn't see him, she could sense him, smell the forest. Cedar and sage. "Callan where are you?" Her voice was little more than a trembling whisper, afraid of summoning whatever monster had conjured the abyss itself in her hallway. But she wouldn't allow fear to freeze her in place again.

Eve let her fingertips slide along the smooth stone wall, memory guiding her footsteps toward her mother's room. She had to get out of this hallway, and she had to see for herself that her mother was okay. Instinct drove her forward, and desperation to know what had happened to her mother had her grasping the handle and pushing the door open.

"Don't go in there, dove." Callan's warning was little more than a whisper at the back of her mind.

Whatever had caused the darkness to engulf the hallway had left her mother's room untouched. Relief had her taking a much-needed breath, placing a hand on her chest as she moved into the room.

It took exactly four steps into the room for Eve's world to collapse around her.

Chapter 19

It had been three days since her mother had died, and Eve hadn't left her chambers once. The scene played over and over in her mind, a waking nightmare.

Callan had tried to stop her but she had barely been aware of his voice, of him reaching for her. The false guard had started laughing, a horrible frantic sound, and she had been screaming because her mother was lying on the carpet in front of her.

The Dowager Queen of Darkegrove lay sprawled on the floor by her writing desk, a wine glass shattered by her feet. Blood still poured from her nose and mouth, only just beginning to thicken. Pale blue eyes that had so often looked on Eve with a sort of pride she could only hope to deserve stared up at the ceiling, unblinking, unseeing.

Riona had been writing while having a glass of wine, common for her in the afternoons when she finally took a few moments to herself. Whoever had poisoned her had then used that very note to draw Eve in. A final warning. One that had her questioning her resolve. For the first day after her mother's murder, she'd done nothing but lie in bed.

Leysa and Valerian had returned around the time Eve had arrived in her mother's room, she later learned, and had come running when they'd heard her screaming. They'd secured the guard, her mother's apparent murderer, whose name she still hadn't learned.

Callan had dragged her from the room, held her close while she wailed and fought against him. Now all three of them remained close by, gathered in the sitting room. Nobody else, save for Sylvie, had been allowed in. She'd taken all of her meals here, in her bed, and had not spoken a single word to any of them.

The kitchens had been searched, staff questioned but no sign of the poison, or who had managed to get it into the queen's wine had turned up. Ert, the healers had discovered, had been used, in line with the traces of red powder they'd found in her glass. Most disturbingly, the one source available in Darkegrove were the blooms of Death's Tears, which only grew in the private royal gardens. Eve's own little sanctuary. It felt like yet another violation, a threat woven within the others. A reminder that nothing she held sacred was untouchable.

A quiet knock sounded at the door, and Eve wondered which of them it would be. Emilia hadn't bothered to speak to her since the incident at the greenhouse, though she and her family had sent a letter expressing their condolences and outright shock and horror at what had happened. Sylvie had already checked in on her twice since breakfast, and Callan and Leysa had left her alone to rest just a short time ago.

"Yes?" she called quietly.

Surprise rocked her as Valerian entered. She'd only been vaguely aware of his presence the day he'd arrived and hadn't bothered to really look at him until now. He was tall, taller even than Callan. The warrior strode into the room with a lithe grace that neither Callan nor Leysa had possessed.

Her look of surprise was met with a warm smile that lit up his entire face. With a complexion that reminded her of newly fallen acorns and deep brown eyes, he was nearly as stunning as his wife.

"I'm sorry, I, uh, thought maybe I should introduce myself since I've been camped outside your room for the last couple of days. Is that alright?" His voice was far more gentle than she would've expected from a trained warrior, especially one with a rather large sword currently resting at his hip.

Eve forced a smile and nodded. Broken as she was inside, she couldn't bring herself to be dismissive of the people who had put themselves between herself and harm. Wood scraping against wood reverberated through the room as he dragged the chair from her vanity closer, taking a seat a few feet from her bed. "I'm Valerian Ashford, but I guess you know that. Leysa tells me that you've already heard the 'Val gets covered in goo' story, so I'm not sure what else to tell you about myself to break the ice." He paused, laughing quietly and patting his leather-clad thighs gently with both hands. "She also tells me that I talk too much."

Eve didn't immediately reply, caught off guard by Valerian's friendliness. They'd each offered her support in their own way. Callan had crawled into bed beside her while she sobbed, holding her until she finally fell asleep. He'd remained in bed beside her through the night, stroking her hair and whispering words of comfort when she'd wake from a nightmare.

Leysa had seemed to understand that Eve needed time. Time to sit alone, to grieve, and to think. So she'd given Eve just that, along with the comfort of her company. Valerian, it seemed, was determined to chat and try to make her laugh.

A kind but pointless gesture. "Hi," she said finally.

Valerian offered her a bright smile that soothed a small part of her shattered heart. "Leysa thought maybe we could talk, as I have unique insight into what you're going through. When I was young, I lost my parents....both of them on the same night." Every ounce of her annoyance was doused like a flame. "They care, but they don't understand, you know? They've both had more than their share of hardships, but not this."

"Can I ask you something?" The covers rustled quietly as Eve shifted, sitting up more fully and turning to face Valerian, who lounged comfortably in his chair. He lifted a hand, palm skyward, an open gesture to encourage her to continue.

"How did you get through it? I...I know that I can't sit in bed and cry any longer. I have to get up and keep going, I have to figure out how to do this without her." Tears welled in her eyes, and she shook her head slightly. She could almost hear her mother's voice in her head, telling her to get up, get dressed and do what needed to be done. A fresh wave of guilt washed over her, nearly drowning out the inner voice that sounded so much like her mother. "But I feel like if I keep going…am I betraying her? They killed her to stop me. What does that make me if I don't let it?"

Warm brown eyes softened with pity, sending a pang through Eve's chest. "I think," Valerian began gently, resting his forearms on his knees, "that you already know what she would say if she were sitting right here." He sighed shaking his head slightly. "And to answer the first part, you just do. There's no right answer, no magic word that'll help, you know? One day, it just hurts a little less, and it goes on like that. Getting a little better at a time. It never goes away but it does stop hurting as much, eventually."

Eve swiped at the tears rolling down her cheek with the heel of her palm. "I know what she'd say. She'd be angry that I'm even considering stepping back and accepting what they want. She'd be furious." She sniffed, groaning slightly. "I'm making a great first impression," she laughed. "All snotty and puffy."

"It's okay," he replied with a grin, sitting back. "You should've seen me covered in the goo." Laughter bubbled forth from her for the first time in two days. Just a little, but it was certainly something. He'd come in with a mission, and he'd succeeded. "See? Leysa was right, as usual."

"I'm interrupting," Callan's voice was light, in stark contrast to the shadows that dwelled in his gaze. The dark circles under his eyes told Eve that he hadn't slept in the last couple of days at least, and another pang of guilt struck her. He hadn't slept because he'd been taking care of her, watching over her. "Valerian, can we have a minute?"

"Of course," he replied, shooting Eve another kind smile. "We'll talk again later."

Eve offered him a smile in return, and this time it wasn't forced. Callan settled into Valerian's abandoned chair with a sigh and looked down at the floor. She couldn't tell if he was avoiding her gaze or simply gathering his thoughts.

Before he could say whatever it was he'd come in to say, she blurted, "What happened in the hallway Callan?" She hadn't spoken a word about the darkness that had overtaken the hallway just before she'd found her mother. Over the last couple of days, lying in bed with nothing but her grief, she'd allowed her mind to wander. More accurately, she'd forced the events of that night to replay in her mind over and over again, searching for something she could have done, some way she could have stopped it.

She couldn't say exactly when she'd begun to suspect that it hadn't been some wayward fae beast or the even less likely angry god, but at some point, she'd realized the timing of the occurrence lined up too perfectly with the moment the guard had grabbed her arm. He hadn't bothered to explain yet, but she suspected it might be at least part of the reason he was here now.

"There are a lot of things you don't know about me, Eve." His voice was quiet, full of something akin to regret.

"Just stop. No more secrets, no more vague promises of protection or cryptic warnings. I can't do it anymore. Just tell me." One hand clenched the sheets beside her, the other was raised, pointing directly at him in command. "You made a promise? To whom? How did the hall get so dark? What did you do to that man? Why are you here, beyond the promise you made? Tell me *something*, Callan."

She hated the desperation in her tone. Hated that she was begging, just so she could feel in control of some part of her life. So something could make sense in the middle of all of this.

When he finally raised his gaze to meet hers, his eyes were darkened, pain etched in his features. "Please don't ask this of me, Eve."

His tone had her faltering. He'd never spoken so softly, used such a pleading tone. The energy for a fight went out of her with a whoosh. "Fine," she conceded, dropping her hand to her lap. "Tell me one thing, just one. Can you do that?"

"That depends on one thing," he replied cautiously.

Eve considered it a moment, weighing the importance of each of her many questions against the likelihood he would answer them. He was giving in because of pity, or guilt maybe, but that didn't necessarily mean he would answer whatever she asked.

She'd seen guilt written on his face the day before, almost as clearly as if he'd claimed it aloud. He felt responsible for Riona's death and had failed to sense the danger lurking within the castle. Of course, he would see it as a failure and take that burden on himself. She could understand his feeling of responsibility, even if she didn't agree it was deserved.

"What happened in the hallway?" she asked finally, deciding it would be the question most likely for him to answer. It was also the one question that would help her make some sense of the situation.

Callan fell against the back of the chair, loosing a breath. "Oh. That." Somehow he looked relieved; as if it was the least troublesome of the questions she could've asked. "I have certain gifts, and that's one of them.

"How is that possible?" she demanded. Magic was gone, taken by the fae and their gods when they'd fled the lower realms.

"That's another question," he reminded her gently. "One you'll have to save for later."

She didn't have it in her to argue. Grief was exhausting, and frankly, if she crammed one more impossible thing into her brain, it was likely to explode.

Deep red curls formed a curtain over her face as she looked down at the hand resting on her lap. A silver band, fashioned to look like ivy encircled her middle finger. A gift from her parents on her last birthday; the last birthday she'd have with them.

The overwhelming desire to run washed over her with a fresh wave of grief. For a moment, she nearly dragged the covers over her head again. Only her mother's voice in her head stopped her from doing so. *"Do not ever let them see you cry."*

"Alright." She straightened, steeling her spine and shoving away the darkness inside her that screamed for her to hide. "I need to decide, don't I? I need to decide if I'm going to keep going or quit."

His voice was rough when he replied, dragging a hand through his dark hair. "Yeah, you do. As much as I hate it, dove, you're going to have to decide soon. Coronation is coming up fast, and they're not going to let you delay any longer."

The council would never allow a delay because she was afraid. Perhaps if she agreed to marry they would, but not with her refusal to fall in line and do as they wished. The voice in her head that sounded like her mother raged at the notion. *No, you can't do that.*

"No, they won't let me delay, and I won't ask them to." Callan's brow rose at the resoluteness in her tone. "They've taken everything from me. What more can they do?"

Callan sat forward in his chair, his ocean-blue eyes meeting hers. "I will find every person responsible for her death, for hurting you, and I will make every one of them pay."

She did not doubt that, not after what had happened in the hall. Whatever they were to each other, as confusing and messy as it was, she knew he would do what he could to protect her.

"They did this to her to stop me, and if I give up now...." She shook her head at the thought. "I have to know who did this, who is trying to stop me."

Dark hair fell forward, hiding his eyes from her as he turned his gaze to the floor. "We'll find out. I have some ideas of where to look already."

The covers were shoved to the side as Eve slid to the edge of the bed and stood up. "I need to see the council. Mother's...," her voice cracked slightly. "Her funeral is this evening. I'll see them afterward."

She could feel Callan silently watching her as she crossed the room and opened the wardrobe. Her heart ached, she was tired, and she was angry. Alongside all of that, she was scared. The bright colors and pretty fabrics that hung inside the wardrobe were passed over as she skimmed her fingertips across them. She was in mourning again; would be for three days after her mother's funeral per tradition. It had been such a short time since her father's passing that her mourning gowns remained alongside her regular gowns. Her only saving grace, the one thing giving her the strength to carry the burden of such heavy losses so close together, was the almost equally heavy burden she'd taken on when she'd decided to take the throne alone. As difficult as it was, her chosen path grounded her. It gave her purpose.

The inky satin gown rustled slightly as she pulled it from the closet. "Are you going to watch me dress, Callan?" She asked, though the humor she aimed for fell short, sounding more hollow than intended.

Callan's eyes darkened as he shook his head. "Not this time, dove."

The corner of his lips tugged upward into the crooked grin that was beginning to make her heart jump around in her chest. By the time a witty response had formed in her flustered mind, he was gone, leaving her alone to dress.

∼

In contrast to the day her father had been laid to rest, not a drop of rain fell as courtiers, friends, and common folk alike gathered to lay Dowager Queen Riona Darrow to rest. The sun above, now showing her last glorious rays of light, had shone nearly as brightly as summer in the Vale for most of the day, a fitting tribute to the woman who had considered Coruscis her true home.

The royal burial grounds lay a relatively short ride from the castle Stoneweald itself, deeper into the forest and far from where any living souls resided. Lovely, with a sort of serene solitude that could only be found in places such as this, the Eternal Gardens were the final resting place for countless kings, queens, princes, and princesses.

Somehow, as if cognizant of what was occurring, the forest around them had gone still, silent. Only the sounds of hoofbeats, carriage wheels rolling and bumping along against the hardened soil path, and the occasional murmur of quiet conversation accompanied the slow procession.

"We're almost there," Eve whispered, casting a glance to Leysa beside her with Callan and Valerian following just behind them. The trees began to thin out as they neared the clearing, ancient pines giving way to smaller scrubby trees before finally nothing taller than grass remained visible near the drive.

The queen's resting spot had been chosen long before her death, soon after her marriage. She'd be laid just beside her husband, in the section designated for their family specifically. A shout from the captain of the guard, at the head of the procession, called a halt. Eve took a steadying breath as the door to the carriage creaked open, exhaling as she descended the small stairs, holding Callan's outstretched hand. His firm grip steadied her emotionally as much as it did physically. She had cried herself dry by the time the carriage had left Stoneweald, yet somehow her eyes still began to sting with threatened tears.

Do not ever let them see you cry. Taking a steadying breath she nodded in silent answer to her own thought and started forward. A simple archway of stone stood as the entrance, the obsidian stone at its apex marking the site for what it was, and serving as a reminder to be quiet and respectful of the dead, lest the goddess of death herself punish you. The warning carried weight in a place like this, even in the absence of the gods.

Watery sunlight streamed through the breaks in the leaves and branches overhead, providing only a meager amount of light for the funeral, held just before the setting of the sun on the third day following death as tradition dictated.

The priest, dressed in the traditional grey robes of his order stood patiently, waiting as the mourners gathered. A fresh wave of grief washed over Eve as she took her place nearest the mound, her guardians, now friends, at her side. The small white stone she carried in her palm seemed to burn against her skin, a solid, tangible reminder of her mother's fate.

Alongside the others carried by those gathered, it would help to ease and guide her spirit into the Otherworld where it would find eternal peace. The priest's prayers were little more than a dull hum in her ears, background noise to the pain that ravaged her.

"May she find everlasting comfort and peace in the forests and meadows of the Otherworld," he intoned.

She had no idea how much time had passed since they'd arrived. Callan was watching her patiently, almost reverently as his fingertips gently grazed her arm. "It's time, dove," he said, for her ears only.

Time to place the stone and say her final farewells. The invisible knife that had plunged itself into her heart three days ago gave a final, painful twist as she leaned forward, tenderly placing the stone on her mother's casket. The stone itself had been small, no more than the size of a cherry, but the weight of it...As it left her hand, another fractured piece of Eve's heart went with it. It had been the same with her father, such a short time ago, in this very same place.

The small piece of white quartz lay flat against the gleaming wood of her mother's casket, unassuming and unremarkable. Roaring sounded in her ears, wave upon wave crashing over her. Her chest ached, and for a moment, she imagined her mother there, arms thrown wide, ready to embrace her. Eve was broken, utterly broken.

One by one the others followed suit until the last stone was placed. Another priest, the young apprentice, began the toning of the bells. One for each day that had passed since her death with complete silence between. Even the horses, waiting beyond the gate, made no sound, keeping still as they waited.

With the final intonation of the bell, the mourners began to shuffle out, finally speaking in low tones as they mounted their horses or stepped into their carriages. They'd be going back to the castle now, to celebrate the life of the Dowager Queen of Darkegrove, and were likely to gossip, drink, and whisper about the manner of her passing.

Eve dreaded it.

"We can wait a while to go back if you'd like." It was Leysa who spoke first, placing a hand gently on Eve's shoulder, and offering her a warm smile. "If you need a little break."

"Or we could skip it altogether," Valerian added, eyeing the courtiers already whispering and glancing Eve's way.

Of course, there would be gossip. Eve's decision, and how she was to blame for her own mother's death. How shameful her behavior was. Not only in deciding to rule, but for how she had carried on with Callan, as an unmarried queen-to-be.

"No," she said quietly, exhaustion creeping into her voice. "I need to go. I have to be seen as strong, even now. Especially now." Straightening, she cast a final glance at the grave workers preparing to entomb her mother. "Let's go."

Within the grand ballroom of Stoneweald, a sea of dark grey and black-clad courtiers milled about, drinking, laughing, and talking. Eve's arrival had silenced them for only a moment, bows and curtsies cast her way. The only sign of deference she'd likely be shown until she was officially crowned.

As she moved through the throng, Callan at her side, she listened to the conversations. Most were dull, people droning on about their minor problems, the weather, and whether or not the yield from their mines would be substantial enough this year. There were a few, though, taking bets on how long it would be before she crumbled; giving in to the council's demands and finally taking a husband. Some even speculated that Callan had been put in her path by the council to ensure just that.

Emilia stopped them only a few minutes after their arrival. "I am so sorry," she said quietly, sympathy filling her lovely brown eyes. "About your mother, but also about the greenhouse. Can you forgive me?"

There was no room in her at the moment to withhold forgiveness, not from someone she had called her dearest friend. "Of course, consider it forgotten," Eve replied with a slight smile.

The courtier practically beamed as she rose on her tiptoes, pressing her hands together in delight. "Wonderful! I have so much to tell you," she began only to be cut off by her name being called in the distance. "Oh, Father needs me. I'll find you later and tell you all the juicy details I've heard about a certain widow and her stable hand!" Wiggling her eyebrows conspiratorially, Emilia flitted away in the direction of her parents.

"That was...something," Callan remarked, taking her hand in his. The casual contact surprised her, given how many eyes were currently on them. So many more tongues would be wagging now.

"That was Emilia," she replied with a shrug, keeping her expression as neutral as possible despite the racing of her heart. "You get used to it."

They walked among the mourners, Eve wincing at every whispered insult. A pair of elderly women hovering near a table laden with pies and tarts leaned closer to one another.

"You know it's her fault. How can she stand the guilt?" one said to the other, with a shake of her head.

"It's a shame, truly a shame. Our dear King Viktor would be horrified," her friend agreed.

Callan's grip on her hand tightened and his jaw tensed. Eve shook her head in silent command and led him toward the balcony. Making a scene now would only make things worse, and coming to her defense against them would most certainly cause a scene.

The double glass doors had been left open to allow the guests access to the vast terrace beyond, though few had chosen to venture out due to the cool temperatures of the fall night. Braziers had been lit along the railings, acting as both light against the darkness and a bit of warmth when the wind blew down cold from the peaks of the Sgiath in the distance. It was cold enough that as they stepped out, goosebumps rose on her skin, even covered by the long-sleeved gown.

Callan trailed a hand down her arm gently, sending a shiver of an entirely different nature down her spine. "Don't listen to them, dove. You know what you're doing is right, and how strong you are." His words were a comfort, despite her doubts earlier.

"I know," she nodded. "But I'm afraid. More than I've ever been. Who knows how many of those people out there want me dead, Callan? Who knows if I'm going to walk into my room tonight and find an assassin waiting for me? Will it even stop once I'm crowned?" Dark red curls bounced lightly as she shook her head, dismissing the thought.

"I will be here for you for as long as you'll have me. Not a single hair on your head will ever be harmed." He stepped closer, gripping her chin gently with his fingers. "I will burn this entire fucking kingdom to the ground before I let them touch you."

A fire burned, low in her belly. Her lips parted slightly as her eyes met his. She could drown in those blue eyes of his, and would do so happily she realized. She didn't know when it had happened, or why. Didn't particularly care either. Eve was beginning to feel something more than a simple attraction toward him. Something she couldn't allow herself to feel because they could never be together, not really. Not in a substantial way, not when he was apparently spoken for and she couldn't, wouldn't marry.

"You...Callan, you have someone, and I–"

The rest of her sentence was silenced as he pressed his lips to hers in a firm but sensual kiss. The kind that had her losing herself in him. For a few all too brief moments everything else fell away. Grief was a distant memory, still there but far less sharp. The hateful gossip of the supposed mourners was forgotten entirely, as was the danger she was in.

The hand that had gripped her chin now plunged into her hair, holding her there as he claimed her mouth with his. Eve's heart sang within her chest as she wrapped her arms around his neck, pulling him closer, needing this, needing to feel him against her. When he finally pulled away, they were both breathless.

"There is *not*, and never will be, anyone else for me, dove."

Chapter 20

The next couple of days passed quietly and without incident. She had barely gotten a chance to speak to Callan since the incident on the balcony. As they'd rejoined the guests, he'd simply slipped away, and Leysa had taken his place at her side, dazzling every one of them with her wit and conversation. Eve had been sure to thank her for her help navigating and even intercepting some of the council members before they could approach her, surely to push for her acquiescence.

By day three, Eve was growing confused by his vanishing act. She had been protected at all times, by either Leysa or Valerian, sometimes both. Something was wrong, but when she'd asked them about it they'd simply told her he needed time.

Time for what? It was a messy situation, but rather than running away, they should've been discussing it. Perhaps he was breaking things off with the woman Leysa had mentioned, whoever she was. A sharp jolt of jealousy rang through her at the thought.

Going through each day without her mother, without her council and the comfort of her presence, had gotten no easier. Distracting herself with preparations for the coronation, avoiding the council, and reading had done little to make it bearable, and she wondered if the ache in her very soul would ever ease.

A knock at the door drew Eve's attention from the filthy romance novel she'd currently lost herself in, and she looked up in time to see Sylvie on the threshold. "My lady, they're asking to see you."

Eve knew exactly who 'they' were. Irritation flared, punctuated by the sound of the book snapping closed as she stood. "Will they never stop?" she said more to herself than anything. "Thank you, Sylvie, I'll be there in a moment."

Leysa, rising from where she had been lounging by the window, snorted. "Old buzzards."

Eve couldn't help but agree, even as she departed to answer their summons. The walk from her rooms to the council chambers had become so familiar that she could have made the trip blindfolded. The council had attempted to insist upon her agreement to marry, citing her inability to think clearly through her grief.

The coronation was now only a day away, thank the absent gods, but until the moment the crown was placed on her head, they would not relent in their tireless mission to see her wed to a man of their choosing. A puppet king they could control, who would give them a new line of kings to follow the old traditions.

"What are you thinking about?" Leysa inquired as they made their way down the grand staircase into the entrance hall of the castle.

"Heirs," she replied with a slight grimace. "I've been thinking about how I can ensure that I am actually enacting change here. If all of this dies with me, then it would have been for nothing. The next ruler after me will have to continue what I've begun, and...."

"You hadn't thought about children," Leysa finished for her. "Well, that definitely seems like a big problem, but probably not one that needs to be worried over just now."

Eve offered a smile to a passing maid as they reached the bottom. "Yes, you're right," she conceded.

The flutter of women's voices drifted across the hall to them. Emilia, surrounded by a handful of other courtiers, passed by just as Eve and Leysa began to cross the hall. Warm brown eyes met Eve's briefly, something she couldn't identify flashing in them, something that might have been regret, before the group continued on, pausing only to offer brief curtsies.

The quick, curious glances at Leysa told Eve well enough why none of the ladies attempted conversation as they may have. Anything to gain more fodder for gossip. They reached the council chamber with little more conversation, mindful of the eyes and ears in this part of Stoneweald in particular.

"I'll be right here," Leysa offered, as they came to a stop outside the doors. Eve smiled her thanks and turned to the door, donning the mask of imperiousness she had learned from her mother for use when dealing with the council.

Sylvie's husband, Dallin, threw open the doors, and a smile lit his kind face as she approached. "My lady," he said in greeting. Lowering his voice, he added, "Tell them to go to the Void, my lady." She had to stifle a laugh at his words and the wink he gave as she stepped inside.

Just as they had been before, the nine men who sought to plan her future sat behind their oversized oak table. This time, however, they watched her with thinly veiled disgust, or in a few cases, outright hatred.

It was Eldred who spoke first, bearing the least animosity of them. "Thank you for joining us my lady, we know you must be quite busy with preparations–"

"Yes, Lord Gray, I am. Which is why I find myself quite perplexed as to the cause of this sudden meeting. Surely there is nothing so urgent to see to that it cannot wait until after the coronation." She interrupted, pausing a breath before offering them a cold smile. "Unless of course, the coronation itself is the matter."

Several of them bristled at her tone, but she paid them no mind. Raising a brow, she waited for Eldred to continue. Unfazed, he continued patiently, "My lady, we implore you to reconsider. Given the unfortunate events that have befallen not just yourself and our beloved Queen Riona, but the townspeople who were caught up in the incident in Forest Haven, we ask that you consider the benefits of sharing the burden of rule. Have the people not spoken, made clear their desire to hold to tradition?"

It was a struggle to bite down on the bitter laughter that began to escape her. "No, my Lord Gray, they have not. What those 'unfortunate' events you speak of, not the least of which is the brutal murder of my own mother, your queen, have shown me is that there are men in this kingdom who will stop at nothing to prevent change." She turned, strolling to the side of the room and back as she spoke. Eve met each of their gazes one by one as she continued, refusing to back down or show fear, no matter how much hatred she found in them.

"Look to our neighbors in the south. Avellon allows the eldest child, regardless of sex, to inherit, given they show themselves to be worthy of rule. Coruscis has not had a male ruler in three generations, and look how they prosper. The time for holding to these dated traditions borne of fear is over." She stopped then, retaking her position in the center of the room. "I will not allow the actions of a few hateful souls to determine the future of our entire kingdom. I will say it one last time, my lords. I will not marry any man of your choosing."

Several of the councilmen rose at once, slamming their hands on the table and shouting. Only a few remained seated, seething or stunned, Eldred Gray and Reynard Ward among them. Guards burst into the room, drawn by the sounds of shouting, and surrounded Eve with Leysa and Valerian coming to stand on either side of her.

When she spoke again, she could hear her mother's voice spilling from her lips. Grief was a shadow, chasing the momentary pride she hoped her mother would've felt, that had her heart aching. *Stay strong, don't ever let them see you cry.*

"My decision is final, my lords. Do not summon me on this matter again."

BACK IN THE WALLED GARDEN AGAIN AFTER DINNER THAT evening, settled on a familiar bench all the way in the back, Eve found herself doing exactly what she'd told herself she wouldn't, hiding.

Valerian had taken on the role of her guardian this evening but had remained nearby the entrance chatting with one of the guards to give her some privacy. She hadn't needed to ask, the exhaustion and stress clear enough on her face by the end of the wake. The exterior entrance that had served as a meeting ground for the conspirators working against her had been sealed after the first bloody warning left in her room, so her garden had once again been deemed safe enough for now.

This late in the year, dusk settled over Darkegrove like a thick blanket early in the evening. It was near dark, and yet the pillywiggins and other little folk still flittered around here and there. As usual, they were hard to spot, but out of the corner of her eye, she could just about make out the shape of an acorn-covered head peering around a bundle of leaves. "I'll be out of your garden soon," she murmured to the faerie.

"Are you talking to yourself or a hidden admirer?" Callan's voice had her heart leaping into her throat. *How does he manage to move so silently all the time?*

"Would it make you jealous if I told you it was an admirer?" she teased, turning her attention to him. The stubble along his jaw had grown considerably, and shadows darkened his blue eyes, in stark contrast with his unbothered tone. He looked like he hadn't slept in a few days. His shoulders were tight and his jaw set.

"What's wrong?" She added immediately.

A humorless laugh escaped him, and he took a seat beside her on the bench. Eve glanced to where the faerie had been, but her little companion had vanished the moment Callan had made his presence known. The shadows had grown deeper now that night had nearly settled in. Perhaps that was what had driven the little one to retire.

Callan dragged a hand through his hair and loosed a shuddering breath. "I had to get some space from you, so I went to check on my home."

Eve stared at him incredulously. After all of the back and forth, all of the pushing away and pulling in, they'd kissed. They'd shared a moment that had seemed like it meant something, and she had just begun to talk herself into believing she could have someone in her life. That a life without marriage in it didn't mean she had to be alone for the rest of her days.

Did he go back to the woman Leysa told me about? How had Leysa described her? The most beautiful woman he'd ever seen. The memory struck her hard, a knife in the gut. She must have been stunning, for just one look to be enough for him to fall for her. She turned to stare at him, hard. "Did you go back to her?"

Callan's brow rose. "Go back to who?" A hawk somewhere overhead cried once, twice, then silenced again. Callan looked skyward and frowned.

Her heart pounded. She felt foolish, like a child, for questioning him this way. Jealousy was a rare emotion for her, yet here it was rearing its ugly head and roaring. "The girl Leysa told me about, the one you saw at a party and instantly fell for." She shifted slightly in her seat, regretting the words as soon as they'd left her mouth, unsure if she even wanted the answer to that question.

Callan truly laughed then, softly, and covered his eyes with his palm briefly. "Leysa and I are going to have a very long talk, very soon." He glanced skyward once more before continuing. "I suppose I owe you an explanation, but this is not the best time for the conversation we need to have. Would you accept it if I told you that you have no reason to ever be jealous of another living soul?"

Her jealousy was abated, if only a little. "What makes you think you get to decide what we discuss and when Callan? And what does that even mean?"

A hawk cried overhead, and Callan cursed under his breath. He waited a few moments before continuing. "I don't want to get in the way of what you must do. I want you, more than you know, but I am afraid of becoming a distraction you can't afford right now. And there are just some truths that I can't share with you right now."

"Do you think I am so weak-minded that I can't handle it?" As usual, she ignored the way her heart raced and the thrill his words sent through her. Right now, he was yet another man making decisions for her life. The anger brought out in her outweighed the singing of her heart at his claim.

Callan huffed a breath and shook his head. "No, of course not," he replied immediately. Meeting her gaze, he gently grazed the pad of his thumb across her cheek. "You could do anything. Conquer all three kingdoms, if you wish. But if I caused a distraction that took even a fraction of fulfillment from you, I would never forgive myself."

Eve considered it for a moment or tried to. His touch was a brand on her skin. Every part of her wanted to lean forward, close the small distance between them and press her lips to his. She wanted to feel those callused hands on every part of her, know what it would feel like to have him touch every inch of her skin. A familiar ache pooled low in her belly, and she found herself moving closer without thought. "Callan," she whispered, letting the flood of desire pull her under.

Their second kiss was everything the first hadn't been. Slow and purposeful, without urgency. He kissed the corner of her lips softly, before claiming her mouth fully, soft and gentle but thorough. His hand that had held her face slid to her back, pulling her body close.

Callan's touch left little shocks of electricity along her skin, even with the barrier of her gown between them. She gripped the front of his shirt as he parted her lips with his tongue, dancing and exploring her mouth slowly, savoring her taste. A quiet moan sounded from her, and he grumbled his approval.

Eve broke the contact first, heat creeping into her cheeks. "I have to go inside, people will talk." Her voice was little more than a whisper, the best she could manage as breathless as she was. It was a lame excuse, they both knew. Rumors about them had already spread like wildfire, and there was little harm, at this point, that could be done. She was losing herself in him totally, and what it meant for her future frightened her.

He nodded, and she rose from the bench, straightening her dress. "Later," he promised.

For a moment, she paused, silently thanking the goddess of the night for the darkness hiding her flushed cheeks. "Later," she agreed, despite the fear.

Chapter 21

Callan

He remained in the darkened garden long after Eve had left. He'd gone so much farther with her than he'd ever intended to, and gotten so much closer than he should have. Before even arriving at Stoneweald this time, he'd been determined to not get involved. They could never be more than friends. Hadn't he learned his lesson already?

He knew Riona was raging in the Otherworld. A promise had been made, a simple one. Protect her, but keep her at arm's length. The mistakes of the past should never be repeated. He knew the consequences better than anyone and had more to risk than most from failing to keep that promise. He was a godsdamned idiot.

A shrill cry sounded overhead. Moments later a small brown hawk landed in the seat Eve had occupied earlier. He didn't bother to look at her as she ruffled her feathers and settled in. "I already know what you're going to say."

With a flash of light, the hawk was replaced by a familiar female form. Leysa snorted. "I highly doubt that, dumb ass."

Callan rolled his eyes, letting the familiar insult slide off him. She didn't mean it, not really. Besides, the jab was deserved. He certainly had been exceptionally stupid where Eve was concerned.

Leysa patted his back gently. She was always mothering him when he did something stupid or needed comfort. If Valerian were here he'd be on the other side, teasing him and probably mocking him truth be told. All of it well-intentioned, designed to get a laugh out of him.

"What have I done, Leysa?" He dropped his head into his palms, elbows resting on his knees. "I never meant for it to go this far."

"Well, first of all, you've managed better than Val or I expected, so that's something. We never thought you'd hold out this long." Leysa's hand on his back stilled. "But seriously, Callan, I don't know what to tell you. I really think she'll understand–"

"She'll understand, Leysa? You really believe that? How could anyone understand that? We all lived through it, the three of us. Are either of you understanding about what happened?" He jerked up, meeting her sympathetic gaze. "She is going to hate me."

Leysa frowned. "We know it wasn't your fault. Have you tried speaking with your mother about it? Maybe she can–"

Callan interrupted her with a bitter laugh. "No, I can't reach her from here, and I know what she'd say anyway. She'd tell me to just wait, that fate has a funny way of working out. "

"I guess. I still think you should try and talk to her."

"I know, Leysa, but as I said, I can't reach her here."

"Not your mother, you moron, Eve." Leysa smacked his shoulder lightly for emphasis.

Callan pinned Leysa with a flat look. "What good would it do? I can't tell her what I am, who I am. You know that. If she knew you were the hawk that attacked her friend, what do you think she would say? I barely managed to get away with not explaining my shadows to her. The rest of this shit," he paused, shaking his head slightly. "No, I can't do that."

Leysa frowned. "So what are you going to do then?"

"Keep her safe. Beyond that, I don't know." He gazed toward the castle, at the lights in the windows. "She will always be surrounded by danger here, and as long as that holds true, I'll do everything I can to keep her from harm."

CHAPTER 22

Coronation day had finally arrived, and Eve felt like shit. It wasn't just the grief, though the loss of her mother played a significant part. Heartache combined with the weight of her future, rolling and blazing, melding within her until it became a ball of lead, heavy upon her heart. Eve's own stubborn refusal to back down. Her mother's support and all it had ultimately cost them both, had led to this day. Eve Darrow would be crowned Queen of Darkegrove. Not Consort, as she would have been called upon her marriage as the council insisted.

The true and rightful Queen. For the first time in so many long years, a woman would truly rule the northern kingdom.

"You look great," Leysa stated, clapping her hands together, startling Eve from her thoughts. The warrior had dressed for the auspicious day in a simple but stunning gown that draped over one shoulder, leaving the other bare. The color she wore reminded Eve of mulberries, and the fabric was as smooth and flowing as the wine made from them.

"Thank you, Leysa," Eve replied. She smiled at Leysa over her shoulder in the standing mirror she'd been looking into. Sylvie stepped forward, murmuring her agreement as she fastened the emerald and diamond necklace around Eve's neck.

It had been Riona's, and though she hadn't planned to wear it before her death, it seemed destined, matching the emerald fabrics of her satin gown perfectly. Corseted at the top, with small sleeves that fell below the shoulder and a flared bottom, it was exactly as she and Riona had planned. It needed no adornment, with the necklace and matching silver ivy earrings that dangled from her ears. Tears welled in her eyes as twin pangs of guilt and grief ran through her. Her mother should be here, helping her prepare not only for her coronation but for ruling a kingdom.

"Don't do this to yourself, my lady," Sylvie said gently, patting her bare shoulder. "Your mother, Otherworld bless and keep her, would be so very proud of you."

Blinking away the tears that threatened to fall, Eve nodded, smiling. Eve wouldn't cry now, not in front of anyone. "Thank you, Sylvie, for everything."

Smoothing her skirts, she stepped back. "Well, I believe I'm ready. Leysa, where is that handsome husband of yours?" she asked, glancing toward the sitting area. She was not going to ask about Callan, who she suspected was in the waiting area, and was definitely not eager to see him, she lied to herself. She willed her stupid heart to stop beating so quickly at the thought of seeing him, of looking into those endless pools of blue.

He'd slept in the living room, apparently concerned with distracting her from the coronation. Later, it seemed, had meant after a certain crown came to rest on her brow. If only she could will time to move a bit faster.

"Handsome? Don't you mean dashing, dazzling, and all-around amazing?" Valerian laughed as he stepped into the room. He did look rather dashing, she had to admit, in his dark suit. Even dressed in such finery, her companions were well armed. It was hard not to notice the sword that now hung at Valerian's back or the shape of the rather large twin daggers strapped to Leysa's thighs beneath her beautiful gown.

"Of course, how rude of me to fail to appropriately sing your praises," Eve teased in return, winning a bright grin from him. "It will be a long day, I'm afraid. I'm expected to greet the council members and their families first, for a private luncheon. Then, I'll have to be prayed over by the priests."

Despite the absence of their gods, these long-held traditions were clung to. Another sign of their lack of progress. Admittedly, the southern kingdoms had also held onto the prayers, so perhaps this particular cling to tradition was less of a failure on the part of Darkegrove. "We should have a bit of a break after that. The coronation itself won't be held until dusk, and then we get to enjoy a rather lovely party."

"Well, the party sounds fun, but can we skip the luncheon with the old codgers?" Leysa asked, wrinkling her nose.

"I think I've pushed as hard as I should for now, as much as I would like to," Eve replied with a laugh. She felt a bit lighter for a moment, surrounded by people who cared for her, and finally preparing to take the throne.

"Are you ready?" Callan stood on the threshold of her bedchamber, watching her. She didn't know how long he'd been there, but judging from the bright grin on Sylvie's face, it had been a little while.

"Yes," Eve replied breathily, ignoring the way her heart danced. "Let's go."

THE LUNCHEON HAD BEEN A BORE BUT THANKFULLY uneventful. Eve, along with Callan and the guards, judging by the wary eyes that had watched over her the entire two-hour-long event, had expected something to happen.

Eve had expected more of the same from the men of the council, or at least snide remarks from either themselves or their wives. While they hadn't been entirely pleasant, they also hadn't said a word about her decision. *Maybe they've just given up*, she thought to herself. Though it was unlikely they were happy about it, maybe they'd simply realized there was nothing more to be done to sway her.

Lord Eldred Gray had failed to attend and had sent a messenger begging forgiveness for his absence due to a sudden illness. It was a shame, she thought, that her father's most ardent supporter and long-time friend would not be present to see her take the throne. Though she doubted he would appreciate the way she had chosen to do it, she believed her father would be proud of her.

Following the luncheon, Eve had been rushed to her rooms to change into a far more simple ensemble for the prayers. The traditional colors were grey and brown, and even soon-to-be monarchs were expected to hold with that particular request by the priests, so Eve found herself in a simple dress of dove grey with short capped sleeves, that dusted the floor when she walked. A darker grey, fur-lined cloak had been wrapped around her shoulders to protect against the cold autumn air.

The prayers would take place at the Black Pool, the last holy place still intact, and Callan would be escorting her alongside Valerian. The pair had slipped away while she had gone to change, with a promise to return before it was time to go, with Leysa remaining behind to oversee the security for the coronation itself.

"Eve, darling!" She had no more than made it to the bottom of the stairs when Emilia's bright voice called out to her. "I'm to escort you to the Pool. Lord Thorne and that delectable friend of his, Lord Ashford, were detained. Something about a crowd gathering at the gates. But there are guards to accompany us, just there, see?" She gestured to the guards standing by the door that led to the eastern terrace.

Eve recognized them both. Devlan, one of the guards from their trip into the city, stood to the left of the door. He'd been one of the men who had escorted her and Callan home and had seen her safely delivered back to the castle. At the right of the door, Edvard, one of her most senior guards. He had been protecting her for most of her life. His presence alone put her at ease.

"You're sure?" she asked as they moved closer to the guards. "Edvard. Devlan, hello again."

Emilia smiled brightly, linking her arm through Eve's. "I'm sure. He'll be just behind you, don't worry."

Devlan nodded in response, saying gruffly, "Hello again, my lady."

Edvard merely bowed, as was typical. She could probably count on two hands the number of times they'd had an actual conversation, but he was steadfast and loyal to her family.

Emilia gestured toward the door. "Shall we?"

The four of them walked slowly down the forest pathway that would lead them to the Pool with Emilia chattering away, telling Eve a story that involved a rather bawdy widow and a quite handsome, according to Emilia, stablehand. It was downright scandalous, Eve had to admit, and drew more than a few genuine laughs from the queen-to-be.

"And have you heard the news about Brodie?" Emilia asked, glancing sideways at Eve.

"No," she replied, tensing. Brodie was a topic Emilia usually avoided, thanks to her utter disapproval of him for Eve. If she had something to share about him, it was going to be big. "I haven't heard much about him in a long while."

"Well," Emilia began, squeezing Eve's arm surprisingly tight. "He's got a baby on the way! Isn't that just adorable? He seems quite content from what my cousin told me. Her family visited Coruscis recently to oversee some trade, something or other of my uncle's.

"Of course, she didn't seek him out. They would never have approved given his low status, but she saw him in town one day." Patting Eve's arm, she added, "I'm so glad you set your sights higher this time."

They were nearing the pool now, the trees finally beginning to thin out. Adorable wasn't the word she'd use, but she was glad to hear that he was happy and had settled well into life there. He was safe, away from all the madness in Darkegrove, and getting what he'd wanted out of life. Maybe she could do the same for herself, somehow. She opened her mouth, ready to confide in Emilia about what had passed between her and Callan, but something was off about the clearing ahead.

They were a bit early for the prayers, but by this point, she would have expected the priests to have gathered. There should have been censers set up to burn the sacred herbs and crystals set in a circle beside the godly waters. None of that had been done. Only the three of them stood in the clearing, now only a few steps from the pool. Fear began tugging at the back of her mind, a quiet voice telling her she needed to move, to run from this place immediately.

A low grunt behind her had Eve spinning as Emilia pulled her arm free. On the path, mere feet away, Edvard was sprawled on the ground, blood seeping from a small cut somewhere at the back of his head. He lay motionless. Dead or alive, she couldn't be sure. Devlan, who must have been standing behind Edvard she realized as a pit opened wide in her gut, motioned for Emilia to come to him.

She could do nothing but stare as her friend moved from her side, taking a place behind Devlan, sidestepping the dead or wounded guard on the ground.

"What–"

"Don't you see?" The voice that had her spinning again belonged to Lord Ward, Reynard the Rat. "Surely by now, you know what we must do to protect our great and beloved kingdom." His hateful, sharp gaze jerked from Eve to Emilia. "Tie him up Emilia dear."

To Eve's horror, Emilia complied immediately, taking a length of rope she hadn't noticed before from the base of a nearby tree.

Devlan moved closer, the two men now cornering her, backing her against the wall surrounding dark water. Predators with prey. She had walked blindly into their trap, alone, and with no hope of salvation. Her hand slid to the hidden slit of her gown, fingertips feeling for the small dagger sheathed at her thigh.

"Save it from what?" she demanded, hating the quiver of fear she heard in her voice.

"From you, whore," Devlan sneered. Pain shocked her as the back of his thick hand met her cheek, the coppery taste of blood filling her mouth. Her fingers closed around the hilt.

"Now, now, Devlan, that is unnecessary," Reynard declared. "She will pay, but there's no reason to make it so...unsavory. We will send her to the gods and let them pass judgment on her traitorous soul."

Before she could realize what he meant, Devlan grabbed a fistful of her hair and began dragging her to the pool. Panic flared, almost as loud as the bark of pain on her scalp as he held fast, pulling her toward the unknown depths. Yanking the dagger free from the hilt, she managed to slash viciously at his forearm, drawing a sharp yelp of pain from the guard. The little bit of relief her successful attack brought was short-lived though, as broad hands wrenched the dagger free from her grasp, tossing it to the side easily.

No. No. No. Not now, not like this.

She clawed, scratched, and kicked as hard as she could, barely making contact with him. Bile rose in the back of her throat as sheer panic flooded her, making it nearly impossible to draw breath.

"Please, don't do this, you don't have to–" Devlan yanked her hair hard, drawing tears and a cry of pain from her. "Emilia, please," she begged.

A glance behind as he dragged revealed, to her horror, Emilia, her friend, grinning at her. "I tried to warn you," the courtier said in a low voice Eve had never heard her use before. With a wink, Emilia raised her hand, revealing a bright red bloom clasped between her fingers. Death's Tears, the flower responsible for her mother's death.

Something inside her broke, just as her feet left the ground.

"This is for Darkegrove, bitch." It was Devlan who spoke, his sickening hot breath against her cheek before he shoved her hard.

Ice-cold water enveloped her so swiftly she'd barely managed to gasp a breath of air before she was under. Kicking as hard as she could, Eve managed to fight her way back up, gasping for air again. A second set of hands joined in, Reynard, gripping her shoulders and shoving her back down.

His grip was strong, surprisingly so for a man they called the Rat. His thin and submissive appearance must have been as much a deception as the very words of loyalty he had spouted moments before. So dark they were almost black, the color of burned charcoal, and filled with unrelenting hatred, Devlan's eyes were the last thing she saw before plunging beneath the water once more.

The deep black water of the pool was all around her, and she struggled, kicking, punching, and clawing. At some point her cloak had been pulled free, floating away in the bleak depths. Instinct and a desperate will to live kept her fighting, despite the futility of it. As she connected with what she thought was Reynard's hands, clawing them desperately, a third pair of hands joined them, Emilia, and Eve knew then that this was it.

I'm going to die.

All at once, she was no longer being pushed under. Their hands still gripped her. Devlan's hands still gripped her hair, Reynard still held her shoulders in his treacherous grip. But now, she was being...pulled? She had to be imagining it. Water didn't pull you down.

Maybe this is just part of drowning. Her lungs still held breath though, so how could it be? Once more she got the distinct sensation of being dragged further into the black depths, and she realized she no longer felt the hold of her attackers.

Eve was pulled downward by some invisible and unfathomable force, lungs aching and burning until suddenly she was no longer being pulled, she was falling. Without thought, Eve gasped, and to her surprise, it was fresh air that filled her lungs rather than water. Before she could do more than utter a surprised curse, Eve landed on something soft.

Jerking to a sitting position, Eve immediately spun, taking in her surroundings. Somehow she found herself in a large, almost empty room.

Every inch of the visible floor was a deep onyx marble, polished so well it nearly mirrored the still surface of the pool above. The soft thing she'd landed on was a chaise lounge she discovered, pure white with gold threads woven throughout.

Looking upward, Eve could see the pool she'd nearly drowned in; somehow suspended several feet above, defying the very laws of nature. She could see nothing of the world she'd come from, as she'd never been able to see whatever this place was when visiting the pool above. The waters of the Black Pool were still as impenetrable as they had always been.

"Have you recovered, darling?" A gentle feminine voice snapped Eve to attention. Seated across from her on a matching sofa that certainly had not been there before were the two most astounding women she'd ever seen in her life.

To the left, a striking, thin woman with dark brown skin and long dark braids accented with tiny gold hoops throughout. She wore a long silken gown the color of warm honey that hung so low in the front Eve thought it might leave her completely exposed if she moved the wrong way. Along her collar bones, twin tattoos of gold, depicting the sun surrounded by shining rays. Bright gold eyes set in an angular face with high cheekbones watched Eve with thinly veiled amusement.

Seated beside her, a voluptuous woman, as pale as Eve, with deep brown locks that fell in light waves just to her shoulders. Her gown mirrored that of her companion's in every way, save for the color. Where the first had been a warm yellow, this woman wore a deep emerald green, the color of a summer warmed forest. Deep green tattoos of vines, filled with leaves and thorns, trailed down her forearms, ending just past the wrist.

"I think she's still quite stunned, my love," the second replied. Eve realized then that it had been the woman to the left who had first addressed her. Her bright, spring-green eyes watched Eve curiously, though with notably less amusement than her companion.

"Well that's a fucking understatement," Eve blurted before she could help it. Followed quickly by a muttered apology, even though she didn't feel sorry.

She'd almost died, and now found herself in what she was beginning to believe was the Otherworld. If so, it surely wasn't the vast natural wonderland the priests claimed it to be.

"Where is my mother?" she demanded, panic seizing her once more. Eve leaned forward, hands gripping the side of the chaise. If she were dead, if this was the Otherworld, then surely her mother was here. Eve scanned the empty room, desperately hoping she would appear as they had somewhere in the vast marble emptiness that stretched as far as Eve could see.

"You are not dead, and your mother is not here." The woman to the right spoke this time, and when Eve looked at her once more she saw that her expression had changed from scrutiny to one of sympathy. "You will see her again, just not here and not now."

"Then where am I? Who are you?"

"Have you all forgotten your gods so completely?"

CHAPTER 23

CALLAN

The prisoner had been annoyingly stubborn. On the night of Riona's murder, Valerian had seen the man brought down from outside the queen's room, while Callan had taken care of Eve. He'd been...mostly whole when he'd been deposited in his cell. Physically, upon arrival, he'd had little more than a few bruises, but mentally.

Well, he might have recovered from that eventually, had he not chosen to be so very uncooperative when they'd begun his questioning. The guard, Arran, had feigned innocence at first, despite the threat he'd uttered to Eve that night. It had taken some creative persuading to get him to admit his role in the plot that had been unraveling around them.

Callan paced in the dank cell below the castle of Stoneweald. It was so damp that moss had even begun to grow on some of the outer walls. Meager amounts of sunlight had managed to break through, either through cracks on the few outer walls that managed to have some space above ground or through the air holes punched through the ceiling in a few places. Even the torches lit along the wall seemed eager to extinguish themselves in this damned place.

"I'll ask you one, more, time," he said quietly, emphasizing each word with a tap of his dagger against the rusted cell bars. If the bleeding didn't kill Arran then infection surely would in this wretched place. "Who is behind the queen's assassination and the attack on the princess in the city?"

Arran wailed hopelessly as Callan's shadows swelled, rising around him like night itself given life. Pain, fear, or some combination of the two had the man muttering useless prayers and begging for release.

Blood already soaked his torn tunic from the identical cuts marring his cheeks, along with more than a few along his torso. Generally, he avoided using such cruel methods to get what he needed but this Void damned fuck had put his filthy hands on her. Nothing Callan could do would be too much for this piece of shit.

The worst had been when he used his gift. Callan's shadows had enveloped him, choking out every minute bit of light that managed to exist in this place. Such unfathomable darkness that it left one entirely unable to see, and it had been left in place for hours without even sound to allow the prisoner to orient himself. He had shown Arran his death, over and over again, playing out in the darkness before him, in as many creative ways as possible.

His surprise at Callan's use of magic had been as genuine as his fear. Callan could be certain of that much, thanks to his empathic abilities. He had never been partial to them, but they certainly had their uses.

"I don't know....anything....about what happened....in the city," he moaned between sobs. "I don't...I don't know about that. But I can tell you about the other thing. The Queen."

Callan stopped dead, turning to face the restrained man. "Tell me." His voice was laced with unyielding command, a promise of utter destruction if he disobeyed.

Arran sagged in his chair, the chains that bound him rattling. "It's the council, or most of 'em anyway. The one they call The Rat, he fired 'em up. Called her a traitor to the kingdom." Callan's answering growl had the man recoiling in fear. "He said she needed to 'see the error of her decision.' It started out just wantin' to scare her, that's all. The animals in her bed, and the note." Arran sighed, shifting in his seat and watching Callan warily through swollen eyes. "You'll give me a clean death if I tell you everything?"

"A clean death, if you tell me everything, and tell me the truth."

Callan inclined his head before casting a glance at Valerian who sat on a stack of crates just outside the cell. Callan really did not want to know what could be inside them. Valerian smirked in response.

Arran nodded once, grunting in pain at the movement. "The Rat, he said it had worked before, in years past, when princesses tried to push back against the marriage rule. I guess the council ran into it a time or two before, so he decided to scare her." He grunted in pain, grimacing as he said, "I guess she doesn't scare easy."

Callan huffed a laugh. "No, she doesn't."

Eve was so much braver than he'd expected at the beginning of all of this. She had been far from the frightened and delicate princess he'd thought he'd have to guard. Of course, he'd known since the first time he'd seen her that she was his mate. But that didn't necessarily equate to love for the fae, not right away. For some, it never did. He'd come to love her in the time that he'd been here, and he knew that it went beyond what the mating bond entailed.

Arran coughed, dragging a bare foot against the wet stone floor slowly. "That's when…Listen, I don't know anything about what happened in Forest Haven." He paused, sniffling. "The Rat seemed surprised too, and then he just…. I don't know. That's the night he came to me though, and told me that if she didn't fall in line he was going to kill the queen, and…." He trailed off, shaking his head. "I love my kingdom, and what that bitch is doing to it–"

His words were cut off instantly as Callan's fist connected with his jaw. He slumped to the side, breathing heavily as he spat blood onto the filthy ground. "You promised me a clean death," Arran rasped.

Callan leaned forward, only inches away from his battered face. "Not if you say one more disrespectful fucking word about her, do you hear me?"

"Callan," Valerian warned. "If you kill him now, you won't get your answers."

Arran leaned back in his chair, rasping a laugh through his bleeding lips as Callan grunted in response. "I'll tell you anyway, just because it's too late for that traitorous whore. She'll be dead by the time you find her." Callan froze where he stood, sheer and unadulterated terror gripping his heart.

Arran's puffy eyes took on a vicious gleam as he continued. "They'll take her before prayers today, and send that ambitious bitch to the Void, as she deserves. "

Callan needed no more than that, to know exactly where they'd taken her. Muttering a curse under his breath, Callan immediately ran from the cell, Valerian close behind. He'd expected her to wait for him, but if what Arran said was true, if he was too late....

He couldn't let himself even consider the possibility. Power vibrated beneath his skin, shadows begging to be unleashed. Not yet, not yet, he thought. If she were harmed, this entire Void damned kingdom would burn for it.

Callan remained silent, tension etched in his features, as they reached the forest path. Having horses brought around and readied would take too long, so they simply ran. "Valerian," he said finally, as they neared the clearing. "If she's gone, you and Leysa take Sylvie, the healers, and that guard, Dallin, and you take them from this castle."

Valerian nodded, catching his meaning immediately. "I will," he agreed.

CHAPTER 24

"Our gods?" Eve repeated lamely, eyes wide. She'd sat there, staring at the pair for a small eternity, trying to wrap her mind around what they'd claimed to be. Astonishment had quickly replaced fear. If she hadn't just fallen into a chamber hidden inside a pool that was thought to be bottomless, she would've thought it impossible. "And I'm not dead?" she asked again, thinking it the only plausible explanation.

The slender goddess smiled patiently, while her companion rolled her eyes. "No, my dear, you are not dead." She folded her jewel-laden fingers on her lap gently, adding, "I'm Helie, by the way. This is my mate, my wife in your terms, Keithia."

Keithia cast a glance at Helie before sighing. "Yes, goddesses of the sun and healing, and earth and life, respectively. Just to get the questions out of the way. We are short on time, you know."

"My mother?" she asked, desperate to know Riona's fate. If she couldn't see her again yet, couldn't say any of the very many things she longed to, then perhaps just knowing she was at peace would be enough.

Helie patted Keithia's leg, a gesture clearly meant to encourage patience on her wife's part. "Your mother rests in the Otherworld, at peace. She is not in pain, and she is not afraid, though she does miss you terribly of course."

Keithia's expression softened slightly. "We have much to tell you and very little time, Evelyn. We must proceed."

"I don't understand," Eve frowned. What could a pair of long-forgotten goddesses want with her? She may not be dead yet, but she wasn't in the land of living either, so what then?

"Listen," Keithia said, leaning forward. "You have set certain events into motion that were foreseen long before your birth. Our departure from this realm was prophesied, as was our return. You are the key to the first lock. Your arrival here, in this room with us, was the first turn of that lock."

Helie frowned, interrupting to add, "I assure you, dear, we would have preferred your arrival here to have been accomplished in a much less....traumatic manner."

Nodding her agreement, Keithia continued. "I cannot tell you everything, as fate is a fickle thing, but I can tell you that you must remain on your current path." Smiling, she added, "I am personally quite proud to call you one of my own."

"One of your own?"

"Your parents longed for a child and failed to conceive. I intervened as I was destined to so that you could be born as you were destined to," Keithia shrugged as if it were the most simple explanation in the world.

"We thought you were all gone." She sagged into the seat. Overwhelmed wasn't even a strong enough word for how she felt.

"Some small interventions have been possible over these many years," Helie explained. "But now that we've said as much as we are allowed, you must go."

"But how will I return?" Eve asked, glancing upward at the ceiling of black water. It was too far to jump, and even if she could, she wasn't sure she had the strength left to swim to the surface. If they were waiting for her up there...Fear spider walked down her spine at the thought.

"We will take care of that, do not worry," Helie replied smoothly. "And you will be safe when you return."

Keithia, as impatient as before, clasped her hands together in her lap and leaned forward. "Our time grows short, darling girl. Hold fast to your path, do not falter. Stay true to your heart. And–"

"Really sister, without me?" A light, feminine voice interrupted Keithia seconds before shadows formed behind the sofa where the two goddesses sat. The darkness rolled and writhed, slowly giving way to reveal a slender feminine form. A crown of obsidian sat atop her head, holding in place a veil that hid her almost entirely from view. "You wound me."

Keithia and Helie exchanged a glance, but it was the goddess of life who spoke. "Macaria," she began with thinly veiled annoyance. "I merely did not believe there to be time for any messages you may wish to send."

A sound above, something that sounded to Eve like a great beast roaring, had all four pairs of eyes looking skyward.

"Time is up, my love," Helie murmured. "She must return or all is lost."

Keithia cursed under her breath, and the pair rose from their seat.

"Wait!" Macaria called, rounding the sofa to stand in front of Eve as she rose from her seat. "Give Callan this message, it is vital he hears it." She leaned closer, lowering her voice to a whisper. "Tell him his mother sends this message of hope–Fate has her ways of working out. Do not despair."

Eve could barely register what Macaria had said before Keithia stepped forward suddenly, placing a palm flat against her right clavicle. "Bear this blessing, my child, may it serve you well, and keep you from harm always," she said quickly.

A rush of heat flooded Eve, starting where the goddess had placed her hand and spreading down her arm to the center of her middle finger. Before she could question the sensation or any of what had been said to her, she was moving. Lifted on invisible winds, rising quickly to the water above. Just as before, her head crashed into the frigid water first, but this time instead of sinking, she was flying upward, weightless and propelled by whatever magic the goddesses had used to send her home.

She could feel the momentum slowing, so she began to swim, kicking hard and reaching for the dim light that managed to break through the surface ahead. Her lungs began to burn just as her fingertips crested the surface. As she rose, breaking through the surface fully, finally, she heard the roar of pain once more.

Callan. Only a few feet away, he knelt, beside the bloodied bodies of Devlan and Reynard the Rat, and a sobbing but unharmed Emilia. Her gasp of air as she reached the wall lining the pool caught his attention. He turned to her with heart-wrenching relief in his gaze.

"Eve," he whispered, her name spilling from his mouth like a prayer. He reached the pool in little more than the blink of an eye. Falling to his knees on the grey stone that lined the pool, he pulled her over the wall, holding her against his chest. His breathing was ragged, as blood-stained hands roamed over her face and body gently as if assuring himself she was really there.

"Your mother says hello," she said through a shaky laugh.

"That's incredible," Leysa whispered, awestruck.

Valerian murmured his agreement, rubbing Leysa's shoulder lightly with the arm that was draped around her shoulder. They'd claimed the loveseat as the four of them crowded into Eve's sitting room after she'd bathed and changed clothes. Eve had spent the last hour explaining everything that had transpired in whatever realm she'd found herself beneath the Black Pool.

The prayers that were supposed to have taken place before her near death had been performed swiftly, and under some duress, by the guards whom Valerian had gone for shortly after he and Callan had arrived in the clearing.

"I'm sure you have a lot of questions," Callan said carefully, seated beside Eve on the larger sofa. She had wrapped herself in a blanket and leaned as close to the fire as she could, and still couldn't quite chase away the chill of the pool. "But I think it might be best if–"

Eve held up a hand from beneath her blanket. "I think the time for secrets is long past, considering the information your *mother* dropped on me." She was too tired to argue much more than that and hoped he wouldn't push the matter any further. The coronation was still a few hours away, but soon enough she would have to go and face the court, her kingdom, and pretend that none of it had happened.

"Fine," he conceded. "But can we hold off on the full unraveling of the story until after you've slept and eaten something?" he asked, eyeing her.

He hadn't stopped fussing over her since she'd come out of the water, and she suspected he wouldn't be stopping anytime soon. The cloak he'd worn had been wrapped around her instantly, covering the sodden gown that clung to her like a second skin, and when they'd finally made it back to her rooms, he'd refused to go farther than the other side of the closed door as she stripped the soaked gown and under-things. The thought of climbing into the tub to bathe sent her heart racing, so she had settled for cleaning herself with the cool water from the basin by the vanity instead.

Eve nodded. "Alright. One secret at a time?" It was becoming their little routine, she supposed.

"Alright," he said slowly, considering. "Macaria, the goddess of death and destiny is my mother, sort of." At Eve's raised brow, she held up his hands, palms toward her. "Not by blood or anything, but adopted in a way. My bloodline was hers, blessed so many generations ago nobody is sure when it started. She occasionally chooses her favorites, for reasons only she knows. I happened to be chosen. Those of us she chooses refer to her as Mother." His tone was matter-of-fact, but Eve's mind was still boggled.

"That's not possible, Callan. I mean, obviously, it happened, but I don't understand how. I don't understand how any of this is happening. The gods are, or were, gone. How did she even interact with you?"

"That's another secret," he replied, watching her closely.

"I'm going to need so much more than one at a time after the coronation, Callan." Everything she'd been taught as a child had been a lie. She wondered if the priests had any idea the gods they thought were lost to them were so much closer than they knew. How would they feel if they knew? Would they be as adrift as she was now?

"What happened in the clearing, while I was gone?"

She had put most of it together already. Devlan and Reynard were dead by the time she'd emerged, and judging by the amount of blood left behind, they had not gone easily. Emilia had been left untouched but was near catatonic from whatever she'd seen by the time they'd gotten her back to the castle. When they'd retreated to Eve's room, she still hadn't spoken a word.

"I thought you were dead," he replied, voice breaking slightly as a shadow crossed his features. "I thought I'd lost you." He dragged a hand through his hair and shook his head. "So I lost my temper. I don't think you want the details."

He was right, she didn't want to know what he'd done. She should feel some sort of guilt for what had been done to them, she supposed, but she couldn't bring herself to feel anything more than relief. They'd orchestrated her mother's death and had nearly killed her. Callan had filled her in on what he'd gathered from the guard in the dungeons. As far as she was concerned, they'd gotten what they deserved, for her mother's death alone.

An investigation would have to happen, now that they knew a council member had been involved and had orchestrated all of it. But that would need to wait until the crown was officially hers. For now, nobody could know what had really occurred. All that they'd told the guards who had come to the pool was she'd been attacked by them and nothing more. They needn't know the full story. It would have spread through the castle, causing a panic they could not afford right now.

Leysa spoke up, breaking the silence that had fallen over the group like a blanket. "You should probably start getting ready soon," she said gently.

"Yeah, I should," Eve agreed, rising slowly. She was utterly exhausted. How she was going to make it through the coronation, she didn't know.

"I want you to know how sorry I am for all of this–" Leysa began.

A sudden burning pain along her clavicle drew a hiss of pain from Eve. She yanked the blanket away and tugged down the dressing gown she wore to reveal the spot where the goddess had placed her palm and offered her blessing. A twisting vine laden with full leaves of ivy was slowly beginning to spread from the place where Keithia had touched her. The burning sensation continued down her arm as Eve tugged the gown lower, as far as she could without removing it. Vines and ivy continued down her wrist, nearly the twin to the mark the goddess herself bore.

"What is that?" Leysa asked, eyes wide.

"I think the goddess did something when she touched me, but I have no idea–"

As the burning reached the tip of Eve's finger, finally coming to a stop, the ground began to shake. The vase atop Eve's wardrobe rattled and danced before crashing to the floor, shattering. Callan and Valerian rushed into the room just as the quaking intensified, giving one final glass rattling shake and then abruptly stopping.

Callan's intense gaze met Eve's and he stepped closer. "What *exactly* did she say when she touched you?"

Eve repeated the words the goddess had said, frowning. "What does it mean?"

"Shit," Callan whispered, hand raising to his temple. "She blessed you." At Eve's flat look, he added, "It's a gift they can give sometimes. Like what Macaria did for me."

"She favors you to an extreme degree, I'd say," Valerian added, eyeing the shattered vase. "That was probably your powers activating."

Leysa gaped. "That hasn't happened in centuries has it?"

Both men shook their heads. "No," they said in unison.

"I've heard of it being done in Darkegrove, a very long time ago," Callan explained. "In a time of great need, but it shouldn't be possible now, especially not here. You'll need training–"

Eve eyed the visible part of her arm warily. "We can't tell anyone about this either," she began, just as her guard, Edvard, burst into the room.

"My lady, are you alright?" Edvard asked.

"All is well," she replied smoothly, tugging up the sleeve of her gown quickly, as Leysa stepped to the side to block the tattoo from view. "Though there is some broken glass here that will need to be swept. Please go and see if anyone has been injured."

When they were alone again, Eve dropped onto the edge of her bed. "Let's get this day over with. We can worry about what all of this means tomorrow."

CHAPTER 25

Servants bustled in and out of the great hall for two straight days, unaware of the chaos surrounding their new monarch. Large garlands of flowers, most grown in the castle greenhouses, hung from the marble pillars that lined the hall. The pale grey marble floors had been polished to a shine so bright that Eve could nearly see her reflection in it. She had been fussed over since just after the quake, nearly two hours before, and had barely resisted the urge to nervously toy with the red curls left loose so the crown could be easily placed atop her brow.

Callan took her hand in his, giving it a gentle squeeze before releasing it. She didn't have the words to express how much his support and protection meant to her, so she settled for a smile. Her heart was a steady gallop within her chest, pounding so hard she could almost swear she could hear it.

Everything that they'd taken from her, every moment of grief and fear, had led to this. Standing just inside the entrance to the grand hall, only a mere fifty steps would carry her to the dais where their most senior priest and Lord Eldred Gray waited to officially crown her Queen of Darkegrove. The significantly smaller-than-planned crowd murmured amongst themselves while they waited for Eve's procession down the aisle. Due to concerns for her safety, only courtiers, councilors, and their families had been invited. Her first official appearance in the morning would be open to the public, but under heavy guard as the coronation itself was.

Somewhere out there, in the sea of faces, Valerian and Leysa were watching along with several other guards hidden amongst the guests, watching the crowd. The priest cleared his throat then, the signal that the coronation was to begin. Raising a hand, he gestured for silence.

With a deep breath to steady her rattled nerves, Eve began to walk down the aisle toward her destiny. Every click of her heel against the tile reminded her of something, of someone, she'd given up or lost to get here. Brodie, given up because she couldn't give him what she knew would make him happy. Her sense of safety, lost because she'd chosen to do what she believed to be right. The most painful of all, her mother taken from her because she'd dared to speak up against an institution that kept women from power. An institution that marked them as lesser than their male counterparts.

The heavy cloak she wore, the traditional white and green of royalty lined with a wolf's fur, rustled as she stopped at the foot of the dais. Callan, who had silently escorted her, stoic as ever, stepped to the side, joining the council members who made up the front row.

Behind the priest who stood just before her, a steward held a pillow, the crown of Darkegrove resting upon it. Forged from silver mined in the northern mountains, shaped to resemble the leaves from trees that made up their great forests, and topped with precious stones from their many mines, it was beautiful and weighty in every sense of the word. Her hands were shaking beneath the cloak, her breath coming in quick bursts. Once more, her mother's words echoed through her mind. *You must stay strong, my love.*

"We are gathered today, mourning as ever, the absence of our beloved gods on this auspicious day," the elderly priest droned. If only he knew the truth, she thought to herself. Despite her nervousness and fear, Eve's expression remained a mask of solemnity, the picture of a righteous queen. "Never before has our kingdom been so blessed. Please, friends, let us offer a moment of prayer, that the gods may yet hear our plea and join us in celebration."

With the priest's gaze now fully on her rather than skyward, Eve thanked the quick thinking of Sylvie for her wardrobe change. Rather than the low-cut white gown she'd planned to wear, one that would certainly have put her new tattoo on display, Sylvie had produced the backup gown she'd set aside. With a high cut, nearly resting against her throat, and a deep forest green color, there was no way it would be visible, even this close to the priest. Sylvie, bless her, had merely blinked, surprised for a moment, but had not pressed for an explanation upon seeing the new brand on Eve's skin.

Mother should be here– the thought darted through her mind for what was probably the hundredth time today alone. Her father should have reigned for many more years, she thought, for maybe the first time since he died, and none of this should have happened this way.

A cloud passed quickly over her features. Nothing could be done to change the past, but she could change the future. Make a better one. One where sons and daughters of the north would have an equal footing to start with in life, neither held in higher esteem than the other from the moment they'd enter the world; before they had even drawn that first precious breath of life into their lungs.

The priest continued droning about blessings and the forgotten gods. Eve kept her face placid, pious, and utterly regal as she held her chin high. Even as she lowered herself to kneel before the priest, signaled to do so by a subtle wave of his ancient, gnarled fingers, she did not let one hint of her thoughts show in her expression.

As she knelt, bowing only before her kingdom and the gods that had supposedly abandoned them, the silver crown was placed on her head, settling against her brow gently. For a moment she could almost swear a collective sigh rushed through the castle. Not from the guests, who remained mostly stony-faced and silent, but the very castle walls. As if the stone, hewn from the mountains just to the north, had been holding its breath for a very, very long time.

The priest, gesturing for her to rise with a wave of his fingers, finally announced, "Her Majesty Evelyn Isobel Fallwen Darrow, Sovereign of Darkegrove, Queen of Earth and Stone."

Finally, she had done it. The first true Queen of Darkegrove in so many centuries. If only her mother had been here to see what she had helped Eve accomplish. Pride and a small amount of joy, tinged as it was with grief, swelled within her only to be dampened by a powerful wave of guilt and grief that threatened to swallow her whole. Though she managed to maintain her outward composure, her heart ached.

Callan was at her side immediately, a hand extended toward her. As she placed her hand in his and began to rise to her feet, the ground began to rumble. A slow, steady sort of shaking, unlike the sudden violent quake that had caught them all by surprise. Guests began to shout as the shaking grew stronger, holding onto one another for stability, some beginning to make for the exits.

Callan, brow furrowed and lips pressed together, held onto Eve's arm tightly, keeping her upright. His gaze roamed the room, spotting the various exits. Guards, as confused as the rest of them, struggled to maintain control of the panicking crowd. It was her duty now, to calm her people, but as she began to speak, the ground began to slow. As suddenly as it had begun, it stopped. People calmed only slightly. Some still cried, and others simply stood and gaped.

The priest, who had somehow managed not to fall from the dais, looked pale and shaken as he raised his hands and called for quiet. "Good people, pray, do not despair."

Eve glanced toward Callan, wondering where this was going to go and finding the mirror of her own thoughts etched into his features.

"The gods," the priest announced breathlessly. "They have....they have sent us a whisper through the very earth. A small rumbling to mark this day. There is naught to fear, good people. Naught to worry yourselves over. Please." He seemed to be talking to himself as much as the gathered crowd, but for whatever reason, his wobbly speech calmed the worst of the panic and they settled. At least nobody was running for the door anymore.

As he fell into silence, Eve seized the opportunity to speak to her people as their queen for the first time. Finally, she ascended the dais fully, turning to face them and holding her head high. The frightened crowd sank into bows or curtsies, not as one but staggered, like raindrops on cobblestones.

"Rise," she commanded gently, and they did, as one this time. "See to your loved ones, take time to recover yourselves. If there has been damage or injury done, please alert a steward and it will be seen to immediately."

Eve paused letting her gaze roam over the sea of faces now staring directly at her. A mixture of interest, curiosity, and some distaste was leveled at her. *So be it.* "Rest yourselves, for tomorrow we celebrate."

Callan gave her fingers an approving squeeze as they departed, still hand in hand, despite the lack of necessity for contact. As their eyes met, just beyond the threshold of the hall, Eve realized she was utterly lost in him.

Chapter 26

Back in the relative privacy of her chambers, Eve flopped onto the loveseat by the grey marble fireplace with a huff. Valerian raised a brow at her very queenlike behavior as he rubbed his wife's shoulders, drawing a slow groan from her. Eve, with barely enough energy left to toss him a light wave in response, offered Leysa a smile where she sat on the floor, her back against the couch between her husband's knees.

"Do we want to talk about it?" Leysa prodded, glancing at Callan, standing by the window. He had been staring into the darkened canopy of the forest since they'd returned to her chambers. Valerian's gaze shifted from Eve to Callan and back, but he remained silent as he worked out the knots that had apparently formed in Leysa's upper back.

"I think," Callan began, not bothering to turn from the window, still surveying whatever had caught his eye in the forest. "That we were getting the very first taste of your powers, princess."

Eve blinked. "What? I didn't do anything."

"What were you thinking? What were you feeling when it began at the coronation?" Leysa asked, the corner of her lips tugging downward.

Eve straightened then, leaning against the back of the loveseat and drawing her legs up underneath her. She'd changed into a pair of leggings she'd borrowed from Leysa. They'd fit well, despite being too long and a little snugger than she'd expected. Leysa's toned, fit body was more slender than Eve's, but she'd still managed to squeeze into them. She had already asked Sylvie to inquire about purchasing several pairs for herself. Buried in the back of her closet, she'd found an oversized knit sweater, the origin of which she couldn't place, in a shade of pale blue she thought more suited to Lia or Emilia than herself, but it was comfortable and warm.

What had she been feeling just before the ground had begun to shake? Almost overwhelming grief and a healthy dose of guilt. Eve sank back against the couch. They waited patiently for her response, as she struggled to find a way to put into words the crushing weight of emotions she'd been feeling all day. A ragged breath passed her lips and she straightened slightly.

"Guilty," she said quietly, her voice barely loud enough to be heard above the crackling flames in the hearth. "Sad. I felt like... like my mother should have been there. She should have been alive to see it, and it was my fault that she wasn't." Her eyes burned, but she refused to let the tears fall. She wouldn't cry in front of them. Later, when she was alone, she would weep and mourn her mother but not now.

Valerian's hands slid from Leysa's shoulders down her arms as a breath whooshed out of him. The latter's eyes had gone soft, filled with the pity Eve dreaded seeing.

"You know that wasn't your fault," Leysa murmured to Eve, curls bobbing lightly as she tilted her head. "You did what was right, and I know that I didn't really know your mother, but I believe she would have been so proud of you today."

She could do no more than nod at Leysa's gently spoken words. Callan, breaking his vigil over the forest, moved to sit beside Eve. His pointed glance had Valerian and Leysa making their exit, claiming exhaustion and making promises to return first thing in the morning to accompany them both to greet the common folk who had come to pay their respects to the new queen.

Once alone, only the crackle of the fireplace broke the silence that had settled over them. Her feet somehow found their way into his lap, and his hands rested comfortably on her outstretched legs. It felt easy, she mused, to simply be with him like this with no need for conversation and nothing but one another for company. The easy silence served as a balm for her aching heart, though her mind still dwelled on her grief, on how much she'd lost, somehow the few moments of peace in an altogether harrowing few weeks helped.

Callan finally broke the silence, asking quietly, "Are you ready for the truth?" He had been silent, withdrawn, for so much of the evening. She had attributed it to the confusion of her apparent powers, alongside the coronation, the mixed feelings that must have brought for him, and the guilt she knew he also carried after Riona's death.

Heart skittering, she nodded. She had repeatedly asked for the full truth, and he had promised to tell her when the time was right. Now that the right time had apparently arrived, a large part of her was afraid, and she couldn't name the exact reason. "Okay," she said slowly, straightening a little.

"I am not...I haven't been honest. It's not that I've lied exactly," he sighed, dragging a hand through his black hair. "I just haven't been forthcoming. About who I am. What I am." It was strange, hearing him stumble over his words. His normally composed, confident demeanor was gone, replaced by doubt, and apprehension.

"What you are?" She echoed, ignoring the dart of fear that ran down her spine.

Moving his hands from her legs, Callan stared at the floor for several heartbeats. Eve watched him in silence as the pieces began coming together in her mind. The shadows in the hallway on the day of her mother's death. Her mouth fell open. He'd moved so fast, gotten to her faster than he should have that day when they'd argued, and his injuries....they should have kept him down much longer, maybe even killed him.

"You're...fae," Eve breathed. A weight settled over her chest. It couldn't be possible, The fae were gone. It had been so long now that the scholars speculated they had even gone extinct somehow. "How are you here?"

Callan lowered his gaze to her legs, still resting on his lap. He did not attempt to touch her, remaining perfectly still, as if afraid to startle her. "There are a few of us still here," he admitted. "I don't know for certain how many. We aren't all in touch, or even on good terms. Your kings and queens are aware of some of us," he added, lifting his wary eyes to Eve. "Your mother knew."

There was a steady pounding in her ears now. Drum beats sounding the alarm within her mind. Her mother had lied. She had known, the entire time, and hadn't spoken a word of it to her. "Tell me everything."

It was a command that left no room for argument. She could see the way his jaw tightened, the darkening of his eyes, but she had to know. Had this secret been a part of her mother's death somehow? She'd been trying to tell Eve something the day she died. But why a note when little more than a brief walk separated them?

"Some of us stayed behind after the fall," he said slowly, choosing his words carefully. "Your scholars and priests only have a portion of the story. There is a lot about what happened back then that they don't know."

"But you do? How old are you?" She straightened, sliding her legs from his lap and folding them in front of her. "That was almost six hundred years ago."

Callan snorted. "Old," he replied. "But I was still young then, a little younger than you are now."

Eve's head was spinning. "How did she know about this?"

"A few of us have dedicated ourselves to helping where we can, a sort of atonement for what our brethren did five hundred years ago, and the things that were done before that. So we made it a point a few generations ago to meet with the human rulers, to explain and offer our help when it's most needed." He glanced to the door through which Leysa and Valerian had departed earlier. "And near immortality makes you a little...restless after a while. We don't fight in wars, but when something truly consequential is happening, we try to help."

Eve nodded. She could guess what they felt they needed to atone for. After all, it had been their king who had started the war. One of their lords had been sent to the human queen and had started a civil war that nearly destroyed the middle kingdoms on his command. The idea that fae walked among them, unknown by the humans, was disconcerting for a few reasons, but not the most pressing matter in her mind.

"Macaria called herself your mother," she said. "Can you still reach her here?"

Callan shook his head. "She isn't. Not in that sense. It's a term her Ravens, those of us blessed by her, use—and no I can't reach her from here."

Her mind turned to what the goddesses had said about her setting certain things in motion. "Do you know what she was trying to tell me about the prophecy?"

"Yes," he said more quietly than she'd heard him speak before. "That's..." He sighed. "I wasn't certain at first, but after what happened at the pool..." The room darkened for a moment, and cold rage rippled off of him. "The prophecy refers to the return of the fae. When the gods left and banished most of the fae from the middle kingdoms, it wasn't for eternity. A time frame was chosen by the gods. The rise of three rulers touched by the gods, to the three remaining human thrones, would signal the time had come."

The newly crowned Queen thought her heart might stop. "Naia Colvari was crowned a couple of weeks ago, and I've just taken mine obviously." She shuddered. "I've heard nothing about Naia having strange powers, and Aldrich Vallyse certainly has none. It's impossible."

Callan lifted a shoulder lightly. "I suppose we'll see, but I wouldn't expect it to be much longer. If they chose to meet with you, they must think it's imminent." The light in the room returned to normal as Callan released the tension from his shoulders, resting his hands on her legs once more.

"Do Leysa and Valerian know about all of this?"

"Not the prophecy, not completely, but I would assume Valerian has guessed. I'll fill them in later."

"I have a question," Eve began, frowning slightly. "My mother claimed you were from Valengard, a region far to the west. Is that even a real place?"

Callan chuckled. "Yeah, it's real. It was once part of the fae territories. It belonged to my mother's family before, and since the fall, I've taken it on. The people there believe they have a Lord who only rarely visits, no more than a handful of times every generation. I'm always the prior Lord's son or nephew. If I'm careful, nobody who has seen me before remains. Leysa and Valerian have played my children a time or two when it was required."

What a lonely life they'd led. Nobody could know their true nature, and because of that, they wouldn't have been able to form meaningful relationships outside of the three of them. The thought sent a little pang through her heart.

They fell into silence once more, and Eve allowed her mind to wander. So many things had been revealed and happened to her in the last few days that she couldn't help but feel her entire world had shifted. It had all but turned on its proverbial head, in truth.

The fact that her mother had known about the fae alone had her reeling. Would she have still chosen this path if she had known her rise to the throne had, in truth, been part of some grand plan by the forgotten gods and not her own choice? She had been so sure of herself, so proud of herself, for making a statement and changing the future. But had it even been her doing?

"Your birthday is on the winter solstice," Callan said suddenly, drawing Eve from her thoughts. "Only a couple of weeks away."

She blinked. "Yes, how did you know that?"

Callan's laugh was little more than a huff. "Do you remember the story Leysa told you about the party and the girl I saw?"

The girl he had fallen for in an instant. *How could I forget?* Rather than voice her jealousy, she simply nodded.

"It was the solstice, and I had been called to confer with the King and Queen of Darkegrove," he began, casting a lopsided grin her way. "They were having a party that night, celebrating their daughter's birthday."

Eve's heart galloped in her chest. She grasped the back of the couch tightly, desperate for something to steady herself. He couldn't mean...

"You were dressed in starlight, I thought, and the most beautiful thing I'd ever seen." His voice was lowered, eyes darkening as his gaze roamed her face. "I think it was that moment," he added, blue eyes drifting to her parted lips. "That I knew I was yours, in whatever way you'd have me."

This time she was positive her heart had stopped. "I never saw you there." She wanted to say more, to say something substantial, but her mouth refused to form words.

His attention returned to her eyes once more, and the look he fixed on her had heat pooling between her legs. "No, I was warned to stay away, so I did. I can't do that anymore."

"Good," she said, barely recognizing her breathless voice. "I don't want you to." Somewhere in the back of her mind, the question sprang forth. *Who warned him away?* Before she could even truly acknowledge it, the thought was quickly silenced, and forgotten entirely.

He moved faster than she could track with her eyes. In a heartbeat, she had been laid flat against the sofa with surprising gentleness. Callan's face hovered over hers, a silent question in his eyes, even as his lips dipped toward her own.

"Yes," she breathed, arching herself toward him.

He claimed her mouth with his own, bruising and thorough. Toned muscle strained beneath the sleeves of his shirt as she slid her hands up his biceps. Eve had known he had to have a warrior's build, but what she felt now, finally able to explore him the way she'd been longing to, she discovered just how right she'd been.

Her sharp intake of breath drew a husky laugh from him as he shifted his attention to the column of her neck, his teeth sliding over her skin toward her collarbone. His warm breath against her skin followed by a light nip sent a shiver through her. "Impatient, dove?"

His grip on her hips was firm as he lifted them from the couch, straightening himself. Hooking his fingers on the waistband of her leggings he began to pull them down so slowly and methodically that Eve thought every slide of the soft material might drive her mad with impatience.

"Callan." The word was a plea on her lips as she gripped his biceps.

Her leggings were swiftly tossed away, leaving only a thin scrap of lacy material covering her most intimate places.

"Fuck," he muttered. His fingers moved to the hem of the sweater, toying with it lightly for a moment before tugging it upward with the same slow, methodical movements he'd used with the leggings.

"Please, Callan."

Callan shook his head, but pulled the sweater over her head, dropping it to the floor. "I want to take my time with you, my queen. I'm going to savor every moment of you looking at me like this, naked underneath me. You are stunning."

My queen. The term had Eve's heart soaring in response. If she hadn't already been half in love with him, she would've been well on her way there from this moment alone. She had been bare beneath the thick sweater, and the tips of her breasts peaked in response to the cold and the sheer desire coursing through her. Callan, still sitting straight up between her bent legs, looked her over slowly, reverently. Finally, his eyes met hers and one look into those sapphire depths sent all rational thought scattering from her mind.

Callused fingers trailed along one breast slowly, patiently. A sharp shock of pain shot through her as he squeezed her nipple between his thumb and forefinger. His mouth replaced his fingers quickly, drawing the peak into his mouth and soothing the little hurt, drawing a low moan from her lips.

Her own shaking hands slid from his arms and began tugging at the front of his shirt impatiently. She needed to see him, to feel his skin beneath her touch. "I want to touch you. I need to," she breathed. She craved him, not only his touch but the intimacy and closeness as well. The desire for human contact, to feel less alone, was almost as powerful as the carnal desire.

Releasing her breast, he tugged his shirt over his head. Laying her palms flat against his chest, she let her hands roam across the planes of his chest, lowering them slowly down his toned abdomen until they came to rest at the waistband of his pants.

"Not yet," he said in response to her insistent tug on his pants. "I want to take my time. I want to touch every inch of you, and taste you."

The apex of her thighs dampened, and she let out a small sigh as he offered her that damned grin that drove her wild. Callan was going to be the death of her, and at this particular moment, she thought it might not be such a bad thing.

"So let's see," he murmured. "We began here." He traced the underside of each breast one at a time with a finger. "Where shall we venture next?"

Eve frowned as he sat back. The space between them was cold, and she barely resisted the urge to tug him back to her.

"Well, this simply will not do," he mused, eyeing her lacy undergarment. "That is going to have to go." In one painfully slow motion, Callan gripped the fabric, rending it in two in one swift motion. Now fully bared to him, her core dampened in response to his darkened gaze as he drank in the sight of her.

Laid out before him she felt freer than she had in as long as she could remember. This was what she wanted, him, this time together. Being with him like this was the first choice she'd made in so very long that was just for her. Taking the crown had been for the future of her kingdom as much as it had been for herself, but that decision had brought with it so many burdens and dangers, a great deal of weight on her shoulders that often left her feeling trapped.

If he sensed the direction her thoughts had taken, he gave no indication as he dipped his head low, raking his tongue and teeth across the planes of her abdomen, in a sweeping path to her hip. Eve lifted her hips in silent demand, and he obliged by lowering himself so that his head rested between her legs.

"So eager," he whispered against her inner thigh. A flick of his tongue against her skin had her breath hitching. Her breasts felt heavy, and her core tightened.

"Callan." His name was a demand this time, driven by desperation for his touch. A single finger came to rest on that bundle of nerves, answered by a gasp from Eve.

"Fuck, Eve, you're so wet for me," he breathed as he slipped his finger inside of her. In and out, he moved at an unhurried pace for several strokes, watching her face as he added a second finger. She whimpered, arching her back to meet his ministrations.

When his thumb met the bundle of nerves at the apex moving in slow circles, she let out a curse that had him chuckling. She was dizzy from him, his scent, his touch. A leaf twisting and turning on an autumn wind, soaring higher and higher as her climax built.

Letting her head fall back against the cushions, she felt more than saw his movement. His tongue replaced his hand, sliding first over the bundle of nerves. She was in freefall now. Her hands plunged into his hair just as he thrust his tongue into her sex, working it in and out. Release flooded her, and she called out his name, an invocation to the gods, what exactly for, she didn't know.

The rattle of her door handle had her freezing in place, as shadows exploded across the room, enshrouding the room in complete darkness. Even the glow of the fireplace had been swallowed entirely.

"Go away," Callan growled, his tone promising a swift death to anyone who dared step through the door.

"Majesty?" The nervous response came from one of her guards, likely alarmed by her cries.

She could see nearly nothing in the darkness that had enveloped the room, thanks to Callan, but she could feel him as he rose to stand beside the couch. "Everything is fine, return to your post. Lord Thorne will see to my security this evening." Her explanation was rushed and winded. A low rumble of approval sounded from her right.

"Very well, Majesty," the guard replied warily.

With the same surprising degree of gentleness he'd shown earlier, Callan scooped Eve from the couch and began to carry her to the bedroom. She couldn't help but wonder, for a moment, how he could see well enough to navigate the distance in the pitch black of her rooms, but the thought was quickly extinguished as he breathed against her ear. "I don't want anyone else seeing you like this. You are all mine."

Desire flooded her once more, and she could manage little more than a hum in response. As they reached the bed, he finally withdrew the darkest of his shadows, allowing candlelight to illuminate his features once more.

Lying back on the bed, she studied the strong lines of his jaw and the cobalt depths of his blue eyes. He was looking at her again, with that intense expression of his that had her wondering what exactly he was thinking, but where he had once looked at her as if she were a puzzle to be solved, now he studied her as if she were a treasure.

"Callan?" she said gently, drawing him from wherever his mind had gone.

"Where were we?" He asked, lifting one corner of his lips in a lopsided grin. "I think perhaps, here?" His hand slid slowly up her inner thigh before meeting her slick apex once more but stopped just short of entering her. "I'm going to take you slowly, dove. I want to hear you beg for more."

She was going to come undone right then and there if he kept talking like that. "So do it," she said, a slight tremble in her voice betraying her faux confidence. The sound of his pants being removed and tossed aside sent another trill of excitement through her.

Climbing the bed, Callan leaned over her, dragging one of her legs upward so it came to rest along his hip and placing his other palm beside her head on the bed. Both out of instinct and a desperate need to close the distance that remained between them, Eve raised her hands, intent on pulling him closer.

Shadowy tendrils appeared suddenly and wrapped around each of her wrists before she could get close enough, dragging her hands back to the bed gently but firmly. Surprise had her eyes widening, even as her core gave a twinge in response. She tugged against the shadowy bonds, finding they held her hands fast.

"No touching, princess," Callan chided, giving her thigh a gentle squeeze. Positioning himself more securely on his knees, he gripped her hips tightly and grinned at her once more. Eve's gaze dropped from his face to his considerable proud length. Her heart sped up, and she bit her lower lip gently. "Ask nicely, princess." He rasped, eyes darkened with lust.

"Please," she breathed. In one thrust, he drove himself into her, to the hilt. Eve cried out, arching her back to meet him as he withdrew, then drove into her once more. If she had been a leaf spinning on the wind before from little more than his touch, now she was dandelion fluff on a whirlwind. Soaring higher and faster than she had thought possible before. She met his pace, meeting each of his thrusts with her own movement.

Her name rumbled from his lips as he grasped her hips, thrusting harder and faster. The invisible bonds that had kept her hands from him vanished, and she wrapped her arms around his neck. As climax found her, drawing a wanton moan from her, he pulled her upward, chests touching as his own release soon followed. "Fuck, Eve," he roared, gripping her back tightly.

Sometime later, they lay side by side on top of the comforter.

Neither had the energy or inclination to move enough to cover themselves. Her head rested comfortably on his chest, arm draped across his abdomen.

"I think, next time, I'll take you against that wall over there," Callan said idly, tracing a fingertip along her arm as he eyed the opposite wall.

CHAPTER 27

The rest of the night had been the most restful Eve had experienced in what felt like years. Even before her father's death, the thought of eventually rising to the throne had made many of her nights long and lacking sleep. Loneliness had long been a companion of hers in the months that had followed her split from Brodie, despite the fact she hadn't loved him, not quite. The comfortable companionship they shared had kept her content for a long time. She hadn't missed him as much as she had missed just having someone, another reason she had chosen to let him go.

Her thoughts turned to Callan, seated beside her on the blanket. She'd asked the servants to prepare a picnic for her and her companions, and despite their perplexed expressions, they'd managed to put together a rather elegant assortment of food and drink inside one of the larger greenhouses. Winter was now approaching Darkegrove with ferocity, and the last few remaining days of autumn had turned near frigid, even in the height of the afternoon.

Would she be able to say the same about him, when inevitably it ended? Eve knew she wouldn't, and had told herself to end it before the attachment became too strong, too painful to break. The thought had even raced through her mind that morning as he kept his promise from the night before, taking her against the wall with such intensity she thought she might not be able to walk correctly for the rest of the day. Despite the warning in her mind, she never gave voice to the thought, though she couldn't say exactly why.

"So, long night, huh?" Valerian was asking, his brow raised as he smirked at them. Leysa chucked a fat grape at him in admonishment and drew a snicker from the warrior.

Callan leaned his head back against his crossed arms and drawled lazily, "I have no idea what you mean."

"He must mean the coronation," Eve offered, narrowing her eyes at Valerian.

Valerian had the sense to remain silent as Leysa poked him hard in the ribs, settling for a bright smile for his wife instead of whatever retort was surely on the tip of his tongue.

Callan rolled his eyes and sat up, resting his elbow on his knee, chin on his palm. "There are some things we need to discuss," he said more seriously this time, casting a glance around the greenhouse. Varying shades of green and fat, bright red roses were the only things that Eve could see, but with his heightened fae senses, Eve suspected if any other prying eyes or ears happened to be nearby he would detect them.

"I've shared our secret with Eve," he began slowly, casting a glance in her direction. "She knows that we are fae, and that Riona was aware."

Leysa's amber eyes widened for a brief moment and then turned to Eve. "I'm sorry we couldn't tell you," she said quietly.

Valerian nodded his agreement, bright smile replaced by a more somber expression.

Eve smiled her acceptance to Leysa, clasping her newfound friend's hand in her own and giving it a gentle squeeze. Forgiveness was easy, in this instance at least. As much as she hated that she'd been kept in the dark about it, she could understand their reasoning. The fae were hated, even more than she was, in this kingdom. Until they could be sure how she would react to the news, they couldn't have risked it.

"The prophecy," Callan continued, "is bothering me. If Eve's ascension is the first sign, then the other two can't be far behind."

Uncertainty played across Leysa's features as she glanced between Eve and Callan; the latter giving her a slight shake of his head. There was more, Eve realized, that she hadn't been told. *Are the secrets never going to end?* Irritation flared, and she turned to glare at Callan. "What else? What else aren't you telling me?" she demanded.

"Eve I–" he began, eyes slightly widened. For a moment she could've sworn worry had clouded his eyes, but it was quickly replaced by relief as Leysa interrupted.

"It's not his secret to tell," she said with a sigh. "I assume he explained the shadows?"

Irritation turned to wariness as Eve turned to look at Leysa. "Yes, sort of."

"Well, allow me to fully explain our gifts then." She was scooting across the floor then, making more space between herself and Valerian. He watched his wife with such admiration in his dark brown eyes that it made something in Eve's chest hurt. "You've heard the stories, about how some fae are, were, special. That we had extra gifts, beyond just the heightened senses, yes?" Eve nodded, and Leysa pressed on.

"Well, Callan and I both have a little of that extra special...stuff," she said, wiggling her fingers as if sprinkling salt on the blanket. "He has his shadows, gifted to him by the Lady of Death and I have–"

"Something that is better shown than explained, I think, my love," Valerian interrupted.

Leysa grinned but said nothing before simply...disappearing. Where she had been, a flash of light appeared, bright and fleeting, almost immediately replaced by a reddish brown hawk. The bird, Leysa apparently, peered at Eve a moment before letting loose a raspy screech and flapping her wings.

"Show off," Valerian muttered lovingly, as he ran a finger along the soft feathers on the underside of her neck.

Eve could do little more than stare for several seconds, while the men, and bird, waited patiently for her to find her voice again. "Oh," she said finally. "Wait, was that you? That day with Emilia?"

The light flashed again, and Leysa, in her more familiar form, reappeared in front of Eve. "Little hard to talk in that form," she grinned. "Yes, and the bitch deserved it. For what she said about me, how she spoke to you; for your mother, and for trying to have you killed. I didn't know about that part then or I would've clawed her eyes right out."

A somber hush fell over them. Grief settled into Eve's chest, a familiar and oppressive weight. She should be mourning, should be preparing her kingdom for the return of the fae, whenever that was to come. There were truthfully a million different things she should be doing right now, instead of this.

"Has she spoken at all?" There was no need to explain who she was asking about as she turned to look at Callan.

"Not a word," he replied softly. "The healers believe she's in some kind of shock. Personally, I think she just doesn't want to admit to what she's done."

Valerian grunted in response, twirling a grape stem between his thumb and forefinger idly.

"They'll keep trying," Leysa assured her as she moved back to her place on the blanket. "But we believe that everyone involved was in the clearing that day. Three members of the council were found to be part of the plan, and have been...taken care of."

Eve shuddered at the reminder. She'd seen just how thoroughly Callan had taken care of the men in the clearing, leaving only Emilia alive, and that was likely only because of the timing of Eve's return. A part of her wished he'd held back, had left them alive so she could ask why. Why they'd killed her mother, why they had tried to kill her. Knowing why wouldn't change anything, but maybe it would at least give her some sense of closure. Or maybe it would make her feel worse. Unless Emilia decided to speak, she'd never know for sure.

"I have to meet with what remains of the council soon, and then there's the reception today." Eve sighed.

It was a necessary part of her rule, dealing with men who may have had a part in the plot that had nearly ended her life. Perhaps some good could come out of the meeting with the common folk at the reception, and the ball held by the nobility should be pleasant if she could manage to avoid having to speak to too many of them. Hopefully whoever stepped into The Rat's council seat would be more reasonable and less inclined to murder. The thought had her snorting a laugh.

Callan's eyebrow rose at that, but Eve shook her head once. The conversation moved on from there, and she found peace for a few blessed minutes, surrounded by lovely flowers and good friends. By the time a guard arrived to escort the Queen to her meeting, the four of them found themselves flushed with laughter and a little wine. Leysa and Valerian remained behind, the shifter giggling lightly against her husband's ear, leaving little doubt that the pair planned to take advantage of their time alone.

A handful of guards led Eve and Callan to the council room where it had all begun such a short time ago. The days had moved so swiftly, and so many tragedies had happened in such a short time. Eve still didn't quite know how she managed to survive everything she'd been through, everything that had happened. She'd had no control of her own life, even after taking the step she thought would secure her own freedom, her ability to control her life, but so far all that had been achieved was the opposite. Taking Callan to bed had been the first decision truly hers since she had taken her throne, and she had no intention of letting it be the last.

Like the last time she'd stood there, the council chamber was dominated by the oaken table surrounded by men of the council, but unlike the last time, light streamed in through the windows, diffused and colored orange by the few autumn leaves still clinging to the trees beyond. The council itself would appoint Reynard's replacement, though if the monarch truly opposed the appointment they had the power to make that person's life unpleasant enough that they more often than not reconsidered accepting the position.

Lord Eldred Gray, followed by his peers, rose from their seats as she strode inside, each bowing low at the waist; save for one. The newest member of the council who had not bowed for the new Queen stood just beside the Rat's former seat.

She had instead settled into a deep curtsy.

The sight of a woman, now rising as the others did, was nearly enough to stop Eve dead in her tracks. Her surprise must have shown clearly on her features as Eldred greeted her with a wry smile.

"Your majesty," he began. "Please allow me to introduce our newest councilor, appointed just this morning."

Eve needed no introduction. She knew the woman quite well. Lady Sophie Hanford had long been a friend of her mother's, one of the few Riona had reached out to for support when Eve had decided to take the throne. Her lobbying had fallen on deaf ears for the most part, but she knew that Lady Hanford's house had at least attempted to help influence the council.

"Lady Hanford," Eve smiled. "How lovely to see you again."

Although Sophie was around the same age as her mother, age had more harshly lined her face than the former queen's; a fact Eve could only attribute to the severe climates of her lands, bordering the northern mountain range. It was a treacherous place to live, rife with snowstorms, many dangerous creatures, and bandits. Somehow her husband's ancestors had managed to make it home for both themselves and the small city surrounding their castle. Eve had never seen the place herself, but she had been told it nearly rivaled Stoneweald in grandeur, despite its smaller size.

"Majesty," was Sophie's cool reply, softened by a warm smile.

"Shall we get to it then?" Lord Gray prompted, signaling the council to take their seats, and for Eve to take her place on the small throne that had been brought into the room for the occasion. "There is the matter of the ball, Majesty, and your audience with the commoners; who will be allowed in later today. The guards tell me they have already gathered outside the gates in rather large numbers. Thankfully there is no unrest to report."

A snort erupted from one of the younger councilmen, seated to Eldred's right. Eve narrowed her eyes at him. "Do you disagree with something Lord Gray said, Lord Sinclair?"

Mason Sinclair bowed his head in what she might have taken for a sign of deference had he not chuckled as he did so. "Forgive my bluntness, Majesty, but are there not more important matters to discuss?" He cast a disparaging glance toward his fellow councilors, who now bore expressions ranging from irritation to mild amusement.

"Continue," Eve replied lightly. Callan shifted at her side, standing far closer than any of the other guards, who had remained several feet behind her. She could feel more than see his presence, making a special effort not to look in his direction, to reach for him. She needed the council to see her as strong, and leaning on him would only serve to undermine everything she'd worked for.

She knew Mason Sinclair by reputation only. He was young but had taken the mantle of Lord from his uncle many years before. He was known to be a bit of a playboy, and quite popular with the ladies at court. She could see why. With short brown hair and piercing green eyes, he was rather attractive. But Mason was far more than that if his rise to the council at a relatively young age was any indication. These nine seats were not easily gained.

"For starters, there is the matter of the noblewoman still housed in your dungeons. I wonder what, exactly, you plan to do with her. Has she spoken of any other conspirators? Are we to be prepared to replace yet another of our number? Is the kingdom, and her people, in danger?" He offered Eve a placid smile that didn't reach his eyes. "With respect, Majesty, certainly those concerns outweigh the planning of a ball."

Hidden within the folds of her gown, Eve balled her fists so tightly that her nails dug into her palms painfully. Of course she had planned to address those matters. Had he given her any time to speak she would have turned the conversation in that direction. His interruption had been purposefully timed to make her look frivolous, like the silly girl they all assumed her to be.

Anger surged, threatening to spill a caustic retort from her lips. She pressed her lips together tightly, inhaling slowly through her nose to keep her composure. Callan tensed beside her, but she ignored it. To glance in his direction would only give Mason more to throw at her.

"I wholeheartedly agree, Lord Sinclair." Eve offered him the cool, practiced smile she'd so often seen her mother use when dealing with the council in her father's absence. "Now, if we can continue with no further interruptions?"

She glanced from each councilor to the other, daring any of them to argue. Gone was the girl afraid of holding her own in front of them, demanding her right to choose her own life. Now she was a queen. Unafraid and unwavering. They may have held power over the monarchs before here, but now she was *the* power in this kingdom.

Wisely choosing silence, the council waited for Eve to continue. "Lord Thorne will apprise you of Emilia Danwell's current status, and then I will inform you of what is to be done with her, and the other prisoner." Finally turning to look at him, Eve schooled her features into neutrality. "Callan, if you don't mind."

Callan bowed, offering her a slight grin she hoped the others had missed. One that had her heart fluttering as he stepped forward to address the councilors. "Miss Danwell–"

"You mean Lady Danwell," a grey-haired and rather thin male interjected. Lord Alinac, Emilia's great-uncle, Eve recalled. Their family had denounced her actions immediately after they had been made public, but the loss of her title would still be a blow to his reputation.

"No, I do not," Callan countered. "Miss Danwell has been stripped of her noble title, as ordered by Her Majesty."

Lord Alinac's face turned a rather impressive shade of red, and as he opened his mouth to argue, Eldred shook his head. "No, Thurstan," the elder said firmly. "Her Majesty has done what is right and what is deserved. We cannot allow treason to stand unpunished." Nodding his head, he added, "Please continue Lord Thorne."

Unbothered, Callan proceeded to detail the conditions of Emilia's imprisonment. She had been given the most comfortable of the cells, at Eve's instruction. She had a bed, though small, and a private area hidden by curtains in which to bathe and see to her personal needs. The former Lady Danwell would be kept comfortable, and questioned only by Callan, Valerian, or Leysa. So far, she had remained silent.

"Do you know how she came to be involved? We are aware of the history of friendship between Miss Danwell and Her Majesty," Eldred inquired when Callan finished.

"To be frank, Lord Gray, we don't know. We assume she was pulled into this plot by Lord Ward," Callan's expression shuttered. Eve suspected there was more.

"Her questioning will continue," Eve stated, ready to move on from the topic. "When we are satisfied we have everything we need to know, and that she no longer poses a threat, she will be exiled."

Collective gasps and noises of disapproval sounded from the council. Only Mason Sinclair spoke up. "Is this to be the example of the crown's justice? Doing little more than burdening our neighbors with a traitor?" More than a few raised brows were turned in his direction at his impudent tone.

"Lord Sinclair, your uncle died....four years ago, yes?" Eve's tone was light as she tilted her head to examine him. The elder Lord Sinclair had never married, nor sired any known children, leaving his deceased brother's son to inherit the title upon his death.

"Yes, Majesty," Mason replied, eyeing her suspiciously.

"In that time, you've risen rather rapidly. You were appointed to the Council of Nine upon Lord Allen's death a year ago. Such a short time, especially considering most Lords serve their families for decades, if not centuries, before rising to the council. Correct me if I'm mistaken, but you are the youngest Lord to ascend to this rank in a very, very, long time."

Pausing, she glanced to the council for confirmation. A smattering of silent nods of affirmation told her she was correct.

"It seems that you and I have something in common then, yes? We have both risen to remarkable heights, and have both blazed new paths for ourselves."

"Is there a point, Majesty?" Mason interrupted, earning more shocked stares from the council.

Eve leaned back against the throne, the picture of bored superiority. "Respect, Lord Sinclair. You will respect my rule, and my own remarkable rise, and I will respect what you have earned for yourself. If you fail to do so, well, I would hate for your own remarkable efforts to be for naught." Eve's heart was pounding in her chest, and she suspected that if she raised her hands from her lap they'd be shaking. She could only hope that the council saw none of that in her face, that the mask she'd donned had stayed in place.

Mason's eyes had narrowed slightly, but like Eve, his expression gave nothing away. If he was angry or frightened by her threat, he gave no indication as he spoke. "Of course, Majesty, my apologies."

She couldn't release the sigh of relief she wanted to and forced her breathing to remain steady, unbothered. "Excellent, now if we're finished with that topic, I believe you had matters to discuss Lord Gray?"

CHAPTER 28

One by one the common folk of Darkegrove came, offering blessings to the gods they thought had abandoned them. Some cried as they reached the throne, reaching forward and offering her tear-filled well wishes, though none were allowed close enough to touch her.

Despite what some had felt about her rise to the throne, many seemed pleased to have a reigning Queen. The majority of those were women, though a good number of men offered kind, or at the least respectful, words as well.

The council meeting had proceeded smoothly after the brief incident with Lord Sinclair. It had taken every bit of her steel to get through that without snapping at him and playing right into his hands. As infuriating as it was, she could show little of what she really felt in that room, even though a king would have been expected to show his fury had he been disrespected in the same manner. Her father had gotten into many shouting matches with the council over the years, and none had dared to call him emotional as they would if she had behaved the same way.

Valerian and Leysa arrived as they reached the throne room, and though there had been little time to speak to them, they had promised to remain in the throne room as extra protection, just in case. Even though the guard they had questioned about the attacks on Eve had insisted there were no others involved that he knew of, her guardians would never take the chance of her being harmed or taken again. Until they were certain of her safety, they would remain close by.

"Bless you, Majesty, and thank you," a young woman curtsied deeply in front of Eve. "My sister found her freedom, thanks to your courage." Rising to her feet, she wiped her eyes with a handkerchief. "When you declared your intent to rule alone, she told my father she wouldn't marry our neighbor's son. His family's mine is successful, and it would've been a good match if he weren't a mean drunk. She told my father, 'If it's okay for our queen to say no to marriage, it's okay for me too,' and you know what, Majesty, he agreed." She sniffled once more and bobbed into a curtsy. "Anyway, thank you, Majesty, for being so brave."

Stunned into silence, Eve could do little more than smile as the woman moved away and the next person stepped forward. As an elderly woman took the young woman's place at the foot of the dais and began to mumble well wishes, Callan leaned across the arm of her throne to whisper in her ear. "You are magnificent."

Heat spread across Eve's cheeks even as she forced herself to keep her gaze on the man who now stepped forward, taking the old woman's place. He was a ruddy man, a farmer by the looks of it, and unlike others who came with blessings or out of curiosity, he looked angry.

"You'd serve your kingdom better spreading your legs for a righteous man and bearing his heirs," he said without preamble. Hatred gleamed in his dark eyes. Her chest tightened, and she couldn't draw breath as her heart raced in her chest. It was another set of hate-filled charcoal eyes staring back at her, and she was being dragged under the water again. "Whore," he spat at her feet.

Callan's furious growl reverberated through the room as he stepped down from the dais. What few shadows the expansive room held deepened and pulsated. "If you dare so much as blink too hard in her direction I will–"

A sudden rumble began to shake the very foundation of the castle as Eve rose from her seat, cutting Callan's threat short. The potted trees lining the throne room began to quake, roots breaking free of the ceramic that confined them, sprawling out onto polished marble. Each click of her heels against a stone stair was mirrored by the quaking of the ground.

Hatred shifted to terror in his eyes, and the man retreated a step. Some began to flee, running past stunned guards. Others remained, fixated on what was transpiring before them. Power flared in Eve's emerald eyes, lips twisting into a terrifying smile.

"Say, that, again," she demanded in a voice not entirely her own. Callan moved to her side, watching closely but not interfering. Those who had remained now edged toward the back of the room, some fleeing entirely. Only Leysa and Valerian stepped closer, instead of moving away.

Callan held up a hand, halting their advance, and murmured gently, "Remember yourself, dove."

His gentle command calmed the worst of her rage, stopping her advance. The ground calmed as she stilled. "Say that again," she repeated.

The man gulped, shaking his head slightly. "I....I apologize... Majesty..." He blanched as the roots moved toward him slowly. "Please, Majesty, I beg you. I-I'm sorry."

Eve considered it, taking his life now. Something in her veins sang, giving her a sense of purpose and strength she'd never felt before. The magic, she realized, but more than that as well.

Her mother had died trying to get Eve to where she rightfully belonged. Riona had been taken from her, she herself had nearly been taken, had nearly been drowned. All for this.

The weeping woman's words echoed in her mind. All of this had happened so she could lay a new path for the women of Darkegrove. The fact that she was the first key to turn an ancient lock mattered as well, but it came second in her mind to the precedent she was setting in her own kingdom.

She could do it, end him right here. There was a dagger hidden within the folds of her gown. Even now she could feel the cool kiss of the bone hilt against her thigh. The depths of her magic hadn't yet been explored, but she knew she could use that too. His life could be snuffed out in an instant and all would learn to respect her, out of love or fear, it didn't matter.

Something within her recoiled at the thought of taking another life. Her mind flashed back to the alleyway and the feeling of another person's blood spraying against her skin, the horror of it still fresh in her mind. He had deserved it, that man. He would have taken her life and likely would have made her suffer too.

She had done what she needed to do to survive in that alleyway, but now? To take the life of this man now would be little more than retribution. It would serve no greater purpose and frankly wouldn't make her feel any better. He wasn't Devlan, despite the same hatred and cowardice she saw mirrored in this man's eyes. He hadn't harmed her, not really. Could she kill another person for simply hurling insults?

It would be mercy then.

Callan was tense at her side, cold, seething rage emanating from him. She doubted the commoners or guards present had noticed the shift in the shadows of the room. They were too transfixed by what was transpiring now to notice something so subtle. Leysa and Valerian would have seen, would know as well as she did what it meant that the shadows seemed to vibrate, to struggle against a leash. Callan was maintaining control of his power, but barely. She needed to end this now before his control slipped.

"You will leave," she commanded, barely recognizing her own cold voice. "Do not step foot on the grounds of this castle or cross my path again. I will not be so merciful next time."

Without another uttered word, the man fled. "Leave us," she said, more gently this time, addressing the rest of those still gathered.

"That's going to be a problem," Valerian remarked as he and Leysa joined them when the last of the petitioners and guards had exited the room.

Too much had been revealed, and she had too little understanding of her new power and how to wield or control it. Turning to meet Callan's gaze, she didn't smile. "I need you to teach me to use my magic."

CHAPTER 29

"It's pointless," Eve huffed. It had been nearly a week since her coronation, and she had only managed to lift a few pebbles from the ground and make small branches grow just a bit longer if she concentrated. In a clearing far enough from the castle to be hidden from view, Callan tried to teach her how to control the magic that now flowed through her veins.

The guards hadn't objected to them leading the queen so far from view. Even though they didn't know the truth about what Callan and his friends were, some instinctual part of them seemed to see the trio was dangerous and more than capable of protecting her, and a small part of her wondered if some of them had allowed it in hopes that something awful would happen and they'd be rid of her.

No matter how hard she'd tried, she hadn't been able to recreate the quaking she'd unconsciously caused before. Callan suggested that though anger had been the trigger before, any deep emotion could cause her magic to break free of her control if she weren't careful, as his had nearly done that day in the throne room.

"You just have to practice. Magic is like a muscle, you have to work to strengthen it. You'll get there." He had been patient, unflappable. Even when she got frustrated and snapped at him, he simply shrugged it off and told her to keep going or offered some advice that usually just pissed her off more. Eve knew it wasn't fair to be annoyed with him, to take her frustrations out on him, but he was the easiest target and the one she knew could handle it.

"It took me ages to stop shifting every time I got angry, or sad," Leysa chirped from her seat on a boulder at the edge of the clearing. "It got easier over time."

"Sometimes she'd even shift if she was really hor–" Valerian's lewd remark was cut off with a grunt. "Ouch."

Callan tossed the pair a glance and shook his head. "Really?" He huffed a laugh and turned back to Eve. "You've been doing the same thing over and over," he said, referring to her need for silence so that she could concentrate, fixing all of her attention on whatever she was trying to move. "Repetition is good, but try something else to help you focus if it's getting stale."

The little bit of sunlight that managed to break through the canopy warmed Eve's face as she turned her gaze skyward. Her hands were freezing, despite the gloves she wore, and woolen socks beneath her boots were doing little to keep her toes from going numb.

The few birds that remained this far north late in the year chirped merrily above her, and she let her thoughts turn to them with some envy. If she could fly away whenever she wished, would she? She had nearly fled once, before her father had died, only making it as far as a village a half day's ride south of Forest Haven.

She had wanted this crown, her birthright, for so long, but when her father had begun to make remarks about choosing a husband soon so that he could be prepared to take the throne, she panicked. Eve had known even then that she had no desire to marry, to be stuck under the proverbial thumb of a husband she wouldn't even be allowed to choose for herself.

Fleeing had seemed like the only option then, even if it meant never seeing her family or her home again. Given everything that had happened, she wondered if maybe she should have kept going. She could have kept riding south until she reached Coruscis. Their neighboring kingdoms could harbor a runaway princess without offending her father, and it was unlikely that either of them would risk it. So she would've purchased passage on a ship heading to the southern continent, or perhaps to the old kingdoms to the east, where it was said dragons still roamed the skies. A sigh passed her lips at the thought of it.

It was folly, this daydream of hers. She would never have been able to abandon her family and everything she'd ever known. Even if she had, her parents never would have stopped looking for her. She would have been on the run for the rest of her life.

Eve was still staring skyward when she realized something had changed in the air. The forest had gone still and silent, as it did only when a predator was present. Her gaze shot to Callan, already stalking toward her, Leysa and Valerian close on his heels. He held a single finger to his lips as the three of them formed a circle around her, facing outward as their practiced eyes scanned the treeline.

Surely nobody would be foolish enough to attack her here, with her personal guards so close. One of the lower faerie creatures? Stoneweald's patrols generally kept them far from the castle and the main roads that travelers and merchants used, but occasionally one or two would slip through unnoticed. Her heart raced as the possibilities of what could be lurking unseen around them flashed through her mind.

They stood there in their small defensive formation for what was likely only a few moments, but felt like a small eternity for Eve. She couldn't understand why they weren't moving, why they weren't making for the safety of the castle. Before she could voice the question, a horrifying sound shattered the silence that had befallen the forest.

Only one creature could be responsible for such a sound, and it was the one creature they could not fight, not with only the four of them and with Eve unarmed and unable to control her magic. They needed to run. She was a liability and would get them killed if they didn't make it back to the castle before the cusith could bark for the third time.

"Go!" Callan's voice was steel as he gripped Eve's hand and began to move.

They had to be fast, so fast. There was no telling for certain how close the enormous dog-like creature was to them, or if it had picked up their scents yet. She could only pray to the gods that it hadn't.

To her side, Leysa wordlessly tugged the bow and quiver she'd worn at her back free and passed them to her husband. Eve dragged her gaze from the pair as they shared a silent moment. Nothing was spoken aloud, but she could feel the love between them, as tangible as the fear that drove them forward. In a flash, Leysa shifted, soaring high in her hawk form.

"She'll try to spot it," Callan explained, still nearly dragging Eve through the underbrush. They couldn't run, not with the roots that grew gnarled and raised from the ground, and the smattering of boulders dotting the forest floor. Falling would slow them down even more, and any delay could cost them their lives.

"Your shadows?" she asked breathlessly. Maybe if they could stay out of its view, that would be enough. The great hounds had a wicked sense of smell and would likely still be able to track their path, but perhaps it could buy them some time.

It was Valerian who answered, "No, we have to be able to see where we're going. Won't slow it down enough to matter anyway, and Leysa needs to be able to see so she can tell us where it is."

As if on cue Leysa cried out twice. Two quick, shrill calls. At once, Callan and Valerian turned right. "What?" Eve asked, stumbling over a root. Callan's firm grip on her hand kept her upright and urged her onward.

"Two for right, one for left," Valerian explained.

Callan paused, turning to help Eve over a fallen log. A small faerie with glistening brown scales and wings that reminded her of a dragonfly squealed angrily as they stomped on what was apparently her home, and Eve muttered a quiet apology.

"She's telling us which way to go," Callan said. "Which means she can see it. It's close."

A second, ear-rattling bark sounded through the forest. Thanking every one of the gods that she'd chosen to wear leggings instead of a gown, Eve ran faster, harder.

It wasn't fast enough. She was slowing them down. Without her, they could have been most of the way back to the castle by now. "Callan," she began, only to be cut off by a sharp look from him.

"Don't even think about it." His tone was firm, leaving no room for argument.

Valerian nodded his agreement as he pulled the bow and an arrow free, notching it as he ran. "We're not leaving you."

Three shrill cries sounded above, and to their right, Eve could swear she saw a moss-covered boulder moving. But boulders didn't move, and they certainly didn't growl.

"Shit." Callan tugged his hand free and stopped. "Valerian take her," he began, as a series of sharp cries echoed above. Leysa was calling out a warning they didn't need. The cusith was close, very close, and they couldn't outrun it any longer. It had yet to bark for the third time, which meant it wasn't going in for the kill... yet. There was nowhere to hide, no more time to run, not for all of them.

"No! I'm not leaving you here, Callan," Eve protested, halting alongside him.

"Cal," Valerian began cautiously. "You can't take it alone."

Callan dragged a hand through his hair. She could see the truth of Valerian's words in his expression, the realization that they were well and truly fucked painted perfectly on his features.

"Stay close to her, you hear me?" He fixed Valerian with an intense stare, before turning to Eve. "If I say go, you don't look back and you don't stop running."

Leysa landed on the forest floor, shifting into a large mountain cat with a flash. Moving to Eve's other side, she snarled in warning.

The sound of underbrush and fallen limbs cracking announced the beast's arrival. It was massive, at least the size of the shaggy cows kept by the farmers nearby. What Eve had mistaken for moss before was actually shaggy fur, grey and green, giving it the appearance of moss on a rock or an old tree.

A low growl emanated from its throat, rumbling the small pebbles at her feet. True terror constricted her throat, a scream threatening to escape. Every instinct within her told her to run, run as fast as she could and get far, far, away from this monster, but she forced herself to hold her ground.

Callan, Valerian, and Leysa stood between her and certain death. Valerian aimed his bow, preparing to fire on Callan's command. Leysa lowered her head and snarled, clawed paws digging into the ground.

Callan had pulled his sword free, holding it in front of him with one hand, as the hand at his side gathered shadows. Slithering and twisting around his outstretched fingers, pure darkness took form. He'd said that it would be useless to hide from the cusith, but perhaps he had something else in mind.

Bright yellow eyes moved one by one over each of them before settling on Callan. A strange sort of intelligence shone behind the beast's eyes. He was sizing up his enemy, she realized, deciding which of them posed the biggest threat. Shadows now clung to Callan's arm fully, and within seconds they wreathed him completely.

Silence hung precariously in the forest. Every animal or faerie that could be prey to the enormous hound had either fled or taken cover. Even the three fae seemed to be holding their breath, waiting.

"I'm sorry we didn't have more time," he said suddenly piercing the silence, voice filled with regret. Before she could process what he was doing, before she could cry out for him to stop, Callan flung his shadow-clad arm toward her. Darkness enveloped her as thoroughly as it had the night her mother had been murdered.

"No!" She screamed, throwing her hands toward him instinctively. She couldn't see, couldn't find him. "Callan!" She screamed, raging against the darkness he'd enshrouded her in to protect her while he sacrificed himself. Fury and terror overwhelmed her, dragging her down into the depths she'd felt only once before. Beneath her feet, the earth began to answer her desperate, unspoken, call.

The great hound's growl rumbled through the darkness to her. Alongside it, the sound of Valerian shouting, a battle cry to draw the beast's attention. Desperation clung to her like a damp blanket. She had to help them, she had to save them. He had shrouded her so that they could distract the monster, and knowing that he couldn't fight it alone, his best friends had remained behind, putting themselves in harm's way.

Something outside her cocoon of darkness rumbled. A harsh, deep sound of something primal awakening. The sound of the mountains when the miners dug too deep, and the very walls caved in around them.

As suddenly as Callan's shadows had appeared, they vanished. She blinked away the last dredges of darkness, and what she beheld fractured something within her chest. Callan was leaning against a boulder, shredded skin and blood exposed through the side of his ripped tunic. He must have been bitten and then thrown.

Leysa was snarling, clawing at the beast's side, blood-soaked paws barely breaking through the thick coat. Valerian was still shouting, raging at the beast as he fired arrow after arrow into its mossy coat. Greenish-black blood oozed from the wounds the three of them had made, vicious gashes and punctures with arrows still protruding from them, but still, the beast gnashed its teeth and snarled, advancing on Callan.

The world stood still as the beast reared its head back, and from its throat, the third and final bark sounded. The predator had claimed his prey.

It wasn't until the ground beneath her feet began to shake that she realized the rumbling she'd heard hadn't been coming from the cusith but from her–from her magic, calling the rocks and roots from beneath them. *Focus*, she thought, *focus and feeling*. A rock the size of her fist flew first, smacking against the hound's skull dully. He barely flinched, ignoring the mild attack as he had the arrows still flying from Valerian's bow.

Ancient roots sprang free from the ground, answering Eve's silent, panicked pleading. Let him be alive, please, she repeated over and over as she watched in horror as the hound grew closer to him. Why it was so focused on Callan and not the ones actually fighting back, she didn't know, and at that moment didn't care. Every thought was focused on Callan and saving him. Another, larger stone tugged itself free of the forest floor and hurtled toward the cusith's head, making contact just below its glowing eye.

More and more roots sprang free. The roots twisted and turned, winding their way around the hound's back legs. A snarl of irritation rose from its maw, but the creature tugged its paws free with little effort. Panic rose like bile in the back of her throat. She was screaming now, wordless anguish pouring forth from her lips.

Without thought, she started toward Callan flinging stone after stone toward the beast with a flick of her outstretched hand. She didn't know how she was doing it, she just *was*. Her magic was a limb, as palpable as her arm or leg, and she used it on instinct.

Callan screamed for her to run as he limped toward her, but she ignored him. Her gaze remained locked on the monstrous hound that stood between them as she moved closer. She was so close now she could smell the damp earthen scent of the cusith. Moldering leaves, loamy earth, and putrid decay hit her like a wall as she stopped mere feet away from him.

"You will not take him," she growled at the monstrous beast, earning a snarl in return. Her torrent of rocks and stone paused only to be replaced by a steady rumble as a shear wall of rock erupted from the ground between Callan and the cusith, effectively shielding him.

Blocked from its target, the beast turned its hyperintelligent eyes on Eve. The small voice inside of her screamed for her to run, but she shoved it back down. To run now would be certain death. She'd made her choice, and though she'd done it without thinking, she would stand by it. Now she had to follow through and hope that it didn't cost her all of their lives.

Another arrow flew then, finding its home just below the beast's shoulder. The cusith howled, finally noting the archer standing behind Eve. Using the distraction to her advantage, Eve called on her power once more, lifting a sizeable boulder from the forest floor and hurling directly at the creature's face. It howled again, this time in pain, and with a final snarl from its now bloodied maw, it turned and ran for the darkness of the forest.

"We have to go now," Valerian was shouting as he ran for her. "It won't retreat for long."

She exhaled heavily, every bit of adrenaline that had been keeping her going draining from her as she turned to Callan. The stone wall that she'd erected to save him simply sank back into the earth as if it had never existed, and the roots she'd called forth retreated into the forest floor. Leysa shifted in an instant, moving alongside Eve as the three of them rushed to Callan's side where he had fallen to his knees on the damp forest floor.

"Callan," she sobbed, dropping to the ground beside him. Shaky fingers ran across his brow before moving to the wound at his shoulder. It was deep, but the bleeding had slowed, thanks to his fae healing. Relief washed over her so intensely that her entire body trembled.

"Are you both alright?" Valerian was already lifting Callan over his shoulder, a warrior carrying a wounded companion from a battlefield.

"We're good," he confirmed, gritting his teeth against the effort of raising Callan. He was exhausted, they all were.

Leysa murmured her agreement, falling into step beside Valerian.

"I told you to run," Callan grumbled through gritted teeth.

Eve snorted. "And you know damn well I don't follow orders from men."

CHAPTER 30

It had been three days since the attack in the woods, and the best hunters Eve could hire had failed to locate the cusith. A blessing, the elders announced, that it had seemingly fled the area. Cusith were deadly, once the beasts set their sights on their prey, there was little that could be done to deter them. Callan could count himself as one of the very few who had survived an encounter, and with surprisingly minor injuries. Both healers marveled that the vicious wound at his shoulder hadn't killed him, exchanging glances and noting how lucky he had been for a second time now, surviving injuries most wouldn't.

They would have to be more careful from now on or they risked gossip spreading about him. It was bad enough the entire kingdom had heard about what occurred in the throne room. After that, there had been no denying the earthquakes had been directly connected to Eve, and gossip and speculation had spread like wildfire. She could hardly walk through the castle without wide-eyed stares and more than a few looks of fear cast in her direction as passersby gave her a wide berth.

Eve had pulled Callan aside, desperate for a break from the stares and whispers, not far from where they'd spoken in the darkened garden soon after he'd arrived. She had been so annoyed by his presence then, felt so stifled by her mother's insistence that she required extra guards.

Now, she only wished that Riona had taken on the extra precaution for herself as well, and she couldn't imagine a life without Callan in it. They'd known each other such a short time. She was terrified of acknowledging the effect his presence had on her–the way her heart sang at his touch, and the word that rang through her mind when he took her to bed.

"What if it's still around?" Eve asked hesitantly, casting her gaze toward the doors to the garden. She had been assured even if that were the case, a cusith couldn't scale the wall, but she wasn't entirely sure she wanted to take the risk, something she'd voiced to Callan no less than three times. It wasn't fear for herself, but fear that she would be forced to use magic again, making her even more of a spectacle than she already was.

"If it were nearby, they would have found it," Callan sighed, for at least the third time. "And I'll have you to protect me, my queen." His crooked grin made her heart flip as much as it made her want to toss something at him. Luckily for him, the hallway had little to offer in the way of projectiles.

"That's My Most Resplendent Queen to you." Her teasing retort fell short of the tone of flip arrogance that she aimed for, the worry she felt seeping into her words.

Callan simply looked her over for a moment, some emotion she couldn't name swimming in his ocean eyes.

"What are you thinking? Planning your next lecture about control?" she asked, only half kidding this time. What she'd managed to do in the forest that day had been a fluke. Or maybe her magic was just so tied to her emotions she simply couldn't use it unless she was in danger, angry, or frightened. Callan had claimed this shouldn't be the case, but she'd still failed to tap into that well again, in any meaningful way at least. The best she'd managed since then was to rejuvenate a few potted roses in the greenhouse beginning to look a little droopy.

Callan's laugh was rough, and he dragged a hand through his dark hair. "No, I was thinking that the ball is tomorrow night, and I'm dying to see you in that dress."

Her heart gave another stupid thump at the desire in his eyes, and her core tightened in response. "Lord Thorne, what an impertinent thing to say to your queen," she said as she moved closer. The scent of cedar and sage hit her, stoking the flame that burned low in her belly for him.

"Mm, why don't you step outside with me and I'll show you just how impertinent I can be." His voice and the promise hidden beneath his words had her toes curling inside her shoes.

"What if someone sees?" She glanced down the corridor in both directions. They were utterly alone. There were guard towers outside with a full view of most of the garden, but there were one or two places inside the walled space that couldn't be seen, not very well anyway.

Callan's grin only widened, eyes swimming with mischief. "I'm willing to take that chance if you are."

If she took the time to think, to worry about the possibilities, Eve knew she'd say no and ask him to take her upstairs to her room instead, but the idea of being outside, with his hands on her, where anyone could find them, was equal parts nerve-wracking and exciting. "Okay," she found herself saying, heading for the door he'd opened already before she could talk herself out of it.

The sharp chill of the air that kissed the bare parts of her skin announced winter's impending arrival boldly. He took her hand in his and led her down the winding pathways to one of the darkest corners of the garden, where detection was least likely. Her breath came quickly, bursting from her lips like tiny clouds in the cold air and barely visible thanks to the dim light cast from braziers lining the walkway. The flames were few and far between, and not large enough to offer any meaningful warmth against the cold night.

Part of her began to wonder what their purpose was when the garden was so seldom used this time of year, but the thought was cut short as Callan spun her to face him before guiding her backward until her back met the stone wall, cushioned with overgrown ivy.

"Impertinent," he murmured as he dipped his head low. His warm breath against the column of her neck sent little bursts of lightning down her spine. "Is that what you called me?"

"Mm, I believe that was it," she said, breath hitching.

He chuckled darkly at that, dropping lower to take the bottom of her pale green skirt in his hand. Kneeling before her, he offered her a grin that drove her mad and said, "My Most Resplendent, Magnificent, Queen, please allow me to offer you a small token of my devotion." His eyes had darkened with desire, and for a moment she swore she could see every dirty thought he had running through his mind.

Dampness pooled between her legs and her breasts felt heavy, tips peaking. Her heart thudded against her rib cage so rapidly she thought it might burst free from her chest. "I am nothing if not a benevolent ruler," she breathed, lacking every bit of the superiority she tried to muster. "Bestow your gift on your queen, Lord Thorne."

He claimed her there in the garden against the cold, ivy-covered stone wall. First, with his mouth, the first glorious climax found her swiftly as she bit her lip to keep quiet. She had barely recovered before he was standing again, dragging her skirt up swiftly. His fingers skated along her thighs slowly, blazing a trail that ended at her hips as he lifted her legs around his waist.

Pinned between the wall and Callan, Eve gripped the tangled vines tightly in one fist, the back of his neck with the other as he entered her, They moved together, each of her breathless sighs of pleasure captured by his mouth, a passionate kiss to keep them from being detected.

In her room, he had been patient and careful with her. Had savored her like she was his favorite delicacy. This time was different, no less intense or satisfying, but harder, more desperate somehow. As if he needed the contact, the connection between them. She'd needed it too, but for reasons she suspected were very different from his. She wondered where his mind had gone, now that he was seated on the bench across from her, staring at the night sky as if it were whispering some long-lost secret to him.

"What's wrong?" She wasn't entirely sure she wanted to know the answer, but the question left her mouth before her brain had time to stop it. She'd known something was on his mind for the last few days, even as he trained her in the woods. He'd been mostly the same as always and had answered her questions regarding the fae surprisingly easily, compared to before at least. But something was off, she could feel it.

"There's more to the story that I haven't told you."

She didn't need to ask which story he was referring to. It had to be the only one that mattered, to her at least. His weary tone, the way he tensed as he spoke and refused to look at her now told her she didn't want to hear whatever he was thinking. Not now, in the afterglow of what they'd just shared. Not while her heart was swelling and that word she'd been avoiding raced across her heart and mind every time she looked at him. She was so close to voicing it, to telling him how she felt, but fear kept her quiet.

"I don't want to know," she said firmly, wrapping her arms around herself.

Finally, he turned to look at her, brow furrowed. "You have to."

"No, I don't. Not tonight anyway."

"Eve, you don't understand, it's important. I have to tell you the whole story. I've kept it from you for far too long as it is, and you've been asking. There are things that would change how you look at—"

"It can wait. Give me one day of peace, Callan." She shook her head as he opened his mouth to argue again. "Just one day, please."

The muscle of his jaw ticked and for a moment she held her breath, ready for him to press on, ignoring her request for one more day of peace. The knowledge that some long-held secret was about to change things, well that alone was enough to taint what had been shaping up to be a near-perfect night for her.

"After the ball," he conceded finally.

CHAPTER 31

There was one thing the nobility of Darkegrove loved more than good gossip, and that was a party at which to spread gossip; especially one thrown by the crown. The best wine and exotic foods were imported from not only their southern neighbors but a few rare delicacies from the continents far to the east.

Night had fallen fully by the time musicians had started playing, signaling the official beginning of the soiree. Each noble guest was announced upon arrival, many followed by a tittering of whispered stories amongst their friends and neighbors already gathered in the expansive ballroom of Stoneweald.

Engagements, business deals, disputes, and even supposedly secret liaisons were murmured about, though none more titillating than those regarding the new queen, what strange powers she might possess, and the mysterious Lord Thorne, serving as her escort tonight. Their reaction had been expected. Whispers began nearly every time Eve entered a room such as this, since the first time she'd been allowed to attend an event. The gossip and curious stares had never fazed her, never given her more than a moment of irritation in the past. Now, it grated her nerves.

The music halted as they were announced. Holding her head high, with every bit of grace that she had been trained to move with since she took her first steps, Eve entered the ballroom.

Only the sound of her heels against marble and the swishing of her charcoal gown met her ears. Too many sets of eyes for her to count watched her from heads lowered in deference.

Callan followed closely behind her, Leysa and Valerian at his side. Thanks to endless meetings with the steward, various merchants, nobles, and mine owners, she'd barely had time to speak to him since their encounter in the garden. It seemed everyone with money or any degree of power wanted to feel out the new monarch and decide how having a reigning queen might impede, or benefit, their businesses and standing. Not that she'd had any idea what she'd say to him anyway.

A lift of her hand signaled the crowd to rise. The music resumed immediately, picking up an upbeat tempo, designed for dancing, as did the whispering. The sheer number of staring faces and whispered voices were more than she'd been accustomed to in the past, perhaps because before her declaration to the council, there had never been much of anything for them to gossip about, not that was true anyway.

Sure they'd spoken about her entanglement with Brodie, but that sort of thing was expected for a girl of her age. Now that she was queen, and unmarried, each and every one of them looked to Callan and wondered if they were looking at their new king. Their relationship remained undefined. The fact she had some unknown and unexplainable power added even more fuel to the fire.

Eve turned to face the male in question, her pulse skittering. In his customary black, his suit had been perfectly tailored to his form. Standing casually with both hands in his pocket, he exuded confidence and a deadly aura that no others in the room could match. Intense blue eyes remained locked on Eve, swimming with some emotion she couldn't identify. Leysa snorted beside Callan, drawing Eve's gaze from him abruptly.

"It's freezing out, and they have the doors opened?" She asked, tilting her head in the direction of the terrace.

"It's tradition," Eve explained, following her gaze to the long row of open doors. "We like to welcome our forest spirits into every celebration, whether it's warm out or not. It's supposed to bring prosperity."

Leysa's expression told Eve clearly enough how silly she found that, but before she could say it aloud, Valerian extended his hand. "Care to dance, my beautiful wife?"

"Do you even have to ask?" she replied, placing her hand in his and tossing Eve a grin as he led her away. Dressed in shimmering cobalt that graced her like a second skin, Leysa could easily have fit right in with the trio of goddesses Eve had met.

"Dance with me." Callan's gruff tone drew her attention right back to him. It hadn't been a question, she noted, scanning his face for any indication of what he was thinking.

Was he going to bring up whatever secret he'd started to divulge in the garden? She couldn't bear to hear another secret, not yet. Whatever this other part of their secret was, it had to be big if he had held onto it rather than share it when he had told her the truth about who, and what, he was.

Eve had no idea what could be bigger than the fact that he was fae, Leysa was a shifter, and she was somehow the first key to the fae returning to their realm, but she knew that for this one night, she didn't want to worry about any of this.

"You promised. One more day, Callan."

"I know," he said, extending a hand toward her. "Just a dance, dove, no secrets."

Eve nodded, placing her shaking hand in his. "Just a dance."

One dance turned into two and by the time the third dance began, Eve had forgotten her nerves entirely. Callan had kept his promise to keep his secret to himself, and as they twirled around the floor, spinning and holding one another close, people openly gaped, not bothering to hide their curious looks or sneers.

"They're staring," she said somewhat breathlessly as they moved across the dance floor. He simply shrugged in response, unbothered. "Some of them will think you're the real ruler," she continued, "making the decisions behind the scenes."

"Then they're fools."

"Maybe, but it could be dangerous for me if that rumor gains traction." It was a concern she hadn't allowed herself to think about, but one she was going to have to face as they grew closer. Whether they married or not, until she did something to prove she was in control of her own decisions and her own throne, people would always think he was the real power.

How she would do that, she didn't know.

Eve collided with Callan as he came to a stop on the dance floor, gripping her chin lightly with his fingertips and turning her face toward his own. "Nothing will ever harm you. Not ever. Not while I am here; and I intend to be here, with you, for as long as you'll have me."

Dancers continued twirling and moving around them, each pair gawking at them as they did. His words settled over her, deafening and blinding her to anything but the weight of them, of the intensity of his gaze, to the way her heart sang at his words. He had made similar promises already, but none had made her feel the way she felt this time. She hadn't loved him then.

"I need air," she said finally, turning on her heel and pushing her way through startled dancers. The word had been flitting across her mind for a while now, hadn't it? So why was she so surprised? Realization struck her as she reached the terrace railing. If he felt the same way, it was real and if it were real, she could be hurt by it.

Someone could take him from her like they had taken her mother. Her chest constricted, and she gripped the railing like a lifeline. Not again. She couldn't face that again. The scent of cedar and sage announced his presence before he had a chance to speak.

"I just need a minute," she said lamely. "It's hot in there."

"Don't run away from me, Eve."

"You're the one who's been telling me this is a bad idea from the start," she retorted.

His hand was at her elbow then, tugging her away from the railing and turning her to face him. "That's why I wanted to talk to you. Why I have to tell you the rest of the story."

He released her arm and looked toward the darkened forest. Eve followed his gaze, her mind drifting to the cusith and whatever else might be lurking out there.

"You promised me a day."

"I know," he sighed. "I can still give it to you, but please don't run from me. Hear me out and then if what I tell you changes how you feel, then fine. But don't run because you're frightened of how you feel."

"And what is it that you think I feel, Callan?" she demanded, turning to face him.

"I think you feel for me exactly what I feel for you. What I've felt for you since the moment I first laid eyes on you, even when you didn't know who I was. I think," he said, stepping closer to her, "that you love me and it scares you."

Eve pressed her lips together tightly, keeping the words that threatened to spill forth unspoken. She should deny it, tell him this was nothing more than a bit of fun between them, but she couldn't bring herself to do it. She had never been very good at hiding how she felt anyway. When she was a girl, anytime she had done something wrong, Riona had known right away. The guilt had always been clearly written on her face, to anyone who knew her well at least.

"I know you're afraid," he said, looking toward the ballroom. They'd remained undisturbed on the terrace so far and had kept their voices low enough to avoid being overheard over the music and conversation inside. "Just give me until tomorrow, until I explain everything, to make a choice."

Eve considered asking him to tell her now. She was beginning to feel like not knowing was worse than whatever this secret he had to share but before she could stop him, he walked into the ballroom and rejoined the crowd, stopping only to send a pair of guards to watch over her on the balcony.

He left her standing there alone, wondering what the fuck just happened as the cold evening air kissed her shoulders, left bare in the strapless gown he'd been so excited to see her in. She followed him with her eyes until he disappeared into the crowd, and her heart gave a squeeze. *What am I going to do?*

Her gaze landed on Leysa and Valerian just through the doors, huddled close together. Valerian was telling Leysa something that had her laughing so hard her shoulders shook. They made such a perfect pair. Happiness and pure abiding love were an aura around them both anytime they were together. It was honestly amazing to see. Her parents had loved one another, she knew, but in a quieter, more content sort of way. Nothing compared to the intensity she saw between her two fae friends.

"It's rather cold out here."

The masculine voice caught Eve off guard, startling her enough that she yelped. A most un-queenlike reaction, she silently scolded herself.

"I apologize, your Majesty," the stranger replied smoothly, holding a hand up in a penitent gesture. He was tall, nearly matching Callan in height. But where Callan was darkness, this man was all light. Short, blond hair and fair skin, with pale grey eyes the color of smoke. "That was quite rude of me."

The mask she donned for the public slid into place easily, as she offered the man a faint smile. "I should have been paying more attention." Her gaze slid to the guards first, ensuring they remained close, and then to the ballroom before she took a step toward the closest door. He was several feet away from her, but given how many close calls there had been, she couldn't take any chances.

"I don't believe we've been introduced," she began, taking a small step toward the ballroom. Having guards close by was good, but having Callan, Leysa, or Valerian would be better.

"Ah, my manners fail me again," he chuckled. "Lord Cathal Vaderyn, Majesty." Offering her a serpentine smile he mirrored her step, keeping his distance, but not allowing her to retreat entirely. "Forgive my impudence, Majesty, but there is a matter I would very much like to discuss with you."

Eve narrowed her eyes at him slightly. His name was unfamiliar, and she knew the names of all of the important families in the north. "You're not from Darkegrove, I take it?"

"Not exactly," he replied with a smile that made her skin crawl. "I can see you're uncomfortable, but I assure you, you want to hear what I have to say."

Irritation at his boldness flared within her, overshadowing the fear that had been driving her inside. "Oh?"

"Mm," he confirmed. "How familiar are you with your kingdom's history with the fae?"

Eve frowned. Why was he asking about that? Did he know, or at least suspect, what Callan was? What about Leysa and Valerian?

Callan had been injured, and by someone who knew how to hurt him. Was he somehow part of it? The possibilities raced through her mind, and true anger flared to life inside her chest. If he had been responsible for the attack on Callan, she would make sure he paid for it dearly.

"Oh, I wouldn't go down that route," he remarked. "I can see that you think you need to protect your...friends," he said, gesturing vaguely. "But I assure you, Majesty, that would not end well for you. Besides, I mean you no harm. I simply wish to have a conversation. "

The trees nearest the balcony began to groan, limbs and roots twisting in response to the magic that yawned to life within her. Despite his claim that he simply wanted a conversation, he'd made a clear threat.

"To me," she said loudly, summoning the guards who moved to her side, ready to protect their queen should the need arise. "I'm certain I have no interest in anything you have to say." She kept her steady gaze on Lord Vaderyn, hoping he wouldn't notice the ivy slowly climbing down the stone pillar to his side. Let him believe the rumbling of the forest was the real threat.

Undeterred by her frigid tone, or by her magic, he continued. "Has he told you who he really is?"

"I'm aware," she replied, jutting her chin upward as she stared down her nose at him.

"Of the whole story?" he taunted, smirking.

"I know enough." *Do I?*

"Then you know the truth about the...unfortunate situation that occurred. How the male in question, the one to blame for all of it in the first place, is your beloved."

His words hit her like a stone dropped in a pond. Thinking back to their conversation and the history she thought she knew. The story of the old queen and the fae male she'd fallen for, the hateful king who had been responsible played through her mind.

"That isn't possible."

"Ask him who he really is," Cathal interjected.

He hadn't noticed the slowly moving ivy, not until it curled around his wrist, ready to restrain him if he made a move toward her. She expected him to be shocked, maybe not by her use of magic, but perhaps by the fact that she'd successfully held him back. Instead, he simply chuckled. With a snap of his fingers, flames erupted along the ivy bonds, burning them to little more than ash in the blink of an eye. The sound of steel scraping against scabbards sounded as the guards pulled their swords free, moving to stand in front of Eve.

Cathal breathed a disappointed sigh. "I warned you that would be unwise." He made no move toward her, simply eyeing her guards with boredom. He had no reason to fear them, she knew.

"You've said what you had to say. Leave." Her tone was calm, belying the pounding of her heart she knew he could likely hear. Where was Callan?

"Of course. I would hate to cause you any undue stress, Majesty." Still ignoring the guards, he tucked his hands in his pockets. "His true name? High King Callan Ryne Vaderyn Thorne."

"I don't believe you." Her heart thudded against her ribcage. She didn't believe him, not really, but a small part of her wondered if this was the secret Callan was so intent on sharing with her.

Something inside caught his attention then, and he smirked. "I would be disappointed if you did. I'm sure you'll see the truth soon enough." He sighed. "Alas, my time is up. Your savior has finally noticed my presence." Cathal sketched a bow, offering her a devious smile as he rose again. "Until next time, Majesty."

Eve turned, following the direction of his gaze. Callan was pushing his way through the crowd, making his way to her. She turned back to where Cathal had been standing, but instead of the sharp-featured fae male, only a wisp of smoke remained. Her guards stood slack-jawed and stunned, swords hanging limply at their sides.

"Where did he go?" the one to her right asked.

"I have no idea," the other replied, scratching his beard. "Majesty, I think–"

Before they could ask questions she didn't know how to answer, Callan arrived, pushing past them to stand in front of her. Rage and fear warred across his face as he looked her over, searching for any sign that she had been harmed.

"Go inside," she commanded the guards. "Please."

Without protest, they sheathed their weapons and made their way inside, still mumbling about the strange man's disappearance and what it could mean.

"Did he harm you?" Callan asked through clenched teeth.

"No, I'm fine. He just...wanted to talk." She paused, glancing inside to ensure they weren't being spied upon by nosy guests. "Who was he?"

Callan's fist clenched at his side. "Someone I thought I had dealt with. What did he say to you?"

"He called you a king, Callan. The fae high king." Eve searched his face for any reaction to her words, any sign that what Cathal had said was a lie, hopeful and desperate she realized for it to be untrue. If Callan had anything to do with the severing of their world when the treaty had been broken...

A shadow crossed his features and he looked downward. It was all the confirmation she needed. "It's true?" she asked, her voice barely a whisper.

"Yes," he admitted. "But–"

A choked sob escaped her lips and she turned to go inside. Betrayal and hurt flooded her. The male she loved, the one she'd taken to her bed, had been the reason behind it all. He had known, had kept it from her.

Callan's choice so long ago was the reason she had had to fight so hard to take the throne that was rightfully hers. It was the reason her mother had been murdered. He had sent an emissary to the human lands to woo their queen—the emissary who had violated the treaty that had kept their world whole in his greed and shattered it.

"Eve, wait," he begged, reaching for her arm. "It's not what you think."

She jerked her arm out of his reach and kept going. She didn't want to hear his excuse, didn't want to give him the chance to explain himself. Not now.

Right now, she needed to be away from him, to think, to figure out what to do. She brushed past Leysa and Valerian, ignoring Leysa's attempt to stop her. The worry she saw only hurt her more. They had known, had befriended her, and had kept it secret.

She had no one left that she could trust.

Chapter 32

Intent on leaving, Eve made it as far as the middle of the room before she changed her mind. There were far too many prying eyes and ears present for her to act on her feelings. Here was their first independently ruling queen, and she was about to make an emotional display of herself, proving the doubters right.

Forcing herself to regain her composure, she moved to the dais that had been set up at the front of the room, taking a seat on the throne. Here at least, she could avoid the conversation she desperately did not want to have. Callan took a place by her side, emotion rippling off of him in waves she could all but feel. Eve could sense his gaze on her, as palpable as his fingertips on her cheek. She ignored him.

"Please," he uttered quietly enough to avoid being overheard. The music was loud in here, but people milled around the dais, close enough to hear a normal conversation.

Not trusting herself to speak without breaking, Eve simply shook her head. Later, she would give him a chance. She owed him that much. He could speak his truth, tell her the whole story, and then she would dismiss him. They couldn't remain what they were now, not with the pain his actions had caused her, however indirectly.

He opened his mouth to speak again, but whatever he had been about to say died on his tongue as a flash of flame sparked in the center of the ballroom. Screams erupted and dancers fled to escape the sudden circle of fire that formed. In the center of the sudden blaze stood Cathal. Standing casually, hands in the pockets of his black suit with a pleased smile gracing his feline features, he could have fit in with any of the gathered nobility, if he hadn't been standing in the center of a ring of flame in the middle of a ballroom.

"I see you've had the chance to ask your question, majesty," he began without preamble. "And judging by the expression on my brother's face, you found my words to be true."

Leysa and Valerian ran from somewhere within the crowd, coming to stand in front of Eve as Callan descended the dais.

"What the fuck are you doing here?" Callan growled, his eyes taking on the gold aura she'd questioned before she knew the truth. Shadows gathered around him ominously. Fear and shock flooded Eve, blood pounding in her ears like warning drums. Too many people were watching, and too many secrets were being revealed. If they fought, how many of her people would be hurt in the process?

"I think you mean *how* am I here," Cathal corrected indolently. "After all, you ordered me imprisoned for the crime of falling in love with someone you believed I shouldn't have." His smoky gaze flicked to Eve pointedly. "The irony is rather delicious, don't you think?"

"Hate to interrupt boys, but is this the place for this?" Leysa interjected.

Eve had no idea how she was going to explain away this display of magic. Explaining her own was proving difficult enough. The priests had conferred with one another, and after days of debate had announced it a rare gift from the gods, declaring that Eve herself must have been chosen to rule. It had quelled most of the more vocal pushback against her rule, but that explanation would almost certainly be thrown out the window now.

"Ah, Leysa darling," Cathal crooned, slaking a lascivious gaze over Leysa's body that earned a warning growl from Valerian. "You look as ravishing as ever."

"Watch your mouth," Valerian threatened, taking a step toward Cathal. The encircling flames flared brighter in response.

"Tsk, tsk. Always so possessive, Valerian," he smirked. "Don't get your hackles up. As lovely as your wife is, I am spoken for." Turning his attention back to Leysa, he shrugged. "I think it's high time the people of Darkegrove knew the truth, don't you? They deserve to know that their new queen is in bed with the fae. Quite literally."

Surprised gasps and fretful conversation erupted throughout the crowd. Some openly wept now, in fear or shock or some combination of the two. The guards who had lined the ballroom made no move toward the fae male in the center of the room, the threat of immolation keeping them at bay as effectively as it had her friends.

"What do you want?" Eve demanded finally, standing now. Her hands were shaking so much that she had to hide them in the folds of her skirts to keep the full weight of her fear from showing.

"Why isn't it obvious?" Cathal laughed. "Revenge, Majesty. And I plan to take it in the form of a life for a life."

"No!" Callan's shout rang through the room. Cathal's words spurred him into action. Darkness erupted from him, turning the room to night and eliciting panicked screams from those gathered.

"Stop." A ring of flame encircled Eve's neck like a garotte, threatening but not burning. She could feel no heat, no pain. Aside from a slight pressure against her throat, there was no sensation from it whatsoever. Ivy lined the floors and terrace doorways, her magic prepared to join the inevitable fray, halting its rapid growth as she issued her strained command.

The shadows remained in place around them, obscuring all but Callan and Cathal from her view. Callan froze in place, barely even breathing.

"Let her go." Callan's words were as much a plea as an order, true fear seeping into his typically sardonic tone.

"A life for a life," Cathal sighed in mock regret. As if he had no choice in the matter. "It is the bare minimum I am owed. If I so desired, I could demand this entire charming kingdom, but as I am in a benevolent mood. I will demand only the life of your love, in repayment for the life of my own." His disinterest in the people gathered, and the lack of care he had for the fear and pain he was causing was evident in his casual posture. "Unfortunately, my hired help was unsuccessful at procuring our lovely queen. As was my attempt to remove you from the equation. You've proven to be more difficult to get rid of than I anticipated, Callan."

Lost for words, Eve simply waited, closing her eyes as she waited for the inevitable. If Callan made a move for Cathal, likely even if he didn't, the necklace of flame would tighten, cutting off her air and if he so chose, parting her head from her body. Her thoughts turned to her kingdom and what would happen to all. Would Cathal stay true to his word and leave them once his blood debt had been repaid or would he decide to conquer her people?

"Please, brother," Callan pleaded.

"How disappointing, I expected more of a fight from you."

Heat began to build from the flames around her neck as the ring tightened. Slowly, torturously. Drawing breath grew more difficult with every agonizing second.

Eve opened her eyes, hazarding a look at the man about to take her life. If he were going to take her life, she was going to make him see her strength and defiance until the last moment. She met his gaze evenly, despite the tears that now flowed freely down her cheeks.

"Stop," Callan beseeched, stepping closer to Cathal's barrier. "Take me instead."

Eve gasped as the circle loosened, allowing her to breathe freely once again, and the heat vanished entirely. Callan's shadows retreated, allowing the light from the chandeliers to once again fill the room. Every guard and guest in the ballroom had been quietly ushered from the room during the darkness, she realized, with Leysa and Valerian positioned by the doors, protecting their retreat.

"Well, now that is an interesting proposition, if a little theatrical." Cathal's attention was fixated on Callan entirely, unaware or uncaring that he no longer had a captive audience.

"I'll go with you, but only if you agree to leave Eve in peace."

From her place on the dais, Eve couldn't see Callan's face, but his shoulders and back were tense, fists clenched at his side. Cathal crossed his arms across his chest, silently considering.

She couldn't breathe, couldn't think. She wanted to scream, to tell him to fight, but all that she could manage was a whisper. "No, please."

Love, regret, and despair swam within the depths of Callan's ocean-blue eyes as he finally turned to look at her. "I'm sorry."

Cathal snorted but nodded his acceptance. "If you try anything, I will come back and end her life."

Callan merely turned his gaze to Leysa and Valerian, watching the scene playing out before them silently, undecipherable emotions playing over their features. "Remember that spring night, when we made our pact? You have been my family, and I will never forget that." Leysa sniffled, and Valerian nodded once. "Protect her," he added.

Why was he talking like he was going to his death? Panic roared to life within her and she stumbled down the stairs of the dais, tripping over her gown and landing on her knees. Reaching a hand for Callan, she sobbed, "No, you don't have to do this."

The circle of flame that had been surrounding Cathal vanished as quickly as it had appeared, and he cocked his head to the side. "Shall we go then, or do you require more motivation?"

Keeping his gaze locked on Eve, Callan backed away from her outstretched hand, moving to Cathal's side. "I wish we had been given more time. I wish I could have made things right. There are so many things I wanted to explain, to tell you," he rasped, his sorrowful gaze on Eve's face. He was staring at her intently as if committing her face to memory. "I love you, Eve."

With little more than a gust of wind and shadows, they vanished.

Eve screamed. All rational thought disappeared alongside Callan. Someone was saying her name, she thought, but they were so far away. A pair of strong hands gripped her shoulders, and a kind face was in front of hers, blocking her view of where Callan had been standing only moments ago.

The ivy that had been hanging near the doorway now grew into the ballroom, encircling Eve like a cocoon. Whoever had been holding onto her fell away from her, his hands releasing her shoulders. Valerian, a tiny voice inside herself told her. Valerian had been trying to help her up. She didn't want it, his help or his pity.

He was gone. He was gone and she hadn't gotten the chance to let him explain, to forgive him. To tell him she loved him too. Callan was gone, and she was alone.

~

With ivy wrapped around her form, she stared at the last spot she'd seen him until her eyes burned, and then she kept them closed for a long while.

Memories played through her mind over and over. Their conversation in the garden, that first time he'd called her dove. The way he'd looked at her the night of the dinner party. When they'd made love the first time, and the last time, in the garden just yesterday.

Finally, she blinked away the dream, staring into reality. The vines fell away, and she was left looking into Valerian's concerned face. It had only been a few minutes but it felt as if Callan had been gone centuries. She had to get him back. It was as simple as that.

"He's gone," she said to nobody in particular, her voice hoarse from screaming.

Leysa lowered herself to the floor beside her husband. "I think I might know where he is," she said cautiously. "What he said about the pact we made, that night was...well, it wasn't important, not in the way he made it sound."

Valerian dragged his hand across his face. "But he wouldn't want you coming after him."

Eve pinned Valerian with a stare. "I don't care. Tell me Leysa." Her throat burned as if she had swallowed fire like the traveling performer she'd seen once as a child. He'd ignited a torch and then slid it down his throat, only to lift it once more with no injury to be seen. Eve had been so astounded she'd spent the entire day asking her tutors to explain how it was done, though she never got a satisfactory answer.

Leysa cast a glance at Valerian, who simply sighed. He disagreed with what they were about to do, it seemed, but he wouldn't stop them. "The old temple of Astraia, the goddess of justice and judgment. That's where Cathal was supposed to have been imprisoned for breaking the treaty."

Breaking the treaty, being the reason Eve and every female heir before her since the Queen of Despair, would be refused their birthright. "I thought that the old king," she began, frowning. "Callan... sent him to do it. Why was Cathal the only one punished?" Saying his name hurt, sending shards of broken glass into her already wounded heart.

For a moment they both stared at her in stunned silence. "What are you talking about?" Valerian asked finally.

"Cathal said that he, that Callan, was the fae king who sent him to seduce the old human queen." Doubt began to seep in, fuel to the twin fires of guilt and regret that burned within her. She should have given Callan the chance to explain, to tell his side of the story.

"That's bullshit." Leysa's voice was cold, sharp as a knife. "Just a story woven to hide the truth."

Shame colored her cheeks and she looked at her hands folded in her lap. How would he ever forgive her for this mess?

"Callan was king," Valerian said, more gently. " And he did send Cathal to meet with the human queen, Mara. But it was only supposed to be a formality, to keep the peace between our twin kingdoms."

"I think that Callan deserves to tell the rest of this story," Leysa interrupted. Her tone had lost some of its sharpness, but her anger with Eve was still present enough to be noted.

Eve nodded once. She had so much to make up to him, so much to say. The least she could do now for the man she loved was give him the chance to tell his story. After she saved him from the mortal danger her mistake had put him in.

"Then let's go get him back."

CHAPTER 33

Arrangements for their rescue mission took little time to complete, though convincing the guards that they must remain behind proved more difficult. They were afraid of the fae now, of the magic they wielded, but they remained loyal to their queen. Eldred had been able to convince them that Eve remained safe when with Leysa and Valerian, and had managed to assuage her of any fear she had about leaving the council in charge during her absence. He was loyal and would not allow her throne to be usurped while she was away, he assured her. Backed by the formidable Lady Hanford and a few others, he was certain there was no need for Eve to worry.

According to Leysa, Cathal and Callan had used a fae ability called pacing to vanish, allowing them to travel through the veil between worlds to appear where they desired. It was a rare gift and one that Valerian possessed, though he had unfortunately never seen the temple itself. Pacing there, especially twice, would be nearly impossible.

The ruins were a day's ride away, Valerian told Eve as they headed out of the gates of Stoneweald, if they rode hard and only stopped when necessary. Half a day into their ride, she was cursing horses, saddles, and Aestera itself. They'd slowed to a trot to make eating easier, and to give the horses a little bit of a break from the fast pace they'd traveled at most of the morning.

"I'm not sure what I can do against his fire," Eve said suddenly, breaking the silence that had fallen over the trio.

"You can control stone, right? He can't burn stone," Leysa offered.

"Sometimes, but it's harder for me than the plants. But it's my best shot," Eve admitted. Hope was dangerous, but it was also all she had left. *It has to work.*

By the time they arrived at the ruins, the cool but clear day had turned into a frigid, rainy mess. Little remained of what had once been a sprawling temple if spacing between the chunks of pillars and archways was any indication. Eve loosed a curse as her boot sank into the mud with a loud squelch. The terrain had grown too treacherous to take the horses any farther, so they had been left by the road. Walking on foot had been the safer, but slower, option.

Valerian, leading the way several feet ahead, stopped and gestured for her and Leysa to join him. Her gaze landed on what he'd found as she slid to a stop beside him, grabbing a tree to steady herself. A small building made of dark black stone sat only a few yards away. The only remaining intact structure.

Callan was inside, he had to be. Resolve steadied her shaking hands, and she began to move toward the opening. How many centuries had it been since mortal feet had met the stone pathway they now walked on? Curiosity had her gaze roaming over everything as they walked, drinking in the rare sight of a standing fae structure.

"I think this was where the priests slept," Leysa whispered, guessing the direction of Eve's thoughts.

Eve opened her mouth to respond, to ask about the priests of the goddess of justice and what they were like. Their priests were less specialized now, worshipping the lost gods as a near singular entity. The names of those they'd once followed were so long forgotten that worshipping them individually as they once had was impossible.

Masculine voices ahead in the gloom of the building silenced her before she could speak. The familiar timbre of Callan's voice reached her ears, but she couldn't quite make out the words. A glance at Leysa told her that her friend's fae hearing had picked up what was being said, and whatever it was, it had both her and Valerian frowning.

Is he hurt? They were close enough now that she didn't dare speak the question aloud. Even moving seemed like a poor decision, given the loose stones that covered the floor. One misstep would announce their arrival as surely as speaking would. For a heartbeat, she hovered in the gloom of the hallway, unsure of what to do.

"Do join us, Evelyn." Cathal's voice carried from beyond the hallway, from wherever they were, still unseen by the trio of would-be rescuers. How he'd known she was there, she didn't know. "Bring your escorts as well, please. I would hate for this to become....unpleasant."

Cursing under her breath, she started forward. There was no alternative. The implied threat to Callan was enough to keep her from taking the risk of running, and pretending she wasn't there was foolish.

She stepped into the inner chamber, into what looked to have been a dining hall at some point, judging from the huge, empty central space, perfect for a long table. A fire burned brightly within the large fireplace at one end, likely the first it had seen in centuries. Cathal stood facing the doorway they had entered through, hands in his pockets casually. Callan kneeled on the floor in front of him, watching Eve with a shuttered expression she couldn't read.

"Well, I must admit this was quite unexpected," Cathal said with a grin. "How invigorating. It's been so long since I've had this much fun."

"Why did you bring her with you?" Callan demanded, gaze fixated on Valerian. "You were supposed to keep her safe."

"He doesn't make decisions for me," Eve interjected before Valerian could reply. "And neither do you."

Rather than anger, resolve fueled her. She was done taking orders from men, even when they believed they were doing what was best for her. All of this time, she'd been bowing to their wants, to their rules and desires, even when she thought she'd broken free of it.

"I have always appreciated strong-willed women," Cathal mused, tilting his head slightly. "I was beginning to think you Darkegrove women had lost all of your fire. Emilia certainly lacked your spirit. Lord Graham Clarke, does that name ring a bell? The foolish girl thought me one of your suitors and happily spilled every secret she could get her hands on." he chuckled. "But you, you remind me so much of my Mara." His gaze darkened at the mention of the woman's name. "And here, we come to the crux of it all. The reason your beloved must die."

Rage blossomed in her chest, sharp and painful. *Emilia.* Had he been behind everything?

"You killed my mother." The accusation came out flat, devoid of shock or any other emotion.

Cathal chuckled once more. "Oh, that? No, darling, that was the work of small-minded men. Emilia acted of her own accord on that account. She was simply my spy and occasional plaything. My plan originally was simply to take my little brother here, to punish him for his crimes. His relationship with you is the only reason I altered my course." He paused, nudging Callan with a knee lightly. "I do love the parallels between us, they are quite poetic, don't you think, brother?"

"Fuck off," Callan muttered.

Cathal sighed, his face the picture of feigned disappointment. "As I was saying, I originally planned to take only my brother in repayment. But his apparent devotion to you, well, punishing him like this will be so much more satisfying. Don't you think?" He lifted a hand, and flame sparked to life within his palm.

Eve couldn't– wouldn't, allow herself to be held captive by this man again. She wouldn't allow Callan to be taken, wouldn't allow Cathal to hurt him by hurting her. Remembering what Callan had told her about control and focus, she held her hands out at her sides. Tears borne of frustration, fear, and rage burned her eyes.

Riona's voice echoed in her mind, *Do not ever let them see you cry.*

She let the tears fall freely. Let him see her cry. If it made him believe her to be weak, then that would be his mistake. Eve allowed herself to feel every hurt she'd endured the last few weeks; but also all of the love and friendship. She'd lost more than she thought she could survive, but she had also gained so much. Callan had claimed her whole heart, and Leysa and Valerian had shown her friendship and kindness even before they really knew her. They had become a second family.

The tattoo tingled, a near-burning sensation running from her collarbone to fingertip as her magic built inside her, rising and stretching from some deep well within her. *Sorry Mother, but fuck that.*

The pebbles and pieces of the ruined wall began to dance across the floor. Callan's shoulders tensed, bracing as his wide-eyed stare met hers. She couldn't risk another quake, not with them standing inside this all but ruined building, but hopefully, she could call forth the stone from beneath them without causing too much damage to the structure.

"Here we go," Valerian murmured, tugging his sword free from the hilt at his side. A bright flash beside told her that Leysa had shifted, into what creature she didn't know.

Cathal's brow rose slightly. "You'd risk bringing the entire building down on us? Perhaps you're not as smart as I thought you were."

"I'll risk whatever it takes to stop you." As she spoke a boulder burst free from the ground between the brothers, giving Callan the time to move to Eve's side. His hands were bound by rope. *Why hasn't he broken the bonds before now?*

"It's ash," he said, answering her unspoken question. Valerian sliced the rope quickly, freeing his hands. "Forgive me," Callan said quietly to Eve, turning to face his brother just as Cathal began to lift his hands. "Mara is alive."

Everything stopped. For what felt like an eternity, nobody moved, even to breathe. The boulder Eve had called forth remained still, her pebbles silenced. Cathal's flames still danced in his palm, but he made no move to unleash them on the group.

"You lie," he said finally. His storm grey eyes had darkened, his jaw set. "She was human. Even if she survived whatever punishment you saw fit to bestow on her, by the time I broke free of my prison, she would have been dead for centuries."

"Not if her punishment was Falias."

Valerian cursed, and Leysa growled from somewhere behind Eve. So she was in the form of a wolf then. Their reactions to his words confused her. The name Falias held no meaning for her, but clearly, it meant something to the fae.

Cathal's hands dropped to his side again. "She's in Falias? That's not possible, she'd have to be–"

"Fae," Callan finished. "Astraia saw it as a fitting punishment."

Valerian snorted at that, and Leysa huffed, noting their disagreement with the goddess' opinion.

"Liar!"

The walls echoed and rumbled with the boom of his voice, with the power within it. He'd been unflappable, utterly calm, and restrained even as he issued threats of violence. The flames within the hearth roared, flaring higher and brighter than the stones could contain.

"Mara did nothing!" He continued, either unaware of or indifferent to the dust that now rained from the ceiling. "The war was between us, she was innocent in the decisions made and deserved no punishment."

Callan's gaze darted upward as the ceiling cracked. "You are right, brother," he said calmly, turning his attention back to Cathal, even as he nudged Eve toward the doorway. "We need to leave this place before it becomes our tomb. Let me take you to Falias, and put the past behind us. Mara is there, I assure you. Cora promised to look after her."

She had no time to ask questions, not now. Later she would ask about Falias, and who Cora and Mara were. For now, her focus shifted from the argument to the quickly destabilizing building. It appeared to be made from the very stone she'd called from the ground before, so maybe she could use her own powers to hold it steady, at least long enough for them to escape. Something collapsed behind them, but she didn't dare turn to see what it had been. Whatever she was going to do, she needed to do it now.

Holding her hands upwards as if prepared to lift the stone herself she threw out every bit of magic she had been building within the well inside herself. She had barely been able to scratch the surface before, but perhaps now, with so many lives at stake, she would hold out longer and dig deeper, no matter the cost.

"Go!" She shouted, straining as the outer edges of the room began to collapse. "Get out," she said to Callan, whose eyes had gone wide with fear. Not for his own life, she knew, but for hers.

"I won't leave you again," he said quietly. His fingertips were rough against her cheeks, and she leaned into them, not daring to lower her hands. She could feel the magic beginning to wane, her strength failing her already.

"You have to get out," she sobbed, arms shaking.

"We're going together," he promised, turning to where his brother was already disappearing on a wisp of smoke.

"Falias," Cathal said as he vanished, fury still etched in his features. "Or her life is mine."

Leysa shifted with a flash, and Valerian took her hand in his. "Let's go," he said, ignoring Cathal's disappearance and threat entirely.

"Right behind you," Callan promised. Valerian and Leysa vanished in a rush of wind. "You have to let go, dove." His voice was calm and coaxing, even as the temple continued to crumble around them.

"I can't." Her voice cracked. Every muscle in her body screamed for her to just let go, let it be over with. But if she released her hold on her magic now, the temple would fall down around them. Would Callan be able to pace both of them away quickly enough? "Go without me. I'll slow you down."

He was so close to her that she could feel his breath, warm against her cheek. "I will never leave you again. Trust me. Let go, my love."

With a breath, she did as he asked and released her hold on her magic. For a brief, glorious moment, all she felt was relief. There was a thundering in her ears, but she was free. There was no more strain, no more feeling like every part of her was being pulled in a million different directions. Boulders had been lifted from her shoulders. A ragged breath escaped her, arms falling to her sides, limp and useless.

Callan's callused fingers gripped hers before she could inhale again, dragging her back to reality. The thundering she'd heard was what remained of the temple walls coming down. Large chunks of granite fell against the unforgiving stone floors, splintering into pieces and scattering.

The bit of ceiling she'd managed to hold back finally splintered above their heads. They were going to die in this temple, and it would become their tomb. Would history remember her? Would her loved ones? Her parents were gone, resting safely in the Otherworld now, and one of the very few people she'd ever really considered a friend now languished in her own dungeons after murdering her mother and attempting to murder her. For what reason, she still didn't know.

Eldred and perhaps Lady Hanford might remember her somewhat fondly, and Sylvie. Sylvie would remember her. Perhaps when she and Dallin had children, they would tell them the story of a queen who tried to bring change to Darkegrove. Maybe even Brodie would spare a kind word. Lia would tell her story, she thought with a smile. Lia would make sure she was remembered. The future queen of Avellon would certainly be sure to tell the story of the Darkegrove queen who ruled for such a short time; the queen who had tried to pave a path of equality in a place where such a thing had not existed in so very long.

The thundering had given way to something different, the sound of a whirlwind. Confused, Eve opened her eyes. There was nothing. No light and no crashing walls. She would have thought they had been buried if it weren't for the distinctive feeling in her stomach. It felt like freefall. Her stomach had dropped, and if Callan hadn't been holding her tight to his chest now, giving her something solid to anchor her, she was sure she would spin away into the nothingness that surrounded her. Maybe that would be better than being crushed to death.

Just as the thought formed, her feet touched something soft and slick. Mud. She was in the mud again. The songs of night birds greeted her ears as she took in their new and sudden surroundings. They were in the forest, several yards from the now completely collapsed temple. Valerian and Leysa rushed over, the latter anxiously analyzing Eve for any sign of injury.

"You made it," Valerian sighed with relief.

"Barely, I thought–" Callan's reply was cut short by the snap of a twig behind them.

"Abyss-spawned demon!" She spun toward the angry shout that sounded from behind her. It was the farmer from her audience with the common folk, red-faced and holding a bow.

Aimed directly for Callan.

He must have followed them all the way from Stoneweald. So wrapped up in their planning, their fear for Callan, they had somehow missed the shadow stalking them through the forest. She had little time to consider how he had managed it.

The next moments happened in a blur. The arrow flew, and Callan shouted. Out of the corner of her eye, the telltale light of Leysa's transformation flashed. Eve turned sharply, spinning to warn Callan, but the words never came. Pain, bright and unending, flared in her chest for a brief moment, and then Eve Darrow felt nothing at all.

Chapter 34

Callan

The farmer was an abysmal shot. The arrow directed at Callan had missed him by several inches, instead finding its home in Eve's chest. There had been no time and no way to save her. Callan roared, his power flaring so intensely that the trees swayed as if a great wind had suddenly swept through the forest. The bright afternoon turned to midnight. Leysa, in the form of a wolf, sprinted after the now fleeing farmer. Callan followed on her heels, leaving Valerian to watch over Eve's lifeless form.

The world had gone silent when her heart stopped beating. Now, the only sound he heard was the crashing waves of fury and grief pounding in his ears. He had seen the light in her green eyes gutter, had heard the life leaving her with her last breath. Guilt settled in his gut, almost as powerful as the grief, slick and oily, adding fuel to the rage that coursed through his veins like wildfire.

He should have known, or at least been suspicious of the man after that display in the throne room. His disrespect of Eve and everything she stood for should have been punished. She had been forgiving in that moment, staying her hand. Even if it were in service to preserving her image, and her standing with the council, she had been far more forgiving than he would have been. This fucker would beg for death before he was done with him.

It took little time for both Leysa and Callan to reach him. He could have paced to him, appearing in front of him like the demon he apparently thought Callan was, but he wanted to savor the chase. Fear, thick and sludgy, flowed from the man like water. So intense it would have been nearly enough for him to feel if he'd been human.

But he wasn't human, and without the steady beat of her heart, there was nothing left in this world to hold back the monster that lived inside him.

Leaping from behind the man, Leysa pinned him to the muddy earth easily beneath two massive paws, letting up only long enough for him to twist beneath her to face his own certain demise.

"I knew the whore was something evil," he spat, his voice quaking with fear even as he spouted more of the same venom he'd thrown at her before.

Callan allowed his shadows to pull closer, encircling him like an aura. Pure darkness like that of the abyss the man had declared him to be from. "Unfortunately for you, you're wrong. She might have shown you at least the mercy of a quick death. I will not." Callan's voice was otherwordly, each word as sharp and cold as the mountain peaks to the north.

The man finally had the good sense to remain silent, all color now drained from his face.

"Take him to the palace, and put him in the dungeons. I'll deal with him when I get back." Callan bared his teeth at the man, an unspoken promise of what was to come when he arrived back at the castle.

Leysa growled low in her throat, her gaze darting from the man to Callan and back. A silent question danced in her eyes.

"Have as much fun with him as you like," Callan replied. "But leave him alive for me."

Chapter 35

Darkness greeted Eve. Pure, black, and unending. She had been standing in front of Callan just a heartbeat ago, and now she could see nothing in front of her, not even her own hand. Whatever she stood on now was solid, in stark opposition to the mud she had been standing in before.

Bone-deep intuition told her where she was, and what had happened. Death had taken her. She didn't remember the pain of the arrow striking her heart. She could barely remember the moment at all. It was a distant memory in the back of her mind, hidden behind a fog she had to push her way through to recall. Callan's face, undiluted terror marring his perfect face, remained clear as a bell, however.

As gradually as the rising sun, light began to filter in from some far-off place, illuminating what appeared to be an endless hallway of white marble. Standing only a few feet away were two figures huddled together in a conversation she couldn't hear.

Her heart would have stopped dead in her chest, had any beat remained. She would have recognized the first woman anywhere, her fiery hair the twin to her own; along with the veiled head leaning toward her.

"Mama?" The single word came out in a strangled sob. Her mother was here. She wanted to fall to her knees or run to her mother and embrace her. But neither happened. Somehow she remained standing as both women turned to look at her finally. Her mother's face lit with the warm smile she'd missed so very much, the other still hidden from view.

As they moved to join her, only silence met her ears. Not even the sounds of footsteps against the marble sounded in this strange chamber.

"Only words here," Macaria offered in explanation. "No distractions, even the most minute. I find it is important for those who find themselves here."

"Hello, my love," Riona said, still smiling.

"Remember that time is short. I can give you a few moments, but no more," the goddess warned gently.

Before Eve could ask what the goddess meant by that, she was gone. She had simply vanished.

"I wish I had gotten to tell you how very proud of you I am." Riona sighed, her eyes beginning to well. "I wish that we had so much more time. There are so many things I need to tell you, to explain and apologize for."

"No, Mama," Eve interrupted, using the name she hadn't called her mother since she was a child. She reached for Riona's hand, needing to comfort her mother and to be comforted, to ease the ache blossoming in her chest.

Riona jerked her arm away, stepping back. "You mustn't touch me. If you do, you will have to remain in the Otherworld forever."

"Aren't I already in the Otherworld?" Eve glanced around at the hallway as if it would yield some answer to her question.

"No, darling. Macaria will explain when she returns, but there are things I must tell you before then, and our time is short." Riona lifted a hand to her temple. It was a gesture Eve recognized well, a sign that her mother was struggling with what to say next–taking a moment to consider her words. "The prophecy, I know you know about it now. That you were the first key, in the first lock. But you need to know, it has already begun. Already, that lock has been opened, and the first veil will lower soon."

The goddesses had told her this much, more or less. She knew soon the fae would return, but had no idea what Riona meant by a veil. Her thoughts turned to Callan, and the secret he'd so desperately wanted to tell her. Perhaps that was part of what he'd been trying to get her to hear, the truth about all of this mess.

Riona pressed on. "I'm...limited, in what I can tell you. Just...stay close to those you can trust and be wary of the winds that blow from the north."

The north wind? Eve shook her head, confusion sweeping her. There was no reason for her mother to be telling her any of this. She was dead, and knowledge of what was happening in Aestera did her no good now. Eve would be watching her loved ones that remained behind live their lives and enjoying eternal peace with her parents, or so the priests claimed.

"Mama, I don't know why–" Movement to her side caught her attention. The veiled goddess of death had returned, as silently and suddenly as she had departed.

"It's time," Macaria said softly. "I am sorry I could not give you more."

Riona nodded once to Macaria before fixing her blue eyes on Eve. "I love you, my darling girl, and I am so very sorry for what is to come."

With a wave of Macaria's hand, Riona rippled out of existence, vanishing entirely.

"Mama!" Eve shouted, reaching for the space where Riona had just been standing. "Mama, no!"

"I am sorry," Macaria repeated.

She probably meant it, but Eve didn't care. She whirled on the goddess. "Where did she go? Bring her back! Bring her back to me!"

"She is at rest, child." A pause, as the goddess considered. "Would you trade your life for it? Trade everything you've accomplished and could accomplish for eternity with your mother?" Macaria asked, veil shifting as she tilted her head. Only the pale column of her neck was revealed, her features remained hidden beneath layers of lace.

"Why do you wear that stupid thing anyway?" Eve demanded rather than answering. In truth, she had no idea how to answer the question the goddess had posed. Could she trade her kingdom and her life in exchange for a few more moments with her mother?

Macaria's breathy laugh caught Eve by surprise. She'd expected ire or perhaps outright anger at her insolent tone.

"Death wears a different face for every soul. Some greet me happily, as a friend. The old man, comfortable and content in his bed, surrounded by his children and his children's children, sees a young woman with a kind face, welcoming him to his well-deserved rest. A warrior on the battlefield, dying from wounds he's earned fighting for what he thought right, in defense of others," she explained, crossing her hands in front of her. "Would see a warrior goddess, beautiful and strong. As battle-hardened as he himself is."

Eve wasn't sure what explanation she'd been expecting, but it certainly hadn't been this one. "And the person afraid of dying? The murderer gone to his execution?"

"The first, it depends. Are they of a pure soul, young, or simply unsure of what awaits them? They might see what comforts them most. A motherly sort, or a young girl of their own age. Those that do evil, however...well," she laughed, the humorless sound sending a chill up Eve's spine. "They see something much, much, more terrifying."

Eve couldn't help but wonder what she would see if Macaria lifted her veil and revealed what face she wore. Was she afraid of death? A few days ago, the answer would most certainly have been yes. Today, she wasn't so sure.

Inside the temple, when she thought she might die to buy time for Callan to escape, the idea of death hadn't frightened her in the least. She would die to save his life without question. But what had happened in the forest had been different.

"So, what will it be?" Macaria prodded, drawing Eve from her thoughts.

"I don't understand." She didn't. She had died and now stood here speaking to death herself. How could giving up her life be an option now?

"It was the reason your mother wouldn't allow you to touch her, to be forced to remain here forever. I can revive you, return you to the mortal world. You can have the chance to continue down the path you've carved for yourself. On the other hand, you can remain here and be at peace with your parents. Either way, there is a price that must be paid."

Live again, return to Callan and her friends, to her kingdom, or be at peace with her parents? An impossible choice. "What is the cost?"

"To remain here, to choose rest, the cost is your life. Your very destiny. Every good thing you might yet bring to the world. To return, to find out what fate has in store for you, the cost is your mortal life."

Fate. She'd had the word thrown at her so many times in the last few weeks that she was ready to scream. If men weren't controlling the direction of her life, fate was. Would she ever be truly in control?

Her gaze drifted past Macaria. The prices the goddess named made no sense. Her life would be the cost no matter the decision she made.

"I don't understand," Eve said after a few moments.

Though she couldn't see her face, Eve could sense Macaria smiling beneath her veil. "If you choose to go back you will no longer be human, child. You will become as one of my own, a child of the gods."

Fae. The word rattled through her, china clattering against a stone floor.

"Will I still be able to help my people?" *Would they even still be my people?* She left the second question unspoken, a fear she wouldn't give voice to. Everything she had done had been in service to something bigger than herself as much as it had been about taking what should have been hers by right. If she succeeded, how many girls after her would have opportunities denied them for so long?

Macaria lifted a shoulder. "What you do with your new life is entirely up to you, if you choose that path."

Eve inhaled deeply, though she suspected it wasn't really necessary in this form, in this place. An impossible choice had to be made. Another decision required her to be braver, and more assured than she thought herself capable of.

In the light of the bridge to the Otherworld, Eve Darrow made her choice.

Chapter 36

"Callan," a male breathed. She couldn't see him but she would recognize Valerian's voice anywhere. Had he noticed she was awake? *Alive*, she corrected herself. He hadn't, because she wasn't. Not yet, not really. Eve hovered within her own body, touching, but not quite in control of it just yet. Before she could try to speak to say, *I'm here, I'm here,* a familiar feminine voice sounded from near where Valerian must have been.

"Take this gift, my child, and use it well. Do not squander what has been given to either of you," Macaria intoned gently. Callan stiffened at the sound, and his head turned in her direction.

Night birds crying out, the pained howl of a wolf, and strong arms wrapped around her shoulders, shaking as they held her close to a male form that smelled of cedar and sage. These were the first things Eve was aware of as she returned to her body, the body that was already beginning to change. With her first intake of breath, the round tips of her ears stretched, growing pointed beneath her loose hair.

With the second, her senses of smell and sound expanded. Before, she had only been able to hear the calls and songs of the nocturnal birds that dwelled in this part of the forest. Now, she heard every note of their song. A chipmunk or rabbit rustled in its den several yards to her left.

She had never heard anything as lovely, or as intense, as the sound of Callan's racing heartbeat next to her head.

Moonlight met her new eyes, not quite as bright as the sun, but still bright enough to illuminate much of the forest closest to her. She could make out the birds she'd been hearing, dotting the branches around them. No sign of the wolf she'd heard.

Callan's attention turned sharply to Eve, his grip on her loosening just enough for him to see her face, and for her to see his.

If she'd thought him attractive the first time she'd seen him, now she thought him utterly divine. It was like seeing his face, his true face, for the first time. Every angle and plane of his face she'd come to know, had come to love, were somehow more defined. He was *more* with her new fae sight. Shadows clung to him like an aura. How blind she'd been as a human, to not recognize him for what he was. Pure, powerful, fae.

"Hi," she said weakly, realizing he'd been staring at her in silence. His expression was somewhere between shock and reverence. Kneeling in the mud, Callan still held her close, only releasing her as she moved to sit up. Her pants were soon soaked thanks to the muck, but she didn't care.

"You're..." he began, slowly, as if he couldn't believe the words coming out of his own mouth.

Alive? She silently finished for him, holding her breath. His eyes began to fill as he lifted a hand to her cheek. *Fae?* The other possibility rang through her mind like a bell. Maybe he didn't want her like this, maybe he preferred her human. She hadn't had time to come to terms with the price she'd paid Macaria in order to return, to finish what she'd started.

She wasn't even sure which unfinished task had driven her to take the deal. Her mother waited in the Otherworld for her, and a large part of her had wanted to take that option instead, but she knew without question that this is what Riona would have told her to do. Even now, she felt a gentle brush against the back of her mind, the caress of approval from her mother's spirit watching over her.

Callan heaved a breath, cupping her cheek gently. "You're my mate," he said finally.

If the world opened up beneath her, and great monsters sent from the Abyss flew free, Eve wouldn't have noticed. At that moment there was nothing, and no one else but Callan and herself. There had been a tug at the center of her chest from the moment she had awoken in her new form, pulling her like a lead directly toward him. The thing in her chest urged her to sit up and face him, to really look at him for the first time with her new eyes.

Yes, there you are, the tiny voice in her mind that had been guiding her for so long whispered. *Mate.* Callan was her mate. The weight of it settled over her like a lead blanket. She was fae now, and the rightful king of the fae was her mate.

Valerian cleared his throat to their side for what Eve suspected was not the first time. "We need to go," he said warily. "Leysa will need help getting our new friend back to the castle."

Callan nodded absently, hardly paying his friend any attention, but rose to his feet anyway. Gripping Eve's hands gently, he pulled her to stand as well. The motion felt strange, every part of her new body feeling foreign. There was a lightness that she'd never known, and strength and power she could feel brimming beneath her skin. She should say something, ask a question, or tell Callan she understood, that she loved him. *Say something, anything,* she told herself.

"Go ahead and help Leysa, we'll pace there. I want to get Eve back to the castle." *In case someone else tries to kill her,* his expression said. Valerian nodded, offering Eve a supportive smile before heading off into the woods.

Callan hesitated as he pulled her slightly closer, those familiar callused hands scraping against her hands. Even her sense of touch had been heightened. The simple contact sent goosebumps racing across her skin. For a heartbeat, he looked as though he might say something more–what, she didn't know. When she remained silent, he simply reached for her other hand and plunged them both into the darkness and wind.

He paced them to her bedroom. Smart, she knew, keeping her from the eyes of her people until they could decide what to do. Mere moments after returning, a brief message was dispatched to her guards, and the council, alerting them to her return.

Now, they found themselves alone once more in her all too quiet chambers.

"Callan," she began, staring out the balcony doors rather than facing him. She could feel his gaze on her back. The thing inside her chest urged her to look at him, to go to him. But she didn't trust her heart, not just yet. Not when so much was changing. If what had happened when her father had died, pushing her onto the path that had led her here, could be called change, then this was upheaval.

"You don't have to say anything," he said, nervous, wary. "I know this is too much, too big. I have no right to call you mine, you have to focus on your people."

He sounded wounded, not physically but in his soul. She supposed he had been when she had died in front of him. Even before realizing she was his mate, he had said he loved her, and she had believed him. It had been in every touch, every look, and every time he had come to her defense.

And didn't she love him too? She had gone to save him not once, but twice, and would have gladly given her life in the temple collapse to keep him from harm. Her choice with Macaria hadn't been because of him, not entirely, but he had certainly been a factor.

Turning, she looked at him finally. "Yes, I do." At the sorrow she saw brewing in his ocean-deep eyes, she shook her head and instinctively stepped toward him. "I am yours, idiot. I have been for a while now, and I've just been too afraid to admit it. Too afraid of what it might mean for my throne."

Not that it's going to be mine much longer, she didn't need to say. Now that she was fae, her claim was gone. A fae would never be allowed to rule over a human kingdom. But this was tomorrow's problem. Tonight, she would fix things with Callan, bathe, and sleep. She needed to recover from all that had happened, and she certainly didn't have the strength left to face the council with this unimaginable news right now.

She was about to say as much when he strode across the room to her. With his fingertips, he tipped her chin back so that she was looking at him. "I love it when you call me names," he laughed hoarsely.

His fingers found their way to the nape of her neck as he pressed his lips to hers. The kiss was slow but firm, filled with a desperate need for her. For a few precious heartbeats, the rest of the world didn't exist. None of the problems that lay just beyond her door existed. There was only this moment they'd been hurtling toward since the day he walked into her life. He had saved her, and she had saved him. Together, they would figure the rest out.

They were breathless by the time they parted. Callan's strong grip came to rest at her thighs, tugging her up until he was holding her close against him, legs wrapped around his waist. One moment she was chest to chest with him, her mate, the next she was on her back on her soft bed, Callan hovering above her.

"Beautiful," he whispered, dragging a knuckle down her cheek. "As you always were."

Eve arched her back toward him in silent demand. Callan's answering laugh rumbled through her own chest, where they touched.

"So impatient," he grinned, teasing her even as he lowered his hand to the front of the tunic she wore.

Eve grumbled, indeed impatient as each blood-covered button popped slowly, so slowly. Every inch of skin left bare by a missing button was soon feathered with kisses. A tantalizing trail leading down her chest to her navel. She arched her back to meet the touch of his lips against her skin, a whimper escaping her slightly parted lips. Need for him coursed through her, fire in her veins.

"Please," she sighed, hands plunging into his dark hair.

Callan growled in response, and in little more than a few heartbeats, every scrap of clothing bearing dried reminders of her death was gone, either shredded or tossed onto the floor. His every touch was a brand, setting her ablaze in the best possible way. Cupping her hip with one hand, he blazed a trail down the tattoo that adorned her arm.

The hand that trailed along her arm moved to her hip, fingers sliding to meet the bundle of nerves at the apex of her thighs. Slow, methodical circles had tension building low in her belly, jolts of lightning dancing along her skin.

Shadow tendrils caressed her breasts and her throat as his tongue replaced his fingers, drawing a sudden and near-overwhelming climax from her. His name was a plea on her tongue, a promise, for everything they had become and everything they would be.

"Callan." Her voice caught somewhere between a cry and a whisper as he rose to his knees between her thighs.

"Mine," he said, ocean eyes darkening. He hovered close, so close that she could feel the length of him pressing against her core, but he went no further. Wrapping her legs around his hips, she urged him closer, earning a low rumble of approval.

As he finally entered her, Eve could have sworn she felt the tattoo on her arm warm in response. Her newly heightened senses had her soaring higher and faster than she'd ever thought possible.

"Yours," she breathed, hands gripping as he moved. "As you are mine."

They moved together, Callan leaning closer, and her arms around his neck, holding him close. "Always," he whispered against the column of her neck. Not another word was spoken between them–the words of promise between them were the only ones needed.

THE DREAM HAD BEEN LOVELY, FROM WHAT SHE COULD remember anyway. Eve awoke with only the memory of a castle of pale grey stone, soaring high above a canopy of winter-bare trees. In the gloaming, the autumn breeze set deep blue flags with silver stars waving. It had been home to her, this castle that stood in such stark opposition to Stoneweald with its dark stone, blending into the mountains in the distance. A trio of towers reached toward the sky, fingers grasping for the darkening sky.

She drifted along, dancing from the highest parapets to the cobbled courtyard just inside the gates, carried on a phantom wind. Utterly alone she traveled, accompanied only by the distant memory of a song whispered to her by the wind.

Though she couldn't quite make out the words, she would know them anywhere. It was a song of love, of finding yourself and finding where you belonged, against all odds. The song of a princess far from home, guided back to those who loved her by the wind, singing a lullaby and whispering encouragement. A song her own mother had sung every night of her childhood, one the wind now whispered in her mother's voice.

Something awoke her with a jolt, yanking her from the beautiful world of her dream.

"Wake up," Callan whispered, his voice low and intense. It had been his hand on her shoulder that had awakened her so suddenly. He was already out of bed, dressed in an untucked shirt and black pants.

"What's wrong?"

What time is it? Judging by the dim moonlight coming through the windows, it had to be the earliest hours of the morning. Even the servants wouldn't be up and about this early, but thanks to her newfound fae senses, she could clearly make out the sounds of footsteps in the hallway. A lot of them, she realized with a start.

Satisfied now that she was sitting up and throwing the blanket to the side, Callan sank to the chair across from her and began tugging on his boots. Something outside, a noise that she couldn't identify even with her fae hearing, caught his attention and he paused, cursing low under his breath.

"Do you have a warm cloak and boots?"

Eve nodded, rising from the bed. The urgency in his tone and expression had her moving quickly, halting the questions that threatened to form on her tongue.

"Good. Get them on as fast as you can, and grab your dagger." Rising from the chair he crossed to her in two short strides, cupping her face and pressing his lips to her brow. "Quickly, my love."

By the time Eve pulled on her furlined cloak and boots, the footsteps outside had shifted into the sounds of running. The shouting started by the time she reached the sitting room where Callan waited by the door alongside one of the guards assigned to stand outside. Where the other was, she didn't know.

Fear had her heart quickening. Something was very, very, wrong. "What's happening?" She hated the tremble she heard in her voice and the fact that she was now asking for the second time, and Callan looked less than inclined to answer. "Tell me."

The guard and Callan exchanged a look before the latter finally replied. "We're under attack, and your men...they're losing."

Her heart skidded to a halt for half a breath. "Under attack? By whom? What do you mean we're losing? We've added so many guards and taken precautions. I don't understand." The words tumbled from her mouth rapidly, a panic-fueled waterfall.

"Look at me, dove," Callan said gently. "Do not lose your strength, not now. We need to get you out of here and regroup."

Eve shook her head, ready to protest. She couldn't abandon her home or her people. How many innocent lives were in danger tonight? Not only the guards, but the council, servants, and visiting nobles. Too many to count.

"I came here to protect you. Let me do that." Callan's voice was rough as he lifted his fingertips to her cheek. "Please, my love, let me keep you safe tonight, and then I will do everything in my power to help you reclaim your home."

Tears threatened to fall, but Eve nodded, wiping them away with one hand as she tightened her grip on her dagger in the other.

"Let's go," Callan said after a moment, pulling his sword free from the sheath at his back. "Stay close to me."

The guard pulled the door open, revealing an empty hallway. Shouting, the clang of steel clashing, and occasional screams echoed off the stone, though she couldn't see the source yet.

"Leysa and Valerian?" she asked, as they hurried toward the wing where their friends' room was located.

"We'll find them," Callan replied, watching the intersection of hallways that lay several yards ahead. "They'll be looking for Sylvie and her husband, if they can. The healers too."

This late in the evening, the corridors of Stoneweald were only dimly lit. Iron sconces adorned the walls every few feet or so, setting strange and almost eerie shadows dancing along the crevices and corners of the hallway as they moved. The sounds of fighting grew fainter as they walked, the invaders either having failed to reach this part of the castle or–

Eve wouldn't allow herself to consider the other possibility. Especially not when her friends' rooms were in that direction. The guard ahead of them remained alert, despite the quiet as they rounded the corner into the guest wing. Callan had fallen into step just behind Eve, allowing the guard to lead the way.

"What's your name?" she whispered, as much out of fear as a desire to avoid detection. Eve had seen him, the man currently leading her and Callan to safety, in the halls several times in the last few weeks. She found herself ashamed she hadn't thought to ask his name before now.

Casting only the briefest of glances over his shoulder with a tight smile, the guard nodded. "Garan, Majesty," he replied in a low whisper.

"Thank you, Garan." She wanted to ask if he had a family in the city not so far from where they stood, but she didn't dare. *When we get out of here, I'll find out and make sure they're safe as well.*

She heard them before they came into view. The sounds of clashing steel and leather boots stomping and sliding against the floor, around the next corner. The fighting must be spreading fast if they'd found their way this far into the guest wing. Garan shifted the sword in his hand as he prepared to face whomever they'd meet when they rounded the corner.

"Stay close," Callan whispered again, keeping at her side, the fighting coming into view finally.

A handful of men she didn't recognize, clad in sleek ivory armor, clashed with a few Stoneweald guards, marked by their slate-toned armor. They were losing, badly. Garan and Callan leapt into action immediately, fighting alongside the guards and dispatching their invaders, but not without losing most of the guards at their sides. By the time it was done, both men stood over the bodies, grim-faced and silent.

Eve could do little more than hope that when death had greeted them, she'd at least worn a kind face.

"Who are they?" None of their known adversaries had armor that shade, and though there were still some troubles with the men of the relatively nearby isles that attacked from time to time, their assaults were limited to the smaller fishing villages along the coastline; never this far inland. Whoever this was had come to conquer, not raid and flee.

"The North Wind," Callan said after a beat. His gaze met Eve's and his frown deepened. "Soldiers of Gorias, far to the north, beyond the Sgiath. I thought they were gone, but apparently, I was wrong."

"Callan–" she started. The warning her mother had given rang through her mind. There hadn't been time to tell him about what had happened to her after she'd died. She had to tell him, but Dallin's voice drew Eve's attention, stopping her short.

"Sorry for intruding, but maybe we should get moving?" She hadn't immediately noticed him in the clamor, especially with the helmet he wore.

"Sylvie?" she asked, grip tightening on her dagger. If anything had happened to Sylvie she would–

"Safe, Majesty," Dallin replied, inclining his head. "With Leysa. She and Valerian are leading as many of the guests and staff as they could find through the west tunnel right now."

Safe, they're all safe. Her relief was short-lived. A million questions and worries coursed through her. She had no idea that anyone lived beyond the Sgiath. The northern reaches were said to be some of the harshest places in all of Aestera to live. The idea that any significant civilization could survive in what had to be almost unending snow and ice, much less an entire kingdom, was staggering.

She wanted to hear more about this Gorias, and why they would attack a kingdom that hadn't even been aware of their existence, but the sound of men approaching stopped her short.

"Has everyone been evacuated from this wing?" Seeing her people to safety was what mattered now, there would be time for the rest later.

It was Dallin who answered, gesturing for his men to head down the hallway that would lead them to the small guest wing library. "Yes, Majesty. We should get to the tunnel. If they find it and follow them out…"

Everyone who had managed to get out that way would be slaughtered. But there were others in the castle who hadn't been in this wing or hadn't been able to be evacuated with the rest. "Callan," she began, finding his gaze already on her face.

"You can't save them all my love," he said firmly, reading the thought so clearly dancing in her eyes. "But if we go now, we can help as many as we can."

She wanted to argue. They should be searching the castle for survivors, she wanted to say. With Callan's powers and her own, if she could get close to a window, they should be able to handle it. Wordlessly, Callan sheathed his sword and bent low. He tugged an arrow from a fallen guard's body with a grunt, murmuring a prayer of peace. Gently opening Eve's free hand, he placed the arrow shaft in her palm.

Ash. They had brought ash arrows. Her hand trembled beneath the terrible weight of it, of what it meant. Whoever commanded these soldiers from Gorias, they had come prepared to kill fae.

CHAPTER 37

Without knowing where their enemy was and with the knowledge they bore weapons designed to kill fae, Callan couldn't risk pacing them out, so on foot, it would be. Each of her steps felt heavier than the next as they escaped, leaving those unlucky enough to be trapped inside to their fate. Desire to protect her people, to save all of them instead of the few Valerian and Leysa had managed to help, roared and thrashed within her. She knew Callan was right, but that knowledge did little to assuage her guilt.

The rest of the way to the tunnel was clear, earning the gods a whispered prayer of thanks from Garan. Hidden behind a tapestry within a seldom-used library, the escape system built by her ancestors was little more than a winding staircase hidden between thick stone walls; a damp and musty place, obviously neglected in the many years of peace they'd been given.

At the front of their little group, Garan carried the only light source: a single oil lamp he had managed to take from the hall above. The eerie quiet was only broken by their footsteps and an occasional drip of water–it reminded her of the dungeons.

"Callan," Eve whispered quietly, breaking the silence that had fallen on the group as they trekked onward. The exit was close, Garan had assured her though she doubted he knew for certain.

At her side, Callan turned to her, brow raised in question.

"We left so many behind, Callan," she breathed, coming to a halt.

Callan stopped beside her. "We did what we had to do."

Eve stared at him. Guilt and anger joined the turmoil of emotions raging within her, fueling her desire to return and fight. "We can't leave them all."

"Have you tried to use your powers, dove?" Callan folded his arms across his broad chest, tilting his head slightly. "You won't be able to. They brought their Samach, their silencers. I can't even reach my own magic here, not with them working to stop me."

Eve frowned. "Okay...that's a problem, but–"

"Your life is worth far more to me and to this kingdom than anyone left inside that castle. No matter how sorry I am for what is happening to some of them." He paused, lifting a hand to her cheek gently. "Do you want to help your people?"

"Of course."

"Then we need to keep going. If you die–" Callan shook his head, as if to drive away the thought. "I will let this kingdom, this world, fall into darkness and ash. It is worth nothing if you are not in it."

Eve let the weight of his words settle over her. Her blood thrummed in her veins in response, her heart pounding. Part of her wanted to argue, to tell him just how expendable she felt she was, but she knew he was right. If she were dead, who would fight for them?

She would give everything she had to protect those like the farmer's daughter she'd met in her throne room just days ago, even if most of them would hate her, now even more than before. No price would be too high to ensure freedom for those who had been so long denied it simply for the fact of their sex.

"Fine," she conceded after a small eternity. "But we're coming back."

"We'll come back, and we will make them pay for everything they've taken from you," he agreed.

The shuffle of Dallin's feet tugged Eve's attention from Callan, though she could still feel his intense gaze on her face.

"Apologies, Majesty," Dallin said somewhat sheepishly. "But we can't afford to stop now."

"Of course, lead the way please, Garan," Eve sighed. Garan nodded confidently and began to guide the group through the damp darkness once more.

Guilt and anger haunted her every step. *Help them later.* For the first time in longer than she cared to admit, her father came to mind. She wondered what he might do in this situation, how he might lead their people to safety. Eve had never been included in any strategy or war talks; she hadn't even been taught the basics of rule. The assumption had always been that her husband would be ruling, so it was wholly unnecessary for a daughter to learn such things.

She had always wondered if he'd wished they had been given a son, either instead of her or in addition. He had never said so aloud, of course. Her memories of her father were largely pleasant. Viktor had doted on her. He loved her, that had never been in doubt, but his life certainly would have been less complicated if he had sired a son or two instead of a single daughter. Maybe the kingdom itself would have been better off–

Voices in the distance stopped the depressing thought short. Ahead of her, Garan and Dallin halted, the former dousing the light swiftly.

"Can you see anything?" Dallin whispered quietly to the senior guard.

"Quiet," Garan said sharply, his voice little more than a breath.

Movement behind her drew Eve's attention to Callan, stalking forward slowly. The passageway was nearly too dark for her to see very far, even for her new fae sight, and would be utterly impossible for the others.

Callan, however, reveled in shadow and darkness, and from the surety of his movements, she suspected he could see better than even she could. Holding a hand up, he gestured for her to wait, pausing just long enough to ensure that she did so.

It took only a few steps for Callan to disappear into the darkness beyond her sight, from the natural gloom of the tunnel or with help from his powers, she didn't know.

She didn't dare move, could barely manage to breathe with him gone. Straining her new senses, she attempted to make out what the voices ahead were saying, but she could catch only a few words here and there, none of it helpful.

"...go now?"

"Don't know...wait?"

"...safe to?"

Two men speaking, and without being able to hear more or see them, she couldn't be sure if they were her own people or the invaders. The ones who apparently carried ash and knew how to kill fae.

A question she hadn't given voice to yet, for fear of the answer, flitted through her mind.

How had they known?

These soldiers of Gorias, whoever they were, had come prepared to kill fae, but how had they known to do so? Cathal had been behind the attack on Callan in Forest Haven, but Callan didn't seem to believe this to be connected. Or he hadn't said so, at least. Was Cathal's need for vengeance so deep that he would call upon this long-forgotten kingdom to destroy the entirety of Darkegrove? Something told her there was more going on than she knew, that Callan knew more than he had said. Once they were safe, she would ask, she decided, adding it to the growing list of tasks in her mind.

When we're safe, I'll get the whole story from him.

The distant voices came to an abrupt stop, and for several moments, only deafening silence met them in the darkness. If not for their breathing and her fae vision being able to make out the outlines of their bodies, Eve might've forgotten Dallin and Garan stood in front of her.

Callan had likely only been gone a few moments, but in the deep darkness of the tunnel, minutes felt like hours.

Something's wrong.

Eve took a step forward just as the voices picked up again, this time much closer. A low curse sounded, from Garan, as both men drew their swords. How they would fight in what had to be total darkness for them, she didn't know, but it seemed they were determined to try. She gripped her dagger tightly, ready to join them. If they were to die, at least they would do it fighting for their home.

"It's me, light your lamp," Callan's voice echoed off the damp walls. A cool stream of relief washed over her.

With a click, the oil lamp flared to life once more, illuminating the area around them. Callan stepped into the light with two utterly unexpected companions.

"Majesty," Mason Sinclair greeted Eve with a halfhearted smirk. His tone was as sardonic as it had been the last time she'd spoken with him when he'd been questioning her ability to rule–but his sharp green eyes had grown far more shadowed. Standing to his side was Silas Morris, another relatively young member of the council, in his mid-thirties by her guess. Like Mason's, his wrinkled tunic was splattered with blood.

Eve let her gaze roam over Silas' bronze arms, bared thanks to rolled sleeves, and his tunic, searching for any signs of injury to the man. The councilman appeared unharmed as he rubbed at his arm as if to brush off the blood and grime that had no doubt been the result of a skirmish with the soldiers from Gorias. Turning to Mason, she spared him a less intense examination.

"Lord Sinclair, Lord Morris. Are you injured?" Her attention darted from one to the other, noting the brief glance exchanged between them.

"No, Majesty," Silas replied. "Lord Thorne found us just where the tunnel opens up in the forest. There's a cave mouth just ahead. We're in the western forest, south of the old Byrne mine, I think."

Eve nodded. That was a fair distance from the castle, far enough to be able to move undetected if Gorias had limited their attack to Stoneweald itself.

"Have you found any of the others?"

"Has there been any sign of the enemy?"

Garan and Eve spoke simultaneously, earning a huff of a laugh from Mason. "Priorities," he muttered.

"Yes, Majesty, but not many," Silas' expression was grim. Too few, she realized. Too few had gotten out.

"Have you seen Sylvie?" Dallin demanded as he stepped closer to Silas. "She's about this tall," he explained, gesturing with his hand at Silas' confused expression. "Black hair, grey eyes. She's the queen's maid. You had to have seen her."

"There might have been a girl of that description, but I can't say for certain. I'm sorry," Silas said, his expression softening with sympathy.

"We've seen no sign of them. Something at Stoneweald, or perhaps in Forest Haven, is burning though, you'll smell it as soon as you step out," Mason said to Garan, ignoring the exchange between Silas and the others.

Silence settled over them as they considered the weight of what had happened. Her home was gone, and many of her people along with it.

"We need to keep moving." Callan stepped closer to Eve, linking his fingers with hers.

"But where are we going?" Dallin asked, shifting. Eve could practically feel the worry and anger surging around him. Worry for Sylvie and the others consumed her, but she could only imagine how much worse it had to be for Dallin.

"To find our friends," Eve answered for Callan. "Right?" Turning to him for confirmation, she narrowed her eyes. Wherever he thought they might go for refuge, to regroup and recover, finding their friends and families had to come first.

"They're not far," Silas interjected. "We can get to where they're hiding in a few minutes."

"Lead the way," Eve directed.

"Of course." Callan's hand squeezed hers gently. "Then we're going to Falias."

CHAPTER 38

True to his word, Silas led them out of the darkened tunnel through the mouth of what appeared to be a cave. For the first several yards, anyone who stumbled into the opening would find what appeared to be a natural cave system, dark and with various branches to lose oneself in. It would be near impossible to know the truth of what their escape route would be.

As they stepped into the watery light of dawn, Eve inhaled deeply. They'd been underground for at least an hour; the sun was already beginning to rise. The forest here was dense, as most of the northern kingdom was. Tall trees, pine, birch, and spruce, that had stood sentinel over the northern lands for centuries blocked most of the view of the sky. Small scrubby plants hardy enough to withstand the lack of light made up the forest floor, with moss growing in every space in between.

The cool air filled her lungs, calming the worst of her frayed nerves. As Mason had said, the autumn breeze carried the heavy scent of smoke. Something was indeed burning at Stoneweald.

What could have happened to those still within the city in the last hour? How many had managed to get out? Her thoughts turned to Emilia, locked away in the dungeons with no hope of escape, and the lack of guilt she felt shocked her.

Emilia had thought herself superior, taking the side of men who had such little regard for women. She had chosen to side with those men, even when they plotted and murdered her mother for showing support for a woman making her own choices in life. All the while, she'd been acting as a spy for Cathal. The entire thing left a sour taste in her mouth.

Thoughts lingering on her former friend, she silently followed as Mason and Silas led them to where the rest of the people who had managed to escape had hidden. Did Emilia still believe Cathal, Lord Clarke as far as Emilia knew, cared for her? It was all but impossible, Eve thought, shaking her head. He had been set on retrieving Mara, with little regard for Emilia or the trouble she found herself in on his account.

"Cover your ears, dove." Callan's voice, so close she could feel his lips graze her earlobe, startled her. The slight contact sent electricity dancing down her spine, as it always did. How his touch still managed to do that, even now in the midst of all this awful, she didn't know.

Shit. Eve tugged her hair forward, raking her fingers through as if trying to remove some tangles. In the chaos of the attack and the darkness of the tunnel, her delicately pointed ears had gone unnoticed. But now, in the early morning light, many eyes would soon be on her, and it would be a miracle if the change in her went unnoticed. She'd need to learn to glamour, as her friends could, and soon. It was how they had managed to keep their secret for as long as they had.

"Dallin!" A cry of joy and relief sounded from just ahead as Sylvie popped into view, stepping out from behind a large boulder.

Dallin's answer was lost in the sound of others shouting words of surprise or relief as the rest of their party neared, and the survivors of the attack on Stoneweald followed Sylvie around the boulder.

Cries of her name mingled with questions about loved ones being posed to Dallin and Garan. Relatives and friends of other guards were desperate to know about their loved one's fate.

Most kept a respectful, and with Callan at her side, likely fearful, distance, but a few women ventured close enough to offer low bows and prayers of thanks to the gods for her safety. She wanted to tell them that it hardly mattered when so many were left behind, but she knew that it would do nothing but make the ones who had survived somehow feel even more guilt than they likely already did.

"Valerian? Leysa?" Callan asked roughly, as Sylvie, Dallin close at her side, came to greet them.

"They're close," she reassured him. "They went to check the woods and make sure we were safe here. A few of the men here are skilled enough with bow or sword that they felt it was our best choice."

Callan nodded, but the tension in his face remained. He worried for them, she knew, as she did. Armed with ash arrows, whatever a Samnach was, and who knew what other manner of weapons, the soldiers from Gorias posed a huge threat to them.

"Do you think they know?" Eve asked Callan, gaze fixed intently on his features.

"I hope so," he said quietly.

"I have questions. A lot of them."

"They'll have to wait, dove," he replied, glancing pointedly at the crowd gathered.

Eve looked, really looked, for the first time at the group of survivors. There were maybe twenty-five in total, ranging from maids and other servants to nobility. Seated on a fallen log, just beyond Sylvie, the healer Celestia. Eve raised a brow in question, and Celestia frowned offering a small shake of her head. Mauren hadn't made it out.

Aside from Mason and Silas, however, only one other councilor appeared to have made it out. By the boulder, in quiet conversation with the other councilors, stood Lord Eldred Gray.

"I need to speak with him," Eve inclined her head in the elder councilor's direction. "He'll know if there is any help to be found in this part of the kingdom. Some villages out this way may be sympathetic toward me, but likely more than a few are not. He'll know which ones we can trust."

Whatever the councilors had been discussing in hushed tones fell away as Eve approached. Callan had remained a few feet away, close enough to protect her if needed, but far enough that it wouldn't appear to them he was the one leading things.

She was still the rightful queen of Darkegrove, despite the attack, and now, more than ever, she had to be seen as strong and in control of herself and her people.

"Lord Gray, I am grateful to see you safe," she said by way of greeting as the elder bowed his head.

"As I am, you, Majesty." Eldred straightened, smoothing the front of his shirt. Like many of the others, he still wore his night clothes.

They had to be freezing, standing in the chill of the early autumn morning without the sun to warm them yet. A fire would have been too large a risk, and none of them had had time to dress for the weather, it seemed. They'd had such little time, and so few had escaped.

"I see your family made it out with you, Lord Morris," Eve said, glancing in the direction of Lady Wren Morris tugging a blanket around the shoulders of her son. The boy couldn't have been more than nine. Just beyond, another noble family she recognized, the Flemings, huddled together. Their daughter, a few years younger than the Morris boy, was cradled in her mother's lap.

Is this all that remains?

With the coronation, nearly every noble family had come to Stoneweald. With both castle staff and those accompanying each family, it amounted to a staggering number of innocent lives–most of whom would have had no way of escape. She could only hope those that remained inside survived.

There had been no warning of the attack, something she couldn't understand. The walls surrounding the castle were high and well-manned, especially now. If Gorias had somehow managed to move through the forests at the rear of the keep or the city to the front and sides unseen, the guards atop the walls should have alerted her soldiers to an impending attack, and yet they hadn't. Too many questions remained unanswered, but for now, the priority had to be finding safety for those who had managed to get out.

"Lord Gray, I am told that we are somewhere just south of Byrne Mine. To your knowledge, are there any villages nearby that might be able to provide refuge and warmth for them?" Eve asked, gesturing behind her. The healer and maids had all huddled together, rubbing their hands for warmth, the few guards who had accompanied them forming a circle of sorts to keep watch.

Mason and Silas shared a glance but remained silent.

Eldred rubbed a hand along his jaw, considering. "Well, Majesty, I believe the village of Roskirk is the closest if memory serves. What I last heard about this region is that it is mostly in support of you, though there have been a few here and there who have been vocally opposed to your reign." Eldred frowned, offering her an apologetic glance. "It may not be the safest option for you, since we do not know for certain who could be a danger to you."

Eve inhaled slowly, pushing down the well of anger and guilt that rose at the idea of her people being harmed even further because of her. "I will not be remaining here, my lord," she said quietly, gaining looks of surprise from all three councilors.

"I am afraid I do not understand, Majesty," Eldred replied.

Eve opened her mouth to explain, only to be interrupted by Mason. "You're going to Falias," he said flatly.

Pinning him with a glare, Eve nodded tersely. "I am."

"Do you even know what that place is?" Mason demanded.

Silas frowned in confusion. Eldred covered his mouth with his palm, eyes widening.

"Do you?" Eve countered, unwilling to admit that she didn't, not really.

"The lost city of the fae," Eldred muttered, glancing sharply at Mason. "What do you know of it?"

Mason simply shook his head. "Only the name," he admitted, kicking at the dirt lightly with his boot.

At least he had managed to dress, or perhaps he had never undressed. If his reputation were to be believed, it certainly would have been like him to be just arriving back to his own rooms in the wee hours of the morning.

"But it's supposed to be nothing more than a ruin on the edge of the gorge, right?" Mason turned an accusing eye to Eve. "So I can't help but wonder why your mysterious...guardian? Fae, lover? Forgive me, Majesty, I do not know the correct term here." He smirked at the rage burning in Eve's green eyes now. "I can't help but wonder why he would declare that you are going there next." He tilted his head, cold eyes narrowing. "Ah, perhaps this title fits best, 'holder of your leash'."

In an instant, so quickly that she had no time to react or respond to the vitriol, Callan was there. One moment Mason stood before her, lip curling in disgust at what he perceived to be her weakness, and in the span of a breath, Callan had the councilor pinned to a tree, hand at his throat.

"A single word from her, and I will rip your throat out," He growled, shadows gathering at his hands. The facade he held in place so carefully had slipped, and gone was the stoic warrior, in his place, the fearsome fae male protecting his mate.

CHAPTER 39

CALLAN

One thought coursed through Callan's mind. He'd fucked up. Royally.

He had been listening to one of the guards explain how Val, Leysa, and the others had all gotten out. How, as frail and elderly as Eldred had appeared, he had rallied the rest of them and guided them to the hidden door in the library. That old man had nearly single-handedly saved the lot of them, according to the guard. Well, except for the fighting, for which he took no small amount of credit, though Callan was sure Val and Leysa were the true heroes of that particular part of the story.

He also had been listening, thanks to his heightened hearing, to Eve's conversation with her councilors. The first in his series of fuck-ups had been mentioning Falias in front of the others. It had been thoughtless, uncharacteristically so.

How many battles had he been in? How many dangerous and stressful situations required a cool head? Too many to count. Somehow those centuries of training and discipline were undone with Eve in danger. His worry for her had clouded his mind, and he hadn't thought before speaking.

That had been the most minor of the fuck-ups though. None of the others had questioned it, hadn't dared question her. Either because they knew her well enough to know she deserved their trust, or from respect for the crown that metaphorically rested on her head.

Callan had been determined to stay out of it. He knew she could handle herself and could put them in their places if needed. She was a queen in every sense of the word, and he wouldn't dare shed any doubt on that in their eyes by treating her as if she needed someone to speak for her, to protect her from every little thing.

But then Mason fucking Sinclair crossed a line.

"...holder of your leash."

The exceptionally thin, and frayed, tether holding his temper in check snapped. Undiluted rage surged through him, and before he could stop himself he used his fae speed to pin the councilman to the nearest tree.

"A single word from her, and I will rip your throat out." He meant it. His magic strained beneath his skin, shadows begging to be let out to play. Already they gathered around his hand at Mason's throat, dancing and whirling. With barely a thought, he could ravage the councilman's mind, with another shred him to pieces.

Callan felt her tense behind him. A subtle, sharp intake of breath. "Callan, stop." Her voice was calm, but he could hear her heart racing.

He'd attacked a member of the Council of Nine, and judging from the absolute stillness that had fallen over the group, all hell was about to break loose. Some of them had likely been in the ballroom the night Cathal had shown up, and those who hadn't had heard about it. Everyone had. It was the reason the number of guards on duty at the castle had been doubled, the reason Gorias shouldn't have been able to get in undetected.

He had really, really fucked up.

With a growl, Callan released Mason, letting the councilman fall to his knees in front of him, as Mason coughed and gasped for air. To Mason's credit, he wisely kept his mouth shut as Silas helped him to his feet.

The other survivors backed away, the mothers of the two young ones in their small company holding their children close.

"Majesty?" The guard he'd been speaking to moments ago looked to

Eve questioningly, they all did. He'd attacked a respected leader, but his status at her side kept them from immediately acting. They'd only act on her orders now.

"Everyone will lay down their arms," Eve commanded. "Lord Morris, has Lord Sinclair been injured?"

Mason waved a hand in Eve's direction, silencing Silas with a glare. "I can speak for myself, Majesty," he rasped. Maybe he had squeezed a little too hard, Callan mused with not one ounce of regret. "I'm fine."

Eve narrowed her eyes at his biting tone but said nothing else to the councilman. Instead, she turned those gorgeous eyes of hers on Silas. "Lord Morris, Lord Gray has informed me there is a village just a short walk from here that should be amenable and capable of providing shelter and assistance to our people." Staring steadily at the guards, she continued. "Please see Lord Gray, Lord Morris, and the others to this village."

Mason coughed again. "Getting rid of the witnesses?" he croaked, nearly earning himself another visit to the tree.

"No," Eve replied calmly, staying Callan's hand with a sharp look. "You will be accompanying Lord Thorne and me, as well as Lord and Lady Ashford when they return, to Falias. I wish you to see for yourself what awaits us. Perhaps that will offer you some insight into my judgment."

It took only a few minutes for the survivors to gather what little they had and begin their journey to the village of Roskirk. Silas, followed closely by a pair of guards, led the way.

Near the rear, Eldred paused, gazing sadly at his queen. "I would have liked to see it," he said, wistfulness clouding his aged features. "The lost city of fae kings. The stories my grandfather told as a boy, things he heard from men as old as I am now, well," he chuckled once, giving a slight shake of his head. "I would have liked to see that."

Eve offered him a soft smile. "Perhaps you will."

"No, Majesty," Eldred corrected gently. "I don't believe I will."

With that, he turned and followed the rest of the group, leaving Callan alone with Eve and Mason to wait for Valerian and Leysa.

Chapter 40

"How long have you known?" Mason asked for the third time in five minutes, flicking a bit of pine straw from his fingers irritably.

Callan growled, barely pausing his irritated patrol of the clearing to offer Mason a glare.

It had been nearly twenty minutes since the main group had gone in search of help, and Valerian and Leysa still hadn't returned. Callan walked back and forth, worried and torn between the desire to go in search of his friends and staying behind to protect Eve. He hadn't admitted it, but it was clear enough to Eve in the way his glance often drifted between her and the eastern sky, the direction that would take them back to Stoneweald, toward danger.

Ignoring Mason's question again, Eve leaned back against the boulder. The rough stone was cold, even through her cloak and long-sleeved tunic. Eve frowned. She had been dressed more warmly than most of the rest of the survivors, and even she was getting cold. Would they make it to the village in their night clothes?

A glance at Mason told her that he was feeling the chill of the autumn air too, try as he might to hide it. Goose pimples covered his tanned arms, and every once in a while he gave a sudden shiver.

"You can go and look for them," Eve said, not for the first time.

"No." Callan's reply was the same as it had been the last time she'd attempted, firm and without room for argument.

"I can at least try to make us a shelter of sorts. Mason's freezing." Mason narrowed his eyes but remained quiet, casting a wary glance in Callan's direction. She'd tried this tactic too, but he'd refused before as well, claiming fear they'd be able to detect the use of her magic somehow.

At Callan's expression, Eve sighed. "We can't sit here and freeze, Callan. I want to find them too, but we're no good to anyone if we freeze to death."

"We wait," he replied, launching into the same spiel he'd given before. "They'll return, and then we'll move. If they aren't back soon, I can pace the two of you somewhere and–"

The sharp cry of a hawk cut him off, and both Callan and Eve turned their eyes skyward suddenly.

"It's just a bird," Mason snorted. "Why are you so–"

"Shut up," they said in tandem, listening for the familiar hawk's cry again. Blessedly, the shifter called again, this time closer and more urgently.

"Leysa," Eve breathed, rising from her seat on the ground. Pine needles and dirt clung to her leggings, but she paid them no mind as Leysa came into view, descending from above the treeline and banking around trees.

Shifting mid-air, she landed a few feet from Eve abruptly, breaking into a run. Eve let out a muffled "mmph" as she was enveloped in a fierce hug.

"You're alive," they said in unison, Eve returning the hug enthusiastically.

Callan, standing beside Eve, waited until the friends had broken apart to crush Leysa in his own arms.

Laughing, Leysa pulled back and looked them both over.

Mason's strangled shout of surprise went ignored.

"Valerian?" Eve asked, frowning.

"He's fine," Leysa assured them. "Just a little behind me. Should be coming through the trees over there any minute. He didn't want to pace in front of the humans, so I was coming to check on them before joining him and shifting. But I saw you guys, and I couldn't stop myself."

"You're both okay?" Callan looked her over once more, nodding to himself.

"We're good," Leysa smiled. Dark curls bobbed gently as she tilted her head to look past Eve to where Mason now scrambled to his feet. "You have a story to tell apparently. Where is everyone else?"

Eve turned to Mason with a sigh. "They're safe. Eldred knew of a village nearby where they could find shelter and supplies. Lord Sinclair and Callan got into a slight...quarrel."

Both men snorted their disagreement with her characterization of the incident.

"Lord Sinclair," Callan added, disdain dripping from every syllable, "has earned himself a trip with us to Falias."

Leysa's attention shot to Callan, chestnut eyes widening in surprise. "Callan, you can't be serious," she said. "We're going home?"

Leysa's questions went unanswered as the sound of someone approaching through the brush sounded. Whomever it was, they were moving quickly. All three fae tensed at once.

"It's Valerian," Leysa said, breath coming out in a whoosh.

Valerian stepped into view moments later, brow covered in sweat despite the cool temperature. His eyes met Callan's first, relief washing over his face before moving to Eve. She offered the warrior a smile, something in her chest warming now that they were all safe, all together again. At last, his gaze landed on Leysa.

With only a few long strides, he came to stand in front of her, lifting broad hands to cup her cheeks gently. "My love," he said in greeting, resting his forehead against hers. "I lost sight of you toward the end, and I thought..." There was no explanation needed. They had all thought the same, each of them worried for the others.

"All is well," Leysa reassured him, palm resting against Valerian's chest. "And," she added, drawing the word out slightly. "We have a guest."

Valerian's attention shifted to Mason, still standing behind the group. His hands dropped away from Leysa's face slowly, as if reluctant to break the contact between them. "Lord Sinclair," he said in greeting, finally turning to survey the mostly empty clearing. "Where have the others gone? Was there trouble?"

"No, they're all okay," Eve answered. "Eldred has taken them to a village nearby. They'll be given shelter and aid there."

"We'll follow them?" Valerian rolled his shoulders, ready for whatever would come next. "Or do we fight?"

It was Callan who answered this time. "We go home, brother," he said, voice thick with emotion.

Valerian stared at him in shocked silence as Leysa took his hand in her own, intertwining their fingers. "Home, Val," she whispered, awestruck.

"Home," Callan echoed.

~

By the time the group had finished discussing the plan, Mason had fallen into what Eve could only describe as total shock. The fae had paid him little attention while they planned, save for Eve, sparing him a few glances on occasion. How strange and likely frightening this all had to be for him. He had known of her magic, and of Callan's, but to hear that the stories they had been told as children of the fearsome fae and their supposedly long-lost cities were real and still existed... It had to be quite a lot to take in.

While Callan worried that any use of their magic could possibly be traced and had argued against pacing at all, Leysa disagreed, saying if that were the case, they would have been discovered when she shifted.

The compromise they reached was simple. They would walk a bit farther, Callan and Leysa agreed, then she would scout from the air to ensure they weren't being followed.

The small walk Callan agreed to felt more like a small eternity. Leysa and Valerian led the way, murmuring quietly between themselves, smiles being exchanged as Leysa occasionally leaned into Valerian's side, the love between the pair as tangible as it always was.

What would it be like, Eve wondered, to live a life so fully with someone who was not only your love but your best friend? She felt such a tremendous love for Callan that it was beginning to feel too deep, too encompassing. It frightened her at times, as much as it comforted her. They had fallen into one another so quickly and amid so much upheaval and fear, she couldn't help but wonder if they would know how to be at peace with each other and simply live.

"They're mates," Callan said suddenly, drawing Eve out of her thoughts. "True mates. It's not very common amongst our kind, but it does happen. They would love each other without it, but it adds another layer of..." He paused, searching for the right word, dragging a hand through his night-dark hair as he did. "Utter devotion. They would literally die for one another, easily kill for one another. And have–" Valerian cast a sharp look over his shoulder at Callan. "Not my story to tell," he said in answer to the question written all over Eve's face.

Mate. The word rattled around inside her, jarring at first, before settling comfortably into some deep spot within her soul she hadn't even known existed. They were mates, he'd said. She had planned to ask him about it when she'd mustered the courage. Eve had been a coward last night. Had planned to continue being one today, in fact. At least until the meeting she'd planned to have with the council had been dealt with.

She'd intended to tell them she was fae, to offer to step down from the throne she'd fought so hard, had given so much, for. Under one condition. The right to choose her successor. A woman. Someone strong and capable. Someone who would ensure that the next monarch would be chosen not for their sex, but for their merits.

But all of that had been swept away in a moment's notice. Now she remained queen of a broken kingdom, a fae queen ruling a broken human kingdom. Walking toward a fae kingdom thought lost to the world, alongside its long-lost king. The thought nearly made her laugh at the ridiculousness of it all.

Fae queen. She chewed on the words, flexing her fingers and marveling at the sensation. There was little difference, really, but something *had* changed. Her senses were heightened, of course, touch included, though not as keenly as her sight or hearing. A strength she hadn't known as a human lay there now, just beneath the skin alongside the magic gifted to her by the goddess Keithia.

Coward on two counts then, she thought. She was afraid of it now, far more than she'd been as a human. The wild magic that flowed through her had been difficult for her to control then. Now, she worried it might just consume her entirely.

"I wouldn't be so sure of that," a feminine voice said suddenly, halting the group.

Ahead, clad in little more than gauzy emerald silk draped over her lush form, Keithia stood on the path. Despite it being fully autumn with few flowers in the region blooming this time of year, a multitude of flowers in full bloom carpeted the ground at Keithia's bare feet. The underbrush, brown and damp, was at once verdant. Life sprang forth around her, *from* her.

At once, the other fae dropped to a reverent knee, leaving only Eve and Mason standing. Mason's head swiveled, attention darting from the fae warriors to the goddess.

"How are you here?" Eve asked cautiously.

Keithia only smiled softly. "Your magic is as much a part of you as the blood that flows through your veins, my darling. If you let go of your fear, you will find that you can do wondrous things with it." Forest green eyes slid to Callan, on one knee in the damp earth with his head bowed. "My sister sends her love, her most favored Raven; and bids you to continue your journey. You are doing what is right, but you must not delay your journey further."

Callan raised his head only slightly. "Yes, my lady, at once."

To Eve, she added. "Trust in yourself, my child." As suddenly as she appeared, she was gone. No flash of light, or any other sign of magic. Simply gone, as if she had never existed in the first place, leaving only the quickly fading flowers as evidence of her short visit.

"Was that...was she...another fae?" Mason asked after a beat, stumbling over the words.

Together, the three kneeling fae rose. "No," Valerian answered, brushing dead leaves from his pants. "That was the goddess of life herself."

Eve turned to Callan, worry settling over her. "Do you think something is wrong? If Macaria sent you this message..."

Callan nodded. "I think something must be very wrong. She prefers to allow things to happen in their own way and in their own time."

"I'm sorry, but what the fuck?" Mason demanded suddenly. "That was the goddess of life. Goddess. You're all fae, apparently," he all but shouted, waving his hand vaguely. "And who is she telling us to hurry along like good children? Another goddess I assume?"

"Of death and destiny," Leysa replied helpfully, earning a snort from Valerian.

"Great. That's just *great*," Mason continued. "So, the fae are still around, the gods have not, in fact, abandoned us all, and we're heading toward the supposedly long-lost fae kingdom, which is apparently in some sort of peril that we must keep moving toward. While our own kingdom is being razed by some unknown enemy."

The late autumn wind swept through the clearing ferociously, sending Eve's unbound hair swirling in its chilly grasp. For a moment, they all simply stared at Mason, reactions ranging from strained impatience on Callan's part to quiet laughter on Leysa's.

"Yes," Eve began, calmly. "It is absolutely...baffling, the situation we're in."

Mason sighed, folding his arms across his chest, but listened nonetheless. So Eve pressed on. "There is so much you do not know, and I know it is overwhelming. If you will just give me until we reach Falias, I will answer any question I am able to. You are owed that much, at least, after what we have been through this morning."

Callan stepped closer to Eve's side, taking her hand in his. "I know you don't trust us, but trust this." Cold blue eyes fixed on Mason unflinchingly. "If we don't go *now,* we will be in danger. *She* will be in danger, and I will not allow that to happen. If you can't get it together long enough to get to Falias, I will leave you here. Do you understand?"

Mason only offered a single sharp nod in response.

Taking that as answer enough, Callan turned his attention to Eve, expression softening significantly. "We need to pace now. Macaria wouldn't be telling us to go if it weren't dire."

"I can take two," Valerian offered, glancing between Mason and Callan.

"What does that mean?" Mason asked finally, loosening his arms. Perhaps to flee, Eve noted with only a little amusement.

"It's like...jumping between two places," Leysa offered. "Only the other place can be very far away, and you have to use magic to do it." She waved her hand vaguely. "It's complicated." Turning to Valerian she frowned. "And no, you can't carry two. I can fly, you can carry him."

"Fuck that, then Callan can take you," Valerian said immediately. "If you're seen-"

"All they'll see is a bird, my love. I won't even use my hawk form, I'll go for something smaller, less conspicuous. We all know that neither of you can take the strain of two people."

Valerian muttered a colorful curse under his breath but nodded.

"Stay low, under the canopy if you can. Be careful." It was Callan that spoke this time, voice laced with worry for his friend.

"Aren't I always?" Leysa replied cheerfully, offering Callan a wink and Valerian a swift kiss before shifting. True to her word, she chose the form of a common sparrow. An unremarkable and utterly common-place sight in the forests of Darkegrove.

"Let's go then," Callan said, taking Eve's hand in his. Valerian followed suit with Mason, in a far less tender way.

"Be safe," Eve said to Leysa, earning a chirp in response before the shifter took to the sky, flittering away westward.

"Hold on tight, dove," Callan said, squeezing Eve's hand once before darkness overtook them. Pacing for the second time was every bit as frightening as the first time had been. Eve inhaled sharply as sheer nothingness surrounded them. A strange, preternatural wind whipped around them, and in the next breath, they were in an entirely different part of the dark forest.

For a moment, she thought they hadn't moved at all. The same types of trees grew here, and the same birds cried overhead, startled by their sudden appearance. But something in the air felt different. It was as if those very trees hummed with some power that called to her own. Indeed, she could feel her power dancing beneath her skin, practically begging for her to use it.

"You can feel it, can't you?" Callan's voice drew her attention, something akin to wonder lighting his face. "We're close to Falias now," he explained. "The magic here runs deep. Most humans can't even tell."

"Well, I'm not human anymore, am I?" she asked, wincing at the bitterness in her tone.

You chose this, she reminded herself. *For the good of your kingdom, for your people.*

A muscle in Callan's jaw feathered. "I know, Eve. But I am damned grateful you're fae and not dead." His tone was harsh, but the emotion behind it eased the sting.

"Leysa won't make it for a while," Valerian sighed from where he'd paced, a few yards away. His eyes remained on the eastern skies, barely visible through the thick canopy.

"Do you want to wait?" Callan asked, casting an uneasy glance to the west. They'd been warned not to delay, but Valerian would want to wait for Leysa. The way they'd spoken of returning home would've told her that if their love for one another hadn't already.

"I could use a minute," Mason groaned, plopping unceremoniously to the ground. His tan skin had taken on a greenish hue, giving him an altogether sickly pallor.

"You two should go ahead," Valerian replied, eyeing Mason now. "I'm going to wait for Leysa. He can stay with me and recover," he continued, smirking at the ill-looking councilman.

At Callan's hesitation, Valerian shook his head. "She said not to delay. We'll be fine, go ahead."

Callan nodded once and turned his attention back to Eve. "Are you ready to see my home?"

"Show me," she said with a smile. As they took their first step toward Falias, her magic began to sing within her veins.

Home, it seemed to say, *home.*

CHAPTER 41

True to Callan's word, the walk to Falias was brief. After a few moments, they broke through the treeline and the city came into view for the first time a massive walled city surrounding a castle. The similarity between the two began and ended there.

While Forest Haven was large, Falias doubled her size. In contrast to Forest Haven's near black stone walls, the pale grey walls guarding Falias gleamed, topped by sentry towers and patrolled by far more guards than the humans could muster. Unlike Stoneweald, in the center of the capital city the fae castle rose high above the canopy of trees. Apparently, there had never been a need to hide her from view.

Eve's heart gave a squeeze at the sight of such security. Would her own people have been spared if they could have matched the craftsmanship and wealth it would require to build such defenses? Perhaps, but without knowing how Gorias had gotten past what defenses they did have, she couldn't be sure.

From this distance, she could only make out the tops of the tallest buildings in the city proper, forming a spiral around the centerpiece of the grand kingdom. The castle was unlike any she'd seen before. Stoneweald was impressive, sprawling, and well-appointed. Sunholde, home to the Vallyse family, was made of so much glass and gold that it was nearly blinding to look at on sunny days, but this...this was something else entirely.

Made from the same pale stone as the walls, the castle soared upward, a trio of towers reaching for the sky as if to pierce the heavens themselves, deep blue flags embroidered with a trio of silver stars dancing atop them. Perhaps the builders had been seeking some connection with their gods, or perhaps they had simply used their skill to elicit the very reaction Eve herself was having now. Awe, pure and simple, flooded her alongside another emotion she couldn't name.

"What's it called, the castle?" she asked, dragging her gaze from the castle to Callan.

Where her gaze had been filled with wonder and surprise, his was full of longing, and to her surprise, grief. Turning to look at her, he chuckled softly, "You know, it doesn't actually have a name."

"I dreamt of it," she said, voice thick with emotion as she turned back to the castle. "Last night, before you woke me, I was dreaming about this place."

"Maybe the gods were telling you something."

Home, the magic within her hummed again.

SHOUTS ERUPTED FROM THE WATCHTOWERS AS THEY CAME into view. Even with her fae hearing, they were still far enough away that she couldn't make out what was being said. As they neared, the great iron gates began to rise, creaking and moaning from disuse. Riders on horseback, a handful at most, raced toward them as soon as the gate rose high enough.

Eve and Callan came to a stop, waiting for the riders from Falias to reach them. Callan stepped in front of Eve protectively, shadows wreathing around his hand, outstretched at his side. Her heart raced, as hard and fast as the approaching riders. Would they attack? Did they not recognize him?

As they neared, Callan's shoulders instantly dropped, shadows vanishing like dust on the wind. At the head of the column was a raven-haired girl, hair flying freely behind her, atop a dapple grey mare and riding hard, straight for Callan.

"Cora," he sighed, stepping forward to meet her as her horse skidded to a stop. She was dismounted in an instant, throwing herself into Callan's waiting arms, joy written onto every inch of her lovely face.

The sharp blade of jealousy pierced Eve's heart, and the pebbles beneath their feet gave a quiver in response to the surge of emotion.

"Callan," Cora exclaimed breathlessly, pulling away to look him over before giving him a not-so-gentle smack on the chest. "Valerian and Leysa, are they?" At Callan's nod, she continued. "You have so much explaining to do." Cora paused, glancing past him to Eve finally, brow raising. "Starting with who *that* is."

The pebbles danced again, drawing frowns from Cora and guards who had finally reached them as well, now sitting atop their own mounts just behind her.

"No need to cause an earthquake, my love," Callan laughed, turning to Eve. "This is my sister, Cora Thorne, Steward of Falias." Heat flooded Eve's cheeks in embarrassment, as Callan continued. "Cora, this is Queen Evelyn Darrow of Darkegrove." Callan turned to Cora with a beaming smile, one of the few Eve had seen. "My mate."

That place in her soul that belonged so fully to him sang. Cora's responding gasp had Eve following her gaze downward. At her feet, flowers had sprung to full bloom, right in the middle of the barren, dusty track where they stood. Returning her attention to Cora, Eve offered a nervous smile. "It's nice to meet you, Cora."

"Same to you," Cora returned with a shaky laugh. "So much explaining to do," she muttered as she turned to her horse. "You can take Starmane the rest of the way. I could use a run anyway."

Eve frowned in confusion. The pale pink gown Cora wore had been ill-suited for riding, let alone running. "A run?" she asked, glancing at Callan, only to find him grinning at his sister.

"You'll see," he said with a laugh as he took Starmane's reigns. "She's a showoff."

Settling herself onto the saddle comfortably, Eve took in the now dirty tunic and leggings she'd been wearing since the night before and grimaced. She could only hope there would be time for at least a change of clothes before she had to meet any more of Callan's family.

A flash of white to her right caught her attention. Where Cora had been before, now stood a large white wolf with the same haunting blue eyes that Callan and Cora shared.

"She's a shifter like Leysa?" Eve asked, earning a huff from Cora.

Callan laughed. "There's a bit of competition between them on that front. Don't worry, sister, they'll be along shortly, and you can do whatever it is the two of you do."

That earned another huff from Cora before she was off, racing toward the city with impressive speed. Taking his seat behind Eve, Callan huffed a laugh at his sister. "Don't let the little competition between them fool you," he explained. "They're best friends. I know she's dying for them to come home too."

As they set off, at a much more leisurely pace than Cora, Eve shifted in the saddle, lifting a hand to her tangled hair. "How long do you think it will take Leysa to get here?"

Behind her, Eve could feel Callan's shrug. "I'm not sure. She's fast as a hawk, but as a songbird, it might take her a bit longer. I'm hoping for no more than half the day."

Eve wanted to ask what could possibly be so wrong that Keithia had chosen to appear to them, to personally deliver Macaria's message, but the presence of Cora's guards kept her silent. She knew nothing of this court, of who to trust and who to be wary of. Would Callan remember? He had been away for so many centuries now, so many things could have changed.

The short ride to the city passed in the blink of an eye. As they crossed through the gatehouse, Eve found countless pairs of eyes watching them in silence. Save for one, the guards who had accompanied them fell back, leaving Eve and Callan to ride at the front, separated and alone.

A lone guard remaining at the head of the column boomed out, his voice carrying on the wind for such a long time and with such volume, only magic could be behind it. "People of Falias, bear witness to the return of the High King of Falias, Callan Ryne Vaderyn Thorne, Lord of Shadow and Darkness."

"Are we safe?" she whispered to Callan, gripping the pommel tighter. Another trip to another city flashed in her mind. Blood and fear, and a desperate race to safety.

Callan's arm came around her waist then, holding her close. "Nobody here will hurt you, Eve." His voice was gentle comfort, his body behind her a shield.

Eve had expected the outer portions of the city to be dirty and rundown. In Forest Haven, only those of the meagerest means lived so far from the castle, and as such, the outer city showed signs of poverty. It had been something she'd wanted to change, given the chance to really rule. Helping improve the lives of the people deemed undesirable by the men who'd ruled before her for so long had been the highest on her list of priorities.

Falias, it seemed, had already taken on that cause.

Though modest in size, the homes in this part of the city were well-kept, showing no signs of disrepair. Some were made from a darker shade of the same stone the walls and castle had been hewn from, others from lumber that must have been milled from the surrounding forests and then painted in varying colors. Pretty flower boxes graced many of the windows, and for a moment she could picture them in the spring, bursting with blooms of every variety and color.

Seemingly every citizen had come out of their homes to watch as they passed. They must have been alerted by the guards and their shouts as Eve and Callan first arrived. The faces that watched in what Eve could only describe as stunned silence were as varied as the pretty homes they passed as they rode through the winding streets toward the center of the city. Even the children, most looking more confused than their elders, did little more than smile. But in their wake, one by one, each of Falias' residents bowed their heads in respect.

The wealth of her residents did seem to increase as they approached the center of the city, homes growing larger and slightly more spaced out. The shift in Falias was far more subtle than at Forest Haven, however, just as she was beginning to expect. Nearing the castle, Eve was stunned to see no walls to separate the royal residence and homes there.

"You don't keep walls between the castle and the city?" she asked as her gaze rose higher and higher, following the impressive tower just ahead of them as it swept skyward.

"Why would we?" The retort came not from Callan but from one of the guards, now riding at their side. "The city of Falias and her rulers, have never had such animosity between them as your human kingdom seems to. If the main walls were to be breached, most of our residents are trained in fighting skills and would assist the guard in defending their homes. As would the royal family."

Eve frowned at the harsh truth laid bare in his words. Callan had stiffened behind her, likely ready to come to her aid if he thought she needed it. "Darkegrove has much to learn from Falias, it seems," she said simply.

Thanks to whichever god or goddess presided over small miracles, the castle had been largely empty when they arrived. Cora was waiting for them just inside the grand entry hall, in the same pink gown, looking unruffled despite her energetic ride, and then run, earlier.

It was all Eve could do not to gape. She was a royal by blood, had grown up in a lavish castle of her own, and had the privilege of visiting what was considered to be the most beautiful palace on the continent when she'd gone to see Lia in Sunholde; yet all paled in comparison to where she now stood. Her gaze swept over impressively high ceilings adorned with chandeliers dripping in crystal, tapestries draping the walls in colors impossibly bright depicting lifelike figures, and tables bearing vases filled to bursting with blooms that had to have been grown in a greenhouse, given the time of year.

She made a mental note to ask about the greenhouses when there was time.

"I'll show you to your suite," Cora was saying, positively beaming. There was a gleam in her eye that told Eve she would be asking a million questions the moment they were alone. But...weren't they alone now? Eve glanced around, finding no others in the immediate area.

Outside, the guards had helped them dismount Starmane. She hadn't seen a single stablehand or any other household staff. In a castle this size, she would've expected to see dozens of staff and courtiers milling about, especially given the excitement of Callan's return.

Guessing the direction of Eve's thoughts, Cora added. "I've asked the staff for space until you're....settled in," she said, gaze dropping to Eve's travel-worn clothes.

"I'm sure I can remember the way, Cora," Callan said pointedly.

"Follow me," she chirped, ignoring both Callan's remark and the frown from Eve as she set off for the sweeping staircase that dominated the space.

"Glad to see you're still bossy," he teased, following her nonetheless.

Eve fell into step beside him. The siblings continued teasing one another as they walked, though she hardly heard them, instead settling her attention on the elegant portraits and tapestries that lined the walls of the second floor.

Finally, Cora stopped outside of a polished mahogany door inlaid with gold stars along the four panels. With a giddy laugh, she pushed the door open, sweeping in with her arm outstretched.

"Cora," Callan said, voice thick with emotion. "This..."

"I know. It was theirs." She shook her head, folding her arms across her chest gently. "A few years after you left, I had it opened up again and cleaned. I wanted it to be ready for you when you came home." Silver lined her eyes, despite the hopeful smile she offered Callan.

The suite was elegant in an understated way. A large setee sat before a huge marble fireplace, flanked by wingbacked chairs, all three in a pale silver color. Deep blue pillows and a matching throw blanket embroidered with the same trio of stars the flags atop the castle had borne, had been artfully placed atop the sofa. A low table in front of the sofa and a small writing desk in the corner completed the comfortable room. As with the hallways, simple yet lovely paintings adorned the walls.

It reminded Eve of her mother's suite, in style more than color, sending a pang of grief and regret through her heart. This had been their parents' room.

Callan had clearly kept other rooms when he'd ruled Falias before the gods had sealed their children away, before he had taken on his self-imposed exile to atone for a crime that wasn't his to begin with. Taking his hand in hers, Eve gave a gentle squeeze.

"Thank you, Cora," he said finally.

"You're welcome," she replied, swiping at her eyes. "Now, you need to bathe, and I have a thousand questions." Moving toward the door, she offered them both a mischievous grin. "Callan, you know where the bathing room is. I'll have clothes brought for Queen Evelyn, and food for you both sent up. When you're settled, we'll talk."

Callan showed Eve to the bathing room as soon as the door to their chamber clicked shut. He insisted she go first, and by the time she emerged back into the bedchamber, equally as lovely and well-appointed as the living area, she saw that Cora had kept her promise. A small table had been brought in and set with two plates covered with silver domes and mugs of something steaming and floral smelling.

Her stomach growled in response, reminding her that she hadn't eaten since dinner the previous night. Nearly an entire day had gone by since they had fled the castle. She wondered about those they'd left behind as she picked up the dress she found laid across the bed, a lovely deep blue gown with stars stitched in silver trailing across the bodice.

As she dressed, she allowed her mind to wander. How many had survived, and how many hadn't? Would she be able to liberate them? And if so, to what end? She couldn't very well remain queen of a human kingdom now nor make demands of them. It would have been difficult enough before they'd been attacked by a fae kingdom.

By the time Callan finished bathing and dressing, Eve had already finished her meal of roasted chicken and vegetables, and what turned out to be hot tea. Guilt and anger simmered low within her as hot as the tea.

"You've eaten?" he asked, settling himself across from her. His own clothes had already been moved to the wardrobe in this room from wherever he'd left them behind.

"The food here isn't as different as I'd expected," she said by way of answer. "I thought it would be…"

"Magical?" The corner of his lips twitched upward as he uncovered his own dish. "Personally I think your Mrs. Elliott is secretly fae. Her tarts especially are something magical."

The reminder of yet another person she'd let down struck her like a knife. Callan's eyes softened at her wince. "I'm sorry, dove, that was thoughtless of me."

"I hate not knowing how many of them survived, or what's happening to them now. I should have stayed."

Callan shook his head, leaning back in the chair, food untouched. "We would have died. Gorias is formidable, even against another fae army. It took the combined army of the lower three kingdoms to push them back last time. They're a plague, Eve." Callan's gaze drifted to the window across the room. Outside, the sun had begun her descent, sinking behind the vast treeline beyond. "They would have killed you, and then taken your kingdom anyway."

Fear simmered beneath a deep pool of anger, roiling and raging within her. "So what do they want?"

"That's what I intend to find out," Callan replied darkly.

Chapter 42

"Where did the city go?" she asked, desperate to sate her own curiosity now, in the relative privacy of their chambers. Cora had arrived not long after they had finished their meal and had promptly begun peppering them with questions. They explained everything, impatiently on Callan's part, from Riona's request for aid to their arrival in the forest just beyond Falias.

"Go?" Cora's confusion was clear.

Seated at the vanity, Eve was attempting to straighten her now damp mess of hair, nearly ready to deem it a lost cause. Setting the brush down, she turned to face her, offering a bemused smile. "Before I... before everything, Falias wasn't here. It was gone, there was nothing but the gorge this far west."

"Eve," Callan cut in, stepping between them. "Wait-"

"It never went anywhere, we've been here the whole time, just sealed and hidden away. The gorge ends a few miles north of here."

Eve went still, hands falling to her lap. "Could you see-"

"Eve, they couldn't have helped him," Callan interrupted gently.

Eve nodded once, gaze locked on her folded hands. "I know," she replied quietly. She did, she knew the people of Falias, Callan's people, couldn't have come to her father's aid. She knew it wasn't their fault that the gods had locked them away, leaving her father and his men to their fate. "Why were they out here?" she asked suddenly, realizing she'd never been given an explanation for his expedition this far west.

"Who?" Cora asked, puzzled.

"Her father, the King of Darkegrove." Callan sank into a nearby chair, frowning. "Did your mother not tell you?"

"No, never," Eve said, raising her gaze to his. "I'm not sure if she even knew."

Cora leaned against the wall, sympathy etched into her lovely features. "I can send a scout or two; perhaps there's something out that way of interest?"

"Thank you," Eve said. A knock at the door drew all three sets of eyes at once.

"Come in." The words had barely left Callan's mouth when the door swung wide, revealing a brightly grinning Valerian, Leysa at his side.

"We're home, brother," Valerian beamed.

Callan was on his feet in an instant, embracing his dearest friend tightly. Leysa pushed past the men, embracing Cora with a riotous bout of laughter from both women.

Eve's heart gave a squeeze at the sight. She was happy for her friends, truly and fully. But she was homesick and left with more questions than answers. Her parents had hidden so many things from her for so long, and now that the truth was beginning to unravel, they were both gone.

Yes, her family was gone, she thought, but watching the three fae who had become more than just guardians, she realized she had found another one. Perhaps, in time, she could find a new home here as well. After she saved what remained of her kingdom and her people, and helped to set them on the right path to a future where all of its people would be seen as equals.

Mason hovered nearby, looking unsure and still a bit queasy despite having regained his normal color. Another outsider in a strange land, bereft and without a clear way ahead. Noting her gaze on him, he moved to stand beside Eve, watching the four of them catching up.

"Must be nice," he remarked.

"They've earned it," she retorted, desire to protect them flaring.

"I know," Mason said more gently, gaze coming to rest on Cora, having an animated conversation with Leysa. "Valerian told me about it on the way here. They deserved to find each other again, to come home."

"They did." The pain in her own heart was mirrored in his, but also the gleam of hope behind his eyes. "So do we. We'll get our home back, Mason." Eve turned her attention to Callan, taking a deep, steadying breath. "And then we'll make them pay for everything they've taken from us."

Coming Soon

'When the gods touch the crescent once more, the lost children will return and herald a new age.'

A new Queen will rise, and the next key will turn.

Coming 2024

Acknowledgments

Where to begin? I have so many of you to thank, and not enough words to express my gratitude.

To Kathy, the amazing editor who helped me battle my bad habits, your help has meant so much to me, more than I can say. I hope you know what a wonderful and kind person you are, not to mention a fabulous editor. Thank you and I hope we get to work together on the next one!

To B.T.B, thank you so much for making me a beautiful map and helping bring the world I created to life. You rock.

To all of my amazing beta readers, and critique partners, you are all incredible, thank you so much. Without each and every one of you, I would've given up a long time ago, and these amazing characters would never have been brought to life. You guys are rock stars.

To my friends from WrA, look what I did! It's hard to believe I came from telling stories of a heartless assassin to those of heroes, from writing in short paragraphs at a time to an entire novel. Without you all, your friendships, your amazing writing, and your outstanding characters, I wouldn't be here today. Thank you all.

To my Platonic Square. Meeting you all has changed my life more than you know, and I am so incredibly thankful for, and to, each of you. All three of you have given me so much encouragement, help, and friendship. Cheers to our little quad, and here's to that commune one day. Love you all.

And lastly, to my absolutely incredible husband. You have been so patient and supportive through this entire, extremely drawn-out, process. I have had so many false starts and without your love and encouragement, I don't think I would have ever made it this far. I love you.

About the Author

Tricia Meyers is an avid reader and writer of fantasy romance, a collector of too many pens, a part-time coffee enthusiast, and full-time mom. Writing has been her passion since childhood and has always been an outlet for her creatively.

Queen of Earth and Stone is her debut novel, and passion project that rekindled her dream of being a full-time author.

Find out more on https://authortriciameyers.com/.

facebook.com/tricia.d.meyers

instagram.com/tricia.m.books

tiktok.com/@tricia.m.books